IT'S
ELEMENTARY

IT'S ELEMENTARY

ELISE BRYANT

BERKLEY

New York

BERKLEY
An imprint of Penguin Random House LLC
penguinrandomhouse.com

Copyright © 2024 by Elise Bryant
Readers Guide copyright © 2024 by Elise Bryant
Penguin Random House supports copyright. Copyright fuels creativity, encourages
diverse voices, promotes free speech, and creates a vibrant culture. Thank you for
buying an authorized edition of this book and for complying with copyright laws
by not reproducing, scanning, or distributing any part of it in any form without permission.
You are supporting writers and allowing Penguin Random House to continue to publish
books for every reader.

BERKLEY and the BERKLEY & B colophon are registered trademarks of
Penguin Random House LLC.

Library of Congress Cataloging-in-Publication Data

Names: Bryant, Elise (Elise M.), author.
Title: It's elementary / Elise Bryant.
Other titles: It is elementary
Description: First edition. | New York: Berkley, 2024.
Identifiers: LCCN 2023048262 (print) | LCCN 2023048263 (ebook) |
ISBN 9780593640784 (trade paperback) | ISBN 9780593640791 (ebook)
Subjects: LCGFT: Detective and mystery fiction. | Novels.
Classification: LCC PS3602.R9474 I8 2024 (print) |
LCC PS3602.R9474 (ebook) | DDC 813/.6—dc23/eng/20231101
LC record available at https://lccn.loc.gov/2023048262
LC ebook record available at https://lccn.loc.gov/2023048263

First Edition: July 2024

Printed in the United States of America
1st Printing

Book design by George Towne

This is a work of fiction. Names, characters, places, and incidents either are the product
of the author's imagination or are used fictitiously, and any resemblance to actual persons,
living or dead, business establishments, events, or locales is entirely coincidental.

For my baby girls,
Tallulah and Coretta

IT'S
ELEMENTARY

ONE

I DON'T SEE HER COMING.

If I had been on top of my game, if I had been *alert*, there's no way she would've got me. I've mastered the swift, no-small-talk drop-off in the years that Pearl has gone to Knoll Elementary. Head on a swivel, sunglasses on, don't make eye contact, keep it moving. I can do it in my sleep. (And, well, I actually *do* sometimes, in this recurring stress dream, which is why my only nighttime companions are a mouth guard and a double dose of magnesium and melatonin.)

But today, I sleep through my alarm. And when I do get up, thirty minutes past the time when I *should* have gotten up, I immediately step into a fresh pile of puppy poop, left there by Polly—our Shar-Pei–pit bull mix—who sits a few feet away at my bedroom door, with her head cocked to the side, all self-righteous like, *You didn't hold up your end of the social contract. What did you expect me to do?* My screech wakes up Pearl, who runs into my room and slides through a separate, secret pile of poop. And though we speed through feet cleaning and tooth-brushing and backpack packing, all the time we've gained is lost when I can't find Pearl's *favorite* silver-and-black-striped knee socks, just her *other* silver-and-black-striped knee socks. So I have no choice but to break several traffic laws on the drive to the school, basically drifting in on two wheels, while Pearl stares resentfully at the impostor socks in the back seat. And when I finally do get my child to the side gate, because it's closer than the front gate, and muster my most cheerful "Have a good day!" she raises her chin and says with complete certainty, "I will not," before swishing her way to her class's line, like she didn't just throw a mom-guilt grenade over her shoulder.

I'm sweaty. I'm exhausted. I'm trying to figure out how many more cups of coffee I'll need to drink to make it through the eight hours of work before me when it's only 7:56 a.m. and I've already lived an entire day.

So of course this is the morning she manages to sneak up on me.

"Hey, Mavis! Just the woman I was looking for!"

Her voice is like a tinkling bell, bright and beguiling, but if you don't know better, it'll suck you in, like those sirens making a snack out of Odysseus's homeboys. I know better. I start looking for the exit points, formulating my strategy. A horde of cooing, crying kindergarten parents are to my left, waving goodbye through the chain-link fence just one more time and blocking the goddamn sidewalk. And a gang of kids on Micro scooters is rolling up on my right, so if I take off that way, I might be risking a maimed toe or two. Which would be inconvenient, but . . .

"Mavis! Yoo-hoo!"

I don't see a way out—or at least a way out that doesn't involve me sprinting or somersaulting or some other wild move that'll definitely get me posted up on the parents' Facebook group.

Trisha Holbrook, Knoll Elementary's PTA president and mother of Pearl's bestie Anabella, is standing right behind me. And I have been yoo-hoo'd.

I fix my face into a tight, plastic smile so my resting expression can't be misread as *unfriendly*—or, even worse, *aggressive*. *Deep breath. Let's get this over with.*

"Oh, hi, Trisha!" I say, turning around. "Were you calling me?"

"Yes, I was! Today *and* yesterday." Trisha reaches up to pat down her hair, even though not a single strand of her flawless brown bob is out of place. "Actually, I've been trying to find you since the first day of school, but you sure are a hard one to flag down!"

It's quick, but a single wrinkle erupts on her forehead, which is usually porcelain—smooth and so pale it must be a part-time job to maintain in the Southern California sun. And I swear there's a flash of something—could it be annoyance?—in her eyes. But it's gone before I can fully clock it. Because annoyance doesn't fit in with the perfect persona that's led her to win every PTA presidential election by a landslide since Pearl started kindergarten at Knoll. Perfect Trisha with the perfect kids and perfect Theory wardrobe doesn't get annoyed—and *definitely* didn't step in puppy poop this morning.

"Sorry, I've probably just been running out of here to get to work." I take a few steps in the direction of my car so she remembers I have to head there now.

"Yes, work." Her blue eyes go wide and she shakes her head, like I've just mentioned some fatal affliction. "I don't know how you do it!"

I do it because I have to, I think. *No one else is going to pay my bills for me.* But I just press my lips into an even tighter smile to fight against the massive eye roll my face wants to let loose.

"So strong," she murmurs, and then claps her hands together, getting us back on track. "Well, I have some PTA business to discuss with you!"

"I paid my annual dues," I spit out, sounding more defensive than I mean to. But I still haven't recovered from the membership drive last year, when the first-grade room mom went rogue and listed all the nonmembers in one of her email blasts. I mean, nobody yelled, *Shame! Shame!* at me during drop-off, but they basically did with their judgy eyes. I put the thing on auto-pay after that.

"Oh, I know you did," Trisha says with such firmness that I'm certain she has the entire membership roster memorized. "It's not that. I just have a really fun, really exciting opportunity for you!"

Okay, now that's unexpected. What kind of opportunity could Trisha, reigning queen of all the Knoll Elementary moms who don't sleep through their alarms and know where the right socks are and not only make small talk at the gate but also continue it at coffee dates after . . . well, what could she have *for me*?

"You see, I met with Debra at Beachwood Council PTA this week," she continues, as if I should know who the hell that is. "And she told me about this new committee requirement, passed all the way down from the state level. She was apologizing for asking *so* much of us, especially in the middle of *such* a busy time. You know how these membership drives go." She pauses and smiles at me, but I know what that smile means. *Shame! Shame!* "I told her, though, no problem at all! Because I know just the woman for the job! In fact, I can't think of anyone else who would do it better."

I have no idea what this is, but I already know I don't want it.

"Well, I appreciate you thinking of me, Trisha. But I already have a job, one that I'm actually going to be late for right now, so . . ." I turn to walk down the block back to my car, but Trisha leaps to the side, nimbly dodging a kid with a rolling backpack, all the while holding eye contact with me.

"Oh, don't you worry about that! You can still volunteer with the PTA even if you have a—a . . . *job*." Her whole body shudders when she says the word. "Felicia, our VP of Ways and Means, has a job, too!"

I take a few more tentative steps. "I really don't think—"

"Please just let me tell you more about it, Mavis," she cuts me off. "If you're in a hurry, I can walk you to your car, maybe? Or can I call you on your lunch break?" *My lunch break?* I know my smile front drops, and this lady gets the side-eye that she deserves at that. *Why is she so desperate to talk to* me *of all people about this?*

"And like I said, I really don't want you to miss out on this great opportunity. I think you'd be *just* the DEI chair that our school needs."

Oh.

Ooooooooooooooooh.

Now I get it.

"DEI, huh? Hmmmm." The smile is securely back in place. And I'm no actress, but I can make my voice sound believably inquisitive and kind after years of navigating conversations like this. "Why do you think I would be perfect for that?"

I know why. It is now abundantly clear *why* she wants *me* to head this new DEI committee mandated by the PTA powers that be. But I'm gonna make her say it.

"Well," she starts, hesitant. "DEI stands for diversity, equity, and inclusion."

My cheeks are going to hurt the rest of the day from smiling like this. "Yes, I know what DEI stands for."

As does every Black woman in the workforce since 2020, when seemingly every industry discovered this magic combination of words.

DEI means diversity, equity, and inclusion, *sure*.

But it also means free labor to be given willingly to fix problems that we didn't create. It means a box checked with no real change made.

For years I've successfully dodged the DEI bullet at Project Window, the teen mentoring nonprofit where I work, only to be caught unawares by Trisha Holbrook at drop-off?!

You really do gotta stay vigilant at all times.

"So . . ." Trisha nods her head, waiting for me to finish the sentence. But I'm not going to finish the sentence. Trisha's gonna need to tell me herself it's because I'm one of the few Black moms at Knoll Elementary—*definitely* the only one she talks to, and even then it's just because our daughters made that decision for us.

I raise my eyebrows expectantly.

"Well, you know . . ." she tries again. "It's because you—you . . ."

I cross my arms and try to hold in the laugh that's bubbling behind my lips. I know seeing Trisha squirm as she tries to navigate this conversation shouldn't bring me so much joy . . . but it's bringing me a lot of joy.

"It's because of what you said at the book fair."

I blink at her, confused, because I was expecting a lot of things—stilted, awkward phrasing; an explanation to me of all people why diversity is important; maybe even a little microaggression thrown in there, just for fun. But not that.

"Say what now?"

"At the book fair," she says, recovering her composure. "You complained about the selections of books we had available. Do you remember that?"

"Well, yes, because it was so hard for Pearl to find something with a character who looked like her . . ." And after thirty minutes of watching her flip through all the books with white kids or animals, only to spend a small fortune on erasers and light-up gel pens, I may have made a snarky comment to the mom at the register.

"Well, we tried to pick books that would be universal." Another small wrinkle appears on her forehead, but it's quickly eclipsed by her blindingly bright smile. "But yes, such necessary feedback for the program! You were so very helpful! As you *also* were at last year's Thanksgiving pageant."

My body tenses at the memory. "Trisha, Ms. Bellevue had those kindergartners wearing headdresses and face paint—"

"And I forwarded her the *several* articles that you sent us afterward. Along with that extremely informative BuzzFeed video and, um—what was it? A Change.org petition?"

Okay, *maybe* the petition was overkill, but I just wanted to make sure the point got across and we didn't have, like, casual blackface on deck for February.

"So . . ." Trisha starts. Any sign of floundering I saw before is gone, and it's unnerving. She knows she's got me and my big ol' mouth—and now she's just taking her time, a lion circling her prey. "It seems like you have a lot of insight to offer our PTA in order to improve our school programs."

"I do, but, Trisha—"

"You're busy," she finishes for me. "I know you're busy. But it's important work."

God, of course it's important work. But it's also *work*— exhausting work—trying to prove to everyone else that you and your kids belong. That you deserve respect, deserve *everything*. There doesn't have to be a special committee to make this happen for the white kids.

"And I also know," she continues before I can think of the polite way to explain this, "that you, like me, would do *anything* for your child. Aren't you so excited for the chance to make things the way you want them to be for Pearl? For all our children? I don't think we can do it without you, Mavis."

And she strikes. I'm gobbled-up gazelle, my guts strewn across the savanna—a goner before I even see her coming.

I got too cocky. I thought Trisha, like so many white people I know, would be so uncomfortable having to even recognize the concept of race that she might give this up and self-reject for me.

But now I'm going to agree to this because there's no way I can say no without forever cementing myself as a Bad Mom. I know I'm not a Bad Mom, but I also need *them* to know I'm not a Bad Mom.

And even if there wasn't the risk of getting the scarlet *BM* stitched onto my Old Navy clearance blouse, I'd do anything for Pearl if it meant she'd grow up happy and feeling like she belonged. Run into a burning building, lift a semitruck . . . run a PTA committee.

"Or I guess I *could* give the position to Angela. She seemed very eager when I brought it up at the board meeting last week."

Angela? The mom who still wears her pilled and faded pink pussy hat on the rare morning it dips below seventy degrees here, and has a lawn covered in variations of that WE BELIEVE sign?

Oh, absolutely fucking not.

"Okay, Trisha."

She nods like that was the only possible outcome. And you

know what? It probably was. I didn't stand a chance against the woman who successfully campaigned for her own lounge right next to the teachers', convinced Principal Brennan to reschedule open house when it conflicted with her family's spring European vacation, and (if whispers are to be believed) got Mr. Richardson put on administrative leave when he didn't admit her son Cayden into the advanced robotics program. This conversation has just been a formality since I was ensnared by the *yoo-hoo*.

"When's the first meeting?" I sigh, resigned to my fate.

And maybe it won't even be so bad. I mean, I'll just be giving my opinions—which, *apparently*, I can't help but do anyway. And Trisha's already made it abundantly clear that she's just trying to fulfill some mandatory PTA requirement. I'll be like that bag of mixed greens you pick up at Trader Joe's every week but never actually use, just there to make you feel good about yourself.

"Oh, it's tonight! But don't worry, it won't be more than two hours. Three at the most! I'll text you the details. Okay, gotta run. Bye now!"

She's dashing across the street, Francine the crossing guard's glaring stop sign as her shield, before I can respond.

Well played, Trisha.

I wish life had a rewind feature, like the constant replays they show during sports to try to make them more interesting. Because I'd like to study that conversation, try to pinpoint the exact moment when Trisha got the upper hand. Lord knows I could use some pointers at work, because I keep walking out of my performance review meetings with new responsibilities and zero new money. Which, I guess I just did. Again.

Shit.

"Oooooooh, girl! I saw that. She got you, didn't she?" A hand falls on my shoulder, and I turn to see my friend Jasmine. Her hot-pink-painted lips are hanging open in amusement, and her eyes dance with delight. All she's missing is the popcorn.

"She did." I let out a long exhale and shake my head. "I wasn't on my game because first the poop and then Pearl's socks—those freaking socks! They look exactly the same! And my brain is just so tired . . ."

I know I'm not making any kind of sense, but Jasmine nods at me like I said something profound.

"Oh, I feel you! Langston here thinks he's grown and doesn't need a bedtime anymore." She jerks a thumb at her son, who beams up at me from her side. He's missing his top and bottom front teeth and looks like the most adorable jack-o'-lantern. "Finally gave him one of those sleeping gummies at eleven, you know, as a last resort, and I still caught him on his Switch an hour later. Turns out this boy hid that thing in his cheek, like he's Jack Nicholson in *One Flew Over the Cuckoo's Nest*!"

"Those things taste like garbage fruit," Langston says, wrinkling his nose so his tiny tortoiseshell glasses rise up. "And also, how did Jack Nichol's son learn how to fly, anyway?"

Jasmine is my one exception to the "head down, keep it moving" rule. We first locked eyes at kindergarten orientation, the only two Black moms in our tour group. And our solidarity has only grown over the last two years as we've consistently been the last moms racing to the gate before the late bell. Except, very much unlike me, Jasmine does it in six-inch heels, exquisitely laid edges, and makeup so on point she could be giving YouTube tutorials instead of working as Beachwood's most sought after ob-gyn.

"Mommy, it's closed!" Langston tugs on her arm and points to the gate I just sent Pearl through. Mrs. Nelson, the librarian, is already power walking away with her ring of keys.

"Really? It's not even *late* late yet. She needs to chill." Jasmine shakes her head, but we both know from experience that there's no use calling after Mrs. Nelson. She'll just shrug like it's out of her control, as if we can't see her clutching those keys on her lanyard like they're precious jewels. Ms. Castillo, the resource specialist, on the other hand, will hold a conspiratorial finger up to her lips while she waves the kids in. Ms. Castillo is a real one.

"Okay, just run on up to the front. That gate has to still be open," Jasmine sighs, taking Langston's Black Panther backpack off her shoulder and sliding it around his arms. "And if they try to close it on you, slide your foot in the gap. They gotta stop then."

I side-eye her advice, and she smirks back at me. "Okay, okay, your lunch pail then! Just, like, fling it in there and roll on in after it. Keep Ms. Mavis here from clutching her pearls." She smooths the baby locs on the top of his head and kisses his cheek. "Have the best day, little man!"

"I will!" he calls behind him, sprinting to the main gate like he slept all night—and with a much more positive attitude than Pearl, I note.

"Now what does Miss Trish have you doing?" Jasmine asks, turning her attention back to me. "Organizing the lost and found? Selling spirit wear?"

"Worse. Leading the PTA's new DEI program."

"Oh lord! Oh no!" Jasmine hollers, staggering back dramatically.

"I know, I know." I groan and hold my face in my hands. "But she started listing all these things I—*rightfully*—complained about, like that fucking Thanksgiving pageant—"

"See, that's where you went wrong. You don't tell *them* when they're being ignorant. You just tell *me* and then we make fun of them."

"*Or*, you know, you can do this whole thing with me, and we can make fun of them at the meeting together tonight." I bat my eyelashes at her and cup my hands under my chin.

"Oh, Mavis. Sweet, sweet Mavis. You know there's no way in hell that's happening. I don't do work I'm not paid for." She makes a face like she smelled something funky. "Mmm-mmm. No, ma'am. I went to one of those informational meetings this summer with the new principal, Mr. Smith, and he tried to get me to join some school advisory committee thing. I was out of there and in my car *with a quickness*!"

She clutches her gold Telfar purse to her side as she mimes running away, and I crack up. The late bell chimes loudly, joining in.

"Hey, how was the new guy, anyway?" I ask.

"He all right." She shrugs her shoulders. "Honestly, he just looks like a younger Principal Brennan. Not totally convinced they didn't get us a clone."

Mr. Brennan had been the principal at Knoll Elementary since I attended this school way back in the day, so it was definitely time for him to retire. But he had a good heart and I felt like I could trust him. Like when Pearl's test scores were just points away from the cutoff for the gifted program at the end of last year, he talked up her organizational and leadership skills. Which, yes, she used those skills to set up a full-blown tetherball betting ring, to the dismay of her first-grade teacher . . . but still. Mr. Brennan saw the positive, and his comments in that meeting were what turned the tide. I'm nervous about what could be in store for Pearl and the school as a whole with someone brand new. I saw Mr. Smith's name at the bottom of all the forms Pearl brought home, and scanned the intro email he sent out, but I still haven't laid eyes on him and don't know what his plans are for Knoll.

"I probably should have gone to one of those meetings. Do you know if he's doing any more?"

Jasmine reaches forward and squeezes my arm, her playful expression changing to one of concern. "Now I know you don't need anything else on your to-do list, Mavis—principal *or* PTA meetings. And that is okay. Put you and your baby first."

She's not wrong. My plate is full—scratch that, *overflowing*. And sitting through a three-hour PTA meeting tonight sounds like the premise of one of my teeth-grinding stress dreams. But also . . . if I don't do it, who will? And clearly, there are some things I'd like to change.

"Mommy, they wouldn't let me in!" We both jump as Langston appears between us. "You need to walk me in, no exceptions. Principal Smith said!"

She shakes a finger at me, her snarky grin back in place. "I take back what I said. He not all right!" She huffs in exasperation but then gently grabs Langston's hand. "It's okay, baby, don't worry. Let's go see Ms. Lilliam."

I wave them off and breathe a sigh of relief that it's not me doing the walk of shame to Lilliam, the school's office manager, today. With one single up-and-down look, that woman can have you questioning all your parenting choices and also whether you're even fit to live on this planet breathing the same air as her. I may have just been conned by Trisha into giving away time that I definitely do not have, but this morning wasn't the *worst* that it could be.

But as I walk back to my car, all remaining hope leaves my body in one last pathetic puff when I realize two things.

One, in my rush to get Pearl to the gate before the late bell, I parked right next to That Damn Sprinkler—the bane of all Knoll Elementary parents' existence because, for some reason, it starts spraying on full blast right when school starts, making your car look like it's gone through a rare rainstorm and creating a river of mud that you have to trudge through to get to your door.

And two, a white-and-orange sedan with the dreaded words *Parking Enforcement* has pulled up behind my Prius, and a man with a bushy mustache—and a rigid interpretation of the rules just wafting off him—is getting out.

Is Mercury in retrograde or something?

But who am I kidding? Mercury is always in retrograde in my universe.

"Oh no. No, no, no!" I dash between my car and his, steering clear of the spray from That Damn Sprinkler so I don't totally destroy my wash-and-go.

"This is a no-parking zone between seven a.m. and four p.m., ma'am," he says, not making eye contact with me as he takes a thick pad of paper and a pen out of the shirt pocket of his uniform.

"I know. I know, and I'm so sorry," I say. "It's just that parents always park here to walk their kids in."

He pauses whatever he's writing on the pad and looks around at the empty curb surrounding us, taking his time to prove his point.

"They do. I swear they do. They're just gone now . . ."

"Hmm." He grips his pen tightly and starts writing again.

"'Cause we all know that the sign's just there to keep the front of the school clear for, like, field trip buses. Or maybe emergency vehicles?" I continue my probably futile attempt. "I don't know for sure. But anyway, we *aren't* going to be blocking anything if we just run in real quick. In and out. So, are you really going to give me a ticket when I was taking into consideration the sign's intended purpose and didn't actually cause anyone any harm? Can't you just show me some mercy, um, human to human?"

"Sign says seven to four, ma'am," he says. "Now can you please step to the side. I need to record your license plate number."

I let out a long, heavy sigh, accepting my fate. I want to do more, but I'm not about to be the mom outside the school arguing and making a scene, confirming all their worst assumptions about me. Even though I really, really want to.

"Fine."

"No, it's not fine." A deep, smooth voice startles both me and my new parking enforcement officer nemesis. We both turn, and for a second I worry that I switched my magnesium and melatonin with my multivitamin this morning, because the vision in front of me can only be a dream.

The still-rising sun is behind him, outlining his broad shoulders and tall, sturdy frame in golden light. As he gets closer, stepping through the rainbow of mist reflecting off the sprinkler's spray, I take in the rest of him. He has tousled, dark blond hair and summer-tanned skin. Thick eyebrows anchor his boyish face, but the salt and pepper sprinkled across his strong jaw and temples whisper of his actual age. His green eyes look serious, but there's a well-worn sunburst of lines next to both of them, so I can almost see how a smile would spread across his face, the lift of his full lips . . .

Which I realize are moving right now. Oh shit. He's talking and may have been talking for a long time while I gawked and had a whole R & B slow jam going in my head.

"—saw you sitting in your car, watching while all the other parents parked on this same block. Yet you only got out when this woman was the last left. I have to question why that is, and why you seem so set on enforcing this rule for her specifically."

Not only is this man walking around here looking like *that*, but he's trying to get me out of this ticket? If this truly is a supplement-fueled dream, I don't want to wake up.

The officer is less impressed.

"Sir, this is not up for debate. Now, I need you both to step aside so I can record her license plate number."

The man turns to me and squints his eyes. Maybe he's considering me, trying to decide whether I'm worth all this—which, let's be real, probably not. Then he nods his head, just barely, to our right, and I think he's trying to tell me something. Though what, I'm not sure. It's time to give up and give this guy my license plate number? Or step aside and let him handle this? It's not clear, but that's also maybe because half my brain is being used to wonder if his lips are as soft as they look.

"Excuse me," the officer barks, clearly out of patience. "Did you hear me? I asked you to move."

Next to me, the man shakes his head and begins to roll up the sleeves of his plaid button-down. My stomach dips when I see his strong forearms dusted with golden hair.

But wait. Oh no. What is happening here? Is he about to fight for my honor? Or, I mean, um . . . my right to not get a ticket? A flush creeps up my neck.

I'm about to tell this beautiful man that it's only seventy bucks and not that serious, when he jerks his head to the side, signaling me again. And my body doesn't even wait for my mind's permission: I jump away from him.

Things happen fast from there. The man leaps over to the pond of mud created by That Damn Sprinkler, dipping the toes of his brown oxfords into the muck. Then he kicks out his foot, spraying my car's bumper with the mud and completely obscuring my license plate. My jaw drops, the officer screams, and the man's face splits into a wicked grin.

"Go, go, go!" he calls, pumping his fist.

So I go.

My hands shake and my heart pounds as I hop into my car, twist the key in the ignition, and speed away from the scene of the crime.

TWO

MY PULSE IS STILL RACING WHEN I PULL INTO PROJECT WINDOW's parking lot. Did that really just happen? Who was that man? And even more urgently, how can I see him again?

I pull out my phone to text Jasmine for intel because she's not antisocial like I am and knows a lot of the parents—half the moms are on the waiting list to get into her exclusive practice. But my fingers just hover over the screen. What can I even tell her about him? He's so beautiful that he looks like a new, evolved version of one of those Chris actors, probably created in a lab somewhere? He might be walking around with muddy pants? The whole thing sounds bonkers . . . and if I tell her now, I'm inviting her commentary. I'm gonna have to deal with her bringing it up and clowning me for the rest of eternity. I don't know if I'm ready for all that yet. So instead I just scroll through the list of members on the Knoll Elementary Parents Facebook group with no success, until I realize it's 8:58 a.m., and I run into the office to avoid the wrath of my boss, Rose.

When my phone buzzes in the middle of our morning team meeting, I half expect it to be the school calling me back for a serious discussion about what I've done (which still strikes fear into my heart, even as a grown woman). Or maybe it's the beautiful man, who somehow got my contact information—not to ask me out for coffee, but to text me a picture of his dry cleaning bill.

It's even worse than the worst-case scenario my mind conjures up so easily, though. It's a text from Trisha.

> Just a friendly reminder that the
> meeting is tonight in the school
> auditorium. Can't wait to see you
> there promptly at 6!

I put my phone facedown and try to focus on the "glows and grows" for last month that Rose is sharing on a PowerPoint instead of just sending in an email. Trisha follows up again when I'm sitting in the drive-through car wash and wolfing down a limp grocery store chicken Caesar salad during my lunch break.

> Hi Mavis!! Just checking in again!
> Can I confirm you for tonight? 😊

I really do mean to respond, but then the rainbow foam stops and the lights flash, and I have to pull out of there while the fans are still going. And Trisha must be stressing, because another text comes in right when I'm walking in the door at the end of the day.

> I checked with the office and they
> confirmed that this is your number!
> Are you okay? Let me know if you
> need anything! And when you get a

> chance can you let me know if you're
> joining us tonight? 😊

I put my keys and purse down on the dining room table (its primary purpose, because we don't do much dining there), pet Polly, who's patiently waiting at my feet, and text her back.

> I'll be there! And goddamn are the
> PTA Police coming to check up on
> you tonight or something?

I delete that last sentence, because today is definitely not the day to intentionally choose violence, and replace it with 😊 to match hers instead.

Half a second later, her response comes in: **Yay!! This is going to be so much fun!**

I snort out a laugh and shake my head. I highly doubt that, but there's no getting out of this now. Trisha would probably send her PTA goons after me, have them checking in my windows for signs of life.

"Maves, is that you?" my dad calls from across the house, and with Polly at my heels, I walk into the kitchen to find him and Pearl sitting side by side at the counter. There's Goldfish, a bowl of grapes, and a stack of papers between them.

"Mommy!" Pearl calls, her face lighting up. And I swear that look contains actual electricity, because even on the days when I'm exhausted down to my bones, seeing her so excited to see me has me recharged and ready to go.

"Hey, baby!" I kiss the top of her head and brush away some orange crumbs that have somehow made it into one of her Afro puffs.

"Okay, I'm glad you're here," Dad says, holding up one of the worksheets. "Because this child keeps trying to tell me this is math, Maves, and this is not any kind of math I've seen before."

"Papa is too old to understand it," Pearl says matter-of-factly.

Dad reels back and clutches his chest in mock offense. "Now, who are you calling old, Miss Thang?"

"You," she shoots back, and then reaches forward to pat his mostly gray beard, to prove her point. "And when you were younger, you probably had to do your math on the cave walls or something. So that's why you don't get my math. But it's okay, I can teach you, Papa."

"Oh, is that right?"

"Mm-hmm."

My dad's head falls back as he laughs, loud and hearty, and Pearl giggles along with him, shaking even more orange crumbs to the ground, which Polly gladly gobbles up.

I moved in with Dad when Corey and I finally stopped fooling ourselves and officially called it, and I was adamant that it was only going to be a short-term solution. Just a beat, a breath, for me to get back on my feet and figure out how I was going to do this whole thing solo. Not that Corey was physically around a lot in the first place . . . That was our problem.

But that was three years ago. I had so many worries at first. Would I feel like a kid again, being under the roof where I grew up? Would Dad respect that I was the parent here, not him? And how would Pearl do with her daddy available, but not *here*? FaceTime is a lifesaver while Corey is out on the road most of the year, working as a touring drummer and hopping from one contract to the next. And he never, ever misses his nightly call. But would Pearl feel the loss of only having one of us there to cheer her on at the awards assembly or cuddle her when she wakes up in the middle of the night from a bad dream?

It's worked out, though, with Dad deferring to me when it

comes to all things parenting and accepting the rent I insist on paying him (even though I suspect he puts most of it in a college savings account for Pearl). He fills in the gaps, taking her to appointments and picking her up from school since he retired from his longtime career as a public defender just last year. Pearl's life is filled with even more love, not less.

"I mean, arrays!" Dad says, waving the worksheet around again. "Tell me why a second grader needs to know about arrays!"

Oh, and there's someone else there to deal with this new math that I, too, can barely understand.

"Let's take a break from the young people math," I say, grabbing a handful of Goldfish to snack on because that grocery store salad faded fast. I hold up my other hand. "Gimme five, girlfriend."

She slaps my palm and holds her hand up, too. "Um. There was supposed to be pepperoni pizza in the cafeteria but there were yogurt parfaits instead, so I'm pretty sure you read the menu wrong." Her first fact about her day—one finger goes down. We started this ritual in preschool, when I would ask her, "How was your day?" and she would just shrug and say, "Good." This helps me get a little more detail from her, even if it's only about how I messed up the menu again. (And it's not my fault that thing is so confusing!)

"Mrs. Tennison read a book about a llama." She puts another finger down. "Joseph found a spider in his desk and he said it should be named Darryl, but I knew it should be named Armando, and then Mrs. Tennison saw Armando and made us put him outside. And, um, and . . . well, we learned about arrays to help with multiplication, which is not even that hard." She smirks at her papa, and he laughs.

"Oh, and my *nemesis*—" Her dark brown eyes narrow and her voice drops low.

"You know things about your nemesis don't count," I remind her. We added this rule last year in first grade, otherwise all her facts would be about this girl who cut her in line one day and didn't say sorry.

"But this is a new nemesis!" she insists, and I shake my head. I wish I could say this comes from her daddy, but a long, petty memory and a list of nemeses is all me.

"Fine. Well, um, Anabella said you and her mom are going to be best friends now." Speaking of nemeses. "She said you're joining the PTA. Five! Done! Now can I go play with Polly outside? I've been teaching her how to play dead!"

I nod my head distractedly, and Pearl squeals and runs out the screen door into the backyard, Polly sprinting after her.

So, Trisha was sure I would say yes, even before we talked. God, am I really that easy a mark? It makes me want to send her a passive-aggressive text of my own. Is being a manipulative mastermind a mandatory requirement for joining the PTA? Please advise ☺

Okay, so that would just be *aggressive* aggressive.

"What happened here this morning?" Dad stands up from his seat at the counter, and I hear his knees pop.

"Yeah, I'm sorry. Were we loud?" Dad sleeps in every morning—a well-deserved luxury after forty years of 8:00 a.m. court appearances—so I try to keep our chaos at least quiet.

"No, it wasn't that," he says, opening the fridge. "There were so many of Pearl's clothes on the ground, I thought that child'd been raptured. And Polly was chewing on the couch leg like a hambone, with a nice little present sitting in the corner."

"Oh god! I thought I got all of it."

He pulls out a Tupperware of the extra spaghetti I made last night and raises his eyebrows, silently asking, *Leftovers for dinner?* I nod my agreement.

"You know, you're supposed to stick their noses in it. That's how they learn."

"Dad, I told you, that's old school."

He grunts and shakes his head. "Yes, I know you're determined to helicopter parent this puppy. I'm just saying . . ."

He defers to me with Pearl but not Polly. Even though neither of us really knows what we're doing with that dog. I didn't grow up with pets; Dad thought it was weird to have an animal in the house "licking you and looking at you all the time," but we both gave in when Pearl begged for this puppy after finding her on a shelter website, all on her own.

And okay, as grateful as I am for the support Dad gives me, moments like these are when it might be nice to not still live with the person who raised me. I mean, I don't want Polly to keep pooping in the house, either, but I also wish I could just make my mistakes without a witness.

"Don't worry. I got it. I think she just needs more activity so she sleeps through the night. I'm going to start taking her out for an extra-long walk right before bed. Speaking of . . . I kind of need to go somewhere tonight." I check the time on my phone. "Pretty soon actually."

"Oh yeah?" He looks out the window, where Pearl is lying on the ground with her tongue out and arms and legs in the air. Polly runs in circles around her.

"But if that's too much to ask, I can totally get out of it, no problem. You know what, that's what I'm going to do. Let me just text—"

"This have something to do with what Pearl was saying about

you and Anabella's mama becoming best friends?" Dad asks with a knowing grin.

"Yes," I mumble, crossing my arms and pouting. What is it about being around your parent that makes you act out the same scenes over and over? I feel like I got caught trying to skip my SAT after-school tutoring session. "She basically guilt-tripped me into joining. She wants me to be the chair for their diversity committee, probably just a formality so they can look like nice little liberals, you know? Because what change are they *really* going to be open to making?"

"Well, you don't know that for sure, right? Because you haven't been to a meeting, so you can't know how it works yet." Dad isn't looking at me as he puts the container of spaghetti in the microwave, but I know his face so well that I can picture what it looks like: pursed lips and raised eyebrows. "Seems like you might be able to do some good for the school, so why not give it a try?" From behind, I see him shrug, like that's the only logical course of action in this case.

God, did Trisha get to him, too?

But I shouldn't even be surprised by this, because the importance of helping others is the code I was raised by. It's why my dad spent his career advocating for the most vulnerable, even though he could have gone into another, more lucrative, kind of law. It's why, when I was growing up, we spent our weekends preparing meals at the homeless shelter and volunteering with the cancer charity that helped Mom in the last years of her battle. And it's why I work at Project Window now even though all my friends from my public policy master's program have landed at these bougie companies with six-figure salaries and insurance that actually covers therapy, and break rooms that are stocked full of snacks that you can just eat without a snarky

Post-it note appearing the next day. It's *the right thing to do*. And now my dad has officially classified being a PTA mom as *the right thing to do*.

He pulls the steaming container out of the microwave and puts it down on the counter. "Like Gwendolyn Brooks said, we are each other's business, Maves." It's a phrase I've heard countless times since I was a kid.

Yeah, I think, *but I've got plenty of my own business*. So much business that the inside of my brain looks like one of those houses filled with a decade's worth of newspaper and expired cans of cat food that they do specials about on TLC. Intervention-level business. I'm not trying to be in anyone else's business, too. Like Jasmine said, I don't need anything else on my to-do list.

But I nod and say, "You're right."

As badly as I want to believe Jasmine—that I can focus on just Pearl and me, that I can put only us first, and that's okay . . . I know I'm going to do this PTA thing after all, and do it well. Because even at thirty-one, I'm still leaning into my dad's approval like a plant toward the sun. I don't know if that instinct will ever go away.

"Good, Mavis. I'm proud of you—AH!"

My breath catches at the sound of his yell, but I start laughing when I see what inspired it. Polly is at his feet, licking one of the knees exposed by his khaki shorts, with Pearl crawling up behind her.

"She's always sneaking up on me," Dad mutters, shaking his head. "She's too quiet. It's not natural for a dog to be this quiet."

I playfully roll my eyes. "Would you rather she bark all the time?"

"Play dead, Polly!" Pearl shouts, and Polly immediately follows the command, flopping down on her side. Pearl lies down next to her in the same position, with her eyes closed and tongue out. "Look, Mommy, we're dead! You and Papa play dead, too!"

And even though we know it's going to lead to at least a couple of ibuprofen later, we both get down on the ground and play dead, too.

THREE

I WALK BACK TO THE SCHOOL, BECAUSE WE LIVE LESS THAN a mile away, and my morning *Fast & Furious* moves are totally unnecessary if Pearl and I can just get it together and leave on time. Before I go in the front gate, though, I text Jasmine a last-resort selfie. **There's still time to join me!**

Her response comes in immediately. **Tell me you did not give in. MAVIS!**

> **I'm hoping it won't be so bad? And I don't know . . . maybe I can do some good for Pearl and a lot of other kids at Knoll**

Okay, Reba

> **What does that even mean??**

She doesn't type anything for a minute, and I'm about to put my phone back in my pocket. I don't want to get there early and be forced into conversation, but I also don't want to get there late and have everyone turn around and look at me. It's a slim window.

A voice note appears on the screen, and I click play, holding it up to my ear. "A single mom who works two jobs! Who LOVES her kid and NEVER STOPS!"

Jasmine wailing in an over-the-top southern twang blasts through my phone's speakers, nearly knocking me over. I quickly cut it off before anyone else can overhear, but her finale comes in as a text a second later: I'M A SURVIVOR!

I laugh as I type back, Girl you are too much.

She responds with a cowboy emoji and a red heart.

God, I wish she was here right now to make this whole thing more bearable, but that's definitely not happening. I check the time, and it's exactly one minute before six, so *at least* I can sneak into the back row right now just as they're starting. Because, yeah, I'm going to do my best at this, but it's going to take a lot more than a quick convo with Dad to make my small talk aversion disappear.

What I didn't account for was the PTA meeting bouncer.

"Hello!" a short woman in a tucked-in Knoll Knights T-shirt chirps, waving at me enthusiastically in front of the auditorium doors. She has thick black hair with bangs and light brown skin, and the tension in my body loosens, just slightly, with the plot twist that there's another person with a drop of melanin here. "I'm Dyvia! What's your name?"

"Mavis," I say, reaching out to shake her hand. And in my head, I'm already envisioning our brown-girl alliance. I may not have Jasmine here, but Dyvia and I are about to be sharing knowing looks at the inevitable moments of Caucasity, hosting a joint fundraising drive to get Colors of the World crayons for all the classrooms. Maybe I won't actually be alone, and this won't be all that bad.

"Well, it's so wonderful to meet you, Mavis!" She squeezes my hand and then caresses the top of it, like she sees our future mom-friendship, too. "We really appreciate your help during the meeting. Now, the other volunteers are already in the cafeteria with the kids. Do you know where that is? And you can come find me at the end, so I can sign your service form, okay?"

Service form? What do I need a service form for—oh. I see what's happening here.

"Um, I'm not a volunteer? Well, I am a volunteer, I guess. But not that kind. I'm a mom?" *Good job. You sound real convincing there, Mavis.*

Dyvia's angular eyebrows press together in confusion, and can I even blame her?

"Of an . . . elementary student?" she clarifies.

"Yes. A second grader."

"Oh! Oh my gosh!" Her hand flies to her mouth. "You just look *so* young!"

I know when people say that—and I hear it a lot—I'm supposed to take it as a compliment, but it doesn't feel like one. I already feel like I barely belong here at these school events, single and Black, so every time I hear this, it's like they're confirming that, too. It makes me want to roll out my whole résumé to justify my place. Like, I have a master's degree from UCLA, lady! I was eight months pregnant with Pearl at the ceremony, but still! I'm grown, just like you! I use Sensodyne, and I have enough white hairs that I can't keep casually plucking them without looking like a "before" in one of those women's hair loss Instagram ads I keep getting, and I'm pretty sure my back hurts more than it doesn't hurt now, and I'm wearing Old Navy Pixie pants. There is nothing more grown than Old Navy Pixie pants!

Dyvia blinks at me ferociously, a nervous smile tugging on her lips. Shit. I hope I didn't let any of that rant actually slip out.

"Thank you," I finally mumble, the correct response to make everyone feel comfortable. The other expected option: a sassy joke about how Black don't crack—but it is after dinnertime on a school night, and I don't have the energy for that.

"Well, um . . . so nice to have you here!" she says, pointing to the open auditorium doors. I give an awkward wave of thanks and quickly make my way toward it.

"And I do really love your pants!" she calls after me. I wince, my cheeks burning in embarrassment.

But you know what, they *are* good pants.

I've been inside the school auditorium only for holiday concerts and kindergarten graduation, so it's a little jarring at first to walk in and see so many empty rows of flipped-up chairs. There are only a couple dozen people in attendance, all sitting up front, and I can tell immediately that my strategy to sit in the back and observe isn't going to cut it. That is just going to make me more noticeable.

I pick a seat in the fourth row back, off to the right, and start scanning the backs of heads. It's almost all women, and I don't think I recognize anyone except for Trisha, holding court with a small group in blue T-shirts at the front, and a curly-haired brunette that may be one of the moms to twins in Pearl's class.

I sigh, feeling my heart fall in my chest. I don't think I even admitted it to myself until now that I was expecting him to be here. The man from this morning, my parking ticket hero. I mean, he has to be a Knoll Elementary dad, right? Why else would he be walking outside an elementary school during drop-off? Well, what other normal, non-creepy reason? Because he definitely seemed normal and non-creepy. But if he's a dad . . . that also means there's probably a mom, too. Or another dad. In which case, it might be best if I never run into him again, because that person probably heard the story and hates me for being the cause of his ruined pants. Or even worse, pities me. Except, did I see a ring on his finger? I don't think so . . . My mind was a little preoccupied by his shoulders and his lips and all that mud, though.

"Felicia! You're here!" a blond woman with bony shoulders and a uniform of Lululemon shouts excitedly, her voice rising above the low din of conversation in the room. She sits down a couple of rows in front of me, next to another woman in a pantsuit, with black hair tied into a tight bun. "I didn't think you could get away from work this early."

"Hey, Ruth! Well, I definitely have another hour or two in front of me tonight," Felicia says, punctuated by a high-pitched laugh. "Hopefully John has the kids asleep before I get home!"

"Oh, Mama, I don't know how you do it!" Ruth coos, placing a hand on Felicia's shoulder. "All that time away from your littles. Even just being here for the night, I feel guilty. I miss them! Oh, I'm so silly, aren't I? I wish I could just turn it off for a bit like you!"

Felicia's laugh goes up another pitch, dangerously close to a sound that only dogs can hear. "And see, I don't know how you do it! I wish I was brave enough to take a breather from the workforce like you and only focus on my family. Your days must be so peaceful!"

"Which one do you think is going to win the Mom Olympics? My money's on Ruth." There's a woman sitting two spots away from me, leaning in over the empty seat. She's wearing lavender sweats with lime-green Crocs, a sharp contrast to the other PTA moms' attire. Her ginger hair is up in a messy bun, and she has a sunburned nose sprinkled with freckles. "I once saw Ruth tell a group of moms with complete confidence that the essential oils she sells on the side can cure depression, heart disease, *and* constipation," she whispers with her hand shielding her mouth conspiratorially. "With that kind of delusion, you can never really lose."

I give the woman a polite smile. I was clocking the passive-aggressive battle of the moms, too, but should I really acknowledge that to this person I don't know?

"Then again, Ruth's husband just quit his corporate finance job to help her sell these miracle essential oils—while Felicia comes home every day to her hot doctor husband *and* their manny. Have you seen that beautiful specimen at drop-off? He looks like he walked right off the cover of a Harlequin Desire paperback. So who's the real winner there?"

I can't help it. A laugh escapes in the form of an ugly, conspicuous snort, and the woman next to me giggles in delight. Ruth and Felicia turn around and give us disapproving looks and then return to their conversation, quieter this time.

"Oh, bless their hearts," the woman next to me whispers at the backs of their heads. She turns back to me and sticks out a hand accented with rainbow beaded bracelets. "Okay, if I'm going to subject you to my running commentary, I guess it would be nice to introduce myself, huh? I'm Corinne Ackerman. And I usually save the snark for myself, but you looked like you were thinking the same thing."

"Mavis Miller." I put my hand in hers, and she grips it strongly. "And oh no, was it that obvious?"

She smiles widely, revealing two bottom incisors that stick up like bunny ears, and pinches her fingers together. "Just a little bit."

"My friend Jasmine says I have resting bitch face."

"Nothing wrong with that. Keeps away the annoying people." She shrugs. "So, I want to know what grade your kid is in, 'cause I'm almost certain I've never seen you here before, but I also don't want to do that annoying mom thing where I ask you about your kid before I ask you about you."

I laugh, making Felicia and Ruth turn around again.

Corinne bats her eyelashes and wiggles her fingers at them, so they both pretend like they were just looking at something interesting on their shoulders.

"It's fine," I say. "She makes up, like, ninety-eight percent of my personality at this point, anyway. I have a second grader named Pearl."

"They tend to do that! Okay, so, second grade? Does she have Mrs. Tennison?"

"Yeah, she does!"

"Good. Love her. My seventeen-year-old, Brody, had her, and let me tell you, that woman needs to be granted sainthood for all that she put up with. Her ban on non-washable markers—yeah, that was all him."

I feel my eyebrows go up when she says her son's age, because I had clocked her as closer to my age than the other fortysomethings in this room. But I try to get my face together just as quickly so I don't do the very thing that I hate so much.

Not quick enough, though. "Yes, I said seventeen! I can't believe it either. Because I look so good." She frames her face with her hands, pursing her lips and posing. "I've also got a fifth grader and a fourth grader, so I've been here to witness all of Trisha's PTA reign." She nods to the front of the auditorium, where Trisha is beginning to make her way to the podium. "I don't know what she did to get you here, but after this is over, remind me to tell you the story of how I barely rear-ended her in the valet line one day, really just a tap, and I ended up being the Fun Run chair for the past six years."

Trisha taps the mic, drowning out my giggles. "I believe we have quorum now. Are we ready to begin, ladies?" Someone clears their throat in the first row, and she adds, "Oh yes, and gentlemen. *Of course* you're always welcome, too!"

"Did you see that? The forehead wrinkle?" Corinne whispers, leaning in again. I nod. "It appears when she's irked but doesn't want to show she's irked—which is a true feat when you consider how much Botox she's got pumped in there. And no shame there, because I've also got a punch card with Dr. Bianchi. Anyway, the way I stay awake at these things is I count how many times that wrinkle shows up."

I snort-laugh again.

"Okay, then, I'm going to officially call this meeting to order. So sorry to interrupt your conversations!" Trisha smiles directly at Corinne and me, her voice its usual cheerful chirp, but the glaring forehead wrinkle reveals her true message: *Shut the fuck up and let me do my thing, peasants.*

"Two," Corinne says softly next to me, and I cover my mouth to keep all signs of amusement from Trisha's almighty eyes.

"We have a real surprise in store tonight, ladies . . . *and gentlemen!*" Trisha continues. She looks regal in her perfectly tailored blue shift dress, the exact shade of her subjects' Knoll Knights T-shirts. "So much of a surprise, in fact, that I didn't even have an opportunity to include it on our agenda. I apologize, of course, for this break in protocol and any confusion it may cause."

I press three fingers into the seat between Corinne and me.

"But don't worry—our recording secretary, Ruth, will make sure it's reflected in our minutes. I see she doesn't quite have her computer out yet, but I know she will soon!"

Corinne gently covers my fingers with four of her own. It takes all my self-control not to bust out laughing, as Ruth frantically boots up her laptop, nearly tumbling out of her seat in the process.

"Wonderful. Now, it is my pleasure to introduce our school's new principal, Mr. Smith, who would like to give a *brief* address at his very first PTA meeting. Let's all give a hand for Mr. Smith!"

As the parents politely applaud, a man in the front row stands up and makes his way to the podium. Principal Smith has dark, deep-set eyes and brown hair that appears to be thinning, if only in comparison to his thick mustache. He's wearing a blue Knoll Elementary staff polo, his paunch pushing at the spot where it's tucked into his blue jeans, and brown tasseled loafers. It's hard to place his age, because his face screams forty, tops, but that 'fit is firmly ordering from the senior menu at Denny's.

"Thank you so much for having me, Knoll families!" Principal Smith smiles at the podium, revealing straight, bright white teeth that seem to shine under the auditorium lights. His voice is different than I expected, warm with a distinct southern twang. "Even in the short time I've been at Knoll, I can already tell that I am just so blessed with this new assignment. Your children and Knoll's wonderful staff and teachers have welcomed me with open arms. I am truly honored to be a Knoll Knight."

There's another round of applause, and he receives it with his hand held out like a polished politician.

"Thank you. Now I know y'all have a lot to get to." He flashes his blinding smile in Trisha's direction, and she gives him a particularly deep forehead wrinkle in return. "But I just wanted to introduce myself to Knoll's most committed parents and tell y'all a little bit about my background. I am new to California and Beachwood Unified, but I am not new to education. I have over a decade of experience back home in Bradley County, Florida, as a fourth-grade teacher, a dean of discipline, and finally as an assistant principal. I come from a family of educators, too, who shared with me the joy of shaping young minds. My grandfather was a professor of history, and my mom taught kindergarten for forty-one years." I don't hear a reaction from the audience, but he pauses and smiles again as if he does. "Yes, I know. A long time, right? She is my why, the reason I am standing before you today, ready to lead this school to—"

The sound of one set of hands loudly clapping cuts him off. Trisha is back at the podium so quick I'm not convinced she didn't teleport.

"Oh, what a treat! Thank you so much for sharing your story with us tonight." She continues to move closer to him and clap, which is straddling the border between enthusiastic and menacing. Principal Smith has no choice but to back down.

"Yes, thank you for having me. I look forward to getting to know y'all better." And he may say something else, but Trisha drowns him out with loud taps and a screech of feedback as she adjusts the mic.

"Now, we'll return to our meeting as scheduled. You all should have received the agenda in your emails today, and there were also hard copies at the front. Ruth, please make note of our last-minute change to our agenda. And if everyone approves of the agenda with that revision, please say aye."

A perfectly in-sync chorus of ayes calls back, except I didn't get the audience participation memo, so my aye is a half second too late, earning me a look of disapproval from Ruth. From the podium, Trisha winks and gives me a placating smile, which will hopefully get her fangirl off my back.

"Great. And with that we'll move forward with item A, or excuse me, *item B*"—forehead wrinkle—"on the agenda, my president's report." Applause fills the room, and Trisha receives it like a gracious starlet just awarded an Oscar. "Thank you, thank you. Ah, thank you. So, as you all know, we have a lot going on right now. The beginning of the school year is busy,

busy! But I have decided to focus this time on an issue that is extremely important to our school community and deserves our prompt attention." She stops to gaze around the room, building suspense. "Many of you may have heard the rumblings over the past year about the gifted school Beachwood Unified is hoping to open. And I have it on good authority that our Knoll Elementary is being considered as the school site for this new, exciting venture within the district."

Gifted school? This is the first I'm hearing about this. And at Knoll . . . what would that even entail?

"Um, hold on," a voice, thankfully, calls out, so I don't have to be the one.

But I'm surprised to see that it's Principal Smith, not a parent, standing up in the front row. Trisha glares at him so intensely that I wouldn't be surprised if he burst into flames. He must feel it, too, because he adds meekly, "I'm so sorry. Excuse me, Mrs. Holbrook, but as far as I know, this isn't a topic for the PTA. This is being decided by administration and the school board."

"You are excused, Mr. Smith," Trisha says in a sharp tone that makes it clear he's anything but. "I wouldn't expect you to know that it is not protocol for me to be interrupted during my address. And yes, I am aware who is responsible for those decisions on the record, but Principal Brennan led our school with a more collaborative spirit and always involved the PTA in decisions that would affect our children."

Two deep wrinkles take over her forehead, and I turn to Corinne with wide eyes to make sure she's seeing this. Corinne's leaning forward, locked into the drama, and when I tap her on the shoulder, she blinks at me, like someone coming off a full-season Netflix binge. I nod toward Trisha and raise my eyebrows in question, and Corinne hurriedly fills me in, her gaze dancing between me and the stage. "Principal Brennan was in Trisha's pocket. Totally terrified of her, just did whatever she said. And I heard he basically promised her that Knoll would be the site of the district's new gifted school. Must have thrown everything off when he retired, and Principal . . . Smith . . ."

Her voice trails off, the quickly escalating scene in front of us winning out. Principal Smith's break in protocol seems to have given everyone permission to break free, because parents are now brazenly shouting out questions at Trisha.

"What year would this go into effect?"

"When will students be tested?"

"Are they going to bus in students from all over the district? Even the Northside?"

I raise my hand with a question of my own.

"Yes, Mavis." Trisha speaks loudly into the microphone. "Thank you for kindly"—forehead wrinkle—"raising your hand."

"I don't know anything about this, so, like, forgive me if this has been discussed already. But what happens to the Knoll Elementary kids that don't test into this, um, gifted school? Do they get moved from Knoll, even if it's their home school?"

Pearl is in the second-grade gifted class, but only because of the exception that was made, only because they looked past her test scores. Who knows if that will happen again next year and the years after? So, then . . . what? She'll just be kicked out of Knoll and transferred somewhere else?

Plus it was glaringly obvious as I watched them all line up on the first day that she's the only Black student and one of only a handful of kids of color. A lot of the pride I felt was overshadowed by guilt, and I've since pored over so many studies about how gifted programs mainly benefit white and wealthy students—not because they're smarter, just because the whole goddamn system is rigged to their benefit. If Knoll becomes a gifted school, what does that mean for all of the kids who don't fit into that box?

"Oh gosh, well, I hadn't thought about that because, you know, that would not specifically impact *my* children, but I love that you're already thinking about how to help *all kids*, Mavis! Very inclusive! Everyone, in case you weren't aware, this is the chair of our new DEI committee, Mavis, already working on the *I*. So on top of it! Can we all give her a round of applause?" Everyone stares at me and begins to clap, following her lead, and I want to fall out of my chair and be absorbed into the floor.

"Mr. Smith, I think I'll pass that one to you," Trisha says, gesturing to him in the front row, and thankfully, everyone redirects their attention to him. Except, he doesn't answer, because he's looking at me. And it's not the look I'm expecting. Not a guilty *oops, we did a racism!* or an angry *and we would have gotten away with it if it wasn't for you, meddling Black woman!* No, he looks like he's seen a ghost. His brow is furrowed, and his mouth is hanging open. He looks scared. Of me.

But I don't get it. My question might have been a little contentious, but it doesn't deserve all this drama.

"Yoo-hoo!" Trisha shouts, managing to make *yoo-hoo* sound like a threat. "Mr. Smith, can you answer this question for our very concerned DEI chairperson?"

Principal Smith continues to stare at me, but now he's squinting and his mouth is twisted.

"I . . ." he starts, finally. "I don't know."

"You don't know?" Trisha demands. "What do you mean you don't know?"

That seems to break him out of whatever trance my question caused. He turns back to Trisha. And I can't see his face anymore, but his voice sounds more confident, maybe even defiant. "I don't know," he repeats. "Because I, along with the administration team at Knoll, have decided not to go forward with the application. The gifted school will be at another site within the district."

The only sound louder than the mic dropping to the ground with a thunderous bang is Trisha's indignant shriek. "WHAT?!"

TRISHA STORMS OFF IN A FURY, MOMENTARILY GETTING caught in the stage's burgundy velvet curtains before she kicks herself free. Ruth rushes to the podium and declares a "short recess." Dyvia passes out Lärabars and cans of La Croix. And Felicia swoops in and thanks Principal Smith for his time, all the while guiding him to the door with a firm hand on his back. They move with such speed and precision that I wonder if this has happened before.

And I watch it all with barely contained glee. First, because Trisha isn't going to get what she wants, and I don't have to worry about this gifted school business affecting my baby after all. But also because it's like the moments of delightful disorder on all my favorite *Real Housewives* seasons (Aviva throwing her leg, Kim rejecting the bad energy bunny)—except even better, because it's real. Eventually, I tear my eyes away to see if Corinne is enjoying this as much as I am, but her seat is empty. I look around the room for her, but I don't see her bright hair or lavender sweats anywhere. I sigh, trying to let out the feeling of disappointment in my chest. *She couldn't even wave goodbye?* But I guess I can't blame her—she saw an out and took it. I was thinking about escape just a little bit earlier, before Trisha went all Ramona and things got interesting there for a moment.

After ten minutes of snacking and polite chatter, Trisha returns to the podium, calm and composed, and continues the meeting as if nothing ever happened. And just like that, it's back to being boring. Except even worse than before, because now I don't have someone to turn to and share a knowing look with when the wrinkle appears on Trisha's forehead as she's trying to look enthusiastic about Muffins with Mom being renamed Pastries with Parents.

I make it about halfway through a lengthy discussion about which film would be appropriate for family movie night (there are multiple spreadsheets, and someone busts out their Common Sense Media premium account) when I just can't keep my eyes open anymore. I make a break for the bathroom to kill time—maybe splash some water on my face and hopefully miss the tail end of Ruth's beef with *Moana*.

The bathroom is empty, so I take my time and check my phone. There are some texts from Jasmine with more Reba McEntire lyrics. And there's also a missed call from Corey . . . which is weird. We don't call each other, just text, mostly because of our schedules, but also because it's just easier that way. There's something about talking on the phone that feels so intimate—probably because that's how we first fell in love, sneaking phone calls late at night in high school. And neither of us wants to be reminded of that now.

He probably just called by accident instead of FaceTiming, and at this point, Dad has definitely connected with him. It's really important to Dad that Pearl and Corey talk every night; he makes sure it happens when she's with him. Whatever it is, I'll just get the details when I get home.

Speaking of going home, it must be winding down now. I'll just pee and take an extra-long time to wash my hands, and then it will be socially acceptable to bounce.

But the bathroom door slams open right when I'm about to flush, and a clattering of heels follows. I freeze, hoping they'll finish up quickly and I can still make my escape.

"I can't—I can't fucking believe that asshole!" a venomous voice shouts. I know immediately it's Trisha, but she also sounds unlike any Trisha I've ever encountered before. I didn't even realize those words were in her vocabulary. "The fucking nerve! Did you see his dumb smug face? Oh, I could just—arghhh!" Her shrieks rival the sounds I made during childbirth, and it's clear who the focus of this tirade is: Principal Smith.

"Just take a deep breath, sweetie," another voice cuts in. Ruth's. "I'm sure you'll—"

"This is all fucking Brennan's fault. We had an understanding. It was almost a done deal. And then he had to go and get gout in his knees and retire earlier than we agreed he would!"

"Here, let me roll these oils on your wrist. It's my calming blend—"

"Me and Chad have a plan for Anabella and Cayden. Graduating top of their classes from *public school* so they look down-to-earth and stand out during Stanford admissions, but if they're not in this gifted program, they don't have a chance, and we are *not* going to commute to another school like some sort of—of—*refugees!*"

Refugees? Did this lady really just say that?

"No. No! This dumb shit from the middle of country-bumpkin-fucking-nowhere will not get in my—*their* way!"

"Smell it. It has chamomile, eucalyptus—"

"I would do anything to help my kids. *Anything.*"

"Lavender, frankincense—"

"I'm gonna fucking *kill him!*"

I hear the door slam open again, as Trisha stomps out with Ruth hurrying close behind.

FOUR

I WAIT A FEW MORE MINUTES TO MAKE SURE THE COAST IS clear and then sprint out of there, waving a quick goodbye to Dyvia, who tries to flag me down on the way out. I know I said I liked the drama, but maybe I'm not trying to live in *Real Housewives* after all. Trisha definitely didn't realize anyone besides Ruth could hear her tirade—there's no way she would've let her mask drop like that if she did—and I don't want to know what she would do if she realized I was eavesdropping. If I had to talk to her now, my face would give everything away.

I power walk home, and before I'm even all the way down our gravel path, I can hear Dad's chain saw snores through the door. I find him and Pearl both asleep on the couch in front of the television, her head on his chest and his arm around her. There's a half-eaten bowl of popcorn on the table, and Polly is hovering nearby with some suspicious crumbs on her nose.

Even though my back is going to make me pay for it when *I'm* trying to go to sleep later, I pick Pearl up and carry her to her bed. I lay her down and pull her pastel unicorn comforter up to her chin, and then I slip her bonnet on over the two simple braids my dad put in her hair. When I kiss the top of her head, though, she stirs.

"Did you have fun on your mommy playdate?" she whispers, her breath warm on my cheek. I can tell she didn't brush her teeth, but if I try to make that happen now, she'll be up for another hour.

"I did, baby."

"Were you nice? Did you share?"

I nod my head, chuckling softly. "And I made a new friend."

"Good job. I'm proud of you," she murmurs, her eyelids falling closed.

I turn off the light and shut the door, and then stand there for thirty seconds, waiting for rustling or a cry of *Mommy*. But it doesn't come. I'm in the clear.

In the kitchen, I rinse the dishes in the sink, load the dishwasher, and go through the stack of mail, leaving the bills to open tomorrow. I fold the load of laundry that was in the dryer and set the musty towels in the washing machine to go for another cycle. I'll remember to move them this time. I open up Pearl's backpack and sort through everything in there: some graded work, a flyer for Saturday morning soccer, and a library field trip permission slip I need to sign. Then I pack her lunch for tomorrow because corn dogs are on the cafeteria menu and I know that's going to be a solid nope for her. If I cut up the peaches and make her peanut butter and jelly the night before, then surely that'll solve all of our morning time-management problems, right?

I notice a note scratched on the yellow legal pad Dad always keeps on the counter. In his all-caps, tilted handwriting it reads *MAVES—CALL COREY BACK*. So, Corey did mean to call me. My mind starts rushing through the possible reasons why . . . He already sent his support payment for this month, with extra for Pearl's new school supplies. So it's not that. Maybe his current tour is going to go on longer than he planned? He did say the next contract was coming up soon . . .

But no. I'm not going to worry about any of this right now. Because I've finally reached the point in the night when it's my time. Pearl is asleep, my chores are done (or done-ish, 'cause they're never *done* done), and I can actually do what I want. I can choose the smart, responsible option and go straight to sleep while it's still possible to get those elusive eight hours (that whole sleep-when-the-baby-sleeps thing stays relevant). *Or* I can grab one of those sour beers out of the fridge and stream last night's *Bachelor in Paradise* now that it's available without commercials. The options are thrilling.

Ultimately it's Polly who makes my decision for me, though. There's a flash of movement in the corner of my eye, and when I turn, she's mid-crouch, about to leave another little present on my dad's favorite rug.

"No! No, Polly!" I hiss, which seems to have no effect. She continues to lower her booty to the ground, looking away, as if that makes her invisible.

"Walk! I'm gonna take you for a walk!" Her ears perk up at the W-word, and she quickly pulls herself up and trots to the front door, where her pink leash is hanging from a hook. I clip it on and quietly open the door so I don't wake up Dad, who's still snoring on the couch.

Outside, the humidity has finally broken, and instead of hot and soupy, there's a breeze and just a hint of a bite in the air. It won't get truly chilly until December, maybe November if we're lucky this year.

"You going out right now, baby?" the sweet honey voice calls to me from across the street, and Polly immediately tugs me that way toward Ms. Joyce, who's standing out at her curb. She's a tiny woman, barely taller than the recycling can she's holding on to, but she has a big, picked-out gray Afro and an even bigger personality. "It's eleven, and you know what they say. Only thing open right now is liquor stores and, well, you know . . ." She presses her lips together and looks me up and down.

"Ms. Joyce!" My eyebrows jump up in surprise and I laugh. "What are you trying to say?"

"Hmmm. I don't know. What *am* I saying? Anyway, I'm trying to bring these bins in. Your little friend next door is about to report me to the FBI, the CIA, the KGB, and who knows all else if I don't have 'em in by her seven a.m. run."

"Ms. Joyce, now you know Mackenzie Skinner is not my friend."

She gives me another assessing look, clutching her cheetah-print robe tight around herself. "Is that not you I see waving to her in the morning?"

"Yeah, but that's just being friendly."

"Hmmm. Well, isn't that nice?" She glances over at the Skinner house, where the windows are dark. "Did I tell you the first thing she asked me when they moved in?"

Ms. Joyce has told me what Mackenzie asked her, like, fifty-'leven times at this point, but I still widen my eyes and say, "No! What?"

"This lady asked me if we had an HOA. Now what kind of person in their right mind *wants* an HOA." She sucks her teeth and shakes her head. "But let me be quiet."

"Can I help you bring in those bins?"

"No, it's all right. I can manage 'em on my own."

But I grab the trash can and carry it to the side of her house, just as I've done for her countless times over the years. Ms. Joyce has been on this street even longer than Dad, and when we moved here—a single dad and a mama-less two-year-old—she stepped in without hesitation, sending over plates of food, showing Dad how to do my hair, and watching me *after* the afterschool program when his court sessions went long.

And she wasn't the only one. There was Mr. Isaac next door, who would mow our lawn along with his own, and Ms. Bernadette, who organized the Labor Day block party every year. Her oldest daughter, Ebony, tutored me in calculus *and* taught me how pads work when my dad just left the box on my dresser. Dad said he felt guilty moving away from where our family began so soon after Mom died, but he just couldn't bear to be in the same house, the same place, where I lived my first years and she lived out her last. But the people on this block became our family.

Now, though, they're almost all gone. Replaced by the Skinners and other young families drawn in by all the glitzy real estate flyers and Redfin ads that describe our neighborhood as "revitalized" and "up and coming." Even though, for Dad and Ms. Joyce and the few original Black owners that are left, it's already *been* here. And the new residents' kids play at Brady Park and go to Knoll Elementary with Pearl—but instead of fitting right in like I did, she stands out. Who knows what Knoll will look like just a few years from now, if Trisha gets her way and all the kids but the "gifted" ones get transferred out.

But no. Principal Smith put an end to that. The man's got some weird staring problems that he needs to get under control, but at least he can stand up to Trisha. Hopefully he can keep Knoll Elementary from becoming completely unrecognizable while Pearl is still there.

As I walk with Polly in the glow of the streetlights, I make note of the FOR SALE signs and houses under construction, soon to be flipped. The prices keep going up higher and higher—I nearly choked when I saw what the two bed, one bath Ms. Bernadette used to live in went for. Now it has gray walls, a designer water-wise lawn, and a second floor in progress, and it'll probably go for double that when the developers are done. Dad could make so much money if he downsized or maybe got a place in that retirement community closer to the beach. The only reason he needs all the space is Pearl and me. Maybe it's time I revisit looking for our own place again. I don't want to be what holds him back.

Polly stops to sniff a tree and do her business again, and I realize we've wandered all the way to the school. I've somehow found myself back here for the third time today, like some sort of messed-up homing pigeon. Oh god, I need to go to sleep. Reset, start again tomorrow, and try to come here only the normal amount of times. I tug on Polly's leash so we can start back, but of course she's lying on the grass, all comfortable. I've definitely taken her too far, and I'm probably going to get stuck carrying her butt for the last block, which is right on track with this too-long, too-difficult day.

"You get five minutes," I say, reaching down to rub her belly. She rolls over some more to help me get a better angle.

I didn't bring headphones—I watched too much *Dateline* and *Law & Order*, Dad's favorite shows, at a young and impressionable age to make that mistake. (Note to self: check to make sure they were streaming Disney and not *SVU* on the TV when I get home.) So, instead of music, I listen to the sounds of the neighborhood: hushed barks, crickets chirping, cars on the distant freeway. It's surprisingly peaceful, and I can see why Polly is ready to turn in for the night right here.

"Okay, Polly, time to go." I gently tug on her leash a couple more times, unsuccessfully. She lays her head on her paws to let me know she's perfectly content where she is, thank you. "C'mon, girlfriend. We are both too tired for this."

All of a sudden, Polly hops up, ears perked, and I think she's decided to do me a solid. But no, her body goes rigid, pointed in the direction of the school's front gate, just around the corner. It takes me a moment, but then I hear what she's hearing. A thud—maybe something big being set down or a heavy footstep?—followed by the long, scratchy sound of something being dragged. It repeats a couple more times, and I start to brush it off as something mechanical. Maybe they've got some giant Roomba going around the place or a loud, busted sprinkler system watering the rose garden in the courtyard. But then there's an erratic clattering that sounds like items falling onto the concrete, followed by a sharp, whispered "Shit."

Someone's there.

Someone who sounds like they're having as bad a day as I am.

Should I help? Would that freak them out if I just appeared out of the darkness like this?

I start to make my way closer, cutting through the grass at the corner, and Polly follows tentatively behind me, her tail between her legs.

"Shit. Fuck. Fucking goddamn it."

That makes me pause. It's late. There's no one else around. Well, except for my puppy, who's only barked, like, six times in her life, so if something happened to me, she wouldn't even alert the neighborhood. I should probably just turn around and go home. This is not my business.

But now, I'm also curious.

I carefully peer around the corner, hidden by the bougainvillea that creeps up the side of the building. And I see the back of the clumsy, cursing person. They have a dark bob and a royal-blue shift dress. It's . . . Trisha?

I don't realize how scared I was feeling until my chest loosens with relief. It's just Trisha. The only threat she poses is tricking me into volunteering for even more school activities.

"Fucking fuck fuck."

Trisha *is* having a really bad day. First, Principal Smith threatens her Knoll Elementary monarchy in a public setting, and now this?

And . . . what exactly is this?

I squint in the darkness to take in more of the details. Her minivan is waiting at the curb, with the trunk open, but the lights off. She's wearing the same outfit as she was earlier in the night, but now it's accessorized by yellow rubber gloves and the kind of blue mesh booties that they make you put on at bougie open houses. The clattering sound I heard earlier was a collection of plastic bottles. They look like . . . cleaning supplies? I recognize the blue and red Clorox label. She reaches down to grab the bottles, putting them in a black trash bag. Near her are two more giant black trash bags. They're bulging, stuffed to the very top with something. Must be something heavy, because I think that was the dragging sound I heard.

So Trisha was, what, cleaning the school? That doesn't fit in with the Trisha I know. Trisha doesn't even clean her own house—I know because she's recommended the woman who does, Gloria, to me multiple times.

But what else could be in the bags? All the contents of Principal Smith's office, because she's already ordered his transfer? Or no, probably Principal Smith himself. Better to dispose of him altogether so there's no chance of him coming back and thwarting her gifted school plans. Ha!

Just then, Trisha turns around, killing whatever laughter was bubbling up in my chest. Her face is unlike I've ever seen it before—instead of cool and composed, it's transformed into a mask of fury. Her eyebrows are arched high on her forehead, rippled with more deep wrinkles than we counted in the whole PTA meeting, and her nostrils flare out as she breathes heavily—from exertion or rage, I can't tell. Her lips curl around her sharp, bared teeth. And in the darkness, her blue eyes look black, like the ashes left over from a blazing fire. I can feel my legs backing away all on their own before I've even made the decision to go. I don't know what's going on, but I know I don't want to be here anymore.

I take a few steps back, keeping close to the wall of the school, but Polly doesn't follow. Instead, she reaches her snout high in the air and lets out a piercing howl so loud they probably hear her clear across town.

Trisha, only yards away around the corner, *definitely* hears her.

"No," I whisper to Polly. "Stop."

And she does. But it's only because she drops down and flips onto her side, her paws limply in the air.

She's playing dead. Just like Pearl taught her.

"Hello?" Trisha calls. "Who's there?"

"Polly," I whisper urgently. "Polly, alive. You're alive. We need to go *right now*."

I lean down and try to turn her over, but she doesn't budge. And now I can hear Trisha's footsteps, coming to investigate. My heart races as I think about her finding me here. Something insistent, something instinctual, tells me I don't want that to happen.

So I scoop Polly up in my arms and take off down the sidewalk, not looking back.

FIVE

"MAVIS, YOU ARE A DUMBASS," I SAY INTO THE MIRROR THE next morning. My neck is tweaked, my shoulders are stiff and sore, and my arms and thighs are aching. All because I picked up my puppy and ran down the street from the, yes, very angry but also totally harmless PTA president for no damn reason.

I was carrying on like a total fool, huffing and puffing and outright exercising like I wasn't the kid who almost failed the Presidential Physical Fitness Test in seventh grade. I mean, I *did* realize how ridiculous I was being about halfway home and put down a very disappointed Polly. But I actually convinced myself I was in danger for a second there. From Trisha! *Trisha!* What did she do, cut up Principal Smith with safety scissors and carry him out in a black trash bag? Was she going to, like . . . *what*? Make me her next victim?

"You deserve this," I say as I pop two ibuprofen and put the bottle in my workbag for later. "You are a dumbass and you deserve this."

The only good thing about staying up most of the night, restless and in pain, is that I don't miss my alarm, and Pearl and I make it to the side gate twenty minutes before school starts, in the right socks. It's a pretty flawless morning, all things considered.

"Have a good day!" I say, squeezing her into a tight hug.

"I will try," she whispers in my ear. "But for your information, Papa and I never finished my math homework, so that may make it kind of hard."

She plants a toothpaste-scented kiss on my cheek and then runs off to her line. Well, I did my best.

I walk toward the corner because I parked in the totally legal (but also totally far) zone across the street, but Francine the crossing guard is absorbed in a spirited conversation with a mom in a straw visor and striped leggings. I catch a few stray words, *gone* and *affair*, and I back up a few steps to give them their privacy. I'm not trying to be involved in anyone else's drama anymore.

I look around—for Jasmine, I tell myself. But let's be honest, it's early. She and Langston are probably still rushing around at home, just like Pearl and I would usually be doing. I'm *really* looking for someone else. But as I swivel my head around—not to avoid other people as usual, but to look for one specific person—disappointment washes over me. I don't see him. Yesterday might have been a fluke, the rare day he drops his kid off. I should probably just let this go.

On the other side of the crosswalk, though, a messy bun, glowing orange in the morning light, does catch my eye. It's Corinne, standing behind two boys with bulky backpacks and matching ginger hair. I wave at her, and I swear we make eye contact. But instead of waving back, she quickly squeezes her boys' shoulders and then turns around and hurries off down the sidewalk.

My heart sinks. I mean, maybe she didn't see me, but I feel a little . . . snubbed? I'll admit, I'm a little wary about making white friends. I've been burned too many times by women trying to make me the Black bestie sidekick promised to them in their youth, the Dionne to their Cher—or even worse, use me as a human shield in their Facebook arguments. ("Well, I have a Black friend, so . . .") But I liked Corinne—*like* Corinne—and kinda hoped it might go further than just snarky comments passed back and forth in a PTA meeting.

"So, where'd you park this morning?" I know who it is before I even turn around, and my stomach does somersaults as I lock eyes with my parking ticket hero. "Because I will fight the establishment with you again, just say the word. But also, I really like these shoes. And these pants."

"I am so, so sorry! I should have just taken the ticket and not made it this whole big thing."

"No, you shouldn't have," he says, waving that away with a crinkly-eyed smile. "He didn't give a ticket to anyone else parked there. It wasn't right." He winces, cheeks flushing. "Though my methods may have been a little extreme . . ."

"No. No, not at all!"

He raises a skeptical eyebrow.

"Okay," I laugh. "So, maybe a little, but—"

"Miss, are you crossing or not?" Francine's booming voice cuts in.

"Uh, no . . . not just yet, thank you," I mumble, scooting away from the corner. "I'm just gonna talk to . . ." I wave vaguely at the man because I still don't know his name, and then start giggling nervously because maybe he didn't even want to have an in-depth discussion with me and was just trying to be cordial and get to work. And now, here I am making him late again . . .

"Jack," he supplies, cutting off my spinning thoughts.

"Jack," I repeat. "I'm gonna talk to Jack. Me, Mavis—I'm going to talk to Jack."

"Okay," Francine says with a smirk, her eyes jumping between the both of us. I already know what's going to be on the agenda for tomorrow's spirited conversation.

"Nice to meet you, Mavis." Jack reaches forward and envelopes my hand with both of his own. His grip is strong and warm—and ringless, I note. I have to look up to meet his gaze, which rarely happens to me at five ten, but he's tall. Tall enough that if we were standing any closer, my face would fit right into the curve under his jaw, the stubble rough on my skin. I am close enough, though, to see that his green eyes have flecks of gold, and they're so open, so inviting, that I have to look away first or I'll fall right in.

"Nice to meet you, too. And thank you for ruining your pants for me."

His cheeks flush a deeper pink, and he runs his hand over his face. "Uh, yeah. Anytime."

"Oh, no. I didn't mean it like—not that *you* were even saying . . ." I cover my face, too, which I'm 99 percent sure might actually be engulfed in flames. "You know what, I'm just gonna stop right there."

"I know what you meant." He laughs, and it's a good one. Low and rumbly, the kind of sound you feel more than hear.

I look down at his pants, self-conscious. I half expect them to still be stained with mud, but of course they're crisp and clean—and slightly snug, the gray fabric falling perfectly over toned legs, hugging him in just the right places.

Okay, so, nope, can't look there either.

I'm suddenly aware just how sweaty I am. I mean, I feel like I've been in a permanent state of sweaty since I had Pearl, but this is definitely another level. I surreptitiously (I hope) swipe a finger over my top lip to make sure there's not some glistening going on, at least, on the mustache I should have gotten threaded . . . like, two weeks ago. Oh god. Maybe I should just hold my hand over my mouth, to be safe. Is that weird? That's weird.

Why am I acting like this? Jack is not my type at all. The closest I've come to dating a white guy is yelling at my screen about which Bachelors are here for the wrong reasons. Not that I'm even looking to date. And I'm definitely not looking to date a dad of someone at my daughter's school.

"So what grade is your kid in?" I ask, bringing us back on the correct path.

He squints at me and then laughs, shaking his head. "No—"

But whatever he was going to say is lost when Ruth leaps between us, clutching my arm. "Mavis! Oh, good, I've been trying to find the whole PTA crew."

"Well," I mumble, glancing nervously at Jack. "I wouldn't say I'm part of the PTA crew—"

"Have you heard?" Ruth asks, eyes sparkling with excitement. It's very clear she's already done this dance many times this morning and is eager for another round. "About Principal Smith? And the whole scene at the office!"

"I don't think I have—"

"Oh, hi, Mr. Cohen!" she says, turning to Jack. "Have *you* heard?"

"Mr. Cohen?" I ask, my stomach filling with dread. "You're a teacher here? What grade do you teach?"

"I'm not a teacher. I'm the school psychologist," he explains quickly. "So if you were—if we . . . I won't teach Pearl."

What, now? He knows who Pearl is? Did he know that before or after yesterday morning? And why would he even need to tell me that? Unless . . .

"But hold on, Mrs. Gentry," Jack continues, his brow furrowing as he looks at Ruth. "What did you say about Principal Smith and a scene?"

"His wife is here! She was waiting outside this morning when the first staff members showed up!" Ruth answers gleefully, delighting in the moment she's been waiting for. "She was yelling, cursing—even *crying*, Felicia's manny said. He was closer and had a better angle than me, so we compared notes. I heard Mrs. Nelson tried to help her calm down, just so everyone could, you know, *understand*—and she got screamed at, too, poor thing! Can you believe that? I mean, *really*." She shakes her head in disapproval, eagerly checking our faces for the same.

"Okay, but . . . why, though?" I ask.

"Oh, well, all this carrying on was because *apparently*—" She presses her lips together tightly and raises her eyebrows. "Apparently, Principal Smith didn't come home last night after the PTA meeting. She's been calling his phone all night long, no answer. She says he's missing!"

Missing. Principal Smith is . . . missing? What the hell?

Did his toe-to-toe with Trisha in the auditorium shake him up that much? Maybe he drove to the closest bar and proceeded to drink away his troubles. I know I might go on a bender if I saw a long future ahead of me of having to fight for my authority with Trisha Holbrook. Could be he just hightailed it right back to Wherever, Florida, and is gonna send for his family when he gets there.

But of course, that's just a funny little fantasy, not real life. This is an adult with a pension and a mortgage. Roots. He's not running away because of some contentious meeting. It's more likely he got in an accident or . . . fell asleep somewhere? I don't know.

It's a sign of how little sleep I got last night that I keep replaying that moment with Trisha outside of the school. The cleaning supplies, the giant black trash bags, the chilling look on her face. And the conclusions I jumped to that seemed so silly in the morning light . . . Obviously, that has nothing to do with this. But still. I can't get her expression of pure rage out of my mind.

"Mavis! Yoo-hoo!"

I jump, and my heart speeds up so fast it feels like it's going to burst right out of my chest. A cold, clammy hand grips my arm.

"I need to talk to you. Now, please."

"THANK YOU FOR MEETING WITH ME," TRISHA SAYS, CLASP-ing her hands tightly on top of her white, glossy desk.

"Of course," I respond, my face stretched into a smile that I hope looks natural.

As if I had a choice.

I mean, it's not as if she forced me to go with her. There was no knife at my side, urging me along. She didn't push me forward or even touch me again. But it was hard not to feel like I was being perp walked by Olivia Benson through the Knoll Elementary hallways as Trisha stood just a centimeter behind my elbow, giving me verbal directions to her lair.

Because that's what this room is. Her lair. I don't care that it reads PTA LOUNGE on the door—this space clearly belongs to her. The walls are covered with pictures of Trisha: shaking hands with the school board president, smiling with her family in matching Adidas outfits at the Fun Run, posing with a shovel at the Arbor Day tree-planting ceremony. The tall bookshelf behind her has only three hardcovers on it (*The Art of War*, *The Prince*, and something by Brené Brown)—the rest of the shelves display golden gavels on wooden stands, with her name and different school years etched on tiny placards, probably some sort of PTA Oscars. I'm counting each of them and trying to will the tiny bead of sweat rolling down my spine to evaporate, when she speaks to me again.

"I wanted to check in about last night."

The one bead of sweat on my back immediately multiplies into ten more, and my pits join the party, too. Is she . . . is she talking about what I think she's talking about?

I start speaking fast. "I was jus—I was going for a walk and it was dark. *So* dark. I could barely see even five inches in front of me. And I wasn't—I *swear* I wasn't trying to like snoop or anything. Honestly! It was just Polly, she gets tired, and then she was playing dead. I don't—"

"Please stop talking," Trisha says, holding up her hand. "Mavis, I have no idea what you're going on about."

My whole body freezes. "Huh?"

"While I would love to hear more about your, uh . . . dog . . . at some point in the future—" She purses her lips as she primly tucks her dark hair behind her ear. "That's certainly not the reason why I called you here. I have a lot of other business to take care of today, as I'm sure you do, too."

I blink at her. "What?"

"I wanted to see what you thought," she says, slowly enunciating each word, like we speak different languages. Which, it kind of feels like we do right now. "About your first PTA meeting? The one you attended last night."

"Oooooh!" I exhale, my cheeks burning. "That!"

"Yes. That."

God, I need to get it together and stop making up these ridiculous stories in my mind.

"The meeting . . ." I start, breathing deeply again to slow

down my speeding heart. I need to be normal, relaxed. "The meeting was, um . . . It was great!"

She nods with finality, as if there was no other possible answer. "I'm just so sorry you had to witness that unfortunate interlude with Mr. Smith. That was very unusual, I can assure you, but don't worry. It won't happen again."

"Because he's missing?" The question escapes from my lips before my brain sends the message that I should probably just shut the hell up.

Trisha leans forward over her desk, narrowing her eyes. "What's that?"

"Um, Ruth just told me. Right before you walked up," I rush to explain. "I guess Principal Smith didn't come home last night? And his wife showed up this morning looking for him? Or, um, something like that."

Her blue eyes flicker like the hottest part of the fire, and the silence goes on for just a beat too long, making me sweat again. Finally, a small smile spreads across her glossy pink lips, but it does nothing to settle my nerves.

"Oh. Well, yes. That is true." She shrugs and leans back in her shiny leather chair. "I don't *personally* know all the details yet regarding that situation. I was only referring to the fact that he hopefully learned his lesson last night—to stay in his lane."

"You mean because of the gifted school . . . how he stopped that from happening?" Another rogue question. I need to just glue my lips together at this point.

I'm expecting another fiery stare, definitely some deep forehead wrinkles, but to my surprise, Trisha beams and then . . . starts to laugh. Like, throws her head back, straight cracks up, until her shoulders are shaking and she's gasping for air. I stare at her, unsure how to respond.

"I'm sorry. Forgive me," she chokes out between giggles. "It's just—stopped? Is that what you thought?"

She throws her head back again, wiping tears from her eyes. And I try to figure out what in the world is going on. Principal Smith said he removed Knoll from the running to become the site of the new gifted school. That was very clear last night, and Trisha was very, *very* pissed.

So why is she laughing? I don't know. But what I *do* know is that I want to get out of here. Right now.

"Well, I better head out to work," I say, tentatively rising from my chair.

Her laughter stops immediately, like someone just pressed the mute button. "To answer your question, Mavis: no, I wouldn't say the plans have stopped just yet. We'll just have to wait and see, won't we?"

She smiles at me slyly, and it makes me nervous . . . but also mad? She really thinks she's going to get exactly what she wants, no matter how it affects other kids at the school. And *of course* she does. That's how it's always gone in the years Pearl's been at Knoll. No wonder I worked up this fantasy in my mind that she did something extreme. Because she would. Not, like, murder, because again this is real life. But she'd definitely try to get him fired.

I need to start looking into this planned gifted school more, maybe actually talk to other parents and organize or something, if we're going to have any chance of stopping her. That's what the PTA's DEI chair should do, right? I can't let this lady change Knoll, and this neighborhood, even more.

"Good talking to you, Trisha," I say, turning away from her toward the door, because there's no way I'm keeping the bitch face on lockdown right now.

"Yes, it was *so* wonderful, Mavis!" she coos. "I'm *so* excited to have you on our team!"

I sigh when I'm outside in the hallway, relief flooding through my body. But then her door swings open, banging against the wall, and I jump like I'm competing in an Olympic event.

"Twin day!" Trisha shouts, eyes wild and smile manic as she peers through the opening. She looks like the dad in *The Shining*—all that's missing is the ax.

"Um . . . what?" I take a single step back, even though my body is screaming at me to run.

"Twin day!" she repeats. "You know, for spirit week? It's coming up quick! I figured that Anabella and Pearl will be twins! And I know you're so busy, Working Mama! So don't even worry about it. I'll get them matching dresses from Hanna Andersson. You can Zelle me!"

"Oh, um . . . thank you, Trisha," I choke out. "That's really nice of you."

See, no big deal. She's just being nice and normal and not creepy at all.

I need to get, like, whatever is the opposite of a venti latte on the way to work today and chill the fuck out.

"Oh, and, Mavis?" Trisha stares at me from the doorway, still smiling, but it's slightly dimmed. Her body is almost unnaturally still. "You should text me next time you go walking at night. I'm trying to get more exercise, too. It's so hard to fit it in during the day."

How did she . . . ? Oh, because, duh. I just mentioned it in my silly little ramble when I completely misinterpreted everything.

"Yeah, okay," I say. "Sure, Trisha."

"We can be walking buddies," she continues. It's quiet in the hallways, the kids haven't been let in yet. But her voice dips lower, her words are slow and steady, and I have to strain to hear her. "It's always better to have a buddy. Someone on your side. Especially at night. It can be . . . *dangerous* out there if you're not careful. You need to look out for yourself."

Her eyes flicker like flames again, and she adds in a singsong voice, "Better to be safe than sorry."

Okay.

Well.

Shit.

It might have been possible to convince myself I was just making things up before, but nope. Now I can't deny it. Trisha did something last night. Something bad. And I saw it. And she *knows* I saw it.

"Oh, and I gave Dyvia your number! For your DEI committee!" She claps her hands sharply and smiles widely again, all of her sparkling teeth visible. But it's like an optical illusion: one blink and she's a woman who's just really fucking pumped about the PTA; another blink and she's an animal baring its teeth.

All I can manage to get out is a squeaky "Yeah?"

"Yes! She's so excited to join you, and I think she has some more recruits, too. Yay! I know you all are going to do *such* important work." Her voice is back to its normal tinkling-bell pitch, and it makes me wonder if I just hallucinated that . . . threat. Or whatever it was. I'm getting whiplash from how quickly her moods are changing.

"Well, bye now!" Trisha flutters her fingers in my direction and then firmly pulls the door closed behind her before I can respond.

I need to slow my breathing down. I need to get my heart rate to something that won't have me keeling over here in the hallway. I try to take a big gulp of air, but instead a giggle comes bubbling up out of my chest. Small at first, but in seconds I'm folded over at the waist, totally overcome by silent and slightly hysterical laughter. Because what is even happening?

I start moving, desperate to be outside, desperate for air. And I slam straight into a brick wall.

Except this brick wall is warm and covered in soft navy gingham and smells like citrus and pine. Because this brick wall is Jack Cohen.

How does this man keep swooping in at my very worst moments?

"Hey." His green eyes crinkle as he smiles, looking for the joke. But his expression quickly smooths into something more serious when he picks up on the unhinged edge to my glee. "Are you okay?"

I can't answer. Because I can't catch my breath. And that must be answer enough, because he gently cups my elbow in his palm. "Let me take you to my office, Mavis."

I let him lead me around the corner and down the hall to a door with SCHOOL PSYCHOLOGIST written in gold block letters on the front. He pulls out a comfortable leather chair and gestures for me to sit down, closing the door behind us, and then he settles in an identical chair across a wide oak desk.

"You need to breathe, Mavis. Are you okay with me helping you with that?"

I try to answer, but it comes out as a weird, croaky chuckle, so instead I just nod.

"All right, let's do this together." He closes his eyes, steadying his hands on the desk in front of him. "Breathe in through your nose, one, two, three, and four . . ." I do as I'm told. "And then hold it in for a count of seven . . . Good, really good, and then you're going to exhale all the way, counting to eight, real big." He lets out his breath in a loud, silly whoosh, and I giggle—this time, though, because something was actually funny and not because I'm questioning my perception of reality and also maybe having a minor breakdown.

"Is that helping?" he asks with a grin, squinting one eye open, and I nod again. "Okay, let's do it a few more times."

I follow him through the breathing exercises some more, and in few minutes, my heart rate has slowed down and my chest no longer feels like I'm wearing a too-tight *Bridgerton* corset.

"Better?"

"Better."

"So, uh . . . what's going on?" he asks, his thick eyebrows pinched together. "I saw you coming out of the PTA lounge."

I consider lying. That would be the smart, sane thing to do right now with a staff member at my child's school. But when that aforementioned staff member just witnessed me completely losing my shit and is also super, unnaturally hot . . . well, I just don't know how I can be expected to perform smart *or* sane right now.

So, before I can talk myself out of it, I tell him everything. How Principal Smith and Trisha argued at the PTA meeting over the site of Beachwood Unified's gifted school, and the threats I heard her make in the bathroom after, which I brushed off as her just letting off steam. I tell him how I saw her dragging those huge trash bags and cleaning supplies in the dark outside the school, and how I took off running when I saw her angry face. And finally, I tell him everything she just said to me now, the innocuous comments that could have also been veiled threats because she saw me last night and she knows that I know. But also how I'm probably making a *thing* out of nothing, because she's helping with my committee and buying Pearl a dress. And so maybe I should just go now, because this is definitely just in my head and, also, sorry for wasting his time . . .

"So let me get this straight." I'm halfway out of my seat, ready to sprint away or possibly just spontaneously combust, when Jack's voice makes me pause. "You think Trisha killed Principal Smith after the PTA meeting last night, carried his butchered body parts out the front gate, and that's the reason why he didn't show up to work today?"

I slap my palm against my forehead, shaking my head at myself. "Well, when you say it like that . . ."

He holds his palms up. "I mean . . . it's not . . . totally outside the realm of possibility."

That makes me sit back down. I study his face, but I can't read him. Is he being serious? "It's not?"

"Well . . . Mrs. Holbrook can be a little, uh, intense. Especially when it comes to her kids." He shakes his head, and a small smile tugs at his lips. "I'll never forget my first year here. There was this assembly—a puppet thing. Paul Perrigrew's Puppets for Peace. It was really called that. He did all the voices, taught the kids to not bully and recycle and everything. Anyway, he needed a volunteer, and Cayden Holbrook raised his hand, but the guy, the poor, *poor* guy, called on someone else. Trisha stood up in the back—and I'm not even sure why she was there, but she shut the whole thing down, quoting a fire code we were breaking, or something like that. I can still hear the wails of the kindergartners as they were led back to class with no puppets or peace."

"No!"

"Yes." His grin grows, and I match it. "And I heard she launched a smear campaign against him all over Beachwood, and he lost his contract with the district. I actually saw him at the library one time after. He was performing to a crowd of maybe three kids, and two of them had their backs to him, laughing together over an Elephant and Piggie book. When I headed out a couple hours later, I saw some felt arms and a miniature top hat hanging out of the dumpster."

"Poor Paul," I murmur, shaking my head.

"Poor Paul," Jack repeats, trying to match my tone. "Poor peaceful puppets."

"And if she could do *that* to Paul . . ."

"Then who's to say murdering a principal is outside her purview?" he finishes, sighing solemnly. But then he snorts, and a tiny snicker follows, seemingly against his will. I'm joining in before I know it, and we both sit there giggling together until all the tension and anxiety that were remaining in my body are gone, and I just feel warm and easy, like I've been lying out in the sunshine. And not, you know, contemplating if the PTA president has murder-y vibes.

"Still, I think that maybe . . ." Jack gently bites his bottom lip and then nods once, his eyes filled with resolve. "Maybe we'll both feel better if we look into it. Just a little bit."

"Yes, just a little minor sleuthing, no big deal," I say, with a smirk, committing to the bit. He throws his head back in a singular "Ha!" and I feel my smile widen.

"No big deal. I mean, kids do it all the time in books, right? Do you think you're more of a Frank or Joe? Or I guess a Nancy."

"No idea who those people are, but I'm definitely an Olivia Benson."

"Okay, then I'll be Stabler." He unbuttons and starts to roll up the sleeves of his button-up, revealing his tanned, muscular forearms. And I don't know if it's those or the *SVU* reference, but my stomach aches in appreciation. "I hope there's some perfectly innocent explanation for all this. And if there is . . ." He mimes zipping his lips and throwing away the key. "But it's not going to hurt anyone if we just . . . make sure. Your gut is telling you that something is wrong, and that's not nothing—I say we listen to that."

I know we're probably just having fun here, but *god*—I barely trust my own gut. How is this man I barely know so willing to follow my truly bonkers gut on this journey? I'm not going to ask him that, though, and break the spell of whatever is happening right now. Instead I say, "Thank you."

"You're welcome," he says, like it's a small thing, when it's enormous. "So, I'm wondering what your thoughts are on this. But I actually *don't* think we should go to the police—"

I'm nodding my head in agreement before he even finishes his sentence. "No. We *cannot*!" I snort and shake my head. "Oh my god, could you even imagine me trying to make a report? 'Officer, Trisha was cleaning up the school after hours. And, and—she offered to run with me!' She'll come out looking like a saint, and they'll laugh me right out of there." And the laughing will continue in the Knoll Elementary Parents Facebook group, probably for eternity. This is not that serious, and *definitely* not call-the-cops serious.

"I think you have a little more than that." I raise an eyebrow, and then he shakes a finger at me, conceding the point. "Okay, okay, so maybe not. But we're on the same page here. No cops. I think we should ask around some more, see if anyone else has noticed something suspicious. Subtly, of course. And there's one person who knows everything there is to know at Knoll . . ."

"Lilliam," we both say at the same time. If there is any gossip buzzing, any clues, Knoll's front office manager will know about it.

"See, the thing is," I start nervously. "Ms. Lilliam kind of hates me."

"Hates you?" he asks with a playful smile. "How could anyone hate you?"

I roll my eyes and shrug. "You ask for just a few late slips . . ."

Laugh lines appear next to his lips as his grin deepens, like another level of happiness unlocked after the starbursts around his eyes. It makes me wonder what other secrets his face has, waiting for me to discover.

"Well, I'll take the lead in that conversation then. And we should probably wait until tomorrow, before school. The bell is going to ring soon, and that's when Lilliam likes to have her second cup of cinnamon coffee."

"Oh, I know because I always interrupt it!"

"And I should probably get your number."

"What?" I blink at him. Did I hear that right, or is my brain already speeding into another fantasy?

"So we can share anything we learn in the meantime. You know, for the investigation."

Right. Because that's what we're doing: "investigating." Conducting a totally innocent, aboveboard investigation into a crime that might not even be an actual crime. That's all this is.

But . . . there's the way he's looking at me right now. Even as he dips his hand into his pocket for his phone, his arm flexing impressively in the process, his heavy-lidded gaze doesn't leave mine. And when he bites his bottom lip again, typing in his passcode, I can feel my whole body flush. I can't remember the last time a man has looked at me like this, that I've even wanted any man to. If this *is* all some ruse to get to know me, to feel out whatever this is between us, well . . . that wouldn't be the worst thing in the world.

"Sure," I finally say, as calmly and casually as I can muster, and recite my cell number to him.

The bell rings, and I take that as my cue to leave, standing up. "Sorry to keep you. I know you have work to do."

"I'm glad you did, Mavis," he says, standing with me. "Really."

I glance quickly around the room, taking in all the details that I was too overwhelmed to notice before. Because what do I *really* know about this man that I've decided to investigate a possible murder with . . . or at least just pretend to, so I can hold on to this giddy, heady feeling? Besides the fact that he is incredibly attractive and is not scared to get his hands (or pants) dirty.

There are bookshelves lining the walls, but in a sharp contrast to Trisha's, they mostly hold books. Thick textbook-looking things like the *DSM*, but also row after row of kids' picture books and novels with bright, colorful spines. I spot a couple of framed degrees from the local state college and a stack of binders—including one labeled *Woodcock-Johnson Tests of Cognitive Abilities*, which I'm positive is just my brain messing with me until I blink a few times and realize that, no, it's real.

I tap his title on the door and turn to face him. "So . . . school psychologist, huh?"

"Yes, that's me," he says, and his chest puffs up, adorably proud.

"I guess I should know this already, but what exactly does a school psychologist do?"

"Well, I handle the assessments for IEPs, consult with teachers. And I also do individual and group counseling with a lot of the kids. This year, I'm planning to start a peer mentoring program, matching the fifth graders with the kindergartners."

"That all must be really rewarding."

He nods. "I like it a lot. This'll be my fifth year at Knoll."

"Then . . . how come I've never seen you on duty before—before yesterday?" There's no way I wouldn't have noticed him, even if I *am* usually racing against the late bell in a sweaty cloud of chaos.

"I was covering for Ms. Castillo. She was out sick."

I want to ask him something else, something that's been buzzing in the back of my mind since we were interrupted by Ruth a little while ago, but I'm probably overstaying my welcome. This man is trying to work and I'm making small talk—even though I *hate* small talk. He squints, giving me a questioning look. "What is it?"

"How did you know Pearl was my daughter then?" I ask slowly. "This morning, you knew her name." *And you also made it very clear you wouldn't ever teach her for some reason I don't want to analyze too much, or else I'll start fantasizing some more . . .*

"I, um, asked around," he says, nervously running his hands over his face and through his blond hair. It makes my whole body feel warm. "I wanted to make sure you were okay."

"That was nice of you."

"It was nothing, really," he murmurs, and it's clear we both know that's not true.

"Well, I'll see you tomorrow, Stabler," I say, walking toward the door again.

He looks me right in the eyes and waves. "Tomorrow, Benson."

I step outside his office, closing the door behind me, and before I make my way to the front gate, I pause against the wall and take a deep breath.

God, what have I gotten myself into? This whole morning has been sensory overload. I've gone through a roller coaster of feelings in what feels like hyper-speed: terrified and embarrassed and understood and also, maybe . . . turned on?

Which is *so* not an appropriate way to feel at my kid's school. Like, at all. I feel like a school security officer is going to jump out at any moment and ban me from the premises.

So I take another deep breath. *Jack believed me.* He didn't laugh or make me feel stupid. I don't know what we're going to find, snooping around. Honestly, I hope we find nothing. I hope

Principal Smith is back bright and early tomorrow morning with some totally reasonable explanation. But it's nice to have this with Jack in the meantime. A reason to keep getting to know him.

I hear someone blow their nose, loud and wet, and it startles me out of my thoughts. I look around to see where it's coming from, and I get my answer when a deep sob follows it. Across the hallway and to the right. The door reads LIBRARY.

I take a few tentative steps, and I can see through the slim crack of the propped-open door. Mrs. Nelson, the librarian, is sitting at her desk, shoulders shaking as she bawls. Her eyes are pink and swollen, and her black mascara is streaked down her cheeks. She looks so different from her tough persona at the gate that I almost don't believe it's her.

Ruth *did* say Mrs. Nelson got caught in the cross fire of Mrs. Smith's outburst this morning. Could she be crying because of that? Or maybe she and Principal Smith were friends? He hasn't been at Knoll very long, but I guess they probably worked together this summer during the transition . . .

Mrs. Nelson lets out another cry, followed by a long honking in her crumpled-up tissue, and I take a step back. I would be mortified if she caught me snooping. And this isn't my business anyway. I put my head down and hurry to the front gate.

Knoll Elementary Parents Facebook Group

Florence Michaelson

Does anyone know what the commotion was outside the office this morning? As many of you know, my Axel is highly sensitive to negative energy and whatever was going on really upset him. I'm wondering if I should keep him home tomorrow . . .

Ruth Gentry

Principal Smith is missing! I was dropping off a doctor note for Ryleigh with Lilliam and Mrs. Smith came to the office looking for him this morning. He didn't come home after the PTA meeting, and no one knows what happened to him!

Charlie Lee

Oh my gosh! This is so terrible! Keeping the Smith family in my thoughts and prayers

Felicia Barlow

It's been less than 24 hours, so the police won't even declare him missing yet

Della Lively

Is anyone else extremely disturbed by this? What do we even know about this man anyway?? I miss Principal Brennan ☹

Florence Michaelson

Well, the school has cameras everywhere. (Never mind the untold harm that the transmission waves and police state mentality are causing our children physically AND emotionally!!!) Anyway, can't they just check those to see what time he left?

Dyvia Mehta

Lilliam told me the footage was deleted!

Ruth Gentry

I heard that too! I really think they need to go door to door. I know Beachwood is mostly safe now, but some parts are still a little, well, you know . . .

Jasmine Hammonds

No, I don't know, Ruth. Please elaborate.

Angela Hart

I think a lot of us have an idea who they should be asking . . .

Corinne Ackerman

Who?

Angela Hart

Sending you a DM now

Trisha Holbrook

Just a friendly reminder to everyone that we're still looking for volunteers to be Room Parents! It's so important to give back to our school during these uncertain times!

SIX

ORGANIC CHAMOMILE OR RELAXING ROOIBOS DANDE-
lion. Those are my options.

I hold up each box of tea bags in the combination break room /
copy room / storage closet of Project Window, weighing which
type is most likely to calm my nerves and least likely to give me
food poisoning. The Organic Chamomile expired in May, so
that should be out, but the Relaxing Rooibos Dandelion has a
suspicious dark stain bleeding from the corner. And also I'm not
entirely sure I want to be drinking those little weeds that Pearl
picks up on our walks and stuffs in her pockets. So, Organic
Chamomile it is. May was only four months ago anyway, and
really those dates are just suggestions, right?

I pour hot water from the electric kettle that's been chipped
since I started working at Project Window seven years ago, and
while it's steeping, I start getting my mind right. Because I'm at
work, so it's time to *be at work*. Everything else fuzzing up my
brain and tightening my chest gets put in a sturdy metal box
while I'm here, locked up tight until it's five o'clock, when I can

open that thing up like Pandora again. I have to do this every day, with varying degrees of success, otherwise all the thoughts about whether Pearl brushed her teeth and if I turned in that field trip slip and is Pearl happy and I'm pretty sure I have to put that load through the washer again and I wonder what Pearl's going to talk about to her inevitable therapist at thirty and maybe I should just throw the whole load of laundry out at this point . . . and yeah. Those thoughts would just take over, and I would never get anything done.

So, along with all that and also my guilt about not checking Pearl's homework this morning, I throw in these new additions.

It's very possible I witnessed Knoll Elementary's PTA president doing something—best case, suspicious, worst case, *murderous*—last night. And she maybe, possibly, threatened me this morning. Plop, in the box.

I am investigating this with the superhot psychologist at my daughter's school, or maybe really just pretending to so we can keep flirting? Plop, in the box.

I want to do *other* things with that superhot psychologist, things that I haven't done with anyone in a very long time, and when I think about those things, my body feels like it's finally waking up even though I didn't realize it was sleeping, and what would I have done if he leaned across the table and . . . nope. No, no, no. Not right now. Plop! In the fucking box.

Throw an extra padlock on there, toss the key into the void. And I'll deal with all that once I don't have a million things I need to get done and only eight hours minus a lunch break to make it happen.

"Oh, here you are, Mavis!" Rose, Project Window's executive director, peeks her head full of blond curls past the teetering stack of boxes half blocking the door. "I've been looking everywhere!"

I hold up the paper cup of tea, which is turning a concerning green color. "Morning, Rose. Just grabbing something to drink."

"Yes, of course! Well, after you get your fuel, can you swing by the conference room?"

I run through my mental schedule, feeling a little panicked. "I'm so sorry. Did I forget we had a meeting?" But no, I'm pretty sure I didn't, because Wednesdays are the only days we *don't* have a morning team meeting, not to be confused with the twice-a-week *afternoon* team meeting or the biweekly *all-hands* meeting. Wednesdays are sacred—the days I can actually, reliably, get something done because my time isn't taken up by *talking* about getting something done.

"We didn't. I just scheduled it." She bounces on her heels and then beams at me with unblinking brown eyes. I swear nothing makes Rose more hyped than meetings. "Don't worry, though! You can have a beat to get settled. We'll start in, say . . ." She checks the sunshine-yellow Apple Watch on her wrist. "Thirty minutes. That good?"

No, it's not good. I have mentor logs to review and a training to start planning for next week, and I have to see if that email I sent out to the Beachwood Black Business Association, pitching them our program, got a response.

"Yep, that's good. Do I need to prepare anything?"

"No, just bring yourself! It shouldn't take more than an hour."

With that, she taps the doorframe and speed walks down the hallway, probably to ruin some more Project Window employees' plans for the day with this impromptu meeting. If I could send a warning flare up into the sky, I would.

Okay, so, make that seven hours minus a lunch break to get a million things done. *Organic Chamomile, it's time for you to do your thing!* I take a sip from the paper cup, and the expired tea . . . tastes expired. Of course. Should've gone with the Relaxing Rooibos Dandelion after all. *Relaxing* was right there in the name! I dump the disgusting green liquid down the sink, throw the cup in the recycling bin, and head back to my office.

Well, *office* might be an overstatement, when these thin dividers that don't even reach the ceiling are the only thing separating me from Sally and the consequences of the shaved brussels sprout salad she brings for lunch every day, and Dane's whispered arguments with his wife that he thinks no one else can hear. If I've only got thirty minutes, then I better make them count.

Project Window definitely wasn't my dream job. I saw myself leading my own nonprofit one day, getting involved in local politics—maybe even going to law school, eventually, like my dad. I was passionate about so many things: rights for the unhoused and police reform, improving public schools and community organizing. The possibilities to do good, to make real change in the world, seemed endless—and I wanted to explore each and every one. But eight months pregnant and newly married at my graduation from grad school, my dreams changed. Or, really, so many of my dreams were coming true that I couldn't be greedy. I needed stability, I needed a way to provide for my baby girl, my new family. And I needed health insurance—especially because we knew that wasn't coming anytime soon from Corey's collection of studio drumming gigs and part-time jobs.

When Rose offered me the position as an operations coordinator right there in the interview, just four weeks after Pearl was born, I accepted it immediately. Partly because my swollen, leaky boobs were about to soak through the nursing pads stuffed into my bra, but mostly because I was just so grateful to have something, some proof that I could take care of us. A good-enough salary and a modest 401(k) contribution and a benefits package that I could hold up to my dad and say, *See, we've got this. I know you think we're too young, I know you think I'm in over my head and maybe rushing into something I shouldn't, but I know what I'm doing.*

I found out later that operations coordinator was just a title for the person who does all the things no one else wants to do, like editing Rose's messy grant proposals and restocking the toilet paper, all great uses of my degrees. But this job carried our little family in those early years, still carries Pearl and me now. And I've worked my butt off to get two promotions in seven years (though only one of those actually came with more money) into my current position as operations *manager*. I'm in charge of all the logistics that keep our program moving smoothly. Processing Live Scans, filing mentor logs, booking venues for our fundraisers, reaching out to new partner schools . . . and yeah, okay, I still have to restock the toilet paper sometimes. I might not be changing the world, but I still am at least a part—a *crucial* part—in doing some good.

I open up Outlook, and there's an email from Rose sitting at the top of my inbox: Can you convert this Word doc into a PDF? I still can't figure it out, ha ha!

See? Crucial.

I convert the file for her, a thirty-second task that Rose could easily learn herself if she just tried to be a little less helpless . . . and I stopped indulging her learned helplessness. And then I take a deep breath and repeat the calming phrase that's been getting me through the past few months: *There is another promotion coming.* It's not a sure thing yet, but Rose and the board sent the internal job listing for program director straight to me and encouraged me to apply. It's a brand-new position, directly underneath Rose, to lead all of the managers and "help usher Project Window to its next chapter." I laughed when I first saw the listing. Like, "next chapter"? That's so vague. What does that even mean? But then I started dreaming about it—on my drives home, after Pearl went to sleep—all the things I'd like to do at Project Window if I was in charge and trusted with more than just converting Rose's files. Finding ways to fund field trips for the mentees, especially when so many kids on the Northside haven't even been to the beach on the other side of town. Partnerships with new and exciting organizations, so we can branch out from focusing so much on college, because that's not every kid's path, and also find more people of color to be mentors. Also, last year I organized an informal gathering with some of our more dedicated mentors and teens, kind of a career AMA, and I'd love to expand that into a full-on career fair. I'd definitely hold *way* fewer meetings.

Because I do believe in Project Window's mission and how life-changing mentorship can be for the kids who need it. There were so many people in my community, like Ms. Joyce and Mr. Isaac and Ebony, who took care of me when my dad was working to take care of me in other ways. And that made me feel supported and empowered and capable—because if those people loved me enough to give me their time, I must be worth something. I want to make sure that happens for more kids. I want to help make this place better.

And I think I have the best shot out of everyone here. Honestly, I can't see anyone else applying. Except maybe Dane, but we all know he can't even make it to midmorning without whisper-screaming to his wife about who's taking their ten-year-old to the orthodontist, or whatever.

My phone vibrates on my desk, and I feel a flutter in my chest. Could it be Jack texting already? Not that it matters or anything, because everything related to him is locked up tight in the box. Still, I better check just in case it's something important . . . and no. It's not Jack.

> Hi Mavis! It's Dyvia! I got your number from Trisha. I am so excited to get started with all things DEI at Knoll! We've definitely got a lot of work to do, but I trust your vision for this important committee. I can't wait to learn from you!

My vision? Learn from me? Now, what exactly did Trisha tell this lady about me? Because she doesn't seem to realize that my only qualification for this job (though, can I even call it that if they're not paying me anything?) is being a Black person who can't seem to mind her own business. She's acting like I'm god-damn Ibram X. Kendi when I haven't made it through even one of those books on the white guilt reading lists that were passed around everywhere in 2020. I'm supposed to have a vision for the PTA's DEI committee? Like, *right now*?

I take a deep breath, pushing down the panic. Another thing to put in the box, to be dealt with later today. I put my phone on Do Not Disturb so I won't get any more notifications, and flip it facedown, too, just to be safe.

But before I can even click open my next email, the phone vibrates again . . . and again.

> I'm looping in Angela Hart to this group because we got coffee after drop off today and she's very interested in helping!

When do you think we should have
our first meeting? I have a few items
I'd like to add to the agenda already.

I check my settings. I'm not tripping, Do Not Disturb was on. So, did this lady really just "Notify anyway" me? The audacity! And is Angela Hart *that* Angela . . . ?

Her response pops up next, also just blazing on through my Do Not Disturb shield.

Angela here! And I'm so ready to get
into good trouble with you, Mavis ✊🏽

Yep, it's pink pussy hat Angela. And okay, now I need to add "white lady quoting John Lewis at me" to the list of things that I hate.

I love the enthusiasm, I type quickly, thankful they can't see my major eye roll through the screen. I'm at work right now and pretty busy, but I'll set up a Google Doc later today where we can start brainstorming our ideas!

Because there's no way I'm about to willingly sign up for more meetings in my life, especially not for this. We can just write up a list of the things we want to change at Knoll, which shouldn't be difficult at all, and then we'll create an action plan that we can pass along for Trisha to implement. That's it—easy, efficient. And honestly, Dyvia and Angela will probably thank me for it—no one, not even the most eager PTA mom, wants to sit through a meeting that could have been an email.

"Something going on with Pearl?" Rose stands in my office's doorway, smiling pointedly at my phone. Somehow I can hear every single bodily function Sally lets loose next door, but I never hear Rose walk up until she's right there, watching me.

"Yes." I put the phone facedown and grin brightly back at her. "Her school needed something." Which isn't an *un*truth, but Rose doesn't need to know that, especially with this promotion decision coming so soon. Her concerned face makes me immediately regret it, though.

"Is everything okay? Do you need to step out?" The exact thing I *don't* want her to say.

"No," I respond quickly. "I'm good."

She sticks her hands into the pockets of her navy blazer and shakes her head, blond curls bouncing. "Oh, Mavis, you have so much on your plate! Here I can barely keep the succulents in my apartment alive, and you have a whole human to take care of. How do you do it?"

On the outside, I smile gratefully, but my stomach dips. Outside of a small picture on my desk of Pearl posing in her Tiana costume last Halloween, I try to keep work a mostly Pearl-free zone. It's nice to hear that my boss thinks I'm balancing things, but I don't like to remind her that things *have* to be balanced. Rose and the board need to see me as completely present, ready to give this place my all, if I have any chance of being promoted to program director.

I shrug my shoulders, hopefully giving off an air of ease, and change the subject. "Is it time for the meeting?"

Rose nods once, rubbing her hands together. "Yes! We're about to get started." With that, she turns and quickly bounds down the hallway, moving double time away from my door. I know Rose loves her meetings, but she seems even more amped than usual. *Could it be . . . ?* I shouldn't get my hopes up, but they *are* deciding soon. There's a lightness in my chest as I walk down the hallway, thinking about what that extra money could mean for Pearl and me. It's not a huge leap in salary, but it would make things a lot more comfortable if we did decide to move out and give Dad his space. And the listing did say they were open to negotiation . . .

I follow Rose into the conference room (which also doubles as another storage room and a shared office for the coordinators, because that's the nonprofit life) and take the open seat next to Sally. I look around at all the faces. It seems like most of Project Window's staff and board of directors are here. Across the table I notice one of the board members I interviewed with, Teresa, an older woman with a perfectly tailored pink tweed suit and a purse that probably cost more than my salary for six months. She smiles and nods at me, and I wave back. I want to play it cool, but my insides feel like a Coke bottle all shaken up, fizzy and frenzied. I don't know if it's excitement or anxiety—they feel the same in my body.

There is one new face I don't recognize, a man lingering at the front of the room. He has dark hair that's just a little too long, slicked down with gel, and he's wearing a striped button-down, pressed khaki pants, and loafers with no socks, putting his pale ankles on display. His hands are moving fast, clenching and unclenching—he must be nervous. Probably a new coordinator, brought into the meeting to take notes, and oh, there's coffee in the middle of the table—real coffee from an actual coffee shop, and not the sludge that we usually begrudgingly accept from the ancient machine in the break room. He must have been in charge of picking it up. (And if they sprang for coffee, this *is* a big meeting.)

His gaze nervously jumps around the room, and I catch his eye, smiling to put him at ease. I pat the empty seat next to me, and when his eyebrows jump in question, I nod him over. I remember what it felt like to be a brand-new coordinator here, knowing no one, and it must be even harder to do in your midthirties, which he looks to be. Maybe this is the beginning of a big career shift for him, a step in a new direction. Maybe I can take him under my wing, give him the lowdown on this place—like how Rose keeps the air-conditioning set at below zero temps, so he should probably invest in socks.

The man sits down in the chair next to me, just blocking Dane from grabbing the spot, and I can almost feel the jitters bouncing off him—or maybe I'm just getting them confused with my own.

"Hi, I'm Mavis," I say, reaching out to shake his hand. "I haven't seen you here before. First day?"

"Nelson. I'm Nelson," he says in a mumbly voice and puts his palm in mine. His grip is loose and clammy. I try to keep my face neutral, but he winces for the both of us, dropping my hand quickly. "Yes, first day. And I'm feeling pretty nervous about it, as you can probably tell. I won't be, uh, offended at all if you need to wipe that on your pants."

He laughs hesitantly, a quiet, endearing snort escaping, and his cheeks flush red. This close, I can see the pattern on his shirt isn't just stripes—it's tiny lightsabers lined up, red and blue. Oh, how precious. I think this new, nerdy coordinator and I are going to be friends.

"No worries at all, Nelson. I'm sure you're going to do great here." I reach across the table, pulling the cardboard carton of coffee and two paper cups our way. "You brought the good stuff, so you're already my favorite person here."

His bushy eyebrows press together, and he looks like he's about to say something, but there's a clap at the front of the room. We both turn to see Rose there, staring out at her assembled meeting with delight and reverence, like a pop star at a sold-out arena show.

"Welcome, everyone," she says, holding her hands out.

"Thank you for making time today, especially at such short notice. Every day, I'm just so grateful to work alongside our dedicated and passionate team."

Rose looks around the room, smiling widely, but when her eyes land on me, something . . . strange flickers in them. Not the excitement I would expect from her, getting to announce my promotion. The fizzy feeling in my body expands to my fingertips and my toes, until I can hardly keep it in. Maybe Rose isn't excited, because I'm getting a little too close to her role for comfort. But we'll work that out. I'll make sure to always keep it clear that she's in charge. I know how to play the game. It's gotten me this far—to *my promotion*!

"And today we're adding a new role to our team, to make us even stronger and better equipped to meet the needs of all the teens whose lives we have the privilege to touch."

Here we go. I take a deep breath and try to keep the smile that's tugging at my lips from spreading. Surprised. I need to look surprised. Even though I know I'm getting this—that I *deserve* this.

"Our new program director comes to us with nine years of experience in the nonprofit world, and I know he's going to help lead Project Window to an even brighter future."

Well, seven, not nine, Rose. But that's just a minor slipup. And it feels like I've been here forever, anyway. Wait, though . . . he? Did she say—

"Please welcome Project Window's new program director, Nelson. Nelson, come on up here!"

The room erupts into applause, and I can feel the air shift next to me as Nelson stands up. Nelson with the *Star Wars* shirt and gross clammy hands. Nelson with no socks! Nelson— fucking *Nelson*—may be new to Project Window, but he's not a coordinator. No, Nelson is walking up to the front of the conference room to accept a much bigger job. *My* job.

He shakes Rose's hand, probably slathering her palms with his sweat, and then turns to the room and begins speaking. I hear phrases like "fired up" and "great honor" and "fresh innovations," but my brain can't process any of it, because this is not how this was supposed to go. I was supposed to be up there acting all modest and "Who, me?" even though *of course* it was me. It had to be me. I put in the work. I go above and beyond. I have given up seven years to this place—and at least three of those years were straight meetings. I never complained about my salary, which is low even for a nonprofit; never even pulled a face when Rose gave me a perfect score at every performance review and gave me only one raise in *seven goddamn years*. Yeah, I never loved it here, but who loves their job? You show up, you work hard, and you're eventually rewarded for it. That's how this was supposed to go. I was supposed to finally get my reward this time.

But no. The reward goes to Nelson, who—oh my god, shouldn't have even been in the running! This was an internal position! Not only did they pass me over, they went outside of Project Window to do it. That might make it hurt even worse. I did everything I was supposed to, and someone else swooped in and easily took what was mine.

Is this the way it's always going to go? Have I wasted my time?

I miss whatever he says, but applause scatters across the room again, and Nelson stands there accepting it with a crimson-cheeked smile and his hands graciously clutched to his chest. Next to me, Sally is clapping so enthusiastically that I can tell brussels sprouts definitely made an appearance in her breakfast today, too.

I jump out of my seat. I need to get to my office quickly so I can be pissed and petty in peace. But someone taps my arm before I reach the door, and I turn to see Rose. Her eyes hold the same strange flicker I noticed just before the announcement, and I realize now that it's sympathy . . . pity. I feel like such an idiot.

"I hope there are no hard feelings, Mavis." Her thin lips are twisted in an exaggerated frown. "It's just . . ."

My throat feels tight and painful like I'm trying to swallow something solid. I wait for her to finish that sentence, but when she just lets the words linger as she worries her hands and frowns some more, it's clear what's expected of me. "No. Of course not."

"Whew!" Rose mimes wiping sweat off her brow. "I was so nervous about that. But you'll get there, Mavis. I know it. Just keep working hard."

I need to get out of this room immediately. Right now.

Rose's eyes light up as her gaze finds something behind me, and I know who it is before she even has to say anything. "Mavis, let me introduce you to Nelson! You two will be working closely."

"We've met." I can't fix my face into a smile, but I think I manage something mildly pleasant.

"Yes, Mavis has already been so welcoming." Instead of looking him in the eye, I look at his ankles. I hope they freeze.

"Oh good!" Rose claps her hands, delighted that this is all working out. That she doesn't have to feel bad or guilty or even worried that I'm going to leave, because why would she? I haven't complained once in these seven years she's been stringing me along. Why would I start now?

"Mavis is going to be such a big help to you, Nelson. She always is."

And a lot of good that's done me.

I'M SITTING IN MY CAR, EATING ANOTHER SAD GROCERY
store salad and feeling sorry for myself, when my cell rings, Jasmine's smiling face lighting up the screen. She's probably the
only non–family member I would actually answer a phone call
from, instead of just responding with a text, because she understands, like me, that talking on the phone is the absolute worst,
and keeps it quick.

"Oh, girl," she says in lieu of a greeting. "We've got a lot to
debrief. It has been A DAY!"

My chest feels heavy with dread. How does she already
know? Did Rose send out a press release to everyone in Beachwood about my failure? Did she hire a skywriter to spread the
message around town? NELSON PROMOTED INSTEAD OF MAVIS. I catch
myself looking up out my car windows, but the bright sun just
hurts my eyes.

"The Facebook group is popping! Talking 'bout Mrs. Smith
was up in the office causing a scene. Florence Michaelson is going on about cameras and the police state. It's wild!"

Yes. Right. Principal Smith is missing. I tried to put all that
in a box this morning, along with Trisha and Jack, and I guess
I succeeded. But now I'm ready to open that baby back up, because it definitely beats spiraling over my place at Project Window, which way too quickly turns into spiraling over my place
in the *world*.

"It really is so crazy. Do you really think something . . . bad
happened to him?"

"I don't know, but people are sending private messages, probably sharing theories. Little Ruthie is on there dog whistling it
up, of course."

"She's actually the one who told me this morning."

"Oh, I saw her! Spreading the news around like it was the gospel, and then offering her little oils for all the havoc she was creating. Me and Langston got there five minutes after the bell, and she was showing no signs of stopping."

I laugh, remembering how Ruth practically ran up to me this morning, so eager to share the gossip. She's Trisha's friend—or the closest thing someone like Trisha has to a friend. So she wouldn't be telling everyone what happened so gleefully if Trisha was involved, right? But also, Trisha's not dumb enough to blow up her spot, *whatever* happened, with a bigmouth like Ruth either.

"So, okay, you were already in and out by the time we got there," Jasmine continues. "Look at you, Miss Early!"

"Well, actually, I was probably still in Trisha's office then."

I can almost hear Jasmine's wide, blinking eyes and neck roll. "You were *where*? With *who*, now?" Her infectious laugh fills my ear. "What—are you and Miss Trish besties now?"

Besties? Definitely not. In fact, I'm pretty sure she wants to off me.

But I can't tell Jasmine about what I saw last night and the conclusions I jumped to—as much as I'm sure there was something more to Trisha's words at the door this morning, some scary subtext I still need to pick at and coax apart, like a hopelessly tangled necklace. I can't present all this to Jasmine as it is now, still a mess of what-ifs and maybes. She would roast me forever for that bonkers theory, and rightfully so. It doesn't make sense, but it was so much easier to tell my suspicions to Jack, someone I barely know. Because if he judges me or thinks I'm crazy, then okay, I could just avoid him for the rest of my life, no big deal. I would miss his pretty face and perfect muscly forearms, but not as much as I'd miss Jasmine—and the high opinion I hope she has of me now.

"We were just talking about my committee—"

"*Your* committee? So it's official then?"

Yes, it's official if the amount of texts I continued to get from Dyvia and Angela this morning are any indication.

> Did you get a chance to send out the
> Google Doc yet? Just want to make
> sure I didn't miss it!

> Sorry to bug, it's just one of my
> agenda items might be urgent?

> I can totally do it if you don't have
> time, Mavis! Google Docs are like
> my spirit animal

That last text from Angela really made me feel itchy with annoyance. Because first, spirit animal? Really? Ew. This lady needs to get *herself* a couple more of those white guilt reading list books instead of shelling out for any more WE BELIEVE lawn signs, stat. And second, maybe I didn't want this committee, but that doesn't mean I want to give it to someone else! I'm in this now. And I'm in charge.

"My committee," I confirm, and then I laugh because I can hear Jasmine's lips popping on the line and can imagine how she's shaking her head at me, sitting at the mirrored desk in her fancy office. It would only be worse if I threw in the whole murder thing, too.

"What happened to you at that meeting yesterday? Some body snatcher shit?"

I snort. "Girl, probably. But honestly, I think it was good that

I went. There was this whole drama with Trisha trying to push through this gifted school proposal. It woulda had all the kids not in the gifted program being bused somewhere else."

"Are you for real?"

"Yes! Principal Smith was against it, so it seems like it's dead now. But if he's . . . going to be out for a while, well, who knows? She's got all this power at the district for some reason. She might try and pull a fast one, slide this change right on through."

Which maybe is exactly what Trisha planned. And why Principal Smith is missing in the first place.

"Someone needs to watch her," I continue, shaking that thought away. "Someone that's not one of her little minions. You know I'm not trying to be one of these PTA moms, but I *do* want to look out for our kids—all of the kids at Knoll."

Jasmine lets out a long exhale. "Of course you have to go being noble and shit, making me feel guilty . . ."

"So that's why you're just so excited to join me, right?" And then I'd have a valid reason to cut Dyvia and Angela loose, be done with all these text messages.

"Mavis, now you already know there's no way in hell."

"We could get matching DEI T-shirts! Or maybe wear all black to the next meeting—like, leather jackets, pick our hair out all big, really freak them out."

"No. Even though it brings me immense joy imagining Little Ruthie's face—no."

"Now imagine the look on her face when I tell her we should rename the school Obama Elementary. The mascots can be the—the . . . owls! The Obama Owls! You know you wanna be there for that!"

"Okay, I'll be there for that, and that only, as long as you promise we're naming it for Michelle."

We both laugh, and it's so light and easy. It always is with Jasmine. But then some movement in the corner of my eye catches my attention, and I see Nelson close the door to his bright blue Kia Soul and stride to the front of our building, his naked ankles shining in the sun. All the good feelings this phone call brought me leak out of my body, like a pool float that's sprung a leak.

I sigh. "Anyway, I better get going. I'm supposed to show around the new guy after lunch . . ."

"Oh, did they finally get *you* an assistant? Wait—girl, did you get that promotion and not tell me?"

"Actually . . ." I start, but I have to pause because my throat is tight again. The one thing I'm not about to do is cry, especially not in full view of my office. "They went with someone else. An outside hire. That's who I'm showing around."

"Mavis, no! No, no, no!" She shouts so loud I have to pull the phone away from my ear. "You gotta get out of there already. I don't understand why you've stayed so long. It's been seven years, and they *don't* appreciate you. They *don't* pay you your worth."

I can imagine her ticking these things off on her palm with one of her pointy gel nails that she gets filled every three weeks. It makes me chafe a little bit. I don't have the flexibility that she has, the money that she has. I can't just *leave*. It's not that simple.

"Exactly. It's been seven years," I huff. "I've put in so much time, and I'd have to start right back over anywhere else."

"Mm-hmm, that sunk cost fallacy is still running you, I see."

"More like my bills are running me. Being the parent with health insurance is running me."

Jasmine's husband, Leon, is a pediatric nurse, with a kind and nurturing personality to match. And outside of Jasmine's mad-dash drop-offs, he does most of the shuttling around with Langston because his schedule is more consistent. He also floated the family when Jasmine had to go without pay for those five months she was setting up her own practice. Jasmine is a force, but she's also got a force behind her.

"You right, you right," she says quickly, and I'm glad. "I'm sorry for being pushy. You know what you're doing. I just love you and want the best for you and Pearl."

"I know you do. And we love you, too."

"Well, keep me updated then."

"I will."

"Okay, I've got a vaginal dryness case walking in in five, so I gotta go, too. Bye."

She hangs up before I can respond. Although what do you even say to that?

I begrudgingly pack up my lunch, reminding myself that I just need to put on a smile for a few more hours. I can do that. My phone vibrates in my pocket before I reach the door.

"If these two don't leave me alone, I swear . . ." I mutter, pulling it out.

But it's not Dyvia asking for the Google Doc again or Angela with another overly eager white lady–ism. It's him. Jack.

Hey Joe! (I've decided you're more of a Joe than a Frank)

I can feel my cheeks stretching into a smile as I respond. I **thought we agreed on Stabler and Benson.**

He doesn't keep me waiting. Just a few seconds later: I **figured we could play around with it, see what feels good**

You know, like Nancy and Ned. Ice-T and that other guy

. . . Hot-T?

It's the corniest of jokes, probably something my dad would think was funny, but I find myself laughing anyway.

> You can be Hot-T

Is this flirting? God, I really have no freaking clue. But that's what happens when you marry your first serious boyfriend. And now here I am with kid dating experience, but grown needs.

So I heard from Ms. Castillo that the
school cameras turned off sometime
after the PTA meeting. The whole
system. And they didn't get turned
back on until Lilliam got here this
morning

My heart starts racing. The school cameras were turned off? Who had the access to do that? And why would they? Unless . . .

> Okay that's weird, right?

Very weird. I think your instincts
were spot on here and it's good
we're looking into this together.

I know I need to keep this in the box. I know I'm just looking for a distraction from work, from what my next steps should be here. But also, it's pretty nice to be distracted right now. By whatever mystery is unfolding here. By Jack.

See you tomorrow, Hot-T!

> No, I'm Ice-T. You're the hot one!

I immediately regret it after sending. Shit. Is it too late to hit the unsend button? Because if we were subtly flirting before, I just unintentionally took things to a whole new level.

But he writes me back before I can make my text disappear— or make *myself* disappear.

Thank you ☺

SEVEN

"MOMMY! HEY, MOMMY!" PEARL URGENTLY TAPS MY SHOULder, pulling me out of my Google Docs trance.

"Yes, baby girl?"

We settled on the couch after dinner and an early bath so she could get her daily dose of screen time. But once she saw me pull out my laptop to work on this DEI list (so Dyvia and Angela didn't escalate to just showing up at my house), she opted for her Chromebook instead of the witch show on Disney+ she's been obsessed with lately. The school just sent home the Chromebooks today, the spoils of some technology grant Knoll won, and pretty much all of Pearl's Gimme Five facts about her day centered around her shiny new toy. ("I can type whatever I want on it! It has internet!")

"Can I check the Daddy Tracker on here?" She pushes a button on the keyboard at an alarmingly fast rate, making the screen so dark it's barely visible.

"Hmmm . . . maybe. But I don't think that's the way to do it," I say, gently lifting her frantic finger.

She frowns deeply. "Well, then how?"

I fix the brightness and then squint at the screen, scanning the limited icons. "Click right there for the internet." She follows directions, her brow furrowed in focus. I lean over her. "Okay, let me type this part in."

The "Daddy Tracker" is what Pearl calls Find My Phone, the app and website that we use to track where Corey is every night. It started out when she was a toddler—aware enough to know Daddy wasn't home, but not aware enough to understand why he couldn't just come home, *right now*! Because how do you even explain to a two-year-old the concept of, like, Cleveland. And how Cleveland isn't in *right now* distance of Beachwood. So we started using this app to show exactly where Corey was in relation to us—kind of like those Santa trackers on Christmas Eve. Just like Santa, Daddy was spreading his music magic all over the world. We kept it up as Pearl got older—and Corey got booked on bigger tours that took him away for longer and much farther, Canada and the UK, and once for months all over Asia. Pearl loves to see where he is that night, especially before their calls.

Except, it's not working on her laptop. I typed in the website, double-checked the spelling, but all I get is this page with ACCESS DENIED in bold red letters.

"I'm sorry, bud. I'm not sure why it's saying that."

"Oh, probably because it's not a scholarly website," she says, nodding knowingly.

"A what?"

"Mrs. Tennison says these are specially for school, so we can only go on scholarly websites. And also send emails to only her or other scholarly people, which is everyone in the class, apparently, so I think that maybe they don't even know what *scholar* means."

"Um, okay. Well, that's good." There was probably an email

sent out from Mrs. Tennison or the school filled with rules about how to use these things. I need to remember to read it later. "Here, let me show you where Daddy is on mine."

I pull up the app on my computer so she can see the enlarged map, and she squeals with excitement when the blinking blue dot for Corey's phone appears.

"Daddy's in . . ." She moves in closer, her nose nearly touching the screen. "New Jersey?"

"Yep. And they're three hours ahead, so it's almost ten o'clock at night there. He might be almost done with his show. He's going to call you after." Corey and I text to coordinate his nightly call because it depends on where—and when—he is. Regardless of where the little blue dot is on the map, though, he never misses it.

Pearl nods, satisfied, and pulls the Chromebook back on her lap. She thinks she's being slick, but I notice how she turns it slightly so I can't see the screen. I haven't really been watching her, instead filling in the columns for positives and deltas (because adults are much too fragile to handle the word *negative*) about Knoll in this Google Doc. "Wait, so what have you been doing on there? Reading Stars? Or Math for Fun?" Those are the two enrichment websites they've been pushing since she was in kindergarten, but Pearl usually gets bored in minutes.

"Typing."

I arch an eyebrow at her. "Typing what?"

She presses her lips tightly together and holds her head high. "A list of my nemeses. I need to add the new one."

"Girlfriend, now I know *that's* not what Mrs. Tennison gave you that thing for."

"It's for learning, and I am practicing my spelling. How do you spell *nemeses*? And also *betrayal*?"

"Oh my lord." I laugh, even though I probably shouldn't, and

Pearl smiles proudly as she hunts and pecks across the keyboard. "Well, just don't email it to Mrs. Tennison. Or any other scholarly people."

"I won't. I promise."

My shoulders shake with another silent laugh. I'm just going to have to let this go for now. At least she's self-motivated?

My attention returns to my screen, where I've organized the document, titled "State of DEI at Knoll," into three columns (positives, deltas, and prescriptions). Is the positive column too short? I think everything I've written is honest, but I don't want the PTA's walls to go up, and to have them get all defensive when they first look at this thing. Hmmm . . . let's see. **Beautiful rose garden**, I add to the positives—though it doesn't really have the same weight as **Martin Luther King Day left off school calendar last year** in the column next to it. Really, I think I better pause and send this document out now before adding anything else. These two ladies already have the extremely wrong misconception that I'm the next Nikole Hannah-Jones or whatever. Better to look more collaborative, open, so they don't expect me to deliver a TED talk at the PTA meeting. Ugh. I shudder at the thought of having to attend the next one of those—and see Trisha again. At least we shouldn't have to hold meetings for this committee. I really think we'll be fine doing everything over email. And text. Dyvia and Angela *really* seem to love text. If I send this through email, hopefully they'll get the hint.

"Mommy, Polly is being silly!"

She was sitting quietly at our feet just moments ago, but now the dog is sprinting back and forth across the room, parkouring off the TV stand, while Pearl watches on and giggles, her nemeses list momentarily discarded.

Pearl and I just threw the ball around with her outside after dinner. I was hoping Polly could wait until after Pearl's bedtime for her last walk . . . not that I'm eager to go out late with her again.

"I'll take her for a walk!" My dad's booming voice makes Pearl and me jump in our seats. "I was already going for a walk anyway!"

He has on a navy tracksuit and the kind of bulky white sneakers that only dads or supermodels can pull off. And dangling from his ears—the same sticking-out-wide ears that Pearl and I have inherited—are white cords attached to earbuds. That's the reason for the yelling, I guess.

"Walk!" he repeats to Polly, but she's already abandoned her stunt show and is patiently waiting for her leash at his feet. Dad points to his earbuds, which I don't think I've ever seen him use before. "Hey, have you heard of this new thing called podcasts?"

"No." I try to hold in my laugh and instead match his wonder-filled tone. "What's that?"

He excitedly leans forward to show me his phone screen and somehow turns on the flashlight in the process. He continues hollering, "They're these crime stories, but with just talking! Like, like—" He snaps his fingers. "Like *Dateline*, but for your ears! And matter of fact, Keith Morrison has one, too! Marcell at the DA's office turned me on to them! Jan's been making him go out walking more since he retired—because of his cholesterol, you know—and he says these make it a lot better! And they're free! Here, let me show you!"

He gestures for me to hand him my phone off the couch.

"Dad, it's okay," I say, the giggles taking over. "I know what podcasts are."

"Huh?!" He pulls out one of the headphones.

"I know what podcasts are," I repeat.

"Well, then why didn't you say so?" he asks, shaking his head. The headphone goes back in his ear, but he doesn't move toward the door, which makes Polly's tail wagging reach a frantic speed. "Well, this one, this one I'm listening to, it's real good! You should look it up! It's about a stay-at-home mom who went hunting for everyone on her, her—" He snaps his fingers some more. "Her mom message board group! Yeah, that's it! After they all banned her or something! Here, I'll help you find it! It's called *The Mommy Murders*!"

"Dad!" I jerk my head toward Pearl, who has completely abandoned her nemeses list and is eagerly listening to this podcast pitch.

"Mommies murder?" she asks, eyes wide with something that could be fear or glee.

"No," I say quickly. "Mommies don't murder."

Although Trisha is a mommy, and she . . . I shake away the thought. We don't know enough—really, *anything* yet. But that reminds me, I need to text Jack and confirm what time we're meeting tomorrow. I have to make it quick if I'm still going to get to work on time. Nelson made sure to ask me before I left today what time he could expect me in the morning, as if it's his duty to keep track of when I report. But I guess he is my superior now. Ugh. I wish I didn't have to go to work at all tomorrow.

"Well, I'm going to head out!" Dad shouts, and Polly eagerly lunges toward the door. Something shiny and royal blue sticking out of his back pocket catches my eye.

"Dad, are those Oreos?" I raise an eyebrow at him. "Your sugar!"

"Papa ate my extra fruit snacks when he was unpacking my lunch box, too, Mommy!" Pearl chimes in, and Dad shoots her a *zip it* glance.

"Dad, you know what Dr. Gelson said—"

"Sorry, can't hear you!" Dad says, pointing at his headphones. "Dawn is explaining how she crossed state lines to—" The door clicks closed behind him and Polly before we can hear exactly what Dawn did to the unfortunate soul from her mommy forum.

I didn't see any Oreos in the pantry, which means he's stashing them somewhere, against his doctor's orders. I add it to my list to find where they're hidden—and also remind Dad not to talk about murder, or any other crimes, in front of Pearl.

I've got a lot of things on my list.

As Pearl goes back to cataloging her nemeses and how they've wronged her, I start ticking through everything else I've still got to get done tonight. Pearl finished her homework, but I need to check my email for anything sent home about this Chromebook—or wait, check that app. Mrs. Tennison sometimes sends stuff on . . . whatever it's called. The dishes need to be taken out of the dishwasher, and that load finally made it out of washer purgatory, so I need to make sure it doesn't just live in the dryer now. I need to check my work email one more time before bed so I'm not caught unawares by anything with Rose or Nelson, and oh yeah, text Jack. But that's going to take me a minute because I need to get it right. I don't want to accidentally get too flirty again . . . or do I? And then the Google Doc— Dyvia and Angela probably haven't seen my email yet, but let me check real quick just in case. And oh . . . *oh*.

Dyvia has not only seen my email but contributed a significant amount to the three columns in such a short period of time, especially in the prescriptions section. I scan what she wrote, and it's good. Really good. Highlighting people of color as school-wide scholars of the month, nonprofits we can reach out to for culturally relevant assemblies, curriculum options we can fundraise for, diversifying the school library—with a color-coded list of specific books! Why did Trisha single me out for this, when Dyvia is clearly informed and passionate and right there? Like, what? The PTA didn't need *me*. Then again, Trisha was probably hoping my extra melanin would get her some brownie points with the PTA powers that be.

There's a little note from her at the bottom. I got started but will add more ideas soon. Hope this looks good to you!

This looks incredible, I write back. I think we already have plenty to pass on to the PTA board! Thank you for putting so much effort into this.

And also, why in the world aren't you in charge of this instead of me? But I guess I'm not in the position to just be giving away leadership positions and promotions, am I? Even the volunteer ones.

She starts typing immediately, and I notice the little icon lurking at the top, Anonymous Badger. Dyvia is ready for business.

Can we meet tomorrow to discuss the library books specifically? There's something I want to talk through with you!

I think over my day, which is already filling up. Shaking down Lilliam for information with Jack, eight hours of being forced to train my new boss. I don't want to really add a PTA-related meeting in there, if only for my own sanity.

Is it possible for us to just chat on here or maybe email? I'm sorry, but I'm pretty busy with work tomorrow. I think about it for a second and then erase the *I'm sorry, but*. Send.

I'd really prefer to talk in person. It's possibly a sensitive matter and I don't feel comfortable discussing it through email.

Okay, now, Dyvia, you've got some great ideas, but what is this "don't feel comfortable discussing it through email" business? This is the PTA, not James Bond or something. Who is going to see our emails? I'm not trying to get involved in whatever this drama is—or, well, *more* drama than I've already stumbled into with Trisha. I have enough.

"Mommy, look!" Pearl says, and I gratefully put my computer down. I'll deal with this later. My phone is vibrating, and a picture of Corey and Pearl holding up churros at Disneyland last summer fills the screen.

"Daddy!" Pearl clutches my phone in her fingers, decorated with chipped sparkly pink polish, and presses the accept button. "Hi, Daddy!" she squeals again, holding the screen so close to her nose it's like she's trying to fall right in.

I get that dip in my stomach, like I have every night for years, the shakiness that comes from absorbing the joy radiating off Pearl mixed with the tornado of feelings that come when I see the person who was supposed to be my forever. Of course, I see him all the time: in my memories, in pictures around the house, in our little girl's face. Pearl has the Miller ears, my tight curls and wide nose—but the rest is all Corey. Chestnut-brown skin, plush lips, and dark, downturned eyes that always look like they're sparkling with a secret. But when they beam those identical smiles at each other, in motion, it really drives home that the face that used to be my everything was basically copy-pasted onto the face that made me realize what everything truly is.

"My Pearl girl!" Corey sings, and Pearl giggles. It's dark wherever he is—probably the bus or backstage—so he holds the phone close to his face, too, nose to nose despite the miles. "What are you doing right now?"

"Making a list of my nemeses. In order," she says, brow furrowed to communicate the severity of this matter.

He matches her expression. "What number are you at now, total? Eight?"

"Ten."

"Ten? That's up from last week!"

"Well, Mrs. Skinner ran across the rainbow I drew in chalk on the sidewalk and made it all smudgy. And then there's a new kid in my class."

"Maves, what's your read on this Mrs. Skinner?" Corey asks, and I can see that my hair and a sliver of my face are peeking in the side of the screen. "She got malicious intent? A beef against rainbows?"

"Well, Ms. Joyce sure isn't a fan."

"Okay, if Ms. Joyce doesn't like her, then we got our answer. Definitely belongs on the list." He shakes his head, reminiscing. "Oh, Ms. Joyce! Remember how she used to give me that look? You know the one—made me start questioning myself, maybe I *was* up to no good. God, I miss that woman."

He keeps it moving, not lingering on the fact that he hasn't seen her, or us, in person for a while, this most recent tour keeping him gone for his longest stretch yet.

"What happened with Armando, the spider? Did you find him today?"

Pearl sighs and shakes her head. "We had a promising lead at first recess, me and Anabella, because Natalie told us she saw a lot, *a lot*, of spiders behind the buddy bench. But there were too many and the bell rang before we could know for sure if he was there."

"Oh, that's disappointing! Did you look again at lunch recess?"

"We *tried*! But Joseph kept calling out 'Darryl,' even though that's *not* Armando's name, and it probably confused him." Pearl lets loose an impressive eye roll, and Corey's howling laugh explodes out of the phone.

I forgot all about that spider, when apparently she had a whole police procedural going on with her friends. (Note to self: I do *really* gotta make sure Dad isn't letting her watch *Law & Order.*) But Corey listens during these calls, to make sure he's as present as can be, that she feels seen and heard. I don't know if it ever really bothered him to leave me—the thrill, the siren song of the road and all of its adventures, was always going to win that competition. But it does bother him to leave Pearl. I can see it in how he hangs on her every word, catalogs every detail like they're something precious. And they are. At the beginning of the separation, my fingers used to itch to text him things—the little milestones, her funny mannerisms—all the quiet moments that make up her life. Like how she declared that her favorite color was velvet. Or how her hands instinctively found her ears after she screamed, as if she startled herself. It was hard to let go of that natural instinct to marvel at our girl together, to want to share the *did you see that?* glance with someone else. I felt like it was all on me to savor, to remember. But while he's there for her in a different way, he's still there. They have moments that are all their own, without me.

"What's that thing right there, baby girl?" he says, pointing into his camera.

Pearl bounces off the couch and picks up her Chromebook, proudly displaying it. "It's my new computer and it's really cool. But also we've got a problem because this thing can't even go on the Daddy Tracker or email whoever I want!"

"Shooooot!" He exhales, giving her the overly concerned face she needed. "What *can* you do with it then?"

"Type lists of my nemeses."

"And lists of Armando's possible hideouts?" he offers.

"Lists of the people I've beat at tetherball!"

"Lists of all the tricks you've taught Polly!"

They continue listing all the different lists she can type on the Chromebook, which is apparently plenty, and the back-and-forth of their voices soon falls into a rhythm, like a rehearsed song. I lean back on the couch and put my feet up on the coffee table, letting the bittersweet melody fall over me.

I knew what I was getting into with Corey. Being a working musician was always the dream. That was the first thing he told me when I met him freshman year in Ms. Canon's geography class, in fact: "I'm going to be a professional drummer and travel the world."

And I loved that about him. I loved his passion, how he knew exactly what he wanted. I loved how he'd stick to his strict, self-imposed practice schedule, turning down invites to parties and hangouts, no matter how much his friends begged. I loved sitting in the soundproof garage his mom set up for him at their house on the Northside and watching him get lost in the music, how he would drum out beats he was working on with his rough fingers on my spine. I sometimes wondered if I was second to the music, but then he'd lock eyes with me in the middle of every show, because I went to all of them, and make me feel so seen and special, and I'd decide I didn't care. This was more than enough for me, more than enough for anyone. And his passion was infectious. For my whole life, I'd been deliberate, careful, trying to follow the exact path that Dad foresaw for me. But Corey made me feel like anything was possible, like there was room for magic. So when we saw that little positive on the pregnancy test and he excitedly, joyfully asked me to marry him, to sprint forward into this new adventure, I said yes. I believed in him, believed in us.

But marriage and parenthood . . . those can't come second to anything. Not if they're going to succeed. The tiny cracks that were there before Pearl was born quickly became deep, vast canyons in her first year, impossible to hop over, to smooth away, so easily. Pearl could never be put down. She always had to be touching me, only me, so I carried her every moment I wasn't working and lay down with her every night. And even then, she would sometimes still cry and cry and cry while I helplessly tried to figure out the reason why. I was so tired and felt so powerless and my back hurt, but I couldn't be mad at her because she was just a baby and it wasn't her fault and I loved her so much. So I got mad at Corey. I rolled my eyes when he said she only wanted to be held by me. I picked fights with him when he left for paid gigs. I could have unlimited patience and grace for Pearl, but it was impossible to have it for both of them. And he wasn't happy anymore either. The girl that always said yes, that approached his music with the same reverence as him, was gone, and she wasn't coming back. Passive digs and petty bickering turned to outright accusations and battles, until everything felt too broken to repair. When he got offered a spot playing drums with a well-known rock band on the European leg of their tour, I encouraged him to take it. I did the same when they asked him to join them in Asia, too. We gave it one last real go when the pandemic shut live music down and Corey was forced to stay put. But being in such close quarters again just made it even more clear how far apart we'd grown. He signed his next contract as soon as he was able, his biggest one yet, right along with our divorce papers. And it felt like failure, but also inevitable.

"Maves?" His voice pulls me from back then to right now— where Pearl has the screen pushed right up in my face, giving him a prime view of the insides of my nostrils.

"Hmmm, you got a few bats in the cave," he jokes, and his smile shows off the slight dimple in his right cheek that I used to find with my finger when I pulled him close. Pearl has that same dimple.

I flare my nostrils bigger, setting off a round of giggles from Pearl. "I don't know. Can you check for me?"

"Hey, did you get my message?" he asks, and I notice the tiny change in his tone. He's always playful, always easy, but his words get a little more precise when something is important to him.

"Sorry, yeah. I've been busy." My voice comes out more tight than I intend, and *he* notices that, understands it's not the time to push.

"I want to talk when you get a chance. Just the two of us. Soon."

Well, he usually understands.

"Can't we just text?"

I don't know what he could want to talk about. Honestly, in this moment, I don't *want* to know. It feels like everyone wants to stake a claim on my precious time today. Don't I ever get to decide who to give it to?

And . . . his voice on the phone. We used to talk late into the night in the beginning, when we were young and it felt like everything was still to come for us. I can't help but think about those calls, his sweet, warm voice cradled in my ear, whenever we have to talk now. That's why I avoid it. The boundaries, the distance I keep between us now—it's fine. I like it this way.

"Daddy, you're moving!"

"What?" Corey blinks, turning his attention back to Pearl.

"You're moving!" she repeats, holding up my laptop by the screen, where the Daddy Tracker was still queued up on one of the tabs. And it's true, Corey's little blue dot is slowly moving across the screen.

"That's because I'm on the bus," he says, twisting his phone around so she can get a better view. "It's taking us to the airport because we're flying overnight to England. I'm hoping I can sleep. They got us those seats that lay all the way down—"

"Are you going to see the king?"

"Probably not, but maybe he'll invite me over? What do you think?"

"If you're nice and say please and thank you! You can have tea and crumpets! But maybe not crumpets, because, actually, I don't know what they are and they might be gross."

In seconds, they're lost again in each other, debating whether crumpets are gross or not and what Corey will eat at his fictional tea with the king, and my chest starts to loosen with relief. I trace the blue dot on the screen with my finger and try to imagine all my feelings and worry funneled into just that small space, contained. It's better that way—for me, for all of us.

As the blue dot creeps its way to Newark, there's a flash of . . . something in my mind, quick and insistent. We use this Find My Phone app as a "Daddy Tracker," yeah, but a lot of other people use it, too. Most people don't even know it's there; it just comes preinstalled. Does Principal Smith have Find My Phone? Has anyone checked it yet? Surely Mrs. Smith has by now . . . but what did she find?

As soon as they're done, I'm going to text Jack. This could get us some real information. It could answer all the questions and put my suspicions about Trisha to bed, where they belong.

I know I'm avoiding. I know I'm looking for a distraction from the things I don't want to feel, the things I don't want to think about right now. But also, is that so bad?

EIGHT

I DON'T WAKE UP WITH THE INTENTION OF CALLING OUT sick from work. But then I make the mistake of checking my email first thing after my alarm, which is, like, never a good idea. And it's an especially *bad* idea when Nelson has sent out a staff-wide blast at 5:30 a.m. about his idea for a career fair for Project Window mentees. And Rose responded just minutes after because apparently these people don't sleep. Love the initiative and innovative thinking! So happy you're on our team!

Before I even put much thought into it, my fingers are already moving across the screen, blindingly bright in my dark room, explaining to Rose that I'm so sorry but my throat hurts. And I'm not even really lying, because my throat does hurt, sort of, but that is likely because of the primal scream I'm attempting to hold in so I don't scare Pearl and Polly.

Rose writes me back quick, tells me to feel better and take it easy. It probably doesn't even occur to her that I might be lying, because I've done this only a handful of times in the past seven years, when Pearl had hand, foot and mouth or scarlet fever or whatever medieval plague was floating around the preschool.

Calling out just isn't in the Miller DNA. But maybe it *should* be, if my nearly perfect attendance isn't going to get me anything more substantial than a printed-out certificate and light applause at a meeting.

And I don't know if it's the freedom of having the whole day ahead of me, Rose-and-Nelson-less, or the buzzing excitement of getting to see Jack this morning speeding me along, but Pearl and I get to Knoll forty-five minutes before the bell, a new record, one that we will surely never reach again.

"Is there school today?" Pearl asks, wrinkling her nose as we walk up the deserted sidewalk.

"Yes, there's school. We had to get here extra early because of a meeting I have, remember?"

She arches an eyebrow and continues to look around suspiciously. "Are you sure it's not a holiday, Mommy? Because you did that before. You brought me to school when it was really a holiday. Remember when you did that?"

"No, it's not a holiday." God, you bring your kid to school on a holiday one time, and she'll never let it go. And how was I supposed to know that Beachwood Unified celebrates Lincoln's birthday and Washington's birthday separately? Like, why is that even necessary? But okay, I guess it does currently look like it did that day we rushed here in our typical frantic fashion, leaving Pearl's lunch box and jacket behind like fallen soldiers, only to realize the school was closed. There are no cars taking all the good, no-danger-of-getting-a-ticket spots in front of the building, and the playground is empty, except for Mrs. Nelson pulling out her precious keys to unlock the gate. I didn't even *know* the playground was open this early—I've never needed to know. But Jack said this would be the best time to catch Lilliam in a good mood, which is definitely a slim window, and he said I could leave Pearl to play on the playground under the staff's supervision. Apparently this is something parents—responsible, early waking parents—do every day.

"See, Mrs. Nelson is here," I say, pointing to the irrefutable evidence that I haven't messed this up, this time. "There is school today."

Pearl sighs and rolls her eyes. She's getting too good at that. "If you say so."

I squeeze Pearl's hand, and together we walk up to the gate. Mrs. Nelson smiles at us, her gaze unfocused, but then quickly does a double take.

"Oh! Pearl . . . Ms. Miller. *You're* here early."

I don't know if I should be offended by her clear surprise.

"Mom says there's school today, but if we should go home instead, that is fine with me." This child. The lack of faith!

Mrs. Nelson giggles and leans down so she's eye level with Pearl. "There's school. And what a delight it is to see you bright and early, Pearl! Are you ready to learn?"

"Yes, but it's not time yet, Mrs. Nelson. First, I get to play." Pearl is eyeing the empty jungle gym, and her fingers are wiggly in mine, itching to go.

"Bye, baby girl," I say, kissing her cloud of curls. "Have a good day!"

"Bye!" She gives me a tight, quick squeeze and then sprints over to the playground without looking back.

"Such a sweet girl," Mrs. Nelson murmurs, and I turn back to her, really taking her in this time. Her highlighted brown hair, which usually falls in smooth, precise waves on her shoulders, is pulled back into a haphazard ponytail, and there are dark, sunken circles under her eyes. Instead of one of the floral shirtdresses she typically wears, she has on wrinkled slacks and a blouse with a fresh coffee stain near the hem.

I want to ask her if she's okay, if she's feeling better after falling apart yesterday, but of course, I wasn't supposed to see that—whatever that was. Our relationship is more her chastising me for my tardiness, not talking about our feelings.

"Thank you, Mrs. Nelson. You have a good day, too."

I walk around the side of the school. My heart rate picks up when I pass the bougainvillea bush, a shock of bright pink flowers, and I don't know if it's because of what I saw there, not even two full days ago, or because of what Jack and I are about to do.

But then I turn the corner and see Jack standing in front of the office in a tailored gray blazer and dark jeans, his blond hair glinting in the early morning sun, and the thumping in my chest speeds up even faster. *Oh.* Apparently this is what he does to me, and I'm somehow supposed to be normal and just keep existing around him, when his mere presence makes me feel like I might need to go to the hospital.

"Morning, Watson," he says, and I watch the smile rise on his face like the sun behind him, the curve of his lips and his eyes that squint into crescents.

"Oh, so *you're* Sherlock?" I arch an eyebrow, and he laughs, that low and rumbly sound I'm already starting to crave.

"I mean, I'm not tied to it. But I am the one who got us this clue about the cameras. Our first major breakthrough." He mimes dusting his shoulders off.

"Well, *I* am the one who thought of asking her about Find My Phone. That's a pretty Sherlock insight, if I do say so myself." I pretend to flip my hair, even though I pulled my curls back into a puff today.

Jack raises his eyebrows and looks me up and down, and I know he's just playing, but it does something real to my stomach. "I think whoever is Sherlock should take the lead with questioning Lilliam."

"You're Sherlock!" I rush out before he even finishes saying her name, and we both laugh.

"Thanks, Watson."

I turn to face the office, though, and the laugh dies in my throat. So far we've just been talking, living in the hypothetical. But actually interviewing Lilliam? Poking around? That's real. We're bringing someone else into this game of ours, and sure, Jack doesn't think I'm crazy for wondering about Principal Smith and Trisha, but a lot of other people will. Do I really want to do this? It's not too late to back out . . .

I take a deep breath in and out, steadying my nerves, and his hand lightly brushes my shoulder. It doesn't really help the nerves, but it fills my whole body with warmth.

"Hey," Jack says softly, "we're just asking her a couple questions. We're not accusing anyone of anything. No one's going to know why."

I nod. "And it's probably nothing," I say, more for myself. "I'm sure Lilliam will clear this up, and then we can move on."

"Yeah, yeah." I want to study his face, to see what the thought of moving on does to his crinkly-eyed smile, but it's probably better if I don't right now.

Instead I flash him a quick smile. "Okay. Let's do this."

Jack leans down with the key on his school lanyard and lets us into the front office, which is apparently locked this early—I'm learning a lot this morning. I hang back as he strides ahead of me, letting Sherlock take the lead.

"Mr. Cohen! Good morning!" Lilliam calls from her perch at the front desk, using a bright, bubbly tone I didn't realize she was capable of, because there's been no reason for her to direct it at me before. The thick pink cardigan that's usually draped over the back of her chair by the time I skulk in here, tardy and ashamed, is still on her shoulders, and she pulls it tight around herself as she finishes chewing a bite of steaming oatmeal, her right index finger curved over her mouth. The room smells like cinnamon and construction paper.

And, like, I know, intellectually, that this is the same woman who I see many mornings, but my brain is having a hard time processing that because . . . she's smiling? Have I ever seen Ms. Lilliam smile? If I have, I don't recall. But it totally transforms her face: the angular penciled-in eyebrows, the thin burgundy lips, the sunken cheeks caked with pale powder—they all somehow look soft instead of smug now. Like one of those optical illusions people get all heated about on Facebook, bunny or a duck, blue dress or white dress.

"I was just thinking about you and your brother, honey," she continues, setting her breakfast down. "How did the meeting with the regional center go? Was he accepted into that program—*oh*. It's you."

And her face clicks back into the disapproving frown I know so well. I've been spotted.

"Excuse me, Ms. Miller?" She flashes Jack an apologetic glance. "Do you need something?" Technically Lilliam is asking me a question, but it sounds like an order. *Tell me how I can help you. Immediately.* "I didn't see Pearl on the tardy list yesterday, but it's possible they missed it. You need to clear that. Mm-hmm, let me check for you." She purses her lips together tightly, making it painfully obvious that she'd rather do anything but.

"Oh, no—I'm not here for—" I start to stutter. "It's just— um, I'm with—"

Jack, thankfully, comes in with the save. "She's with me, Ms. Lilliam. We, uh, have a meeting, shortly." Lilliam narrows her eyes and turns her assessing gaze back at me. I can almost hear her thoughts. *Are you sure you want to be fraternizing with this truant woman?* But then Jack smiles and it seems to work the same magic on her that it does on me.

"Mm-hmm." I mean, it's no warm welcome, but at least she's allowing me to remain in her presence.

"But yes, Derek did get into that program, thank you for asking," Jack continues, and Lilliam's frostiness melts a little more. "It was such a relief after being on the waiting list so long, and they're going to provide transportation, which will be really helpful. Cut down on my commute in the morning, you know."

My own curiosity is piqued, and I want to ask more about his brother. What program is this, and why does he need transportation? But no, it's better to stay quiet and let Lilliam forget I'm here.

"Oh, good. I'm so glad." Lilliam nods understandingly and gently pats his hand. "I know you have so much going on, and I worry about you. It's a lot for one person to manage."

Jack winces, just slightly, but then he smooths out his face into a gracious grin. "That's very kind of you, but you don't need to worry. Derek and I are good." It rings a little hollow to me, but Lilliam doesn't seem to notice. "You, however—*you* I do worry about. I heard about what happened yesterday, and I'm sure a lot is falling on you. What with Principal Smith being out, and everything."

And *that* is why he's Sherlock.

"Oh, you don't even know the half of it." Lilliam sucks her teeth and then sighs dramatically, closing her eyes to demonstrate her exhaustion. "He'd only been here since July, so I was still training him on how things should be done, and now, what was that all for? I have to do everything myself again, anyway. And that wife!" Another long, weary sigh. "She came in yesterday morning yelling, accusing everyone. And it wasn't the first time. No, mmm-mmm. Between you and me, I wouldn't be surprised if he left town just to get away from her."

She shakes her head, laughing bitterly, and then freezes, seeming to remember I'm there, an interloper. My eyes shoot to the ground, making it clear that I wasn't eavesdropping, not at all, and then I wander a few feet away for good measure, staring intently at the pens she's decorated with fake flowers and displayed in a clay pot.

Moments later, Lilliam continues, quieter this time. "The cameras were off that night. Did you know that?"

"I did," Jack responds, leaning in. "Has that ever happened before?"

"Oh yes, plenty of times. Sometimes I feel like those darn things are off more than they're on, with all the trouble they give us. All the system restarts and software updates—and it's all on me, of course. I told Principal Brennan for years that we needed something new, but you know how he was always putting things off. Really, they were just for show, because no one checked the footage anyway."

"Did they see anything on the cameras before they shut off? Mrs. Smith or the police—"

"The police!" Lilliam laughs and slaps the front counter. I can feel her eyes burning on the back of my neck, checking to see if I'm listening before she starts again in a whisper. "The police aren't looking into anything, though that woman wants them to, that's for sure. But there's no evidence that something . . . untoward happened. He lives close, you know, walks to school, so his car is still sitting in front of their house. But he took his phone, wallet. Between you and me, I think there's some issues going on in that marriage and he needed a breather—excuse me, Jonathan, can I help you?"

I startle at the quick change in her tone, the same question-but-not-really-a-question she asked me earlier.

"Ms. Lilliam. I throwed up. On the playground! I throwed up!" A sweet little boy with tan skin and black, spiky hair stands in the middle of the office, clutching his stomach. His Pikachu shirt is covered with the evidence of his claim.

"Mm-hmm, and that's why I told Mom to keep you home three days with this stomach bug, but I see that you are here." She clicks her tongue, assessing him, but then smiles sympathetically. "Mm-hmm. Okay, Jonathan. Let me go ahead and call her.

"So sorry, Mr. Cohen," she adds, patting his hand again. "Give me just a second."

Lilliam scoots down from her high-perched chair and walks over to her desktop near the back of the office. She tuts to herself as she pulls up her glasses from the rhinestone chain around her neck and searches for Jonathan's mom's number.

"Do you want to sit down, buddy?" Jack asks the boy, and he nods and scoots into one of the chairs in the corner.

"Hello, Mrs. Garrido? Mm-hmm, yes, this is Lilliam at Knoll, and it seems that Jonathan was dropped off today *even though* he is still sick . . ."

Jack clears his throat, getting my attention. And I raise my eyebrows at him. Is that the signal to get out of here? He hasn't asked about the Find My Phone app yet, but we did find out some more about the cameras. They probably weren't even turned off on purpose, which is another point for Team This Is All Nothing and Mavis Is Just Being Paranoid. Maybe that's enough for today.

Also, I'm not trying to get whatever Jonathan has.

But Jack raises his eyebrows back at me and nods toward the

principal's office on the opposite side of the room from the entrance . . . and Lilliam's call to Mrs. Garrido. I've been in that room before—the last time was that meeting with Principal Brennan about Pearl's placement in the gifted program. Now, of course, there's a new brass plaque with the name PRINCIPAL SMITH instead, and the door is slightly ajar, the dark office beyond it. Does that mean something? A clue?

I look back at Jack, and he nods toward the door again, more urgently this time.

Wait. Does he want me to . . . *go in there*? My brow furrows in confusion, and he widens his eyes conspiratorially, giving one last decisive nod. Oh, I can't do that. It's one thing to ask Lilliam some questions, but go into Principal Smith's office? What if I get caught? What would everyone say?

Except . . . the way Jack is nodding right now, urging me along, it reminds me of how we just met, and how he leaped into helping me. Even though he didn't know me at all, and there was nothing in it for him. He took that risk anyway. He acted.

Sneaking into the principal's office is decidedly *not me*. But maybe it could be? Just for this moment? I'm already playing hooky from work, taking time for this silly fantasy with Jack. Would it hurt to lean in a little bit more and hopefully get some definitive answers? I can get in and out, no harm done. I can show Jack that I'm willing to be a little daring, too.

Lilliam's back is to us as she faces her computer, and Jonathan is staring at his equally ruined Pikachu shoes. There's no one else here yet. Before I can overthink it, I make my way to Principal Smith's door in three quick strides and slip in silently. In the darkness of the room, I wait for Lilliam's inevitable outraged screams, but there's nothing. I did it. Now . . . what *am* I doing exactly?

Right. Looking for clues. Anything that's suspicious or

points toward Trisha. But what would that even be? Her Lulu-lemon rewards card left behind, a signed note that reads *I did it!*? When I saw her that night, she was wearing rubber gloves and carrying Clorox . . . whatever happened, she was thorough.

As my heart pounds, I scan Principal Smith's sparse book-shelf and the degrees hung on the wall. There are three of them: a bachelor's in elementary education and a master's in school leadership, both from the University of North Florida, and some sort of national board accreditation. So . . . he is who he says he is? *Okay, yeah, great insight, Mavis.*

I creep toward his desk, and it definitely doesn't look like the scene of any foul play. It's tidy and mostly empty, just his sleek iMac, screen dark, and a silver-framed photo of him and a bleached-blond woman with thick black mascara and filler-plumped lips. That must be Mrs. Smith. And they look happy? Or at least, not like he skipped town to run away from her? But I know pictures can be deceiving. There are lots of happy family photos of Corey, Pearl, and me, taken right in the thick of our worst fighting. I pick up the frame to look at their faces closer, knocking the white mouse next to his keyboard in the process. His large computer screen turns on, like a spotlight on me, the intruder. I freeze. Did Lilliam see that? Am I caught? But I hear her voice continue—the sweet one this time, so she must be talking to Jack again. Hopefully he can keep her distracted.

I turn down the brightness on the screen, casting an eerie glow across the room. And it takes me a second to process what I'm seeing. Principal Smith reading *The Cat in the Hat* to a group of kids. Okay, a picture of himself as his background. Extremely cringey. *But* it also means his computer isn't password protected, which is also extremely good for me because as much as I'm try-ing to take a leap here, that doesn't mean I can start miracu-lously cracking codes or whatever. This isn't a TV show.

The folders look pretty ordinary—this year's budget, grade level curriculum, School Site Council agendas. Nothing titled IF I GO MISSING READ THIS, or anything else that'll make things easy for me here. I notice an extra icon for his internet browser on the right side of the dock, though, something that was minimized. I click on it, bringing it full screen.

It's an email account, but there aren't any markings of Beachwood Unified. So, his personal one. On the bottom right, there's a draft of an email that he started writing, but he didn't get very far. It's blank with no subject, just the address field is complete with a name: Paul McGee. I search my brain for a flicker of recognition, but no. I don't think it's someone from the school, at least not anyone I know. There's an alert at the top: DRAFT LAST SAVED 8:32 P.M. So he started writing this after he was escorted out of the PTA meeting . . . and a few hours before I saw Trisha leaving with her cleaning supplies and trash bags that night. Why did he need to contact this Paul guy right then? Is it related to the PTA meeting, the gifted school debate . . . or is it totally unrelated? This is his personal email after all . . . But my chest feels tight as some more pressing questions rise to the top of all of them: Why is this draft here, incomplete? What stopped him from finishing this email . . . and is it the same thing that made him not show up for work the next morning?

I consider continuing to go through his email. Maybe there's a threat from someone, a travel itinerary that reveals an escape? But then I'd have to click out of this draft email and tamper with evidence even more. If the police start taking this seriously and actually *do* get involved, that might be noticed. It's probably better that I don't muddy things more than I am. I need to remember to wipe away my fingerprints before I leave, too.

There's another tab open to the right, though, which means he must have opened it after the email. If I click on that, it won't do anything to the email screen—I can easily return things to how I left them . . . right? My curiosity wins out over my conscience, and I navigate to that tab.

There's a Beachwood Unified logo on the right corner, and a long list of names. The top reads Knoll Elementary, and right underneath that, a name in bold font, Ms. Laguna. She teaches the fourth-grade gifted class—I remember her presenting at one of the school events, maybe open house or Back to School Night. And all these names . . . oh, they're students. This is a roster.

I carefully trace my finger down the screen, reading all the names and trying to get into Principal Smith's head. Why would he have this open that night? Did he open this after he stopped working on the email to Paul McGee at 8:32 p.m.? River, Nora, Jaxon, Arya, Tessa, Sebastian, Khaleesi . . .

I hold in a little snort. Two *Game of Thrones* names? Really? Was this kid named before or after that series finale? I guess I can't talk, though. Pearl was named after a brand of drums.

I keep looking. Delilah, Owen, Dexter, Harlow . . . and then one name right in the middle of the list makes me stop cold, goose bumps erupting up my arms. Cayden. Cayden Holbrook.

Trisha's son is in this class. The class that Principal Smith was looking up, for some reason, right before he disappeared . . .

The door hits the wall with a loud thud when it opens, flooding the room with fluorescent light from the main office.

"Ms. Miller! *What* are you doing in here?"

NINE

I KNOW FOR DAMN SURE THAT LILLIAM DOESN'T BUY MY "Oh, I thought this was where Mr. Cohen and I were meeting!" playing-dumb routine. But she *does* think I'm dumb, so that goes a long way toward her allowing me to be ushered out of the office by Jack without, like, alerting the authorities or whatever.

We silently speed walk to his office, looking at the ground instead of each other, but as soon as the door shuts, the giddy exhilaration bubbles up out of me.

"That was—oh shit! That—"

"Just happened," he finishes, and it's clear from his wide eyes and slack jaw that he feels the same as me.

"We did it! I can't believe we actually did it!"

"*You* did it! I can't believe you went into his office—"

"Isn't that what you were telling me to do, with the little—" I jerk my head to the side, mimicking his head nod.

"Hey, I didn't look like that!" He laughs. "And well, yeah, but then you went and actually did it, all spy-like—" He takes long, dramatic strides across his office like some deranged super-model.

"Now, I did not look like *that*!"

"Okay, maybe not, but—" Something else crosses his face as he rubs the side of his jaw, eyes on me. If I was having a particularly feeling-myself day, I might call it awe.

"Let's regroup then," I say, sitting in the chair across from his desk. He follows suit. "Do you know anyone named Paul McGee?"

"Paul McGee." He bites his lip, thinking it over. "No . . . no, I don't think so. Why?"

"There was an email started on Mr. Smith's computer—"

Jack's hands fly up. "You broke into his computer? How are you so good at this?!"

"No, no, hold your applause. I didn't have to. There was no password. But there was an email draft on the screen to someone named Paul McGee. And get this—the draft was last saved at eight thirty-two p.m."

"Wait, eight thirty-two? Lilliam said the cameras went out around then. Eight or nine . . . she couldn't remember for sure."

"Okay, so that could be something. If they didn't just shut down on their own, I mean."

"Did you get this Paul guy's email?"

My stomach drops. So much for being good at this. "No. I didn't even think of that. See, I told you to hold your applause."

"It's fine. Don't even worry about it. I'm sure we can look him up. But hey, I asked Lilliam about Find My Phone, and you were spot on there—"

"He has the app? Well, then where is his phone? That could solve everything."

Jack sighs. "That's the thing. He has it turned off. I guess that was part of Mrs. Smith's rant yesterday morning."

I sigh, too, leaning back in my chair. Another dead end.

"Hey, we still made some progress here," Jack says, with an

overly enthusiastic tone that he probably uses with his students. "Let's recap, one—" He counts off a finger in his palm. "Principal Smith was at Knoll until at least eight thirty-two, sending an email to someone named Paul McGee. And two, the cameras went off at around that time. On accident or . . ."

"On purpose."

"On purpose. Yes. And three, he doesn't want his wife, at least, to know where he is. This is all . . . It's not nothing."

But is it something? Do we have any evidence that *something* happened here, really? Or are we still just playing around . . . wasting time? I feel a sharp pang of guilt in my chest. I should be at work, trying to prove myself with Nelson, my new boss, instead of distracting myself with pretend. But also—"I found something else on his computer." I almost forgot in the rush of escaping from Lilliam. "He had a roster pulled up. For Ms. Laguna's class."

"Okay . . ."

"Do you know who's in Ms. Laguna's class?"

Jack shakes his head, brow furrowed.

"Cayden Holbrook."

We sit in silence, staring at each other, both of us hesitant to take this piece of information to its conclusion.

Finally, Jack leans forward on his hands, and starts slowly. "So, that means . . ."

"Does that even mean?" I cut in quick, my voice as frantic as my heartbeat. "I don't know! Am I assuming way too much?"

"It's definitely odd," he concedes. "I don't know if it means *that*, but . . . my mind is catching on it."

"Yeah. Yeah . . . right?"

"Right."

Before we can sit and ponder any further if Cayden's name

on a list means Trisha did something to Mr. Smith or nothing at all, though, the bell rings.

"I'm really sorry, Mavis, but I have an assessment to do right at eight."

I stand up fast, and the chair makes an annoying screech. "Oh, it's okay. I have to . . . Yeah." Do absolutely nothing, because I'm playing hooky from work *like a child*. But he doesn't need to know that.

"So, game plan," I continue. "We're both going to look into Paul McGee?"

"Yes," he says, standing up. "And I'm going to keep poking around with the teachers and staff, see what comes up. Oh, and actually, are you in the parents' Facebook group? I've heard that it's pretty active?"

"I try to avoid it at all costs, but I can make a sacrifice for this." Jasmine did say that people were discussing Principal Smith on there. Maybe there *is* something useful, outside of the usual petty drama and Mom Olympics.

"Okay, good, well." He makes a move around his desk toward me, and for a second, I think he's going to hug me. I . . . would like a hug. What does that blazer feel like, I wonder? And does he smell even better up close? But then I realize with a flash that he's just moving toward the door and I'm blocking him all goo-goo eyed, and I jump back and pull it open before I can make this any more weird.

"Bye, Nancy."

I laugh. "Bye, Ned."

As I walk down the hallway, I realize I forgot to ask about his brother and the funny look on his face when Lilliam made that comment about all he had to manage. Next time, I guess. Well, if he wants me to know. It's possible that to him, this really is just about figuring out what happened to Principal Smith. It's definitely not just about that for me.

"Don't tell me they already got you working early morning hours for them? Now, *what* does Trisha have on you?"

Corinne stands at the other end of the hallway, but she quickly closes the space between us. She's wearing the same lime-green Crocs and rainbow beaded bracelets from when we first met, but her curly red hair is out of the bun and down to her lower back. She's wearing ripped jeans and a fuzzy yellow sweater, even though the temperature is probably already creeping up outside.

"You can tell me! Don't worry, I can keep a secret," she says with a wink.

I'm confused. Did I totally make it up, or was she giving me the cold shoulder yesterday? This is much more aligned with how she was in the PTA meeting, though. She might have just been having a tough morning. Lord knows I have those, like, every other day.

"Actually, I was just talking with Mr. Cohen," I explain. "But PTA has already been . . . a lot. You left the meeting too early to warn me about the sheer amount of texts involved. But I don't blame you for sneaking out of there when you—"

"Oh, I just keep them all blocked unless I need to talk to one of them about something specific," she says, waving her hand as if it's a normal solution. "So, Mr. Cohen, hmmm? Does your daughter have an IEP?"

"Uh, no, she doesn't, but—"

"My fourth grader does, and I'm not one of those parents who tries to keep it secret—well, clearly. Mr. Cohen, though, he's great. A real advocate. And also pretty drrrreeeeeamy." She shimmies her shoulders as she trills that last word, and I can feel my neck heat up.

"Ooooh, I saw that! But I will pretend I didn't." She mimes zipping her lips. "Hey, what are you doing right now? Do you want to go get coffee?"

From how fast she's talking, I'm surprised she needs any more.

My excuse is right there on the tip of my tongue. *Sorry, I have to go to work.* Except: I don't today. I have nowhere to go. And actually, I can't just go *home*. Because then I'm going to have to explain to Dad why I'm home, and then I'm probably going to have to get into the promotion that I didn't get, and Dad will most likely give me a lecture about how this isn't the way to get the next promotion, and it'll be a whole thing. I feel exhausted just imagining it.

I've always felt like I was above *those* moms, the ones who can get coffee in the middle of the day. Go to the gym, grocery shop alone . . . have friends. But I've also secretly wondered what it would be like to be one of them. And here I have the whole day in front of me and a chance to find out. Corinne is a bit much, but it's also pretty infectious. I wonder what it would be like to go through life with such a carefree, comfortable spirit. She seems like she's read and internalized all those white lady books about washing your face and not giving a fuck, subtly. Hell, she could probably teach those ladies a thing or two.

"Yeah. Yeah, that sounds fun."

"I thought I heard your voice, Mavis!"

I jump at the sound of Trisha's voice, and the jump scare continues when I see Dyvia standing there next to her. Trisha because, you know, the whole possible murder thing, and Dyvia because I think I forgot to respond to her last message. How messed up am I that they strike almost equal amounts of terror in me?

"Good morning, ladies!" Corinne chirps, waving at them.

And I don't know if I'm giving off clear *HELP ME* vibes, but Corinne seems to pick up on something. "Sorry, but we were just running out."

"I thought you were working today," Dyvia says, frowning in confusion. "If you do have just a moment, can we have a quick chat?"

I want nothing less right now . . . well, maybe the only thing less is being left alone with Trisha. But now that I've made this commitment to one of the coffee-and-wash-your-face ladies for the day, I don't want to work on anything—work-work or PTA work.

"Well, we were going . . ." I start, but is it really going to hurt me so much to stop and talk to her right now? This *is* important. And Dyvia has put in a lot of effort already. Really, she could be doing this all on her own, without me . . .

"It won't take that long," she adds with a kind smile. "Just a quick meeting to touch base."

I cringe at the M-word, but Trisha cuts in before I can say anything else. "I'm sure Mavis knows what she's doing, Dyvia."

Her voice is soft, pleasant. And if I wasn't looking at her, I might write it off as playful teasing between friends. But her eyes are filled with the same blue blaze as yesterday, and my skin prickles with unease.

"It's PTA, not life or death," she adds and then erupts into a high, frenzied laugh, like shattering glass. It sends a chill racing up my spine.

"Uh, ooooh-kay," Corinne says, her eyes dancing between them. "Well, we better go."

"Yeah, Dyvia, I'll text you soon." I smile at her apologetically, and then Corinne, thankfully, whisks me away.

———

"I JUST REALIZED I NEVER ACTUALLY ASKED," CORINNE SAYS, taking a sip from the paper straw in her iced honey latte. "What did you have to go in early to talk to Mr. Cohen about?"

We're sitting outside of a cute coffee shop with scalloped pink and white umbrellas, which I always drive past but never actually get to stop at.

"Oh, just—" I can't tell her what we were truly talking about, of course. In fact, it's probably better to avoid talk of Principal Smith and his disappearance altogether. That way, none of my bonkers conspiracy theories can slip out. So I lie. "I was just checking in to see if he had any insights about Pearl, what with her being in the gifted class and everything this year . . ."

It rings false, even to my ears, so I can't even blame Corinne when she narrows her eyes and smirks at me. "I'm sure Mr. Cohen offered some great insights. And it doesn't hurt that they come from those perfect, pouty lips—"

"No! No, no. It's not like that!" I say, shaking my head. But it probably isn't very convincing as I laugh at the dramatic duck lips she's making, reminiscent of the Myspace profile pictures of my youth.

"Okay, but if it *was* like that, no shame! You're single, right?" She glances knowingly at my empty ring finger, and I nod, putting my hands up to my burning cheeks.

"He's hot," she says simply, like it's an inarguable fact. "I say you *make* it like that, and soon! Have you noticed all the moms circling him like prey at the school events? Even the married ones! Mavis, stake your claim." She waggles her thick eyebrows and shoots me another devilish grin. "Hell, if my husband doesn't get home soon, then I might need to join right in with the cougars!"

My eyes must go wide, because her palms are up fast, giggles shaking her shoulders. "I'm kidding, I'm kidding! Mr. Cohen is all yours, ma'am. I wish y'all a happy life together."

Lord, I need to change the subject now, or my whole body is going to burst into flames.

"So, your husband's out of town?" I venture.

"Yes, allllll the time." She rolls her eyes and lets out a long, weary sigh. "Ben travels for work. He's in sales for a tech company. And during the busy season, he's gone Monday through Friday most weeks."

"That's gotta be tough."

"It's a miracle I haven't already lost my goddamn mind." She slaps her forehead. "But here I am being all woe is me, and you probably know better than anyone."

I smile, grateful that she recognized that. I never try to engage in the Mom Olympics, because I know we all have it hard in our own ways. Nothing about raising another human is *easy*. But still, it's nice to have it recognized that I don't have a partner to relieve me, even if only on the weekends.

"Is Pearl's dad around?" she asks, and I nod.

"Yes, when he can be. He travels for work, too. He's a touring musician, so he's gone for months at a time sometimes, and currently, he's gone. But they talk every night. They're close."

"That's good. It's important for a girl to have her daddy." She points at me with her drink, the paper straw already drooping to the side. "I say that as a daddy-less girl! And let me tell you, I went looking for every long-haired boy in SoCal, with a troubled soul that only I could fix, to fill that void!"

My eyes go wide and a surprised giggle escapes from my lips, and Corinne beams in delight. It's becoming really clear, really fast that everything that pops out of her mouth is probably going to make me react this way. But I don't hate that. It's refreshing to be with someone who doesn't have a filter and doesn't seem to judge—at least not me.

"Watch out for long-haired boys. Check," I say, pretending to mark it off an invisible list.

"Still, the day-to-day is all on you. I know that gets over-whelming fast."

"It does, but I live with my dad. Papa, Pearl calls him." I smile, and she matches it. "And he's a big help. He picks her up from school, makes dinner some nights. We've become a real team in the past few years."

"Ugh, that's so good! Protect Papa at all costs! I wish I had that kind of help. The boys' nana lives fifteen minutes away, but she just shows up once every few weeks to make comments about how I fold my laundry and bank some content for her 'I love being a glamma!' Facebook posts."

I laugh as she pretends to gag. "Your mom?"

"No, mother-in-law. My mom's dead."

She says it, just like that. I usually hesitate to talk about my own mom with most people, especially those I don't know that well. So often, after telling others that my mom died from breast cancer when I was just a baby, I feel like I have to perform the grief they expect—grief that sometimes, I convince myself I haven't earned, because the only memories I have of her are re-told from Dad. Or worse, I end up having to console them, tell them it's okay, I'm okay.

But the way that Corinne just gets right in there, digs around without worrying about getting dirt under her fingernails, it makes me feel less scared to be open.

"My mom died, too."

"What! Dead Moms Club!" She shoots up her right hand to give me a high five so fast that she winces. "C'mon, you can't leave me hanging."

Again, my eyes go wide, but then I reach up to slap her palm gently because what else can I do? And soon my nervous giggle blooms into full-blown laughter, Corinne joining in easily, her ginger curls falling back over her shoulders and chair as she throws her head back in loud, hearty chuckles.

We sit there for over an hour, the conversation flowing easily from motherhood to our kids to Knoll and all the PTA gossip over the years—of which she is very informed, like a historical scholar. I let the laughter come instead of holding back or over-thinking too much. It feels good to do so, to let myself go along for her ride. And it feels like that ride just goes on into infinity, with Corinne's endless supply of energy. I almost want to check her for a battery pack or a USB plug-in, because how is she this happy, this spirited when her husband has been gone all week, and with three boys? I barely keep it moving with just Pearl and me. I tell her that, and she slaps the table.

"Well, I'm glad it looks that way, but I feel like I've been chewed up and spit out, the way these boys are running me." She smiles, and I can already see her gearing up to tell another joke. But there's also a flicker of something else in her eyes, and I notice for the first time the dark circles hidden with concealer, the exhaustion that she's covering up. "I was driving down the PCH yesterday after picking up Mason from karate," she continues. "And Brody was complaining about my music on the radio, you know, being a typical teenager. Does he really think it's going to wound me if he calls me cringe? I will wear cringe like a badge of honor! And then both River and Mason thought it would be funny to start banging on the back windows of my van, and mouth, 'Help me,' to the car behind us, like I was kidnapping them or something?"

"No!" I shout incredulously, joining her easy laughter. But something also tugs at my mind, something I can't quite pin down. Maybe because she said "*the* PCH"? I've never heard a Southern California local call it *the* PCH. That *the* sounds all wrong. I wonder when she moved here, and from where.

"God, if someone pulled me over, I would have said, 'Here, you can have them!' And then maybe I could get some rest for a day!" She shakes her head and throws back the last of her drink, crunching on the ice. "And then they broke the lock on their bedroom window on Monday, River and Mason. River claims that they weren't playing ball inside. They were just cleaning up and it got tossed a little too enthusiastically into the toy bin. As if I was born yesterday! Now, I can't get the goddamn thing to open, so that's another thing on my to-do list."

There's that tug again. But what is it? I'm not sure . . . I think she told me about her boys at the PTA meeting, the high schooler and the two at Knoll. I saw the two younger ones across the street with her yesterday morning, so that must be Mason and River . . .

River! That was one of the names on the roster in Principal Smith's office. First on the list, which makes sense, because Corinne's last name is Ackerman.

"River. He's in Ms. Laguna's class, right?"

Her brow knits in confusion. "Right . . ."

I tap the side of my head, playing spacey, because I can't outright say, *Um, your son is in the same class as Trisha's kid, which I know because I was doing a little light entering without breaking in our missing principal's office, trying to suss out if Trisha had something to do with his disappearance.* At least not without her instantly regretting her decision to get to know the new PTA mom and, like, backing away slowly. No, I've got to lie again. "Oh, it's just Trisha was talking about a kid named River in her son's class. I just made the connection right now."

But that just makes Corinne's brow furrow deeper. "What was she saying about River, exactly?"

I tense at the sharpness in her voice. "Nothing specific, really. It definitely wasn't anything bad."

She shakes her head and sighs. "Sorry, didn't mean to go all mama bear there. It's just . . . Trisha has a lot of power at Knoll, as I'm sure you know by now. So I don't want my kids anywhere on her radar, or in the way of what she wants."

"What does that mean?"

Corinne stops and looks around, and the sudden shift in her vibe, the wariness in her eyes, makes me shiver despite the bright sunshine. When she confirms that it's just us on the patio, she leans in closer. "So, Ms. Laguna teaches the gifted class for fourth grade, and . . . Cayden wasn't in the class originally. I don't know what happened, so don't quote me on this, but I saw Trisha talking to Ms. Laguna after school. And she was real upset, you know, not yelling, but—" She scrunches up her forehead and points to the wrinkles there. "The next day, Cayden was in the class. I found out because River came home complaining that his best friend, Ulysses, got moved somewhere else."

Corinne shrugs her shoulders and gives me a meaningful look. "Trisha has a plan for her kids—never mind if that's what's right for them. And she doesn't care what she has to do to keep them on that path, or who she hurts. No one's about to get in her way."

Trisha *would* do anything for her kids. She said it herself when she was venting in the bathroom to Ruth after the PTA meeting . . . after Principal Smith went against accepted protocol and boldly stood in the way of her plan.

And what does *anything* include, exactly? Would she actually try to get rid of him? Could she have tried to have a conversation with him like she did with Ms. Laguna, and it somehow went . . . wrong? Led to an accident?

"Anyway, that's why I get nervous if that woman is even mentioning my child."

"I get it," I say, trying to keep my voice steady and calm so there's no hint of the unease I'm really feeling right now . . . the fear. "And if I thought it was like that, *at all*, I would tell you. Promise."

"You know what, I know you would," she says, nodding decisively, and then her playful smirk reappears like it never left. "I think this is the beginning of a beautiful friendship, Mavis."

And even though my nerves are going haywire, I'm also grateful that I said yes to this coffee, for this new connection. I'm usually firmly in the camp of no new friends, but Corinne is shaping up to be a good one to have. "I agree, Corinne."

A little while later, we're ready to leave, and when Corinne throws her big tote bag over her shoulder, I notice that she winces again and gently pats her arm.

"You okay?"

Corinne grins quickly and waves me away. "Just got into a fistfight with Trisha, trying to get her to release me from my PTA indentured servitude. No big deal."

I laugh along with her, and I hope she can't hear the difference in my laugh, the shift in my energy.

"Oh my god, could you imagine? Trisha in a fistfight? Trisha doing *anything* remotely improper or unpolished at all!" She snorts and shakes her head at the ridiculous idea.

But it's not so ridiculous to me, because I can. And I don't think it's funny at all.

Knoll Elementary Parents Facebook Group

Della Lively

Was Principal Smith back today?

Dyvia Mehta

No, not yet 🙁 I checked in with Lilliam again this morning, and she said there's no word yet on his return date, or even what happened!

Charlie Lee

Is there a MealTrain set up for Mrs. Smith? I can't imagine what she's going through.

Felicia Barlow

The 24 hour period has passed, so I'm sure the police are getting involved

Corinne Ackerman

Is that 24 hour thing for real or just what happens on TV? Because I ran into Lilliam this morning too and she said she doesn't even think they're looking into it because there's no signs of foul play or something

Ruth Gentry

I really hate all of this. Foul play? Police??? What is happening to our community? This is NOT okay!

Florence Michaelson

I've seen a lot of comments to DM, and I think it's better if we're transparent with each other. This affects all of our kids! Please share what you know!

Ruth Gentry

She's just jealous because no one will tell her anything

Ruth Gentry

Please ignore that, meant to post in another group I'm in! Moderator please delete!

Corinne Ackerman

You can delete your own posts

Jasmine Hammonds

What group was it meant for, Ruthie?

Della Lively

Is someone going to step in as principal until this man decides to return? Our children deserve consistency!

Trisha Holbrook

I've just received word from the district that Michael Reed, esteemed curriculum specialist and school board member, will be stepping in as our interim principal until Mr. Smith returns from his leave of absence. And what a small world!! Principal Reed just happens to be a longtime family friend. He's played golf with Chad for years, and our families vacation in Maui together every June! Isn't that a fun coincidence? 🙂 So I hope I can alleviate some of your worries . . . we're in excellent hands!

TEN

"MOMMY, THE SKY LOOKS . . . DIFFERENT," PEARL SAYS, scrunching her nose over her bowl of Cheerios.

"That's because we're up early today, even earlier than yesterday."

She blinks at the window suspiciously and takes another big bite of her cereal. "Why do we keep doing this?"

Or at least that's what I think she asks. It's hard to be sure with her mouth full.

I woke up before my alarm, and Polly heard me moving around, so she launched herself onto my bed and made it clear she was ready to start her day, too. Pearl followed soon after. Is this all it took for me to get my morning shit together? Restless nights, because I'm replaying every one of Trisha's moves over the past seventy-two hours and analyzing every clue Jack and I have managed to find? And how many days in a row does it take to build a habit? Because I think we're on our way there now.

I have to admit, the mornings *are* much more pleasant when I don't start them already behind. Pearl's dressed and her backpack and lunch are packed. Polly went out before the sun even came up, so she didn't have a chance to leave us one of her little presents. And my heart is beating at a normal speed, and I'm not already drenched in sweat before we've left the house. I even offered to make Pearl bacon and eggs and toaster waffles—a real breakfast like the moms lovingly make every morning in movies—but she declared that was weird and asked for her Cheerios instead.

"I'm done. Can I play with my princess stickers?" Pearl asks, sticking her face close to mine. I wipe a drop of milk off her squishy cheek and then kiss it for good measure.

"First, brush your teeth, and then you can—" She's up out of her seat before I'm done talking, so I call after her. "The whole two minutes, Pearl! I'll know if you don't! You don't wanna go to school with crusty teeth!" She speeds to the bathroom, and I hear her electric toothbrush buzzing seconds later. She's always hyped to play with this dress-up princess sticker book Corey brought her home from one of his trips—she'll sit and change their outfits and make them talk to each other for hours. But there's probably even more of an allure to playing with them *before* school—a true novelty in our household.

I take a sip of my coffee—which is hot and fresh and delicious, because I didn't have to settle for the leftovers in the pot from yesterday, due to lack of time. Another novelty. And now . . . what am I going to do? We don't have to leave for a bit, and I'm all caught up on the dishes and laundry. One more minute with that toothbrush, and then she's almost all ready. The only thing left is her hair, and we're keeping the two cornrows I put in last night until wash day on Sunday. I just need to smooth down her edges with some Eco Styler, and that'll only take a second—on the most hectic days, I can even leave that step for the car.

So, I have . . . free . . . time? Time that is free? I can barely process the concept.

I guess I can check my email. Except that didn't go so well yesterday. No, better to deal with work when I get to work. Program directors send early morning emails, and they made it clear I'm not *that*.

And wait. Paul. Paul McGee. That's what I need to do. I got a million results after googling just his name yesterday, and then I had to let it go because Pearl needed help with her homework and the fridge was making a troubling sound and then Corey called. I need to try again and narrow the search some more to get actually helpful results. Maybe his name and Principal Smith's together?

"Mommy! My teeth aren't crusty, so—so, I can play with my stickers?"

"Yes, you can, baby girl," I confirm, and she squeals in excitement, pulling them onto her lap on the couch.

What is Principal Smith's name anyway? I search my memory for what those degrees in his office said, but all I can recall is North Florida . . . Okay, well, it's gotta be on the school website, right? I scroll around there for a second, and yes, there at the bottom, his full name: Thomas Smith. Reeeal distinct name there. That's gonna make this easy, I'm sure.

"Mommy! This princess has a pink crown!"

"Oh, that's cute!" I call over my shoulder, and she smiles and returns her attention back to the book, whispering a conversation between two of the sticker princesses. Thankfully, that's the only contribution she needs from me for now.

I type both of their names into the search bar, and still, there's too many results. Their names are both pretty common—the only thing somewhat unique is McGee. I scroll through the links and the pictures, scan a couple of news hits, but nothing is really standing out—they're all about other Thomases and Pauls. I'm on my fifth LinkedIn profile when I decide to give up on that. If this is going to be helpful at all, I need to add some other criteria . . . but what?

"Mommy! Hey, Mommy! And this one has a purple crown!"

"Purple? Love it!"

Maybe Mrs. Smith's name, too? But I don't know how I'd even find that, at least not right now. Or, where was Principal Smith from again? I know he said it in the PTA meeting when he was running off his résumé. Somewhere in the South, I think . . . oh, Florida! Like his degrees. I don't remember the exact town, but North Florida might help?

"They're going to a ball together, but they're hiding their se-cret swords."

"Oh, that's exciting."

And okay . . . this looks slightly better. More LinkedIn, more Facebook, but there's a news article that stands out. "Bradley County Teacher Awarded Florida Teacher of the Year." I click on it, and sure enough, there's Mr. Smith, a little younger and slimmer, but that's him. I speed-read the article, and there's nothing about Paul McGee—just a Paul Schneider who served on the nominating committee and a Karen McGee who wrote the article. But Bradley County sounds really familiar . . . Yeah, I think that's what he said at the meeting. What if I try that?

"Mommy!"

"Yes, baby?"

I wait for more, but she doesn't say anything else, her atten-tion back on her stickers. So, just the usual proof-of-life "Mommy!" rather than the I-need-something "Mommy!"—and they're both preferable to the I-have-an-emergency "Mommy!" I wonder how many times I hear "Mommy!" per day. I should count sometime, for science.

One of the first results for their names plus Bradley County and Florida is a Facebook event: Bradley High Bears 15 Year

Reunion. Could that be something? That would make Principal Smith . . . well, not much older than me? I *guess* he could clock as thirty-five, if he stopped tucking his T-shirts into his jeans and wearing shoes with tassels.

I click into the page, and it's public for some reason. I guess it's good for my purposes, at least, that some people still don't understand privacy settings. It looks like the reunion already happened a couple of years ago, but all the posts are still up. **Do you remember Ms. Lockwood's crazy Hamlet impersonation?** and **Has anyone kept in touch with Brenda Phelps?** And lots and lots of pixelated photos from the mid-2000s. I scroll through the sea of low-rise jeans and pastel polos and trucker hats, searching for whatever made Google bring up this page, and I'm about to click back to the search results, when I see it. Posted by Alberta Fraser, back in May: **Remember when Paul and Tom tied for Homecoming King junior year? Still not convinced it wasn't rigged!** And below that is a picture of two teenage boys posing back-to-back in powder-blue and orange *Dumb and Dumber* suits, pointing to their matching crowns. The one in orange is definitely Principal Smith. His hairline is taking up additional real estate, but I recognize his deep-set eyes and sparkling white, schmoozing smile, which apparently came pre–principal job. The guy next to him has dark brown hair down to his chin and striking blue eyes, like a real-life Shawn Hunter. I check the tags, and there it is: Thomas Smith and Paul McGee. I've found him.

"Mommy! Mommy, Mommy!"

"Give me a second, Pearl! I'm just finishing one thing."

So Principal Smith was emailing his high school friend that night? I sigh, feeling like my chest has sprung a leak and all the hope is trickling out. I don't know if this lead—if I can even *call* it a lead—is going to amount to anything after all. I click on Paul's profile, and his location is still Bradley County, Florida.

Looks like he's a lawyer and maybe does something in local politics. So he probably wasn't anywhere near Beachwood . . . and it's unlikely that Principal Smith was emailing him to be all, Help! A hatchet-wielding PTA mom is coming for me! He was just catching up with an old buddy, and then . . . got distracted? But with what?

I should send him a message. The thought pops into my head in between several *Mommy, Mommy*s that I'm tuning out in order to think straight. I just need to complete this task, see this through, and then I can perceive whatever color of princess crown Pearl wants me to. What would I say in a message, though? Hey, what do you and your buddy Thomas talk about? Has he mentioned anyone hating him lately? I wonder if Mrs. Smith even started informing their family and friends that he's missing, anyway. Because I shouldn't be the one to tell Paul, so . . . shit. I can't really message him on here, can I? Because then he'd see my profile and my location in Beachwood, and then this whole thing would no longer be under wraps between Jack and me. But wait, okay, here's his email address attached to his account. Should I make a separate, anonymous email? Maybe I should talk to Jack again about this first.

"Mommy! Hey, Mommy!"

"*Yes,* Pearl." My voice is tight, like my nerves.

I tear my attention away from the computer screen and blink a few times to process what I'm seeing. Pearl is standing in front of me, her princess stickers long forgotten. Instead her hands hold a brush and two sparkly scrunchies. And her hair, which was in two neat braids just seconds ago—because I've only taken my attention off her for mere seconds, surely—is now completely undone and sticking out at the sides. She looks like Frederick Douglass—who is great, of course, love him—but I'm not trying to send my seven-year-old to school looking like Frederick Douglass.

"Pearl, what did you *do*?"

"I want a different style like—"

"We don't have time for that! Pearl, oh my god, now we're gonna be late!" The anxiety and frustration make each word sound louder, harsher, and I immediately regret it when her bottom lip starts to tremble.

"You're using a mean voice, Mommy. I don't like when you use a mean voice," she whimpers, and I crumble into a million pieces onto the ground, which then get swept up and dumped into the trash. Where I belong. Or at least that's what it feels like.

I take a deep breath, trying to force the calm that I desperately need right now.

"I'm sorry, Mommy shouldn't have used a mean voice. It's just—we don't have . . . Doing another hairstyle is going to take a lot of time."

Her frown deepens, and her eyes well up. "But I wanted two buns. I tried to tell you, but you were only looking at the computer. So I helped to start it." The first tear falls. "I'm sorry, Mommy."

The guilt knocks me out like a wave, and I'm underwater before I even know what's happened. She couldn't get my attention because I was too busy playing Nancy Drew, and then I was so on edge that I snapped at her, which she didn't deserve for doing a normal seven-year-old thing. And now the whole morning is about to go to shit because I keep looking for other things to do even though the universe keeps trying to remind my dumb ass that I already have plenty, thank you very much!

I take another steadying breath and then squeeze her little body close to mine. "It's okay, baby girl. I'm not mad. We can do the buns."

She sniffs, hugging me back. "And a zigzag part?"

I laugh, and shake my head at the audacity, but we both already know I'm going to agree. "And a zigzag part. But next time, ask me first. Okay?"

"Okay."

We get into position, with me sitting on the couch and Pearl between my knees. And as she's pulling on her black and silver socks and hollering all dramatically every time I pull the brush through her hair, I can't help but think about my own mom. How would she handle all of this?

I don't have memories of her on my own, just vague, hazy outlines colored in by Dad and the stories he told me before bed every night as I was growing up, like prayers. How she would sing "Isn't She Lovely" to me when I cried until her own voice went hoarse. Or how she would carry me on long walks around our neighborhood, introducing me to the world. "Hello, sun. Hello, trees. Meet Mavis." I know from Dad what a good mom she was—and would have been, given the chance. She wouldn't roll her eyes at her tender-headed little girl or snap at her for no reason.

I feel so much pressure to be perfect, to get motherhood right because I'm here and have the chance. I have to do it for both of us. But I'm definitely not perfect. Not even close. Even if I was, it still wouldn't be good enough. Because Pearl deserves more than that. Pearl deserves the whole world.

I'm letting all these other things distract me—work, PTA . . . a goddamn missing person investigation. I've got to focus. I can't lose sight of what's most important. What should come first, always.

One zigzag part and two scrunchie-adorned buns later, we're running out the door. The bell is going to ring in five minutes, but we'll make it, just barely. Mackenzie Skinner is jogging past our house in a neon-orange spandex set, and I wave at her as I jump in the car. As we drive away, I clock the rustling of Ms. Joyce's curtains—I'm gonna get an earful from her later about my "little friend."

"It's Friday, so that means movie night!" I say, giving Pearl a hug at the side gate. "Maybe we can even get an extra treat when I get home from work? Do you want boba or ice cream?"

I'm not above bribes.

"Boba," Pearl says. "And, Mommy, just so you know, you moved up my nemeses list for using your mean voice, but you're not at the top."

I hold in my laughter and fix my face into the serious expression she expects. "That's good to know. Who *is* at the top?"

"That is confidential." She reaches up to pat my head. "Have a good day, Mommy."

And then she skips through the gate before Mrs. Nelson can close it on her.

"Oh, that girl has been here before." Jasmine appears at my side as Langston runs ahead and expertly slips through the gate at the last second, too.

"Right? Like, where did she come from?" I shake my head.

"Now I gotta run to the hospital because they just told me this lady is seven centimeters dilated, but first: How was work yesterday?" Her eyebrows press together in concern as she squeezes my arm. "I've been thinking about you."

"Still . . . blah," I say with a huff. "I actually took a sick day yesterday. I just needed a beat, you know?"

"Oh-kay, self-care! Oh-kay, boundaries!" She raises her hands up and snaps. "Because for real, they think they can jerk you around and not give you the titles to match. Uh-uh. It's about time they realize what it might be like without you there."

"I don't know about that. Seems like this new guy is stepping right in and doing everything better." I get a sour feeling in my stomach, remembering Nelson's email about the career fair and Rose's excitement, but no. I shake my head like I can toss those thoughts right out of it. They're not paying me to care before I clock in. If they want to keep me as a mid-level employee, then that's all I'm gonna be.

"But it was good to rest. I got coffee with Corinne—"

"Corinne?" Jasmine asks, making a face like she smelled something funky. "Who's Corinne?"

"She's this mom I met at the PTA meeting." Her mouth falls open, but I already know what she's going to say. "She's not like them, though," I explain quickly, with my hands up. "She's really funny and sees through all that silly . . . mom posturing. I think you'd like her, too."

"Hmmm. I don't know about that." Jasmine crosses her arms and shoots me a playful smirk. "Corinne. Huh. Sounds like someone who leaves their cart out in parking lots."

I snort. "What does that even mean?"

"Or, like . . ." she continues, her face a mask of mock concern. "The kind of person who talks about their Starbucks order like it's a personality trait?"

"Girl, you are too much!"

"Am I? Or am I just speaking the truth?" Her serious expression finally cracks, and she throws her head back, laughing at her own joke. "Okay, I gotta deliver this baby. Where you parked?"

I point across the street.

"Oh good, me too."

The front of the school is mostly cleared out—all the other responsible, punctual parents dropped their kids off on time—so when we get over to the crosswalk, Francine's stop sign is hanging at her side as she talks to that same woman in a straw visor from the other day. And they're a lot louder this morning.

"I mean, do you really think she didn't know? She had to, the way they were carrying on! When I dropped off Scout's registration packet this summer, that woman was in his office with the *door closed*. Can you believe that? Some people have no shame!"

"So, do you think his wife kicked him out then? That's what Angela is running around town telling everyone—that she kicked him out and is trying to cover it up with this whole 'mysterious disappearance' thing, to save face. That doesn't make one bit of sense, though."

"It really doesn't. Ruth told me that she heard he left on his own. That him and Mrs. Nelson are planning to run off together."

"But that doesn't make sense either. Run off together after, what, two months? If that? And anyway, Mrs. Nelson has been here crying and carrying on. You know Ruth. That woman just likes to talk, don't matter what is coming out of her mou—*oh*, are you two ready to cross?"

Jasmine and I both nod, with matching wide eyes and strained smiles. I grab her arm and squeeze as we follow Francine across the street, communicating silently, *Oh my fucking god did you just hear that!*

"Thank you," I say, when we reach the corner, and Francine waves, eagerly heading back to her gossip buddy. We walk a safe distance away, look around for any witnesses, and then properly freak out.

"What!" I scream whisper.

Jasmine runs around in a little circle and squeals instead of responding.

"What did we just hear?!"

Her lips are pressed together so tight they've disappeared.

"Mrs. Nelson and Principal Smith!" I say, eyes bugging out.

"Mrs. Nelson and Principal Smith!" Jasmine repeats, finally able to produce coherent words. "So *that's* what they were talking about on the Facebook group!"

"They brought up an affair on there? And you didn't tell me?!" God, I need to start looking at that thing more.

"No, not *directly*, but Angela was sending people DMs and Florence was mad because no one would tell her and then Ruthie—"

"And you say I've been body snatched?" I ask with a laugh. "You're talking about them like they're the Real Housewives!"

"And just like the Housewives, I watch their foolishness from the comfort of my own home, okay!" Jasmine says, twisting her neck around. "Oh, and there was another thing on there, too! I meant to tell you. Miss Trish was bragging about how she knows the interim principal they're bringing in, talking 'bout 'We vacation in Maui together!'" She swans around, doing her best Trisha impersonation.

"What? There's gonna be a new principal? Already?" Trisha didn't waste any time, and she's not even trying to hide her intentions here. If this new guy is her bestie, the gifted program decision is probably going to be reversed in no time.

"Yep, that's what she said." Jasmine exhales sharply and shakes her head. "Mmm-mmm-mmm, we've got some Real Teachers of Knoll Elementary going on here. Affairs! Missing principals! What is happening up at that school?"

But I'm only half listening because I already have my phone out, texting Jack this newest development. Principal Smith was having an affair with Mrs. Nelson, and it's possible his wife didn't know . . . until now. That would explain why his Find My Phone app was turned off at least.

Where does Trisha fit into all that, though?

The only thing that is clear is that something *is* going on here. I didn't conjure all this up in my mind—it's not just some wild fantasy, some little game with Jack.

And this mystery is way down on the list of things I should be thinking about right now, but I can't stop reaching toward it, like cold hands toward a fire—or really, more like a moth flying straight into a bug zapper.

Knoll Elementary Parents Facebook Group

Florence Michaelson

What time does the PTA meeting start tonight? I saw the flyer outside the office, but I forgot to put the details in my Passion Planner @Trisha Holbrook @Ruth Gentry

Trisha Holbrook

There is no PTA meeting this week, as we just held our monthly general meeting last week. Just a friendly reminder that the schedule is always posted on our website! 😊

Della Lively

Then what parent meeting was that flyer for? I saw it too.

Ruth Gentry

Mrs. Smith is holding a meeting about Principal Smith's disappearance in the auditorium. Lilliam told me that all the flyers were up when she got here this morning. I heard Mrs. Smith wants to share what she knows so far and also put out a formal call for any information or tips from Knoll Elementary families

Trisha Holbrook

This is the first I'm hearing about this meeting, and I typically handle all requests to use the auditorium . . .

Charlie Lee

I know that our school community can come together to help her in this trying time. This is all so awful!

Della Lively

I heard she doesn't want police involved—why? It's not like we know anything and they're much more qualified to handle something of this magnitude.

Angela Hart

Maybe they already looked into it and found out that there's nothing to investigate . . . 👀

Francine Brown

I really don't think it's appropriate to gossip about what may be going on until we hear directly from Mrs. Smith. The woman is going through enough. We're better than this!

Trisha Holbrook

Just so there's no confusion, this is NOT a PTA sponsored event. The agenda has NOT been approved by the board and attendance is NOT mandatory for PTA members.

Leslie Banner

Sorry, I'm new to the group! My Julian just started TK this month (and I'm still crying at drop off . . . but that's another story lol)! Angela, would you mind filling me in as to what the police found already? I didn't realize it had gotten to that point. I feel so out of the loop!

Angela Hart

Sending you a DM . . .

Florence Michaelson

Enough with the DMs!!

ELEVEN

THE AUDITORIUM IS MORE PACKED THAN I'VE EVER SEEN IT. More than even Pearl's kindergarten holiday pageant, and that was standing room only *and* resulted in a tussle between two dads with bulky cameras on tripods in the front row.

And the energy is the same—the fizzy, frenzied anticipation that something memorable is about to happen. Except now instead of a bunch of five-year-olds warbling along to "I Want a Hippopotamus for Christmas" in construction paper costumes, the anticipation is for the juicy details of Principal Smith's disappearance.

The conversations buzzing around the room create a wall of sound, making it almost impossible to hear what anyone is saying unless I get right up in their business. But it's easy to figure out what they're talking about without being all conspicuous and eavesdropping. It has to be the rumors that are spreading on the Facebook page. I've been checking regularly since Jasmine mentioned it, and she's right—those moms really are just putting people's business all over the internet. Jack and I texted all weekend, which was quite the feat considering my heart stopped and then sped up double time every single time his name appeared on the screen. Still, I managed to fill him in—without needing, like, medical intervention—on what I saw on there and what I overheard Francine dishing out on her corner: about the affair between Mrs. Nelson and Principal Smith, and whether or not Mrs. Smith knew.

I search the packed auditorium for an empty seat or a familiar face. Jasmine was on call and couldn't make it (though she asked me to report back all of the tea), and I don't see Corinne's signal flare of a messy bun. My eyes do land on Dyvia's shiny black ponytail in the front row. She's sitting in between Angela and Ruth, her head pinging back and forth between them as they both talk animatedly, probably sharing the latest updates. But I quickly duck to the side with my hand over my face, hoping she didn't spot me. My stomach feels tight with guilt because I still haven't responded to her, even after a whole weekend. She's so committed to this—and in the *real* way, not the usual "listening and learning" way that just makes people look and feel good instead of getting anything legit done. And here I am, not following through, putting her off, getting close to becoming that kind of person myself. I feel like I barely scrape by to the end of each day, overwhelmed and exhausted, but when I look back, I can't even put my finger on exactly what I got done. For real, I'm going to text her back, though, and actually get some things moving. Tomorrow. Or by Wednesday, for sure.

All the ancient, padded chairs that flip down are full, but someone has put out some metal folding chairs for the overflow of people. I spy an unclaimed one against the right wall and speed walk over, getting there just milliseconds before a pissed-looking mom in a gauzy sack dress and wide-brimmed hat. I pull out my phone and pretend not to notice her shooting me daggers.

There's a text from my dad. Pearl says you told her she could have two desserts because she didn't eat the dessert in her lunch box.

Desserts don't carry over, I text back. I shake my head and laugh, but there's a flicker of that same guilt, the tight squeeze in my stomach. Because I really should be home, giving her the side-eye about that dessert logic and tucking her in. Not here, playing detective—or really just rubbernecking like all these other parents. And I did consider that, staying home, leaving this to Jack—even letting this all go completely! But as soon as I'd resolve that's what I should do, what I *needed* to do, that little what-if would start tapping on the edge of my mind, like a fly on a window. *What if Principal Smith needs help? What if he doesn't come back and Trisha gets her way? What if Jack misses something small, but crucial? What if I'm the only one who can figure this out?* The what-ifs are steady, persistent . . . and really fucking annoying.

My phone lights up again with another text, this time from Jack.

Hey Scully, eyes on Trisha in the
front row

My lips curve into a smile all on their own at the nickname, because we're not investigating aliens here. But then I glance up at Trisha and my smile quickly dies because she's more alarming than anything that ever showed up on *The X-Files*.

She's sitting in the very last seat, on the opposite side of the auditorium from me. But even from here, I can feel her energy, like the static you can sense buzzing in the air right before you get shocked. Her arms are tightly crossed over her blue lace blouse, and her right foot taps furiously, as if it's trying to run right out of this place. Is Trisha impatient to get out of here? Or maybe she's . . . nervous? About seeing Mrs. Smith or whatever information she might give? And see, that's why I couldn't miss this. Who knows what Trisha will give away, returning to the scene of the (probably, maybe) crime.

I look around the room for Jack, trying to be casual about it, and my eyes snap onto his like magnets. I feel another smile tugging on my lips, but I keep it locked down. While we were texting this weekend, we also decided it's best to keep things between us under wraps here at Knoll. And if that means "things between us" as in snooping around together, or . . . something else, well, I don't know. I've been out of the game for a while, but I remember enough to know you don't clarify. What I *do* know is that I don't want to be the next hot topic of the parents' Facebook group, whatever is going on.

Jack is sitting in between Ms. Castillo and Mr. Duval, one of the first-grade teachers. And actually, the whole back row is teachers and staff, here for information just like we are. I wonder if . . . No, I don't see her there. But I guess I wouldn't show up, either, if the entire audience knew I was having an affair with the missing man. Allegedly.

As if he's reading my mind, another text lights up my screen. **I saw Mrs. Nelson still in the library when I was walking over. Don't think she's coming.**

Yeah, Mrs. Nelson is definitely avoiding Mrs. Smith, but also . . . maybe she's avoiding Trisha, too? I rack my brain, trying to see if I can place them together in the past week. No, I don't think so. If Mrs. Nelson and Principal Smith were having an affair, it's possible she could have been waiting to see him that night, for a little rendezvous after the PTA meeting. What if she stumbled onto something she shouldn't have? Is that why she was crying in the library and looking a mess all week—

because she witnessed a murder and is too terrified to tell anyone?

Okay, this is reality, not *Law & Order*, so Occam's razor or whatever. The simplest explanation is the most likely. And most likely, she was just crying because her married boyfriend is gone.

The man sitting behind me gasps, startling me out of my quickly spiraling theories. And it's easy to tell by the hush that falls over the room what inspired that gasp.

Even though I saw Mrs. Smith in the picture on Principal Smith's desk, I almost don't recognize her walking up the steps to the stage. Her face is free of all makeup, and she's wearing a simple dress in a color that can best be described as dirty dishwater. With her bleached hair pulled back into a limp braid and sickly pale skin, she looks like some weird Instagram filter sucked all the color out of her.

Could she have done something to him? And all of this is just a ruse to distract from the fact that she offed her husband? I mean, he did cheat on her, according to the Greek chorus on the Facebook page, and that's motive number one in every book and TV show, right?

Mrs. Smith steps up to the podium and adjusts the microphone. She winces as feedback erupts from the speakers, and then keeps her eyes closed for a moment . . . and then another one. The room is so silent that I swear I can hear the long, shaky exhale she lets out before she finally opens her eyes and begins to speak.

"Thank you all for coming." She takes another steadying breath as she gazes around the room, like she's trying to memorize each face. "As you all surely know at this point, my husband and your principal, Thomas Smith, went missing last Tuesday night. It's not uncommon for my husband to stay late at work, so I wasn't worried at first. I went to sleep, thought I'd see him in the morning. But when I woke up and saw he wasn't there—and he—he didn't even answer his phone, I—I knew—" Her voice cracks, and she swallows, tries again. "I *knew* something had happened to him."

She pauses and leans forward, clutching the podium tightly like it's the only thing keeping her standing.

"I want to be transparent with you all. Our marriage wasn't always a . . . happy one." The man behind me gasps again like he's watching a soap opera, and he's not the only one. "And I did find a letter in his nightstand . . . suggesting we—we . . . take time apart. But it wasn't finished! And he didn't leave it out for me. He didn't even sign his *name*."

The last word comes out as a sob, and her pain is so raw, so palpable, that I have to fight the urge to run up on that stage. To throw her over my shoulder and whisk her away from here. This isn't anything anyone wants to admit in public, let alone to a room filled with judgy parents you don't know.

"The police haven't been helpful," she continues, and it sounds like every syllable is a struggle to get out. "They say he has a right to take some time away as an adult. But this isn't like him. I know it's not. His work means everything to him. So even if he would leave me . . . he wouldn't . . . he wouldn't l-leave . . . *Knoll*."

The tears begin to flood down her cheeks then, and soon her shoulders are shaking with the effort. And again, I'm struck by the fact that she just doesn't seem like a woman who could kill. She looks heartbroken and in shock. Like someone was taken from her, not like she did the taking.

I glance at Jack, in the back row, and his face is a mask of concern.

"I want to make sure that Thomas is safe. That he's okay. I'm *worried* about him." She looks around the room again with pleading eyes, as if she's searching for something. "And that's why I'm going to offer a reward of twenty thousand dollars for any information that leads to him being found—to him coming home!"

The gasps and yelps of surprise around the room nearly drown her out. Did I hear that right? Did she offer money—and *that* much money?

"Hopefully this shows how serious I am about this," she chokes out, and there's an edge to her words. I wonder if she's seen the rumors online, too. "How much I really l-love Thomas. Thank you."

Hands shoot up across the audience, while others give up on niceties and just start shouting questions. I can hardly make out what anyone is saying, and Mrs. Smith doesn't seem like she can either. Her gaze goes wide and unfocused, and she stumbles backward, unsteady on her feet. "That's all I can do. For now. I'm sorry," she mumbles, clutching the podium tightly. "But there are flyers. Outside. They have my email address, and the number for the tip line."

With that, she rushes out of the room, but the cacophony of questions and concern continues, almost as if the parents don't realize she left. I can't even focus on any of that, though, because twenty thousand dollars.

Twenty thousand dollars! Of real money!

Who just has twenty thousand dollars to throw around at the drop of a hat? Is that, like, a normal adult thing? Am I really that behind in life? Because even a hundred dollars would be a stretch for me some months.

But I guess this isn't a normal situation . . .

This isn't pretend. This isn't a game.

A real *crime* happened. *Real* money is being offered as a reward.

And Jack and I are ahead of everyone else. We have more information than anyone.

Is that information enough, though? Enough to get all that money?

Because I could do a lot with that money, even half of it if I split it with Jack, which I guess is only fair because we *are* in this together. Even though I am the one that witnessed the crime, the actual and verified crime, and so maybe that should earn me at least 60 percent . . .

But regardless, I could move out of my dad's place and give him the retirement he deserves. It might even give me a little freedom, a little wiggle room, to start looking for a new job, a job that makes me happy.

And also I could help find Principal Smith, of course. *Of course.* And that's the most important part.

"Thank you all for coming out tonight." The voice makes my whole body tense up. If Mrs. Smith looked like she was falling apart, Trisha looks refreshed, brand new, as she steps up to the podium. She's practically glowing as she holds her hands out over the crowd, like she's the one we came to see and that was just the opening act. It's chilling. "I think I speak for all of us when I say I hope Mrs. Smith is able to get the help that she needs and that Mr. Smith returns very soon. And I'm very grateful we have Principal Reed, our interim principal, steering the ship in the meantime. I know we will be in very good hands."

She gestures to a man in a gray suit in the back row, a few seats down from Jack. He has a helmet of glossy brown hair, ruddy pink cheeks, and light eyes that are blinking fast, like he's a robot that just achieved sentience. He stands up, hand outstretched in a wave, as if he's going to address the room, but Trisha is already moving on before he gets a chance.

"And just in case anyone's been concerned like me, Principal

Reed *was* able to get our application to be the site of the district's gifted school back on track. Mr. Smith was still ruminating over the idea, as some of you may have heard, but luckily Principal Reed saw the great benefits this would bring to the Knoll community and made the right decision before the deadline passed."

Still ruminating? He straight up told her no. I look around to see if anyone else is outraged by the outright lie, or suspicious about how all of a sudden this new guy is pushing through Trisha's will after her adversary, Principal Smith, conveniently disappeared. But it doesn't look like most of the room is even listening to her announcement. No, they're still discussing all of the bombs Mrs. Smith just dropped. And normally Trisha wouldn't stand for that, but tonight she's probably counting on it. She probably *planned* it this way.

"Unfortunately, now we need to clear the auditorium for the rest of the evening, as this is the janitors' regularly scheduled deep cleaning time," she continues, rushing things along. "Please, let's thank them for being so flexible with their time and patient with this interruption tonight." She starts clapping, but only Ruth and a few other PTA moms join in on the half-assed applause. Everyone else continues their concerned conversations. So Trisha leans into the microphone, her voice booming over the interruptions, like the voice of God. "And just a friendly reminder, if anyone is ever curious about the auditorium schedule, I'm always happy to provide that information! Good night, now! Drive safe!"

I FOLLOW THE SEA OF PARENTS DOWN THE AISLES OF THE auditorium in a daze, and by the time I step outside in the warm evening air, my head is spinning with questions.

I text the first one to Jack. **Can we debrief? Because that was A LOT.**

My office in 5?

I send him a thumbs-up and then start walking over, the rest of the questions flooding my mind.

Could Mrs. Smith be lying? Did she do something to Principal Smith in a fit of rage after finding that letter and knowing he was on his way out? But then why offer the money? And why did she look so heartbroken, so innocent, while Trisha was practically parading around with a neon sign flashing SUSPICIOUS! LOOK AT ME! I mean, she basically outlined her motive like a *Scooby-Doo* villain, bringing up her gifted school plans just now. What else can explain Trisha's conspicuous behavior *except* that she is involved somehow? . . . But *how?*

"Are you okay?"

I blink a few times and process that Dyvia is standing in front of me. Just down the hallway from Jack's office. And oh my lord, I really hope I wasn't muttering any of that out loud to myself again. She probably already thinks I'm nuts after the goddamn Old Navy Pixie pants rant.

"Just your face," she clarifies with a kind smile. "You looked . . . worried. Which, why wouldn't you be, right?" She sighs and shakes her head. "Can you believe all this is happening?"

"No. It's wild." *And you don't even know the half of it.* "Hey, and listen, I need to apologize to you. I'm so sorry I haven't gotten back to you yet about the DEI stuff. It's just been—"

"No," she says quickly, reaching forward to pat my arm. "Don't even worry about it. There's a lot going on, and I don't want to step on your toes. I get a little . . . enthusiastic sometimes, and I can see how that might be a little off-putting."

"No, not at all, Dyvia! Step away! Truly." I laugh. "Honestly, I'm not even sure why Trisha insisted I take this job, when you were, like, right there."

Dyvia looks down, smiling modestly, though we both know it's true. I wonder if she resents my appointment at all, like I'm some outsider encroaching on the PTA, taking what's rightfully hers. Oh my god . . . am I Dyvia's Nelson?

"There *is* something that's a little time sensitive. It was in one of my emails. The books I mentioned?" She gestures down the hallway behind her, where the library door is closed. There is light beaming out of the window in the door, though. "We don't have to talk about it now, of course. I just wanted to get it on your radar soon."

Her voice is so sweet and patient, but if I'm Dyvia's Nelson, then she's probably boiling inside. Having to go through some PTA nobody to do what she knows needs to be done? Dealing with the insult of someone else swooping in on her turf? And I didn't even want this job! Should I acknowledge that to her, see if she wants to be DEI chair? I mean, yeah, I want to try to do some good with this title that I was guilted into, but maybe it's best to pass the baton to someone who could do that good even better? *Nelson* could take some notes.

"You know, Dyvia, if you want to be . . ." My voice trails off as my gaze is pulled behind her again. The library. The light is on. And Jack said that he saw Mrs. Nelson there . . .

This could be the perfect opportunity to talk to her alone. To ask her some questions, subtly of course, without the pressure of the school day about to start and Rose checking for me at my desk. Because it's clear that Mrs. Nelson knew Principal Smith, well . . . *intimately.* Maybe he texted her that night promising he was on his way? I just have to meet with Mrs. Holbrook first, you know how she is 😑 Or Mrs. Nelson could have seen something that night on her way to, like, get it on in his office, or wherever they conducted their business. On the cafeteria tables? Against the copy machine in the teachers' lounge? Ew. I should have protected my psyche from that visual. But anyway . . . maybe she saw something that scared her.

". . . and the tracking information says they arrived." My eyes jump back to Dyvia, and I have no clue what she was talking about. It's clear from her lowered brow and wringing hands that it was something serious. I should ask her to repeat herself and really listen, but also . . . I need to get into that library before Mrs. Nelson goes home. This might be my only chance to see if she knows anything about Principal Smith's disappearance.

And this isn't just a hypothetical anymore. He has disappeared, officially. There's a tip line. Reward money. Money I could really use . . .

"I'm so sorry, but can we talk about this tomorrow? I have to—" Interview a person of interest? Conduct a missing person investigation even though I'm an unqualified, mid-level non-profit worker? "Talk to Mrs. Nelson. About a book Pearl wants to, um, check out."

I can tell she's unconvinced and more than a little bothered, but thankfully she's too nice to make it a thing.

"Yes, definitely. Just . . . email me back when you get a chance."

"Thank you, Dyvia. I will. I promise." My eyes are locked on Mrs. Nelson's door, and my body is already moving. "Tomorrow!" I add over my shoulder, for good measure, but I don't look to see if she's even still there.

My first knock on the library door goes unanswered, but I know someone is in there. There's a blind pulled down behind the window in the door, blocking whatever's happening inside from view, but when I press my ear against it, I can hear muffled music. I knock again. "Hello? Mrs. Nelson?" But there's still no answer.

I don't want to just walk away, though, not when the answers might be right there. Better to ask for forgiveness after, right?

When I open the door, I'm nearly knocked over by Adele. The music is so loud that I'm surprised I couldn't hear it all the way from the auditorium. What kind of magical librarian sound-proofing does Mrs. Nelson got going on here? And where is she?

I scan the room as the music makes my eardrums pulse, and quickly spot her in front of a bookshelf in the corner. She's pulling books from a cart and swaying along as Adele asks if she'll ever love again, and it's clear from her shaking shoulders that she feels every one of those words.

I shouldn't be here. This lady is clearly going through something. But I *am* already here, so . . .

"Mrs. Nelson?"

She lets out a wail along with the music, but it sounds more like gibberish than any one of Adele's lyrics.

"Mrs. Nelson?" I try, louder again this time. And it just happens to coincide with the fade-out of the song, so it's very loud. Too loud. So loud that Mrs. Nelson jumps and all the books that were in her arms crash down to the floor.

"Ahhh!" she screams.

"Ahhhhh!" I scream back, for some reason. But listen, what else are you supposed to do when someone screams at you?

"Ms. Miller, you—you scared me," she says, clutching her chest. She quickly strides over to the speakers sitting on her desk and cuts off Adele before she can sing another ballad. "Can I . . . help you with something?"

"I, well . . . there was this book Pearl was asking for." If I'm gonna keep lying, it's better to keep them consistent, but I can see that goes over about as well as it did with Dyvia.

"Pearl needs a book . . . right now?" she asks, her eyebrows raised. "It's after seven, Ms. Miller. The school is closed."

"Oh, I know, it's just—it was a special book. An important book." *Yes, very convincing, Mavis. Not suspicious at all.* "And I was already here for, you know, the meeting."

Her eyebrows drop down at that as her eyes narrow at me. She's going to send me on my way real soon if I don't get to it. But I need to be careful here. Subtle.

"Trisha!" I blurt out, very carefully and subtly. "She, uh, recommended the book to her. Trisha Holbrook."

I search her face for *something* at the mention of Trisha's name. Fear. Anger. But she just looks . . . confused. And slightly irritated.

"Okay, well, I guess I could look up what Anabella or Cayden have checked out," she says, walking behind her desk. "But I really have to go home soon, Ms. Miller."

She sighs heavily as she begins typing on her computer, and I walk closer, racking my brain for how I'm going to keep this ruse going. I should have come up with a plan before just barreling in here.

And that's when I see it. Sitting on Mrs. Nelson's desk in a thin brass frame. A picture of Mrs. Nelson in a white dress, with her dark hair pulled back into a chignon. And next to her, a familiar face.

"Nelson?"

She looks up from the computer screen. "Yes?" But then she follows my gaze to the picture on her desk. The picture of her and Nelson, Project Window's newest employee and number one on my nemeses list (if I ranked them like Pearl).

She frowns at me. "Do you know him?"

"Yeah, we . . . work together."

"At Project Window?"

I nod.

"Oh, I didn't realize . . . Yes, he just started. Well, you know that, I guess. He's really excited, has all these ideas about how to turn things around."

I have a lot of questions. Like why is he under the impression that things need to be turned around? And how did he apply for the job, anyway, if it was supposed to be an internal position? But the question at the very top of my mind is: *How the hell do you know Nelson?*

I look at the picture again, processing more of the details this time. Mrs. Nelson is in a white dress, and Nelson's in a suit. And between them is a towering white cake adorned with sugar pearls and buttercream roses.

"You . . . and Nelson . . . are married?"

She jolts upright, crossing her arms tightly around her body. Her eyes narrow as she looks me up and down. "Oh, that's why you're here, is it? Came to get some gossip firsthand, so you can pass it on to all the little bored women who have nothing better to do?" Each word drips poison as it falls out of her snarling lips. "Do you think you're the first one?"

"No, I—that's not what I—"

"We didn't plan for it to be this way!" she shouts, throwing her arms out. "Go back and tell them that. Tell them I'm not the goddamn villain Mary is making me out to be."

"No. No, no—"

"God, I could just—arghh!" She slams her hands onto her desk, sending papers fluttering. And just as quickly as it arrived, the rage dissipates, and now she's crying. Ugly, booger-y crying, as I stand here looking on awkwardly.

"Okay. Well, um . . ." I reach forward to pat her back, and she lets out a long, loud moan that seems to channel every feeling that Adele has ever sung about.

"We were going to be together! But not yet! We had a plan!"

"You really don't have to—"

"He wouldn't leave without me! Something happened to him, I know it. It's only been seven weeks, but . . . *we were twin flames*! One soul split into two bodies! Do you understand what that means? You can't just run away from that! We both had never felt something so intense before—emotionally and *physically*. I mean, when we connected, our *energy* chord—"

"Nope, stop. Please stop." I wave my arms around wildly like one of those inflatable tube guys outside of a car dealership, because I desperately don't want to hear the end of that sentence. "I just, I was asking—Nelson." I point to the picture. "I thought that was his first name."

"It is," she says, looking at me like she wasn't just ranting about twin flames and I'm the weird one here.

"So. His name is . . . Nelson . . . Nelson?"

"Yeah," she says, waving that away. "It's an old family name."

"Um. Okay."

So Nelson from work is married to Mrs. Nelson, who was sleeping with Principal Smith . . . but where does Trisha fit into this?

Mrs. Nelson shakes her head and keeps going before I can even think of a not-so-subtle way to ask that. "Yeah, yeah, go ahead and judge me, but you don't know what it was like. We met so long ago, back in high school, me and Nelson. We didn't know what we were getting into, not really. And we were different people, you know, still growing." Her eyes get misty as she looks past me. "And you either grow together, or grow apart. I knew we were growing apart, but it's like Nelson was too afraid to admit it . . ."

And actually, I know exactly what that's like. It didn't lead me to sleeping with my boss. (But also, my boss was Rose and I was too sleep-deprived anyway.)

"I had nothing to do with this, you know." Her tone sounds so familiar, and it takes me a beat to place it. Mrs. Smith, she sounds like Mrs. Smith just did a little while ago in the auditorium. She sounds just as sad, just as desperate. Her eyes even have the same pleading insistence. "I miss him. I love him. And I was home alone that night, not that you even deserve to know."

"Alone? But—so, where was Nelson?" The question falls from my lips before I can decide if it's a good idea.

"I don't know. He was out! Why do—do you—" I can see the exact moment she processes what I'm really asking. Her nostrils flare and her eyes pop out, like weapons being deployed. "Are you fucking kidding me?!"

And if her eyes *were* weapons, I would be dead on the ground right now. More than dead: dust. "Get out, Ms. Miller!" she screams, shooting her finger toward the door. "Right now!"

TWELVE

I FOLLOW MRS. NELSON'S DIRECTIONS, SPEED WALKING TO the door, and once I hit the hallway, I figure it can't hurt to upgrade to a light jog. I'm sweating and shaky, and it's fairly likely my heart's going to thump right on out of my chest, and those feelings only intensify when I slam right into another body.

"Ahhhh!" I scream.

"Ahhhhh!" the body screams back, because apparently that's protocol.

The body also has bright red hair and arms full of jangly beaded bracelets. Because the body is Corinne's.

"Why are you screaming?" I ask, pulse racing. "What's wrong?"

Is Trisha stalking the halls, bloodthirsty for another victim? It *is* after another parent meeting and Corinne hates her even more than Principal Smith does, so this fits right in with her MO. And maybe I've stumbled onto something much larger here, a goddamn serial—

"Lady, what else am I supposed to do when you come careening into me from around the corner, like a bat out of hell?"

Yeah, okay. Well, I guess that makes a little more sense.

"Mavis?" Corinne's eyebrows draw together in concern as she searches my face. "What's going on? Are you okay?"

"Oh, yeah. I'm fine!" I say, trying to fix my face into a totally chill, completely normal smile, but she frowns back at me, unconvinced. It might have something to do with the fact that I'm breathing (and sweating) like I just ran a marathon.

"Absolutely fine. Nothing wrong at all," I add, but that doesn't seem to do the trick either.

"Mavis . . ." she murmurs. Her eyes flick behind me, searching for the answer there. "Now, we both know you do not look fine. What's wrong? You can tell me, you know . . ."

Sure, I'll just go ahead and tell her that not only have I decided to investigate Principal Smith's disappearance but the PTA president is my prime suspect, and oh yeah, I just got kicked out by the librarian for maybe alluding to the fact that her husband, who just so happens to be the man that stole my promotion, could've had something to do with it, too. I'm sure that'll go over real well with this brand-new friend who doesn't know me well enough yet to give my sanity the benefit of the doubt.

"I was going to the restroom, after the meeting, and I—I . . . thought I heard a noise. I got scared." Better to think I'm a little jumpy than insane. Also, better to change the subject. "What are you doing here?"

Her gaze drifts behind me again, for just a moment, and then she's groaning, her face an exaggerated mask of exasperation. "PTA business. You know how it is."

"Oh no, what does Trisha have you doing now?" I hope she doesn't pick up on how my voice quakes, saying that name.

"I got put in charge of the Great ShakeOut. You know, that California-wide earthquake drill that's happening next month?"

I don't know, but I nod anyway.

"Trisha wants these huge signs painted on butcher paper to hang up everywhere, and she also has all these rules about the snacks allowed in the sample emergency preparedness kits the teachers will be showing the kids. Organic, gluten-free, no added sugar, and on and on and on. So we can 'lead by example,' or something silly like that." She does a pitch-perfect Trisha impersonation and then rolls her eyes. "I don't remember the earthquake kits being so fancy when I was in elementary school. Pretty sure I just had a Chewy bar and some jelly beans thrown in there."

"They had earthquakes where you grew up, too? I thought that was just a California thing."

She wrinkles her nose and cocks her head to the side. "I *did* grow up in California."

"Oh, right. Okay."

She smiles brightly, her bunny-ear teeth on full display. "Yes, SoCal, born and raised! And if the big one comes, let me tell you, we are not going to be worried about artificial dyes. No, uh-uh, we're gonna be too distracted by the freakin' canyon deeper than Trisha's forehead wrinkles that opens up on the 110 freeway—"

I laugh, my nerves finally starting to settle, but they spike right back up when I spot movement behind Corinne. It's Jack—eyes wide in questioning, and then worry. Because we were supposed to meet before I went off book and decided to question Mrs. Nelson all on my own.

Corinne can't see me with Jack. She already thinks there's something happening there, and this'll just confirm all that and bring on even more eyebrow waggles and suggestive smirks. Plus, I don't *think* Corinne is one of those moms scavenging for scraps of gossip to post on the Facebook group. Her name only popped up a few times on there when I was scrolling. But regardless, I need to be careful here if Jack and I are going to stay under the radar like we want to.

I shake my head, just barely, and then link my arm in Corinne's, pulling her the opposite direction.

"She's got you working too hard."

"You're telling me. You make one little dent in her precious Tesla."

"I thought you said it was just a tap . . ."

She shrugs. "Eh, tomato, to-mah-to!"

Later, when I'm lying in bed, Pearl fast asleep and Dad chain saw snoring on the couch, Jack sends the text I realize I have been waiting up for.

Can I call you?

I don't wait. I call him.

He's already chuckling, soft and low, when he answers. "I know some people don't like talking on the phone."

Me. I am some people. But I don't know . . . maybe this won't be so bad.

"Well, it *would* be a lot to type," I say. "Plus, is it just me, or does the screen get smaller and harder to read the later it gets? Am I going to have to finally crack and get some of those old people glasses at CVS soon?"

He laughs again, and it feels like a prize won. "Old people glasses, huh? Well, what if I tell you I'm wearing some right now?"

"Oh lord, oh no. Are they red? Why are so many of them that, like, bright lipstick, clown red? Like that talk show host from when we were kids."

"No, they're not red. They're green, um . . . How would I

describe this green? Maybe a forest? Fern? I think they bring out my eyes."

I can picture him in those green glasses that bring out his eyes. I can imagine how endearing it must look when they start to slip down his nose and he has to push them up in the middle. There's a rustling of . . . something on his end, and it sets my mind off even more. Is he lying in bed like I am? Maybe in a well-loved white T-shirt, with rumpled hair. The secret side of him, Mr. Cohen off duty, that most probably don't get to see . . . but I want to.

I clear my throat and say a little prayer that I wasn't doing something completely cringey like heavy breathing. "So . . . this is . . ."

"Real?" he finishes.

I sigh. "Yeah, it is."

"Twenty thousand is . . ."

"A lot of fucking money."

I sigh again, and this time he joins in, right in sync.

After a beat, he continues. "I guess I did think there was *something* there, but . . . there was a distance, you know? Like when it rains here, and all the streets flood and the roads are a mess anyway because no one knows how to drive in the rain." I turn on my side, cradling the phone closer to my ear. It's almost like his voice, every single sound wave, is a physical thing, and I'm greedy to keep them for myself. "But when you're at home, maybe because it's the weekend or you don't have work, you can forget all that. Read a good book and be, I don't know . . . cozy? I feel like, until tonight, we've been inside, and now we have to walk out into the storm and reckon with the fallen trees, car crashes on the freeway. You know, like . . . what's *really* happened."

"That's a—a pretty poetic way of saying shit just got real."

He laughs. "I mean, I *was* a creative writing minor in college."

I wish I could bottle his voice up. Or record it for one of those sleep stories on the meditation app I always forget is on my phone. I would use it every night if I could listen to him . . . but I can't tell him that.

"Yeah, that doesn't surprise me. Now, on the other end of the spectrum, I was forced to take a creative writing class in high school because all the other electives were full, and the guidance counselor didn't want to listen to my objections and insisted it would be a good outlet. But *then* I broke out into hives during the first workshop, reading this stupid poem I wrote—and I'm talking *hives* hives. They were everywhere—my eyelids, my armpits, the bottoms of my feet! They let me drop creative writing after that."

"Armpit hives! No!" I can feel the smile in his voice. "That sounds like a trauma response. What did poetry *do* to you?"

"I don't know, but it won. Poetry, one; Mavis, zero. And there will not be a rematch!"

I try to keep my laughter quiet so I don't wake up Pearl and Dad. But pretty soon we're cackling together, the kind that goes on so long you can't even remember why it started. It feels like a release after this long day and especially intense evening. And when it finally settles down, my cheeks aching and my eyes wet, the silence is even nicer. It's comfortable.

I hear him exhale and again imagine where he is, what he looks like. In the darkness of my room, it's even possible to trick myself that he's right here.

"Okay," he finally whispers. "So, what happened after the meeting? You were with Corinne?"

"Well, I may have gone rogue. Just a little bit." I press my thumb and pointer finger together even though he can't see me.

"And how does one go *just a little bit* rogue?"

I fill him in on my detour to the library, and how much Mrs. Nelson misses her twin flame and swore she had nothing to do with it. And how I sorta believe her, even though she doesn't have an alibi. And oh yeah, how her husband, who I *know* and *hate* (though I leave out the hate part because I'm not trying to reveal the depths of my pettiness to this man) doesn't have an alibi either.

"I still think Trisha did this. I think her little *oh, by the way* about the gifted school she just slid on in there tonight made that pretty clear," I conclude. "I don't know *how* she did it. Like . . . at all. So, we still need to keep digging there. But maybe it's worth it to look into what Nelson was doing that night, too? Just to rule that out. I can talk to him at work tomorrow—"

"Are you sure that's safe, though? I mean, what do you even know about this guy anyway? Do you think he could be dangerous?"

"Nelson is not going to do anything to me," I scoff. *Except take my job.* "And our office is so small, I could tell you with frightening accuracy how many times the lady across the hall farts per day. Surely someone will step in if Nelson starts confessing or, like, goes for my throat."

He laughs, but then his voice takes on a surprisingly serious tone. "All right, I just want to make sure you're safe."

My stomach wobbles at that, and my whole body feels warm and heavy, like I just threw on a weighted blanket right out of the dryer.

"Well, thank you, uh . . ." I start to mumble, but it's cut off by a jarring noise on his end.

"JACK, YOU NEED TO COME RIGHT NOW! IT'S STARTING SOON!"

The voice is so loud that it's almost like the person is yelling directly into the receiver. Who is that?

"Okay, man, just give me a second," Jack says, his voice muffled. "Sorry, Mavis, I—"

"YOU KNOW THE RERUN COMES ON AT EXACTLY TEN P.M. PACIFIC, TWELVE A.M. CENTRAL TIME! IT'S THE SAME EVERY DAY."

"I know, Derek, and I'm excited to watch it, too, but I want to finish this phone call first. Can I have five minutes to finish?"

"Yes! Five minutes!"

I can hear stomping footsteps through the phone and some rustling. "Sorry, Mavis. That was my brother, Derek, and as you can see, we take game shows very seriously in this household."

"Oh, your brother. Lilliam mentioned him last week? And some program?"

"Yeah, she was asking about this new program we've been trying to get him into forever. My brother has Down syndrome, so after he aged out of the school district at twenty-two, me and him started looking for a day program for adults with disabilities that he would like. To, you know, work on social skills and life skills and keep making friends. But the good programs, they can be hard to get into, and Derek is picky, too—which he should be! Plus, he lives with me because . . . because, well, that's just what worked better. So it had to be close or provide transportation, because I've gotta get him there before work."

Okay, so that answers some of the questions lingering in my head since last week. Well, except for . . . "You made a face when she was talking to you. Lilliam, I mean. Something about how it's a lot for one person to manage . . ."

"I did? Usually I'm better at keeping that under control." I can almost see his expression, how he's probably biting his lip, his thinking face. "It's just . . . I really hate when people say that. Because we're not one person managing, we're two. And it's hard for both of us some days, a lot of days, especially when we have to fight to get him what we know is best for him. But it's also not hard a lot of the time, too—it's great."

I want to ask him more: where they live and how long it's been this way, what they do together on the weekends. I feel like I've turned to the next page of Jack, and I want to read, to memorize, every single word. But we're out of time tonight.

"JACK! IT'S BEEN FIVE MINUTES!"

Jack laughs. "I'm sorry, but you heard him. He doesn't get to watch *The Price Is Right* live anymore because of his new schedule, but they show it again on cable at ten every night. We watch *The Price Is Right* kind of like how other people go to church? Or CrossFit? Missing it is not an option."

"*The Price Is Right*? Who hosts that again? . . . Wayne Brady? Pat Sajak?"

"Um, excuse me?" he asks, voice dripping with mock outrage. "How can you just erase the long and truly remarkable legacy of Bob Barker like that? Or Drew Carey, who is a game show legend in his own right?"

"So . . . not Wayne Brady then?"

"No, definitely not," he declares, and then he sighs, and I can feel a shift. "But, Mavis . . . just be careful, okay? If you're going to talk to Nelson?"

And there's that warm, heavy feeling again—like I'm cared for, looked after. I haven't felt that way in so long, but it would be nice to have someone to lean on again. To drop the ball and know someone is there to catch it. Or to interview a possible suspect and know someone is there to report the details to the police if I get offed, too.

"I will. I promise."

"Thank you. Good night, Mavis."

"Good night, Jack."

BUT, IT TURNS OUT, THERE REALLY ISN'T MUCH TO BE WOR-
ried about when it comes to Nelson.

"Is it cool if I sit here?" I ask, gesturing to the table with the
peeling wooden veneer where Nelson sits in the combination
break room / copy room / storage closet. My head is spinning
already, as I try to think of a game plan. Because how, exactly,
am I going to find out where he was last Tuesday night when I've
been avoiding him since he started at Project Window? Maybe
I should have thought this through more last night, instead of
dreaming about Jack in his green glasses.

"So you can ask me about my alibi on the night that fucking
snake went missing?" he asks, arching a bushy eyebrow.

Well, that makes it easy.

I slide into the plastic chair across from him.

"Uh . . . Mrs. Nelson told you then?"

"Yes, Mavis. Of course Rebecca told me." He pulls one of his
legs up over his knee, flashing a pale, sockless ankle. "Our marriage is . . . over, as I am sure you are aware. But no matter how
much she's lost her mind, thinking she has a twin soul, I hope
my wife of the past fifteen years would tell me if I was under
suspicion for murder."

The word *murder* hits me like a blast of cold air.

"I didn't say that. Murder, I mean. He could have just, you
know . . . gone away for a bit." Despite the call that Mrs. Smith
put out last night, I don't think I want people knowing that's
what I'm looking into. I've barely even admitted it to myself.
Has everyone else already jumped to that conclusion already,
too? I doubt it . . . It's still so early. And if that means Jack

and I figure things out first and get the reward money, well, so be it.

Except, I must not sound very convincing, because Nelson drops his head down, looking at me like, *really?*

"He had this shiny new job with all the prestige and attention he so clearly needs, plus his wife *and mine?*" He snorts and wags his head. "He didn't run away from that. No way! It's much more likely that someone he messed with finally caught up with him."

My pulse starts to speed up, and I feel sweat begin to gather at the base of my scalp, all signs from my brain telling my body to get the hell out of here. Someone Principal Smith messed with. Someone like . . .

"Not me!" Nelson shouts, falling back in his chair. "God, I know you don't like me, Mavis, but do you honestly think—"

"I never said I didn't like you."

He gives me another one of those *really?* looks, and I laugh awkwardly, studying the pattern on the table.

"And that's okay," he continues. "I know that you were probably shooting for this job, too. Hell, likely even deserved it—I've heard you're very good at what you do. But I promise I'm not here to go on some kind of power trip or act like I know best." The fake wood grain on the table is fascinating. I could stare at it for hours, days . . . the rest of my life. "And, hey, if it'll help things between us at all, I can tell you that I was at Boards and Brews—that bar with all the board games, over on Flower Street. My D&D group meets there every other Tuesday night. Ask Carl at the bar—he'll vouch for me. He's the one with the top hat and white handlebar mustache."

Okay, now, that makes me look up.

"He's going for a Mr. Monopoly aesthetic," Nelson explains with a shrug, as if that's a totally normal aesthetic to go for.

"Anyway, Rebecca probably didn't know where I was because she didn't want to . . . or maybe I just stopped talking about it. She doesn't really approve of my nerdy habits, thinks I need to grow up already. And I guess . . . that's probably why we are where we are right now."

He sighs and turns his head, swiping at something under his eye. And I almost feel sorry for him. I mean, if he wasn't the guy who swooped in and took my promotion and made me question if I wasted seven years on a job that will never value or appreciate me. If he wasn't that guy, *then* I would almost feel sorry for him.

Could he be lying to me? Could he have done something to Principal Smith? If he did, then he has me fooled. Because I can't see him hurting anyone, outside of, like, an orc in a tabletop role-playing game. Still, I shouldn't just take his word— Nelson, Mrs. Smith, Rebecca Nelson . . . I can't completely rule them out, no matter how obvious the *real* suspect here seems to be.

"Thank you, Nelson," I say, awkwardly reaching forward to pat his wrist. But it's giving more anxious toddler at the petting zoo than *there, there.* "And I . . . didn't think you did anything. Not really—"

"Yes, you did." He cuts me off, smiling gently. "But that's okay. I heard there's some big reward money now."

"There is." And I want it. I want the security that money could bring, and the freedom it could give me to start searching for something else, something better. So I don't have to sit in a cluttered break room / copy room / storage closet, eating a sad salad with a new boss who admits I probably deserve his job, though there's nothing he can really do about it, because that's just the way things worked out.

"Okay, but there's one thing I need to ask," I say, cracking open the plastic on my only slightly wilted Caesar, because there's nothing else I can do about my situation right now. "Why didn't you tell me your name is Nelson Nelson?"

He lets out another snort of a laugh. "I'm pretty sure I did when we met. And that's definitely how Rose introduced me. I told her to. I always try to get it out of the way, so people can make their jokes."

I think back to last week. Did he? No, I'm sure I would have remembered that. It's not like you meet many Nelson Nelsons in your life.

"What jokes?" I ask. Maybe I can tell them to everyone in the office, get a little bullying action going on here, so he's forced to resign. Just kidding, of course.

He shakes his head. "Wouldn't you like to know?"

Knoll Elementary Parents Facebook Group

Charlie Lee
Are we really going forward with Back to School Night this Thursday? I'm worried it may be insensitive with everything happening with Principal Smith . . .

Florence Michaelson
I would like to make it known that I am really uncomfortable with the increased police presence on campus. My Axel came home and told me, "Mama, I wish I knew how it would feel to be free!" I'm so worried about his sensitive soul.

Jasmine Hammonds
Girl, that's a Nina Simone song. Mr. Forest probably just had it on deck in music class this week.

Florence Michaelson
That still doesn't explain the troubling police presence . . .

Felicia Barlow
As far as I know there hasn't been any police presence?? Are you talking about my manny? He's been going to auditions after drop-off and sometimes he likes to get into character and wear costumes. I think it was a Netflix cop show this week . . .

Ruth Gentry
Ooooh Felicia, how fun!

Trisha Holbrook
Back To School Night is a very important event for our school and the teachers have been hard at work preparing for you to visit the

classrooms and get to know them! I'm sure Mr. Smith would want us to keep up our time-honored Knoll Elementary traditions to create a sense of consistency and comfort despite his current absence. And don't forget: we still need donations for the bake sale that night!

Leslie Banner

Oh, I can definitely bring some of my famous chocolate chip cookies!! What is the money being used for? Just curious! Maybe we could give some of it to Mrs. Smith to help contribute to her fund?

Trisha Holbrook

That is a great idea, but I've already promised the funds to the PTA's new DEI committee!! I think we can all agree that's a very worthy cause! @Mavis Miller

THIRTEEN

"SO I HEARD YOU ABOUT TO COME INTO SOME MONEY!"
Jasmine exclaims with a sly smile. She and Langston are the first
people I see when Pearl and I walk out of Mrs. Tennison's Back
to School Night presentation. And normally that would be a
comfort, seeing their faces in a sea of unfamiliar ones. But instead my heart stops. How does she know? I've tried to keep it
under wraps that Jack and I are working toward solving this.
Because the money *does* make it all a little more legit, but not
enough that I want to go broadcasting my intentions around
town.

"Um, what?" I ask, trying to delay the inevitable roasting just
a moment longer.

"Lord, tell me Miss Trish at least informed you about this
bake sale fundraiser before just broadcasting it on Facebook! I
thought she tagged you."

Oh, okay. So, false alarm. My spot isn't completely blown, at
least not yet. Dyvia texted me before I even saw the notification,
about the bake sale that's apparently raising money for the DEI
committee. She was hyped, which confused me because, well . . .

it was a bake sale. But apparently they're big business at Knoll and can bring in hundreds. Dyvia talked about getting assigned the bake sale like it was some high honor bestowed upon us by royalty, which I guess in Trisha's PTA kingdom it is.

But still, I jerk my head to the side, directing Jasmine a safe distance away from the door, while Langston and Pearl giggle and play some hand game, already bored with their grown-ups. Because Miss Trish is in that room behind me, interrogating poor Mrs. Tennison about her grading policy, or maybe one of the read-aloud books—she asked so many "minor clarifying questions" during the ten-slide PowerPoint that I lost track. I definitely don't want Trisha to hear me talking about her. I know—or at least, I'm pretty sure I know—what she does to people who do anything but step in line behind her.

"She did tag me, but that was the first I heard of it. Seems like she didn't want the money to go to Mrs. Smith . . ." I roll my eyes so I can have plausible deniability, but I do want to know if Jasmine noticed that waving red flag like I did.

Jasmine just laughs and rolls her eyes back, though. "That lady doesn't want anything stealing her spotlight, even a missing principal. But are we surprised? Mmm-mmm, no we're not."

I laugh along with her, as if that's all I meant by it, too.

"So, what you got planned for all the big bake sale money? DEI about to do its thing?"

I throw my head back and groan. "I have no idea. I haven't done much of anything yet, and I feel so bad. Dyvia—she's the mom that's really stepped up—she has all these ideas, and I've just been too busy to really sit down and make a plan of action—"

Jasmine is already assuring me before I can properly explain why I'm the worst. "And that's okay, Mavis! You've got a lot going on, and they can't expect you to save their asses and fix all their problems in a matter of weeks! You gotta be realistic with yourself."

"I know. But I should have done *something* at this point. I've really been dropping the ball . . ."

"Is it the job search? 'Cause that's a damn good reason. Get yourself settled first in a job you *want* and *deserve*, and then you can worry about doing everything for everyone else, okay?"

Except, it's not the job search. The only time I even pulled up LinkedIn was to search for Paul McGee. I haven't stopped to think of what I would be qualified for, let alone what I might want. And I've been putting in the minimum with Project Window, too, since they passed me over. But I find myself smiling and nodding, feeling guilty . . . but not guilty enough to be real. Thankfully, we're interrupted before I have to lie any further.

"Pearl!" It's the only word except for *Mommy* that cuts through everything and makes my whole body go on high alert.

"Hi, Pearl!" A little girl with two strawberry blond pigtails and a face full of freckles smiles at Pearl, waving excitedly. But when my eyes find my child, I realize, with horror, that her arms are crossed and she's giving this little girl the stank face. Like, a totally annihilating, world-ending stank face . . . that she may or may not have inherited from me.

"Pearl!" I say, rushing to her side. "Wave back at your friend!"

But she doesn't wave back, she doesn't even move, until eventually the girl skips off, seemingly unaffected.

I get down on Pearl's level. "Now, I know you know better than that. Why didn't you wave back at that girl? She was being nice."

Her stank face falls because she's not about to direct that at me, but its impact lingers. "She was showing her teeth at me."

"Um, do you mean *smiling*?"

Pearl shrugs but doesn't say anything more. Jasmine leans down toward her ear and whispers conspiratorially, "I get it. That smile had bad vibes."

I whack her shoulder. "Jasmine!"

"I agree." Langston jumps in, very unhelpfully.

Jasmine pats his head approvingly. "That's Angela Hart's daughter, right? Sojourner?"

My eyebrows nearly reach my hairline at that. "Wait, her daughter is named *Sojourner*?" I whisper to Jasmine. "I didn't— *how* didn't I . . . Are you even allowed to name a white girl Sojourner?"

"Maybe they give you permission when you buy a Black Lives Matter lawn sign," Jasmine says between her teeth, a hissing laugh escaping in the process, and I know I need to get this conversation back on track.

"Okay, but, Pearl," I say, giving her my most serious look. "You need to acknowledge people. That might have hurt Sojourner's—"

"I think they call her SoSo," Jasmine cuts in.

"That might have hurt *SoSo's*"—I feel my composure flicker, but I quickly fix my face—"feelings."

Pearl frowns and then opens her mouth, as if she's about to say something, but then her lips clamp shut when someone walks up behind me. And then my lips do the same, and there's also something fluttery and wobbly going on in my stomach when I see who it is. Jack. But not just regular Jack. Jack in a tie, which immediately zips up to the top of the rankings of my favorite Jacks.

"Hey, Langston, hi, Pearl." He smiles at them and then turns his attention to Jasmine and me, nodding. "Ms. Miller, Dr. Hammonds." He should wear that tie all the time. Except, no, he should not, because then my stomach would be doing backflips and somersaults like this all the time, too. It's too powerful.

"Hi, Mr. Cohen!" Langston shouts. "You look fancy."

"Yes, I like the tie." I hope my voice doesn't give away the full gymnastics routine going on in my belly, but it's clear from the eyes Jasmine is making at me that I'm not being slick at all.

"I had to watch a YouTube video to get this thing on, and even then, Derek had to offer his assistance," Jack says, straightening the tie in the most endearing way, and now there's a whole-ass crowd *watching* the gymnastics routine and going wild in my chest, my heartbeat thundering like applause.

Oh lord, I cannot be like this *in front of my child*. I'm a grown woman, not a lovestruck teenager. *Get it together, Mavis!*

Luckily, Pearl tugs on my sleeve. "Mommy, can I go play with Anabella?" she asks, pointing at the playground, where Anabella is waving excitedly from the top of the jungle gym, in a crowd of other kids.

"Mm-hmm, go ahead!" I say, and she runs off, not looking back.

"And we'll leave you to it!" Jasmine says with a smug smile, her eyes still dancing between us. She tugs Langston with her, and when she gets behind Jack, she holds her hand up like a phone and mouths, *Call me*. And then she throws a little shimmy in for good measure.

"Sorry, should I not have—" Jack starts.

"No. No, it's okay. She's cool." I look over his shoulder, where Jasmine is still shimmying and waggling her eyebrows as she walks backward. "Usually."

"I just wanted to tell you some things. About, well, you know—"

"Oh, did you find out something else?"

"Yeah, it's about Paul—" There's another flash of movement

behind him, but this time it's not Jasmine being all conspicuous. It's Ruth in a Knoll Elementary PTA shirt, rolling a little glass vial of essential oils on her wrist. And there's no mistaking it, her narrowed eyes are locked on us, ready to report everything back to the Facebook group. I reach forward and touch his arm, which—*shit* . . . probably isn't the best thing to do, either, with her watching.

"Ruth Gentry at six o'clock," I whisper.

His head starts twisting around, which also really isn't helping with the totally chill and not at all suspicious vibe. "Six o'clock? Where is six o'clock?"

"Actually . . . I'm not even sure why I said that, because I don't know where six o'clock is either. But it sounded like the right thing to say—just—behind you. Ruth Gentry is behind you, and she's watching us."

"Well, Ms. Miller, I can definitely show you those forms, but they're in my office."

I wrinkle my nose at his change in tone. "What—uh, huh?"

"I apologize for not sending them home with Pearl last week, but I can be quick! This will only take a minute," he says, his voice jumping even louder. Ruth doesn't even have to strain to hear him now, and—*ooooooh*. That's the point. Okay. I can do this.

"I guess I can go with you. If it's quick! But I really wish you weren't so forgetful, Mr. Cohen!" He raises an eyebrow at me and I flick my hands up at my sides like, *I don't know.* "But what about Pearl?" That's a real question. She's not gonna want to leave Anabella after I just gave her the go-ahead—there's a whole multistep process involving timers and legally binding pinkie swears when it comes to leaving a playground.

"She'll be fine," Jack says, using his normal voice now. "The school hired playground helpers for the night." He points at some teenagers with matching polos and whistles on the edges of the yard. "They'll watch her."

I catch Pearl's eye and wave at her, gesturing that I'll be right back. She waves distractedly and then takes off after Anabella toward the slide.

"Well, let's go get those, uh, forms!" I declare, leading the way. My eyes flick to Ruth, and she's talking to one of the other PTA moms, but I know she's still listening. I hope we have her fooled.

The giggles bubble up out of my chest as soon as he shuts his office door. "Did that help our case, or did it just sound like the beginning of a bad porn?" My hands shoot to my mouth, realizing what I've said before my brain has even processed it, and Jack's cheeks are already turning an alarming shade of red.

"I—I don't know why I said that."

Jack lets out a garbled noise that may be a word, but not in any language I know.

"In fact, let's, uh . . . pretend I *didn't* say that."

He starts coughing, his whole face flaming now, and he puts up a finger before picking up a water bottle from his desk and taking several large gulps. He seems like he's going to be drinking forever—and you know what, I would be just fine with that—when finally, he chokes out, "Yes, let's."

"So, what did you want to tell me?" I ask, as if I didn't just make things incredibly awkward—and also as if I don't have . . . related images currently playing in my head.

He takes another sip of his water and clears his throat. My stomach does the fluttery, wobbly thing again as he leans against his desk in his tie. "I emailed Paul McGee. Yesterday. And he just got back to me this morning."

"You did? What did you say?"

"I just told him I was a school employee, helping to catch up with Principal Smith's correspondence, which really doesn't make sense at all if you think about it too much—and ugh, I'm realizing as I'm saying this out loud, *definitely* wouldn't hold up if he decides to pass it on to Mrs. Smith. But he didn't really ask too many questions, so hopefully we're in the clear there."

"So . . . what did he tell you then?"

"Oh yeah, of course," he says with a startle, running his hands through his hair. "He said he hadn't heard from Thomas in about a month. And okay, I *also* looked into Mrs. Smith's alibi yesterday evening—"

"You *what*?" My jaw drops in surprise.

He holds his hands up. "Well, don't get too impressed here. I recognized the street she lives on because of a student I used to do home visits with last school year—it was just a couple houses down. And I knew it was a long shot, but there was this sweet old lady who lived across the street. One of those curious types, you know—always pulling back the curtains when I drove up, or out watering her garden."

Sounds like a Ms. Joyce type—and Ms. Joyce *would* know everyone's business on our street, especially if something juicy like one of us going missing happened.

"So I decided to walk down the block with Derek, just a casual evening stroll, you know. And sure enough, as soon as Derek and I doubled back, the lady was out there watering her hydrangeas. Derek got things going—he's a real charmer when he wants to be, and when I casually dropped that my boss lived on this street, she started talking. Dot was happy to tell me what Mrs. Smith was up to that whole week, not just that night. And according to Dot, who I believe is an incredibly reliable source, Mrs. Smith was watching *Bachelor in Paradise*—a special three-hour episode—and then fell asleep on the couch in front of her bay window, in clear sight of the *whole* neighborhood.

Dot is not a fan of reality TV, by the way, thinks it rots your brain."

My stomach is doing something weird again, but it's not because of how good he looks—though that's still very much true. No, this time it's because he's been doing detective work here. *Real* detective work. And I've just been—what? Interrupting Mrs. Nelson's Adele sobbing sessions? Eating salad with Nelson Nelson?

"Wow. You—wow. *Wow.*"

Jack smiles, seemingly charmed by the fact that my vocabulary has shrunk to two words. "I know we still don't have anything concrete here, but . . . it made me feel better to follow those loose ends and tie them up. I think Trisha has something to do with this, too, don't get me wrong, but I want us to be sure. Especially before we tell Mrs. Smith any—wait, what's wrong?"

I thought I was hiding whatever this feeling is—disappointment, maybe jealousy?—but apparently not well enough. Or maybe Jack can just read me better than most, after less than two weeks.

"You've just done so much," I say, immediately feeling stupid and immature. *God, this isn't a competition, Mavis. A man is missing, and we're trying to help.*

But before my self-loathing can completely take over, Jack reaches forward and brushes his finger against my wrist. It's barely a touch, I could convince myself I just made the whole thing up . . . except for the fact that it has my whole body buzzing with an energy so intense that I may just start running up and down the halls, hands in the air, like the ladies at church.

"Mavis, I wouldn't be anywhere without you." Yep, full-on praise dancing. "If you hadn't been so perceptive and—and *brave* to tell me what you thought was happening . . . well, Derek and I wouldn't have been going all George and Bess."

"George and Bess?"

"Um, Nancy Drew's sidekicks, obviously," he says with a playful smile. "Because you're the boss here. I'm just trying to keep up."

"Thank you."

"And hey, let's look into Nelson's alibi together. Boards and Brews, you said, right?" He clears his throat again, and his gaze shifts to something very interesting on his desk. "Maybe we could even . . . uh, get dinner there? If that's a thing they do."

Dinner. Dinner . . . as in a date? It sure sounds like a date. I *hope* it's a date. There's no way in hell I'm about to ask, though, because I can't handle the kick in the teeth it'll be if he looks at me all confused, and then pitying, to tell me it's not.

So instead I just smile—innocently, unpresumptuously—and say, "I'd like that."

But okay, maybe it would be good to know how exactly he feels about me, right this second, instead of putting it off any longer. Whether it's the same way I'm feeling, or if I'm tragically off the mark . . . just so I can prepare my heart either way.

"Is this a—"

My phone starts buzzing in my pocket, and when I pull it out, I see Corey's name and smiling face. The moment, if there even was a moment, is gone—deceased. And all the church ladies have stopped dancing to throw themselves over the casket.

"Sorry, it's my ex," I say, ready to put it on silent. Why is Corey FaceTiming me now? We have our schedule for a reason, even though he's been trying to expand it lately with these phone calls. Maybe we need to have another talk about boundaries— except . . . shit. He's calling because it's the time we scheduled. We, as in both of us . . . together. But I must have gotten the time zones confused or forgotten to tell him about Back to

School Night. So, even though this is not convenient at all, we don't skip these. I press accept.

"Hi, Corey," I say, trying to keep the screen tight on my face. "Listen, I'm not with Pearl right now, but I'll go find her and call you right back."

"Not with Pearl?" His nose wrinkles. "Was I supposed to call your dad?"

"No, you were supposed to call me. We're at Knoll for Back to School Night and she's on the playground—"

"Well, then where are you?" His eyes bounce around, scanning the few clues available on the tiny screen.

"I'm just with someone from the school, but his office is close by. Don't worry, I'll—"

"His? I thought her teacher was *Mrs.* Tennison. Who are you meeting with on Back to School Night if it's not her teacher, Maves?"

Annoyance flares in my chest at his questioning, and I try to let it out with a long exhale. But I can still hear it in my tight, clipped response. "You don't need to worry *who* I'm meeting with, Corey, because I've got everything with Pearl's school handled. Now, I'll call you back."

I know it's petty and I'm going to feel guilty about it later, but I hang up even though I see his mouth open, about to say something else. I let out another breath and rub my hands over my face, resetting. I'm scared to look at Jack, but his face doesn't have any of the judgment I'm expecting.

"So, that was Pearl's dad." I sigh. "And I'm sorry, but I better go find her. They FaceTime every night, and it's important."

"You don't have to say sorry, Mavis," he says gently, holding the door open for me. "It's cool. I'll walk with you."

It's silent as we make our way down the hallway, and that

lightness, that hopefulness I felt just moments ago quickly shifts to dread. If that wasn't the perfect demonstration of what Jack would *really* be getting into. Because dinner with me wouldn't just be dinner—it would involve organizing childcare and Face-Time calls, a curfew, and, *oh god*, me telling my dad. None of this with Jack will be as easy as I want it to be.

As I scan the playground, looking for Pearl among all the kids running and hollering in the dusky evening light, I try to think of the right way to let him off the hook. This doesn't have to be weird. We're just friends investigating a disappearance together . . . the least weird thing ever.

"I don't see Pearl." I turn to him, and he squints, surveying the crowd. "Do you?"

I keep searching, waiting for the familiar tug of her two puffs or her sunflower-printed dress on my attention. But . . . no. I don't see her. Pearl isn't here, I realize as my heartbeat starts to speed up. Where's my baby?

"There's Anabella." Jack points to the little girl with the long, dark ponytail and purple overalls. I don't say anything. I run to her side.

"Anabella?" She's waiting in line for the monkey bars, but I kneel down in front of her, forcing her attention. "Anabella, where's Pearl?"

"She's with my mom."

It's possible she says something more, but those words rise in my head like a massive wave, drowning out everything else.

"Pearl?" I'm moving before I've even decided to, my voice frantic and frail. "Pearl? Where are you, Pearl?"

"What happened? What did she say?" Jack is somewhere behind me, but I can't stop, can't talk to him. I need to find my daughter right now.

"Pearl! Pearl!" I know I'm making a scene. I know people are staring. Let them, though. That woman has my baby. And if she's capable of what I think she is—what I *know* she is, in my bones—what will she do with her? Is she just trying to make a point, or is she willing to take a much bigger risk?

Sharp pains strike my chest like bolts of lightning, and the world spins as I run around the perimeter of the playground. And then when there's nothing there, from classroom to classroom. "Pearl!"

"Mommy, what's wrong?" The voice cuts through the chaos of my mind, and then I'm on my knees, hugging my baby, my precious baby girl, smelling the coconut scent of her curls and stroking the soft skin on her shoulders because she's here. Safe and here, right in front of me.

"Mommy, why are you so sweaty?" My laugh comes out in a long, gasping sob. I squeeze her tighter as I choke out, "I couldn't find you. I thought I lost you, baby girl."

"I had to go potty. Mrs. Holbrook took me to the bathroom 'cause I didn't want to go alone."

"Sorry, Mavis. If I knew you would be so upset, I would have texted you." The voice is like an ice cube slowly trailing down my spine. When I stand up to meet her, face-to-face, I expect a snarl, lips stretched over bared teeth—something ugly and dangerous to match what she is. But instead, Trisha is smiling at me.

"We're friends. We help each other. Right, Mavis?" She sounds perfectly pleasant, but I can hear the sharp edge of warning. "I will *always* be here to look out for Pearl, don't you worry."

FOURTEEN

I SCOOP PEARL UP INTO MY ARMS AND TAKE OFF TOWARD the front gate. Ignoring Jack's calls, ignoring the scene I'm probably making. Ignoring all the screaming, straining muscles in my neck and back that are going to require extra-strength ibuprofen later.

Because there's a low, insistent thud pulsating in my ears, punctuating each one of my steps, and I know it won't let up until I get us to safety. And absolutely nothing about Trisha is safe.

She kept it cute because there were witnesses there, but that was a clear warning. A threat. I'm running out of time to figure this out, to prove that she's guilty—without any doubt, so she can't smooth it over with her PTA powers and make me the crazy one.

And what will she do to me if I don't? To the school . . . to Pearl?

I can't let her get away with this. I can't let her win.

The drumbeat in my head gets even louder as I drive home, and it makes me feel nauseated. I've gotta get this feeling out. I've gotta release the anxiety thrumming in my blood somehow, or I'm going to throw up. Or explode. Or maybe do both at the same time—a whole-ass *Exorcist* display that will scar Pearl for life and also take forever to clean up. But luckily, when we walk through the door, my dad's hunched over the kitchen counter, his phone to his ear, chatting with the perfect candidate to absorb all these goddamn feelings. Already I can sense the familiar shift happening in my mind, anxiety transforming to rage, a fire catching, like so many arguments of our past.

"And she stayed on the message board the whole time! Can you believe that, Corey? At night she was writing their usernames on the walls in their blood, and during the day, she was talking all DH and DD and FTM and all those little mom online codes. They had a whole language—"

"Dad," I say sharply, cutting off his podcast recap. "I need to talk to Corey."

He looks me up and down, wrinkling his brow in concern, but he hands me his phone without any questions.

"Mommy, are you okay?" I realize I'm still holding her, pulled her right out of her booster seat in the back and carried her to the front door. And it's possible that's not the first time she asked. I was hoping the Kidz Bop blasting in the car would distract her from Mommy going into full fight-or-flight mode, but it's clear from the way she's biting her bottom lip that isn't the case. Of course it isn't.

"Yes, I'm fine, baby girl," I say, setting her down. I stroke her cheek with my thumb and give her my brightest smile, but her eyes are still narrowed in suspicion. "I need to talk to Daddy real quick before you do. Do you want to play on your Chromebook while you wait?"

That seems to do the trick and wipe the slate clean. Her eyes light up and she squeals as she runs into her room, Polly bounding after her to see what all the excitement is about.

My dad's not so easily distracted by a Chromebook. But I ignore his assessing stare and stomp into my room, closing the door behind me. And then I go into my closet and shut that door, too, just in case.

I swear I can feel steam shooting out of my ear when I finally put the phone up to it to speak. "You have a lot of nerve, Corey Harding, giving *me* the third degree like that, questioning *my* parenting!"

"What, I—"

"As if *I'm* not the one keeping everything together. As if *I'm* not the one showing up every day, *sacrificing*, so that Pearl can have the very best life possible!"

"I know, and I—"

"And who cares if I was talking to someone other than Mrs. Tennison? Who cares if I was talking to a man? Because that's none of your business! *You* don't get to pop in and be all *concerned parent* whenever you feel like it!"

"You're right."

"I don't deserve to have anyone interrogate—wait . . . what?"

I catch my breath, feeling like an untied balloon that just twisted through the air. Did I just hallucinate that?

But he says it again. "You're right."

"I'm . . . right?" The words feel strange on my tongue, like a foreign language.

"You're completely right, Mavis," he repeats, and I can hear the smile in his voice. "I'm sorry. I know I shouldn't have pushed like that. I know it's not my business if you're, uh . . . seeing someone." He clears his throat, rushing into his next words. "And I know you always keep Pearl safe, no matter what. You're an awesome mom—the best there is. And I'm sorry for being a dick."

My stomach churns with guilt because I did just *lose* Pearl.

Only momentarily, yes, but, uh . . . with a possible murderer. Or whatever. Otherwise, though, what he's saying is true. I *am* an awesome mom.

"You were being a dick." That's true, too.

"Fair." He laughs, high and hearty, and for just a moment, I'm transported back to other whispered phone calls in this very same closet, after my dad called lights out and listening to that laugh was so much more important than sleep. I shake that feeling away.

"Thank you, Corey. Now let me go get her for—"

"I wish I could be there, Maves," he says hurriedly, cutting me off. "I really do."

Lord, and I was feeling better, too! But now the anger is flaring right back up again. Because that's a choice he's made—*not* being here. He acts like it isn't one, but it is. He *chooses* to put work first. He *chooses* to be somewhere else, pursuing his passion. And I shouldn't even let myself get sucked into this same old argument tonight, but maybe it'll feel good. Maybe it'll be the distraction I need from the fear, the anxiety, of what the hell I'm going to do about Trisha.

"Well, you love your work." I spit out the familiar fighting words and then brace myself for what I know will come next.

"But I love Pearl more."

It feels like the air is sucked from my body. That . . . that's not following the script. Yes, he loves Pearl. I know that without a doubt; that's not the surprise. It's just . . . that line usually comes later, after endless excuses and justifications. Why is he going off book?

"And something's gotta change, so I can be there," he continues. "I don't think—no, *I know.* I can't do this anymore. That's why I've been trying to get you on the phone . . . to tell you that."

"W-what?" That's all I can manage to stammer out, because this is brand-new territory.

"The next contract is coming up, and I think I might turn it down and take a break. I can always do local shows when they come up, maybe find a house band that's hiring? And it won't pay the same, but I can pick up some studio work to pay the bills, too."

I can't believe what I'm hearing. Is this real life? Because I know how much he hates studio work, how he lives for the rush and energy of a live audience. I saw how restless he became during lockdown, how the spark left his eyes. It's what made me so certain, finally, that we needed different things. Different *lives*.

"I can put down some roots again. It's about time. It's *been* time." His voice is heavy with emotion, insistent. "I know you know that. You've *always* known that. And I think I'm finally catching up to you, Maves. I want to be there for Pearl—*really* be there." He pauses and I hear him hum, like he wants to say something else. Like he's starting and stopping. Finally, he lets it out. "I want to be there for you, too."

"Okay," I say. Because what else can you say when the person you used to love most in the world is saying everything you've ever wanted to hear? What do you say when you're finally hearing the words you've needed to heal your heart, the words you've hoped and prayed for, years too late?

"Okay?" he asks.

"Okay." That's all I've got for now.

"Well, okay." He sighs, but he knows me enough not to push. "I get that it might take some time, but I'm going to prove to you that I'm serious this time. I promise."

"I . . . hope so, Corey." I stand up from the floor of my closet, and the weight of everything nearly knocks me back down. I have to prove that Trisha did something to Principal Smith. I have to keep my baby girl safe. I have to get that reward money.

I have to find *a new job*! Do I really have time to process how I feel about my ex coming back into my life? I shake the Magic 8 Ball that's my jumbled brain. All signs point to hell no.

"I'm gonna get Pearl. And—don't tell her yet. Please? Not until it's one hundred percent happening."

"Oh, it's happening."

I feel a growl in the back of my throat, the last ember of the raging anger I felt toward him just minutes ago.

"But all right." I picture him holding his hands up in defense, and he should.

When I walk into Pearl's room, she shuts her computer screen. She's biting her bottom lip like before, and her eyes are stormy with worry. Oh god, could she hear me yelling all the way in here? That's why I went in the closet—I need to protect her from all this. But it looks like I'm failing once again.

I hug her, hoping that communicates all the apologies I can't say right now.

"Ready to talk to Daddy?" I ask, and she smiles. It looks like a real smile. Though I could sit here for hours, analyzing every secret it may hold.

It's better to give them space. I need it right now, too.

I switch my dad's phone to FaceTime and then go back to my room, ignoring my dad's curious glances on the way. My own phone lights up in my purse, and there's a text waiting there from Jack.

Are you okay?

It's the same question Pearl asked me earlier, but this time I'm honest.

I don't know

———

"WHAT'S YOUR DEAL WITH TRISHA ANYWAY?" CORINNE asks, and I almost swallow one of the lemon wedges floating in my glass of iced tea.

I'm sitting on a wooden stool at Corinne's kitchen counter, while Pearl, River, and Mason run around outside, basking in the magic of an impromptu playdate. Project Window had a half day today for a leadership summit—which I didn't have to attend, because it has been clearly decided that I'm *not a leader*—so I was able to make it to pickup. And when we walked past Corinne, she invited us over for some sweet tea and time in their big backyard—in front of Pearl, so there was no way I could turn it down. It didn't matter that she had never met the Ackerman boys and had no idea who this lady was: playdate invitations are sacred. And not that I *wanted* to turn it down either. It's just, normally Pearl and I have movie night on Fridays, which is a lot less work than dodging playdate mom small talk—and dodging out-of-the-blue questions about Trisha.

I cough, hold up my finger to let her know I need a second, and then cough some more.

"What do you mean?" I finally ask, casually, as if I didn't just almost need emergency services.

"Well, that, for one," Corinne says, gesturing at me with a playful smile. "And when she walked past us on the way here and said hi. You jumped five feet in the air and then grabbed Pearl like there was a train moving at her, full speed. Instead of . . . oh, I don't know, waving back?"

I can feel my cheeks heat up. God, was I really that obvious? But it's not like I can tell Corinne the *real* reason I'm so jumpy.

"I'm slacking a little bit with my PTA duties . . . You know, this DEI committee? I didn't want to deal with any questions about that today. Now that it's the weekend, I mean." Hopefully that was believable. "Hey, you have that pan! I keep getting Instagram ads for that pan. Is it any good?"

I point to her stovetop, which is cluttered with a kettle and a spoon still crusted with last night's red sauce—and a bubblegum-pink ceramic pan that I keep almost pulling my debit card out for when I'm scrolling and I see that cute video. Except, it's not the whole pan, I realize, just the lid.

When I turn back to Corinne, she winces. "It *was* good, before the boys did something to the rest of it—though of course, they deny it! I'll probably find it hidden a month from now." She laughs, shaking her head, and then she sticks up her pointer finger. "And actually, it's too quiet right now. That's never a good sign."

"Oh no, you're right!" I laugh and follow her to the sliding glass door that leads to her backyard. It's a little kid's paradise. There's a tree house, painted all black, with a rope swing hanging from the same sturdy oak tree. Next to it is a combo swing set and slide that Pearl squealed in delight when she saw. And there are piles of enough scooters, skateboards, and bikes that the Ackerman boys could probably outfit the whole neighborhood. But, suspiciously, there are no actual little kids in sight.

"Hmmm. Now where could they be?" I ask loudly, tapping my chin for effect. I know this game well. "What's their go-to hiding spot?"

But when I turn to Corinne, she doesn't look amused at all. In fact, she looks panicked—her brown eyes are saucers, and her jaw is tight. She stomps straight over to the wooden fence separating her backyard from her neighbors' on the right side and flips up one of the wide slats—just wide enough for a kid to fit through.

"Mason! River! You better get your behinds back over here

right this second!" Her voice is stern, but there's a frenzied edge that makes my pulse speed up. "Y'all, this is not funny! I mean it, right now!"

"Corinne, what's—" I start, but it's interrupted by the giggles of Mason, River, and Pearl as they come barreling through the opening, extremely pleased with their prank.

Corinne, though, still isn't smiling. "Boys, I told you not to go over there again, under any circumstances." She fixes them with her mom glare, the one we've all mastered to let our kids, specifically, know that we mean business and they better quit playing. Corinne's is so fierce it makes me start sweating and questioning whether I've also done something wrong.

Mason, at least, is not so affected. "But, Mom, there's no one there! And we didn't go inside the house."

"It doesn't matter. I told you—"

"Okay, fine. I'm sorry," Mason says quickly. "We won't do it again or whatever."

"Yeah, I'm sorry, too!" River pipes in, and then they both run off, a blur of red hair and freckles, just like their mom. Pearl looks at me for permission, clearly aware that an apology like that wouldn't fly in our house, and then she runs off toward the tree house, too, when I give her the nod.

Corinne lets out a long sigh and then holds up her glass. "Is it too early to switch to wine?" she asks. She throws her head back in an easy, self-deprecating laugh, but her eyes flick to the fence once more before she plops down in a patio chair. "Sorry for freaking out there for a second."

"You don't have to tell me sorry," I say, sitting next to her. "I think, uh, *don't break into the neighbor's backyard* is a reasonable boundary."

"You would assume, huh? But with Mason, I probably should have told him, 'Please go in the neighbor's abandoned backyard!

Have fun!' if I really wanted him to stay out. So, like, my bad."
She runs her free hand through her hair and groans. "No one's
lived there for a year, and it's been under construction for almost
as long. So, it's basically just a dirt pile full of nails and splintery
wood and who knows what else back there—and of course that
means *my kids* want to sneak back there every day."

"No! That long?" I groan, too, in commiseration. "God,
there's so much construction going on around here. It's constant!
I feel like I hear drills and hammering more than birds. And the
neighborhood is changing so much from what it used to be. The
people moving in are—"

I stop myself. I don't know how long Corinne has been here.
Maybe she's one of the new people, too. Maybe she and Mackenzie Skinner are besties.

But she finishes my sentence. "Really fucking annoying?" I
snort in surprise and delight, and she smiles proudly. "I swear,
these richie-rich, entitled tech people moving here from wherever they already jacked up the prices so bad even they can't
afford those houses anymore—" She wrinkles her nose and
shakes her head. "Uh-uh, can't stand them! We got that Whole
Foods over on Flower Street—that was the first sign that they
were coming! Once the Erewhon arrives, it's a lost cause."

"Oh no, do you think it's going to get Erewhon bad?"

"These people next door," she says, jerking a thumb in the
direction of the busted fence. "Like I said, they bought this place
a year ago and immediately started a total gut job. They were all
excited to tell me about the movie theater they were adding, and
the"—she switches to an unidentifiable accent that I think must
be rich-people speak—"*temperature-controlled wine room.* But a
couple months later, she files for divorce, construction stalls because he was funding the whole thing and now he's being petty.
And it's been sitting empty since then, no end in sight. What

kind of people can afford to just keep an empty house they're not living in? Especially a house they bought for the inflated prices these things are going for lately?" She purses her lips, fixing me with a knowing stare. "People who shop at Erewhon."

"Ugh, no! Make it stop!" I cross my arms in front of me like I can fend them off with my bare hands, and Corinne cackles.

"Mom, can I use the car?" The low voice so close makes me jump in my seat. I knew Corinne had a teenage son, she told me that at our first meeting, but it's another thing to have him standing right there. Brody looks nothing like Corinne. His eyes are bright blue, and his frame is more waifish than the sturdy stock that Corinne and her other boys seem to come from. His hair is dark instead of ginger, and it's styled in what I only know as a mullet, though I'm sure it's called something new and perplexing, like everything else about Gen Z that makes me feel nearly geriatric. He does have her signature freckles on his nose, though, which she reaches up to boop, clearly to his annoyance.

"Say hi to my friend Mavis," she instructs.

"Hi, Mavis," he mumbles, like it's physically painful to get out. Then he turns back to his mom. "Now can I use the car?"

"Where are you going?"

"To Penelope's house."

"Is Penelope's mom home?"

"Yes," he says, but even I—as a mom to a non-teenager—can tell the veracity of that claim is murky.

Corinne smiles at him. "Sure you can go. Just put Penelope's mom on the phone when you get there, or I'll get so worried I'll have to come over and check."

He sighs heavily, making it clear how much she's inconveniencing her. "Okay, but I probably won't leave for an hour, actually."

"Oh, change of plans, okay! Thanks for letting me know!" Corinne says cheerfully. He disappears back into the house in a sullen cloud.

What's it going to be like when Pearl has hormones and a driver's license and even more attitude? Everything already feels so hard now. I start to ask Corinne about it, but her question comes first.

"Was your divorce like that?"

Wait, what? I rack my brain, trying to identify what beat of this conversation I missed, because that feels like it came out of nowhere.

"Did it take a long time, I mean," she says, pointing toward her neighbor's house. "Like them. Was it contentious?"

"No. No, it wasn't. No empty houses for us." My eyes instinctually find Pearl in the tree house, to make sure she's out of earshot. "I remember it feeling so wrong, actually, with how long we were together. Everything over, just like that. But I let him go when it was clear that he wanted to be gone."

And was it too soon? I wonder, thinking of last night and the conclusion Corey finally reached. The one I always hoped he would. Would he have gotten there faster if I had just hung on a little longer? My throat feels tight, so I take a sip of my tea. But it doesn't help.

"Sorry, I didn't mean to bring up a sore subject." Corinne touches my arm, and I blink away the itchiness in my eyes.

"No, it's okay," I say, waving away this awkwardness that I've caused. "But yeah. I don't really want to talk about him right now. Things are . . . weird." And if I ignore them entirely, maybe they'll eventually be less weird. Because that's how it works, right?

Corinne nods understandingly. "Got it. Change of subject."

"Thank you."

"Well, don't thank me yet," she says. She bites her lip and pretends to pull on her collar. "Listen, I'm just going to say it. And I hope you don't hate me, but . . . I know what you're doing with Trisha."

Yeah, that's not the change of subject I was hoping for.

I squint at her, trying to find the joke, but her expression has shifted to something much more serious.

"You do?" Surely, she can't *really* know.

"You're looking into Principal Smith's disappearance. You think she has something to do with it."

Shit.

"How do you—"

A little dip appears between Corinne's brows as she leans in close, her voice barely above a whisper. "That night after the parent meeting, when Mrs. Smith offered the reward. I saw you sneaking around the hallways, right outside the PTA room, remember? And then how you acted with her today? Am I—am I wrong?"

Well, that seems like quite a few jumps for someone to make. Like, *Olympic levels* of jumps. And that's not even what I was doing that night—I was investigating my *other* possible, though way less likely, suspect. I'm about to start denying, lying— whatever I need to do to keep my secret under wraps. But something in my face seems to confirm everything for her.

"So, I'm not wrong." She nods definitively. "And I saw you and Mr. Cohen whispering at Back to School Night. Are you two working together or something? To figure out what happened?"

Shit. Shit, shit, shit.

How in the hell did she make that connection? I didn't see her that night, and Jack and I were going out of our way to be subtle. But maybe we aren't being as slick as we thought . . . I definitely didn't leave there anything even remotely close to slick.

I could lie. I *should* lie.

But also it's a Friday evening after a long week of parenting and working and detective-ing. I'm tired.

"God, does everyone know?" I say, falling forward and hiding my face in my hands.

She pats my back gently. "I don't think everyone knows," she says, and I groan in response. "Really, I don't. I promise I would tell you if I did—*clearly* I can't be delicate about anything. It's just, I'm pretty perceptive. I pick up on a lot of things, nuances. I've had to . . ."

It's clear that she's weighing whether to say something more, and I'm grateful for anything that takes the attention off me playing detective. "Oh yeah?"

"Yeah. It's probably because . . . I. Well, I, uh, used to be in an abusive relationship."

That makes me sit up.

"I had to notice his little tells, that subtle shift in energy, you know? That's what I relied on to keep myself safe."

"Oh, Corinne, I'm so sorry. When—"

"It was another life," she cuts me off, waving it away, and I can tell from the way her face quickly shutters and then shifts into another smile that she doesn't want to say anything more, maybe regrets even bringing it up in the first place. So many questions linger, but I have to respect that.

"Anyway, you should be careful, Mavis." She's still smiling, but her eyes are unblinking, unnerving. "I know I've joked about it a lot, but Trisha *does* have a lot of power around here. She'd do you real harm if she knew you were even thinking she was involved in this somehow. Better to just stay out of it . . ."

"I saw her that night." I immediately want to suck the words right back in and start talking about my divorce again or some other trauma of mine or literally anything else. This was not the plan—this is the opposite of Jack's and my plan.

Corinne tenses and her eyebrows shoot up. "You did? With him?"

"No. She was by herself, outside of the school. She was wearing yellow gloves and dragging these giant trash bags to the back of her minivan. One was full of cleaning supplies, but the other two . . . I don't know."

Corinne leans back in her chair and lets out a long whistle.

"So, isn't it the right thing to do? Look into this?"

Corinne runs her hands through her hair, chewing it over. And then her nose wrinkles and she begins to slowly shake her head. "Why don't you just tell the police you saw that? Tell them—" She wipes her hands together and then pushes them away from her. "And be done with it."

"I want to be sure first. Imagine she didn't do it, and I got it wrong? She really would destroy me then."

She lets out another whistle as she meets my eyes, but she doesn't disagree. We both know I'm not wrong.

"Just . . . be careful, Mavis," she repeats, resigned. "Ask yourself: Is this really worth it?"

I nod my head and make the same promise I made to Jack. "I will. I'm good."

For some reason, though, it feels different this time. Probably because I know, deep down, I'm being anything but.

FIFTEEN

THE LAST FIRST DATE I WENT ON TOOK PLACE AT THE BEACH-
wood AMC. We saw *27 Dresses*, even though Corey didn't want
to, and shared a large popcorn and a cherry Icee with two straws,
because that's all we could afford with our combined cash. And
when Corey walked me up the steps to my house, I realized I
forgot to wear deodorant, and if he got any closer, he was going
to realize it real quickly, too. But it didn't even matter, because
my dad opened the door and fixed Corey with a death glare he
was probably practicing the whole time we were gone. And Corey was so scared he shook my hand instead of risking his life to
kiss me and then sprinted back to his mom's station wagon,
which was waiting a respectful distance down the block.

So, really, the bar isn't very high when it comes to first dates.

Not that this is a date.

Because no one said it was a date. Definitely not me.

It's just two friends investigating a suspect with a weird
name's alibi at a restaurant that specializes in beer and board
games. There's nothing even remotely date-like about that.

"What do you think's good here?" Jack asks, peering at me very adorably over the Boards and Brews plastic-covered menu.

"I mean, mozzarella sticks are always a good idea, right?"

See, that's how I know it's not a date. Because as I get older, I'm less able to convince myself that I'm not lactose intolerant. And if I eat even a single, delicious mozzarella stick, I'm going to get so bloated that the buttons are going to pull on these tight, high-waisted jeans I wore. Because I liked them, of course, not because this is a date.

"Right." He nods decisively. "And this soft pretzel with cheese sauce is calling my name, too."

Also decidedly *not* a date food.

"Pearl went through a big soft pretzel phase last year. I ended up getting the frozen ones from Costco, and she'd devour two, sometimes three a day . . . until we got that big stomach flu that blew through Knoll." I wrinkle my nose. "So, sorry to, like, yuck your yum or whatever, but I can't even look at them anymore without getting triggered. Seriously, I will need to leave the table."

His eyes squint into starbursts as his head falls back in laughter. "Now I don't know if *I* can eat them anymore without getting triggered."

I laugh and twiddle my fingers together. "All part of my master plan."

"Is she with your dad tonight?" he asks, setting the menu down.

"No, my friend Jasmine is watching her. Uh, Dr. Hammonds? We trade sitting sometimes when we need it, and my dad told me last minute he was going to this live recording of a podcast with one of his old lawyer buddies." I widen my eyes and press my lips tightly together to show what I think about that.

"Um, wow? So your dad is cool?" he says with another perfect, rumbly laugh that I feel in my chest. "I don't think my parents even know what a podcast is."

"Well, to be fair, he went from discovering what a podcast is to getting me to enter my credit card information into their Patreon in, like, the span of a week. They got their claws into him *real* quick!"

He arches one of his thick eyebrows. "*Your* credit card information?"

"He's weird about putting in his own anywhere," I say, shaking my head. "He thinks they're going to steal his identity, but . . . doesn't care if they take mine, I guess?"

"Why are they like that?!" he shouts, pointing at me in recognition. "My mom is the same way! But then she had no problem whatsoever giving her social security number to the nice man on the phone just checking in from 'the IRS.'" He curls his fingers into quotation marks.

"No!"

"Yes. It was a whole thing." He runs his hands over his jaw as he laughs, and I join in.

"And these are the people who raised us! But I guess Pearl will probably be talking shit about me, just like this, to her friend soon enough."

My voice wobbles when I say *friend*, and for a split second I'm terrified he's going to call me out on it, set me straight that this is not a date—*which I know*. He bites his lip, eyes flicking to the table.

"So, Pearl's dad . . ." he starts. "Feel free to shut me up if this isn't my business. But . . . is he in the picture? It's always you—at drop-off, I mean."

And it's a totally normal question to ask, whatever we're

doing here, right now. "Yes, Corey's in the picture," I say. "He's a drummer, and he mostly works on tours. So he's gone a lot, traveling all around the world."

"So your ex-husband is a rock star?" He mimes wiping his brow, and I laugh.

"My ex-husband is a rock star." I shrug. "It's what he always wanted, so I'm happy for him. That he gets to live his dream . . . not a lot of people do. And he always makes sure he's here for the big things with Pearl—and all the little things, too. They're always talking."

Without even thinking about it, I find myself giving the same highlight reel explanation that I always do when telling someone new about Corey, because I don't want them to think badly of him not being here for the day-to-day. I don't want them to jump to any of the negative stereotypes that so many are eager to grab on to. Because regardless of what happened between us, Corey is a good man. A good father.

"He . . . actually, he may be coming back to Beachwood soon. For a longer break than normal."

"That's good." Jack's tone is even, but I can tell by the quirk of his lips there's a question there.

"Yes, it is," I confirm. "For Pearl. She's going to be so happy once I tell her."

For me, though? I don't know.

Corey *did* say he wanted to be there for me, too. But what did he mean by that, exactly? And what did I *want* him to mean by that?

"Okay, I may be getting him confused because he does have a pretty common look. But I think that's the guy Nelson told you about. Carl, right?" Jack has a playful grin on his face, and it's clear he's trying to shift my suddenly stormy energy. When I follow his subtly pointing finger to the bar, though, it works. I

crack up. Because that's Carl all right. Black top hat and an impressive white handlebar mustache—made even more ridiculous
by the faded *Star Trek* shirt, puka shells, and baggy cargo pants
he's paired them with.

I try to hold in my giggles, but then my eyes start streaming
and a loud snort shoots out, which sets Jack off, too. We must
be making quite the scene, because Carl looks up and narrows
his eyes at us. He wipes his hands on a dice-printed towel at his
waist and then ambles over to us.

"Sorry for the holdup, folks." His voice is surprisingly deep
and low, like Lance Bass's, whenever NSYNC let him sing a
line. "We're short-staffed today. There's a big board game convention this weekend over in Anaheim, and most of my waiters
called out."

"A board game convention? That sounds like fun! Hey, uh, I
wonder if Dungeons & Dragons has a booth at that convention
because it's a . . . role-playing tabletop game—" Jack clears his
throat and taps a beat out on the table. "We've, you know, uh—
been looking for a place to play that D&D. With others—play
with them, and yeah . . . could we do that . . . *here?*"

Oh. Oh no. I just realized we never talked about our strategy
for interviewing this guy. I didn't think we *had* to when Jack was
so smooth with Lilliam in the office. But this awkward word
vomit appears to be Jack's strategy . . . ? How in the world did
he talk to Mrs. Smith's neighbor without arousing suspicion?
Lord, Derek must have taken the lead there.

And judging by the way Carl's looking at us right now, I'm
going to have to do the same.

I smile widely at Carl and hope the right words will come out
if I just start talking. "So, I work for Project Window? Have you
heard of us? We're a program that pairs teens with mentors, and
I'm . . . currently working on outreach. I'm looking for adults

with, um, interesting names? Yeah, interesting names . . . to help the, you know, youth in . . . similar positions feel less alone. Would you, um—would you happen to know . . . someone like that? Someone with an interesting name?"

Okay, I guess I can't judge Jack after all. Carl clearly isn't buying *that* either. He sets his jaw and crosses his arms in front of Spock's pointy eyebrows on his shirt, looking between us with eyes that are nearly squeezed shut. Finally he points at Jack and then his finger trails to me. "Are you the people coming to check up on Nelson? He told me to expect you."

I sigh, but Jack seems to think there's still a possibility to salvage this.

"And . . . if we were . . ." he says slowly. "What would you tell us?"

Carl shrugs with one shoulder. "He was here two Tuesday nights ago. Late."

"But if he told you we were coming, that is what you'd say, isn't it?" Jack locks him in a gaze that's clearly supposed to turn up the heat in this interrogation, and I stifle a giggle. I *really* got all in my feelings, thinking he was better at this than me. No, we are both *equally* bad.

Carl doesn't make an effort to hide his amusement, though, and lets out a loud chuckle. "Hey, if you don't believe me, you can check the Instagram, man," he says, with another shrug. "We post pictures from all their sessions. You know, THAC0 Tuesdays? With a zero on the end?"

It's clear that's supposed to mean something to us, but judging from Carl's long, belabored sigh, we don't give him the reaction he expects.

"They have a huge following," he adds, shaking his head at our ignorance. "Now are you going to order or not? You are taking up our best table."

I look around. The place is empty except for two guys in the corner, huddled over an intense chess game, and a woman nursing a dark beer at the bar.

"We'll have the mozzarella sticks to start, please," I say, handing him my menu. "And a pint of that blond you have on tap."

I raise my eyebrows at Jack, who is already reaching for his phone. "I'll have the IPA. Thank you, Carl."

"No problem," Carl mutters, his tone revealing that he thinks we're all of the problems.

As Carl walks away, Jack puts his phone in the middle of the table and scrolls back to the Tuesday in question on the Boards and Brews Instagram page. And sure enough, there's Nelson at a table full of other middle-aged white men, declaring something animatedly from behind a plastic screen perched on this very same table, from the looks of it.

I sigh. "That was easy."

"Too easy?" Jack asks hopefully.

"No. Just easy."

This was really a formality anyway because we know—or we are at least *mostly* sure—that Trisha did it. Now that we've fully ruled out everyone else, we need to focus on her, the real threat here. We need to prove, without a doubt, that she's behind Principal Smith's disappearance, which we'll do by . . . well, I'm not sure. But I mean, there has to be evidence *somewhere*, right? Murder is messy. It's not like she just gave him a little ride in those plastic bags and locked him up somewhere. No, she *killed* him. So where did she take those bags? Her backyard? Should we wait until she and Chad are out one day and then see what we can dig up?

My body shudders at the thought of that.

It's so easy to make this into a little game and Trisha into some cartoon villain. But body parts possibly buried in the dirt next to her David Austin roses? That's some real shit. Shit I don't want to think about when there are mozzarella sticks on the way and Pearl is safe with Jasmine and Jack is sitting across from me with his rolled-up sleeves and kind smile, and there's nothing I can actually do right here, right now.

But is that selfish? A man may be dead, and I want to sit here and enjoy my maybe date?

I run my hand through my curls and let out a long, frustrated exhale.

"What should we do?"

Jack grins and points to the overflowing shelves of board games next to the bar. "Well, I feel like Clue might be a little too on the nose. So, Battleship or Sorry?"

Two hours later we've played rounds of both, and we're deep into an intense game of Candy Land.

"Take that, Princess Lolly, you bitch!" I shout, slamming down a double blue card.

"Wow, you get really into this, don't you?" Jack asks with exaggerated concern, as if he didn't have to get up and do a lap around the bar when I sunk his last battleship.

"Is there any other way to play Candy Land?" I smirk and move my little red gingerbread man along the rainbow path. "And c'mon, you know you want to call her a bitch, too, the way she trapped you in the Lollipop Woods for five turns."

"First of all, it was only three," he says, holding up a finger. "And second, I mean, I don't know the context of that decision, her life circumstances—"

"Her life circumstances!"

"Yes, her life circumstances. Maybe she's lonely. Maybe she's holding some residual trauma from her childhood. It must be difficult growing up in the shadow of Queen Frostine and King Kandy."

"Well, it's about to get even more traumatic when I get to that finish line and conquer this kingdom. Princess Lolly is going to have to get a job and eat some broccoli!" Jack's blue gingerbread man is where mine is supposed to land, so I knock it over and claim my rightful spot. Except, okay, maybe I am being just a *little* dramatic, because not only does his gingerbread man fall on the floor, but mine shoots out of my hand, too, clattering on the ground.

"Hey!" Jack holds his hand to his chest, wounded.

I shrug. "Can't get in the way of the future queen."

I go to pick them up because I'm not, like, a total monster, but Jack is out of his chair before I can do anything. He kneels in front of me, scooping them both up. And then, with his green eyes locked on mine, he gently places my piece on my knee.

"Here you go."

It's a quick movement. He sits back down, and his hand is gone before I can even process it. But the warmth of his touch remains.

"Um, thank you." My voice sounds too breathy, and my skin is too flushed. But that's just because I'm on my second beer. Not because of anything else.

"Do you—uh, remember where we were?"

"I think—" I reach forward to take his piece from him, letting my fingers brush against his, letting myself have another fix and linger. It's a feat to make myself break away. "I think you were back here."

I put his gingerbread man back at the start, by the weird-looking tree, and he laughs low and warm.

"Well, then you were there, too." He takes the gingerbread

man from my hands but doesn't even follow through with the pretense. Casting my little red piece aside, he slowly threads his fingers through mine, linking us together in the middle of the board.

My pulse raises and my stomach dips as he bites his bottom lip and holds me with a gaze full of meaning. And it's nice. I forgot how nice this is. Holding hands with someone new, the thrill of every little first.

I could get used to this.

The smile spreading across his lips makes me realize I said that out loud, but he starts talking before the embarrassment even has a chance to take hold. "So why don't you? Get used to me."

I squeeze his hand, pulling it closer to me.

"Maybe I will."

I'M STILL RIDING ON THE HIGH OF HOLDING JACK'S HAND like a giddy middle schooler, but that feeling soon dies when I see Jasmine's face.

Her mouth is set in a thin line and her eyes are dark and serious, especially in contrast to the bright yellow of the Hammondses' front door. I notice she's opened it just enough, instead of the wide-open welcome I usually get.

"Hey, girl, can I talk to you outside?"

I nod, confusion and anxiety already swirling in my stomach, and she slips outside and firmly pulls the door shut behind her. With just the faint glow coming from her porch light, all of Jasmine's features transform from cheery to somber, and my mind speeds off to the worst conclusions.

Did Pearl give her a play-by-play of the fight between Corey and me the other night? Did she tell Langston the whole plot of

Dad's podcast, or maybe a *Law & Order: SVU* episode, and now he's scarred for life? But, like, it happens, right? And I didn't say anything when Langston showed Pearl one of those terrifying Roblox games he plays, and she ended up sleeping in my bed for two weeks and turning around all her stuffed animals to face the wall . . .

"Did you have a nice time?" Jasmine asks, but I only nod in response. We both know it's a formality.

She clears her throat and looks me in the eye. "Listen, I think Pearl is being bullied."

That isn't what I was expecting, and the news hits me in the chest like a cannonball.

"What?" I croak out. "How do you know?"

Pearl is being bullied? My Pearl? How would Jasmine know that before me? Because if Pearl, *my* daughter, was being bullied, she surely would have told me first? Or I would have noticed . . . *something*. There must be some confusion here.

"The kids were on their Chromebooks, doing that Reading Stars app. You know how Leon is—they wanted to play on the Switch, and he said they had to spend an equal amount of time working their brains before rotting them." I do know, and that's why I sent Pearl's Chromebook with her in the first place. "So, anyway, I noticed, just, how she was when she was on it. She kept . . . frowning and looking all miserable, which surprised me because Pearl usually likes all the school stuff. So, I checked it when she and Langston went off to play *Mario Kart*. It was just an instinct. And sure enough, there were these emails pulled up on one of her tabs, all from SoSo Hart, saying just the meanest things—"

"Like what?" I can't get the answer fast enough. I wish I could scoop it right out of Jasmine's brain and plop it into mine, all this information she knows about my baby that I don't.

"Like that she was stupid." Jasmine's eyes flick to the window, where I can see the blurry colors of Rainbow Road through the curtains. Still, her voice hushes lower. "That she didn't belong in Mrs. Tennison's class with all the rest of the kids. That she—she was ugly."

"No!" The word escapes from the fire already burning inside of me. I want to storm right over to the Harts' house right now. I want to fling open the door and stomp through the hallways, banging pots and pans, and demand that this child explain herself, right this instant. Why she thinks she's qualified to have *any* sort of opinion about my brilliant, beautiful marvel of a girl.

"That little shithead."

And okay, I know. I probably shouldn't call a seven-year-old a shithead, but luckily Jasmine doesn't balk.

"That little shithead," she concurs.

But also, right along with the anger is a deep sadness. Because I couldn't protect my baby from this pain. Because she didn't even feel like she could tell me. My heart aches as I think about her navigating this alone.

"How far back do they go?" I ask.

"To the second day of school," Jasmine sighs. "And it seems like it's been really affecting Pearl. She had this nemeses list? Like a list of people she hates. And SoSo Hart was number one, bolded and underlined. Did you know about this list?"

"Yes, she told me about that. I knew she was typing it up on her computer. But I—I didn't look at it . . ."

"Why not?" I can tell Jasmine is trying to keep her tone neutral, but I can feel the confusion there along with something else. Judgment? And why *didn't* I look? Why did I just laugh and blow that off? Pearl's always talked about her nemeses, but she escalated to a goddamn list—a document right there on her computer, a computer that's almost always sitting on my kitchen counter in plain view . . . and I couldn't even be bothered to take a peek?

I feel like a total idiot. I feel like the worst mom who's ever lived. What in the world was I doing?

Well, I was probably coming up with a new theory about Trisha or dreaming about Jack in his green glasses or responding to an email from Nelson or wondering if I've wasted my life in a dead-end job or avoiding Dyvia or looking up rent prices in our school district or spiraling over the fact that Corey might be moving back to town and what that even means for me if I'm holding hands with someone else . . .

I was distracted. I still am distracted.

"Oh, Mavis. I'm so sorry. And if you need backup when you go to square up with Angela, just say the word." She gives a half-hearted chuckle, pounding her fist into her hand, but when the joke doesn't land, her face cracks into the concern she was trying to mask. "Listen, I know this is a lot right now. This and everything with work, too." She sucks her teeth and shakes her head. "Lord knows your plate has *been* full! But you are strong, and you've got this. You're a great mom, and now that you know what's going on, you can step in and fight for her and get this little SoSo in check, oh-kay? And this work stuff is manageable, too. I told you Leon has a friend who runs the Rosso Foundation, right? Though I don't know if you want to stay in the non-profit world . . ."

I run my hands over my face and let out a deep groan. "I don't care about work." In fact, work is the absolute *last* thing I want to be thinking about right now.

"You don't? But why—" Jasmine's lips press shut before she can finish that question, like she realizes she doesn't want to know the answer. Her brow wrinkles, and she reaches forward to squeeze my shoulder. "Listen, sis . . . maybe it's not the best time to be dating. I'm glad to see you having some fun, but if you're already feeling this stressed . . . maybe it's better to keep your head on straight. Just for right now."

My skin bristles under her touch, and I feel the flames in my chest swell again, her judgment like gasoline.

"I feel like that's easy for you to say from your position," I spit out, waving toward her big, beautiful home with her loving, supportive, equal-partner husband inside. "And that's not even what—what this thing with Jack is . . ."

Which is not *exactly* true, but true enough.

"Okay, you're right, you're right, and I'm sorry," she says quickly, holding up her palms. "I don't know what it's like to be a single mom or in your situation at all, so I should probably just zip my lips and keep my advice to myself." She mimes zipping her lips but then immediately unzips them and smiles at me softly. "But if Mr. Cohen—*Jack* is the right person for you, and I *do* think he seems pretty great, well, then he'll wait—"

"But there isn't time to wait!" The words come out in a strangled shout, and Jasmine reels back with wide eyes.

"Girl . . . what?" She purses her lips and narrows her eyes at me, giving me a subtle up-down. Like she's checking for all the signs she's missed that her friend lost her goddamn mind.

"We're not seeing each other. Or at least, that's not all we're doing . . ."

Her perfectly arched eyebrow tells me I'm gonna need to give her more than that.

"You know Principal Smith's disappearance? Well, we've been looking into it. Together. And I think we might be getting close because we've already ruled out Mrs. Smith and Mrs. Nelson and Nelson Nelson—that's Mrs. Nelson's husband. She was cheating on him. And really, looking into their alibis was just a formality anyway because I think—no, I'm almost positive—that Trisha did it. Because I saw her that night outside of the school, me and Polly did, and she was carrying out *something* in these, like, big black garbage bags. And I know it sounds crazy—I *know* that, *believe* me—but I think it may have been Principal Smith in those bags. Like . . . killed. *Cut up.* Because he was the one person in the way of her getting this gifted program she wants, and now that he's gone, look! It's back on track again. And it's extreme, but we know Trisha. She'll do *anything* for her kids. Even kill for them."

When I finally get all of the words out, I feel breathless, but I also feel relief. Like I just pulled something grubby and grimy out from my belly and then wiped all my insides down with Clorox, leaving everything shiny and new.

But that good feeling vanishes when Jasmine starts to laugh. Low and throaty at first, but soon she's slapping her leg and hollering, her cackles echoing down the block.

It takes her a long time to realize I'm not joining in, and then the silence is overwhelming.

"Oh, Mavis . . . no."

I bite my lip and look away from her, trying to hold in the fury and embarrassment combining into something toxic, something that's making my throat burn and eyes well.

"I'm not—I'm not saying it's not plausible . . . all of this with Trisha." I can tell she's choosing her words carefully, trying to be delicate, and I hate it.

"I get that you're stressed," she starts again. "And . . . trying to figure your life out. But can't you just do what most of us do, and, I don't know . . . walk around T.J.Maxx for an hour? Why do you have to try and solve a whole-ass mystery that doesn't even involve you?"

"Mrs. Smith offered a reward—to anyone who can figure out what happened to him. Twenty thousand dollars. Even split with Jack . . . that money could help me and Pearl out. A lot."

I know I don't have to convince her. This is my decision, not hers, and I'm a grown woman. But still, I want to. I want her to know I've thought this through.

"But what about Pearl, Mavis? You were so preoccupied with this that she was being bullied and you didn't even know. Is this really what's best for you both?"

And I can't even argue with that. My baby was hurting, and I didn't even know. I failed her.

The flame of anger goes out, doused by a bucketful of guilt.

"Thank you for watching Pearl," I say, keeping my voice polite, precise. If I don't, the tears prickling behind my eyes, making everything blurry, are going to fall. "I need to get her to bed now. Sorry for this, um, inconvenience."

"Mavis, don't be like that. You know I'm just trying to look out for you." Jasmine sighs and reaches for me, but I dodge her hand, going for the door.

"I can see that, and I love you. But I'm fine. I can look out for myself."

And I put on my best act when I walk into the Hammonds house—gathering Pearl and her Chromebook, waving at Leon and Langston, giving Jasmine a tight smile on the way out. So maybe on the outside, at least, it'll seem like that's true.

SIXTEEN

I SQUEEZE PEARL'S HAND BETWEEN BOTH OF MINE AS WE walk home, listening intently as she tells me every last detail about each round of *Mario Kart* they played, as if that can make up for what I missed. When we get home, I run her a warm bath, filling it with chamomile-scented bubbles from Lush, which I'm always too scared to actually use because they're so expensive. And then I wrap her up all cozy and clean in my bed and read her a picture book, the one I usually hide behind all the others because it's too long. I find myself putting the back of my hand to her forehead, like a reflex. And I almost wish it was something like that—a cold, a fever—because then at least I would know for sure what to do.

We need to have this conversation tonight. I can't let these feelings fester in her for a day longer. But how do I bring it up?

And then Pearl rips off the Band-Aid.

"Did Ms. Jasmine tell you about SoSo being mean to me?"

"How—did she . . . talk to you about it?" But even as I ask the question, I know that's not right. Jasmine wouldn't step in like that.

"No, Mommy," she says, sighing to show her great patience. "I saw her sneaking on my computer when she thought I wasn't watching her." She crosses her arms over the comforter and juts out her chin. "*Without* my permission."

"I understand how that could be upsetting, Ms. Jasmine looking at your personal stuff." I nod and wrap my arm around her shoulders. "One time Papa read my diary and I was so mad. I gave him the silent treatment for a whole week."

"Papa? Really?" Her mouth drops open in outrage.

"Mm-hmm, but sometimes parents do that, look at personal things, because they want to make sure you're safe and happy. It's not okay all the time, but *sometimes*, we have to make exceptions."

She scrunches her face up, thinking it over, but it's clear she's unconvinced.

"And from what Ms. Jasmine told me tonight," I continue, "it doesn't seem like you are . . . safe and happy. Are you, Pearl?"

Her bottom lip quivers as she shakes her head, and she quickly cuddles in closer to me, tucking her face and soft hair into my neck. We used to lie like this when she was a baby, and I'd inhale her sweet scent and marvel at every one of her features, from her deliciously wrinkly knees to her tiny, sharp fingernails. Back then I worried endlessly over her sleep patterns and my milk production and developmental milestones and wonder weeks. Everything was a possible problem, an emergency—but they feel so far away from the problems we have to reckon with now.

"I'm so sorry that this girl is being mean, baby," I whisper into her hair. "The things she's told you aren't true at all. You are smart, but even more important than that, you work hard and do your best. You belong in that class. And when Daddy and I first saw you, we both said you were the most beautiful thing we'd ever seen, and you've only gotten more and more beautiful every day."

"Then why would she say those things? If they're not true, why would she say them, Mommy?" Her voice is so small, so wounded, and my chest aches with the need to take all of her pain as my own.

"I don't know what's causing her to be so hateful. But sometimes when people are mean, it's because something bad happened to them. So even though they hurt us, we can feel sorry for them and hope they feel better."

She sniffles. "And also plan our revenge?"

I cough to hide the big laugh that nearly escapes. I almost want to say yes and start plotting how we're gonna get back at little SoSo and her mom, too. But . . . I've got to be the adult here. I guess.

"We don't want to give her any more of our minds or our time," I say, sounding like a very convincing adult. "She doesn't deserve that. You just have to be kind back to her and tell an adult if she keeps on with this, so we can handle it for you. It's called being the bigger person."

Pearl lets out a long, weary sigh. "Sounds hard."

This time I do let myself laugh. "It is. But you can do hard things, baby girl."

She lifts her head up, giving me an epic side-eye—which I can only blame on myself, because it's exactly like mine. "Are you sure?"

"More sure than anything in the whole wide world." I stroke her hair and kiss her forehead. She immediately wipes it off and then falls back on the bed, rolling her eyes. My limbs loosen in relief, seeing that little glimmer of her sass, her spark.

I've got one more question, though, that I know will keep gnawing away at my insides if I don't get it out now. "I'm wondering . . . why didn't you tell me?"

She covers her face with her hands. "I'm sorry."

"No, no. You don't have to be sorry," I say, gently pulling up a finger so I can peek through. I smile at her. "I just want to know how I can help you better in the future. Because Mommy messed up here, too. I should have noticed this was going on."

"I didn't want you to notice, though." She sets her jaw, eyes full of determination. "I could tell you were busy. And stressed out."

"You could?"

"Yeah, because you always do this when you're stressed out." She sighs dramatically, flopping her body to the side. "I need coffee! I'm so tired! The laundry!"

I didn't ask to be dragged like that, but okay. I roll my eyes at her and sigh . . . and then immediately regret it when she giggles and points at me. "See!"

"I don't know what you're talking about."

"Also, also—I wanted to fix it by myself like you always fix everything by yourself."

I can tell she means it as a compliment, but it lands like a mom-guilt missile. Is that the message I'm sending my kid? That I have to handle everything myself? That I have to be stressed out and stretched thin and exhausted all the time because there's no one I can go to? I don't want that for her . . . I don't want it for me either.

"I really am bad at asking for help, aren't I?"

"So, so bad!" She purses her lips and nods emphatically.

"Well, I want to get better at that. Because I need help sometimes—we all do. And it's always better to tell someone and reach out to others if you need it. You don't have to do anything alone. You have a big group of people who love you, like me and Daddy and Papa and Ms. Jasmine."

"And they can help you, too. Right?"

"Yes, they can. And they do. When I let them." My throat gets tight as I think about my argument with Jasmine, but I push those feelings down. I'll have to deal with that later.

"And my most important job is always being your mommy, Pearl, so even if I seem stressed—"

"And are drinking a lot of coffee?"

"And I'm drinking a lot of coffee." I smile. "You can always tell me what's going on. Always. I'm never too busy for you."

But I'm already questioning the words as they come out of my mouth. Is that really true? That I'm never too busy for Pearl? Yeah, that's what I want to be the truth, but is that the way I've been operating for the past two weeks? I've been distracted and overwhelmed, chasing something that doesn't even involve me, like Jasmine pointed out. And my child has suffered because of it—there's just no way around it. I need to put this mystery down and focus on Pearl and decide if I want a different job and figure out how to navigate this transition with Corey and maybe start volunteering in Pearl's class so I can keep my eye on little SoSo and stop obsessing over what could be buried in Trisha's backyard. That's what a *good* mom would do.

And yet . . . is it even worse if I *don't* see this through? I've already wasted so much of my time. Does it make it even more of a horrible, selfish, Bad Mom offense if it was just . . . all for nothing?

THAT QUESTION FEELS JUST AS FRESH, JUST AS URGENT, ON Monday morning, like a deep cut that just won't scab over.

"Mommy, stop looking at me like that," Pearl whines, tugging on my hand outside Corinne's front door.

"Like what?"

Pearl juts her face forward, widening her eyes and curving

her lips into an exaggerated frown. "Like that. It's annoying a little bit, no offense. I'm okay, Mommy."

So . . . Pearl seems to be doing okay. Or whatever. But I *am* going to keep watching her closely to make sure she stays that way. I'll just be a little more subtle about it.

"Come on in! I'm in the kitchen!" Corinne's faint voice floats through the door, and Pearl opens it without hesitation, bounding inside to play with River and Mason. She's so excited for this bonus playdate with her new besties, the Ackerman boys, that it's almost possible to forget why it's happening in the first place. I called all the numbers and emailed all the addresses I could find for everyone of importance at Knoll—the interim principal Mr. Reed, Mrs. Tennison, even *Ms. Lilliam*—demanding that we have this meeting with Angela Hart before school started this morning, because there was no way in hell my kid could safely return without it, and did they really want to be responsible for keeping her, the victim, away from her education? Which, I admit, was a little extra, but if there's ever a time that a mom is able to be extra, it's when her kid is messed with. Luckily (for them), everyone agreed, and I had to ask Corinne to watch Pearl so I could go to the demanded meeting. Because I don't like to interrupt my dad's well-earned sleep-in mornings unless I absolutely have to, and the only other person I'd feel comfortable asking is Jasmine, and well . . .

Corinne barely even let me finish asking for the favor before she agreed—no, insisted. And I'm still getting to know Corinne, of course, but there is something about her that's so warm and inviting, just like her house that we're walking into, right now, for the second time in less than a week.

"Oh, Mavis, you look beat!" Corinne calls from behind the counter, which, okay . . . may contradict that whole warm-and-inviting thing I was saying.

"Thank you?"

"I'm sorry! I need to just shut my big ol' trap, but you look like you haven't slept at all. You poor thing." She sticks the knife she was holding into the jar of peanut butter in front of her and walks toward me with her arms out and sympathy shining in her eyes. "Come here."

I let myself be hugged by her and feel the tightness in my body loosen as she rubs soothing circles on my back.

"This sucks."

"I know."

"And what if she's scarred by this forever?"

"She won't be."

"I should have caught this from the beginning."

"Should've's don't help nobody. You caught it now, and you're gonna make it right."

"Mom! Have you seen my econ textbook?!" Brody calls from somewhere in the house.

"Have you checked the bathroom?!" Corinne shouts back. She pulls away and squeezes my shoulder. "I'm sorry. Give me a sec."

She strides down the hallway, where I can hear Pearl giggling with River and Mason, and I'm already feeling so much better than I did just moments ago. I'm gonna make it right. I can handle this meeting. And I don't have to leave for another five minutes, so maybe I can help Corinne, too, since I'm already intruding on her morning, the most chaotic time in every mother's day.

I walk over to the counter, where she has an open bag of carrot sticks and the makings of three PB&Js set up. I quickly divide the carrot sticks into three small plastic containers and then get to work finishing the sandwiches, adding the jelly and then cutting them up—hopefully the Ackerman boys like triangles.

"You're so sweet. Thank you," Corinne says as she walks back into the kitchen, and Brody follows her, carrying a backpack so heavy it looks like it's going to topple his thin frame right over.

"Bye, Mom, love you." He kisses her quickly on the cheek and then jogs toward the door.

"Wait! You forgot your lunch!" I call, stuffing a sandwich in a plastic baggie and holding it out to him. He looks at it like I'm presenting him with a dead rat or something.

"Um, I buy lunch in the caf," he mumbles, shaking his palms out, as if I'm gonna force it on him or something. Then he waves awkwardly and heads out the door.

I raise an eyebrow at Corinne, and she smiles, taking the sandwich from me. "I make an extra for myself so I don't forget to eat," she says. "So . . . I know you gotta go, but is there anything new with . . . well, you know." Her eyes flick to the hallway. "I haven't been able to stop worrying about you. You're being careful, right?"

"Yeah, I am. Jack and I looked into another alibi on Saturday night, actually. Mrs. Nelson's husband. Turns out he's all clear, too." I shrug. "I don't know. I feel a little stupid right now for being so distracted by all this . . ."

I also can't get Jasmine's knee-jerk laughter at the whole thing out of my head. It makes my body feel hot with shame and makes texting her feel like an impossible mountain to climb. Not that it's just on me, though . . . She could text me, too.

But Corinne didn't laugh. No, she thought this was all serious enough to call the police, and I can see that worry etched all over her face right now.

"You shouldn't feel stupid," she insists, her voice hushed to keep the kids from hearing. "I keep replaying it in my head, what you said you saw that night." She shivers and presses her palm to her chest. "It's important that people know . . . if she did what it seems like she did. She's around our kids *every day*."

She looks me in the eye, telegraphing the gravity of all this, and goose bumps sprout up my arms.

"I need more proof first—"

"Oh yes. Of course, of course!" she says, waving her hands like she's dusting away the tension. "Because you're like me, Mavis, and we do what is best for our kids. No matter what. And I know it might be a little, well . . . *unpopular*, but you're gonna do what's right to protect our kids."

My chest feels a little tight as I think about what's actually right in this situation, but I smile and chuckle awkwardly. "Yeah, first I have to go to this meeting, and then I can move on to proving Trisha's guilty."

"First, this meeting!" she repeats with a nod. "You've got this. It's gonna go well."

THE MEETING GOES ABOUT AS WELL AS IT CAN GO CON-sidering Angela opens it up by saying, "Just so you know, Mavis, we're not racist."

"I . . . didn't say you were?"

And I swear Angela, Mr. Reed, and Mrs. Tennison all let out a perfectly synchronized sigh of relief.

"Because I've taught Sojourner to be kind to Black people. We *celebrate* Black people in our home. Clearly."

Maybe that's the problem. That you see my kid's race first, when you should just be seeing a little kid. That you think a specific name and taking pictures for Instagram at one march and a ten-dollar sign stating your beliefs stuck into your lawn is enough protection from the anti-Black beliefs that can seep into kids' brains like poison, from the TV shows they watch and the toys they're given to play with and the books you read them and our entire fucking culture. Maybe the reason that you thought this was about race, your kid bullying mine—the only Black girl in the room—is that you know, deep down, it is, and that's just too big a burden for you to bear.

Which is what I *could've* said if I wanted to make this a whole thing and have Angela chasing me, trying to earn her not-racist gold star for the rest of the girls' time in elementary school.

But I decidedly *do not* want that.

So instead I just smile and nod as the three of them apologize profusely and promise to never let this happen again and emphatically agree with each of the solutions I ask for: a restorative conversation for the girls, loss of technology privileges for little SoSo, and increased supervision at school and online.

By the time I walk out of there, I'm all tense and tight from holding my face in neutral and keeping the anger boiling in my belly from reaching the surface. Because I know how that would go. I know how quickly I can switch from being the victim to being the problem, as a Black mom, when I show any emotion. So I did what I had to do to get my baby what she needed, and I just hope I have some time to scream in my car before I have to put on another mask at work.

Of course, I bump into Dyvia right outside of the school gates.

"Oh, Mavis! I was just about to text you!" she says, smiling brightly. "Do you have a minute?"

I don't stop moving, because I can feel the clock on my non–bitch face and good home training about to run out. Better to deal with this later once I can regroup.

"I'm so sorry, Dyvia," I say, walking backward. "But I promise I'll—"

She shakes her head, cutting me off. "Yeah. Okay. Whatever."

It's so out of character that my body freezes all on its own. I blink at her. "Uh . . . excuse me?"

"I'll be here when you get around to it. Really. It's okay," she says, but her pinched face and tight tone make it clear that it really isn't.

My neck starts to get hot with embarrassment because I know I've dropped the ball. "I'm sorry, Dyvia. It's just . . . I've been really busy."

"Yes, I got the message," Dyvia says, her voice taking on a sarcastic edge, and then, hello, annoyance enters the party of emotions I'm currently trying to repress. "But why did you even take on this job if you weren't actually gonna do it? Why be the DEI chair if you're so *busy*?" She spits out "busy" like the four-letter word it is.

"I didn't take it on. Trisha forced it on me," I explain, my jaw clenched, my nerves tight. I know I need to walk away now if I want to be able to keep all these feelings on lock, to be the nice, neutral person they all expect me to be.

"You couldn't just say no? And leave it for someone who actually deserved it?"

"You're acting like this is some big honor!" And there it is. I'm yelling. At Dyvia. It's like a release valve for all of the anxiety and guilt and shame and fear and anger that's been billowing up in my chest like a cloud of toxic gas for the past two weeks. "DEI is just something they assign to us"—I slash a finger toward my skin—"to cover their asses, not because they want any real change! But at least at a real job, there's money attached to it. This is a volunteer position for the PTA, Dyvia! If you want this, you can have it!"

"So that's what it is for you, isn't it?" she asks, her lips pinched tight. "You think you're better because you *work*? You think we're just silly moms aimlessly trying to fill our days?"

"I didn't say—"

"You didn't have to!" she shouts, jerking her head. "I know Trisha is a lot, and who knows what her intentions were with this DEI committee. But the PTA does good work, *important* work, for the school!"

"Listen, I think we're—"

"The money raised from our Fun Run pays for the music teacher and the art teacher because the district didn't think they're important enough and cut the funding. We run tutoring sessions after school so the already overworked teachers don't have to do it. Field trips, book fair, family movie nights, assemblies—all that extra stuff? Yeah, that's all us, too! And I got us thousands of dollars' worth of new, diverse books for the library, through a grant that I applied for. Books that are currently missing, which is what I've been *trying* to get your help with for almost two weeks now, but you can't be bothered because it's not a real job. So, if you think our work isn't valuable because we don't get paid for it, if you don't want to be a part of this—well, then you can give it up right now, Mavis. No one is begging you!"

I didn't *say* anyone was begging me. And okay, maybe I didn't realize that the PTA paid for all those things. I thought those were just, you know, basic elementary school provisions . . . And what did she just say about books?

But no. I can't get into all this right now. I just can't. After this weekend and that meeting . . . it's clear I need to get focused. Because all this multitasking and spreading myself thin is just making me shitty at a lot of things and letting a lot of people down. Pearl is my top priority. And after that, solving this mystery, once and for all. Like Corinne said, it could be dangerous if I don't. Maybe if I let everything else go, just for a little while longer, I'll have the clarity I need. That doesn't mean I can't come back to the PTA and do this DEI thing right. But it just can't have my energy in this moment.

"Dyvia, I'm sorry, but it's just—I have a lot going on right now."

"Oh, okay." She huffs, rolling her eyes. "Well, let me know when your schedule clears up."

With that, she storms off down the block, leaving me alone. And that's when I notice the small crowd of moms that has formed, whispering behind their hands and sharing glances of concern and delight.

Knoll Elementary Parents Facebook Group

Della Lively

Who was that yelling at poor Dyvia this morning?

Ruth Gentry

That was Mavis Miller, the chair of the DEI committee

Della Lively

Well, that explains it 🙄

Ruth Gentry

I agree it was quite the scene, especially in front of the school! We have a responsibility to set a good example for our children. They are always watching!

Leslie Banner

Does she have a pattern of acting so erratic? I'm pretty sure I saw her screaming and running around at Back to School Night

Angela Hart

I had an unfortunate run-in with Mavis today, too. Our daughters had a little tiff that—don't get me wrong—definitely needed to be resolved!! But I was surprised by the aggressive energy she brought into the conversation, and sadly she didn't show a commitment to the restorative justice model as much as I would have expected. Dyvia and I are both on the DEI committee with her too, but so far we've felt very let down by her leadership ☹️

Florence Michaelson

Are you all sure you have the right one? My Axel has been in her daughter's class the past two years, and from my experience Mavis has always been pleasant, if a little quiet

Jasmine Hammonds

Honestly, fuck all y'all

Trisha Holbrook

Just a friendly reminder that this is supposed to be a safe, fun, and informative space for all Knoll parents! We will, unfortunately, have to remove group members that repeatedly use any foul or hateful language.

Jasmine Hammonds

FUCK. ALL. Y'ALL.

SEVENTEEN

I HOLD MYSELF TOGETHER ALL DAY, EVEN WHEN NELSON asks me to join *his* career fair task force at work, even when Corey tells Pearl he's getting a break from this tour soon and then texts me afterward to explain it's an indefinite break. Even when I see what the moms are saying about me on Facebook.

I make it until eight, after Pearl is in bed and I'm starting a load for its infinite cycle in the washer because I forgot again, and my dad walks up and pats me on the shoulder with one of his warm, heavy hands.

"Why don't you rest, Mavis? I'll finish this. You're gonna run yourself ragged."

And that's when I break.

"Rest? I can't rest!" The words fly out of me in one wild, weary sob, and then I'm crying. Finally crying.

"Hey. Hey now," Dad whispers, his forehead creased in concern, probably because I *never* cry. But it's like now that the floodgates have opened, my body wants to release every last drop I've been holding in for weeks, for longer—immediately. My shoulders shake and I can't catch my breath and my eyes go blurry with a stream of tears.

Dad pulls me close to his chest and doesn't even flinch at the snail trail of snot that smears across his T-shirt. He leads me to the living room couch, most likely to keep the sound of my crying from waking up Pearl, which just makes me cry more. And he lets me, rubbing my back and murmuring words that I can't even make out because all the tears and the snot are spilling out and filling up my ears. It makes me feel like a kid again—five-year-old Mavis with a deep splinter from that old bench in Brady Park, or twelve-year-old Mavis who wasn't invited to Kathy Donnovan's boy-girl party—when the only thing that could make me feel better was one of these good, long hugs from my dad. If only it were so easy now.

Still, I cry and cry, until it feels like I've emptied my entire self out and my blubbering has slowed to hiccups and sniffles. And that's when he finally pulls away and fixes me with that gentle, searching look I've always sworn could see right into my brain.

"What's going on, Mavis?"

"I just keep screwing up. Everywhere! With work and my friends and this stupid PTA stuff . . . and—and mostly with Pearl. I'm so worried I'm not making the right decisions for Pearl."

And I thought I was all done, but another round of tears begins to roll down my face. Dad reaches forward to wipe them away.

"I think you're being too hard on yourself here," he says, and then shakes his head. "Which, don't get me wrong, I get. I'm like that, too. But not making the right decisions? Well, that just sounds like parenting to me."

"Bad parenting!" But it comes out more like "Ba-*sniffle*-d par-*sob*-rent-*sniffle*-ting!"

But he's already waving his finger, so he must have understood. "No. Uh-uh. *Normal* parenting. Because none of us know what's right. We just make the best decisions we can in the moment with the information we have and adjust when we *do* screw up. Because that's inevitable and *okay* as long as we keep showing up." He puts his hand on my shoulder and looks at me, his eyes wide and imploring. "And you do, Maves. You show up for that girl every day. You give her your all—don't try and convince yourself different."

"But I don't! I haven't been!" If only he knew what I've been so distracted with, how much I've truly dropped the ball. "She was being bullied at school. Another little girl was sending her mean messages on their laptops. I found out Saturday—from *Jasmine*! I didn't even see it on my own. That's how much I've been screwing up."

His eyebrows pinch together, and I can feel the worry for Pearl. But he keeps his tone steady. "Okay, and once you found out, what did you do?"

"Well, I had a meeting with the school this morning, and we came up with a plan to fix things—"

"So, two days after you found out, you did what was best for Pearl?" He gives me the *I told you so* look I know so well—because it looks just like mine.

"You need to give yourself grace," he says. "I screwed up all the time. I let you watch *Law & Order* in elementary school and probably scarred you for life. I had your hair looking so crazy, even with my best efforts, that Ms. Joyce just showed up one day saying she was gonna give me lessons. And I didn't know how to handle your feelings at all. I remember once you came home crying about some girl's party in middle school, and I called that mom up the next day, to explain the consequences of her daughter's behavior, you know. But once she answered, I got so tongue-tied, I just said, 'Your daughter is a jerk' and hung up."

"Dad! You didn't!"

"I did. She star-sixty-nined me and everything, and I had to answer and pretend we were a pizza place, to get her off my trail." He closes his eyes, laughing at himself, and I feel a smile that felt impossible moments ago breaking through. "And see," he continues. "I'm scared to even ask this, but what did you think about me? Was I a bad dad?"

I'm already answering before he finishes the question. "Of course you weren't! You were the best—*are* the best."

"And you are a wonderful mom, Mavis." He says it like it's fact, like there's not even a possibility for debate. "That girl feels loved, she has consistency and structure . . . She has a soft place to land. You are creating a beautiful life for her. For both of you."

My eyes burn and then fill up with a new wave of tears, but this time they're because I'm overcome with a different emotion, and I let them come. Because maybe it's true. I'm making the best decisions I can in the moment, for Pearl's and my future. I'm keeping us safe. I'm a good mom.

"Hey, and whatever you do," Dad adds, already smirking at his own joke. "You're better than these ladies on *The Mommy Murders*." He lets out a long whistle. "And I haven't even told you about season two."

I laugh and wipe my slimy, swollen face on my shirtsleeve, which is gross but necessary. "I never asked you. How was the live taping you went to?"

"Oh, real good. I got my T-shirt signed." He points down to the T-shirt he's currently wearing, also christened by my snot and tears, and I wince. "It's all right, it's all right. *And* I got my question answered during the Q and A session. Almost didn't make it up there, but Bert waved his hands around and was hollering all loud—got the attention of the woman with the Post-its."

I laugh again thinking of Bert, a mild-mannered tax attorney, making such a scene.

"What did you ask?"

"I asked what recording equipment they started with, because I've been looking and it's real expensive—"

"Oh my god, Dad! Are you going to start a podcast?"

"Well, me and Bert were talking about it. I think people would really dig a *Law & Order* recap podcast." I don't have the heart to tell him that there are probably already a million. Plus, those aren't hosted by Dad and Bert. "I just want to keep enjoying this retirement. I know your dad may be getting old." He stretches out his right leg, letting his knee pop for effect. "But this old man's still got a lot of life left!"

"I know, Dad. And I want you to enjoy it." My voice sounds wobbly, and if the tightness of my throat is any indication, some more crying is about to go down. (God, is this just my life now?) But I swallow and take a deep breath, trying to will my face to look more collected than I feel. "I was actually thinking of looking for something other than Project Window, maybe something with higher pay . . . outside of the nonprofit space. So me and Pearl can maybe . . . move out."

A new job with higher pay—and, if I can finally figure this out, a split of some significant reward money.

Dad wrinkles his nose and curls his lip up. "Now why would you go and do that?"

"So . . . you can have your privacy. Your own space, you know? So you can really enjoy your retirement without us here cramping your style."

"Well, first of all—no one's cramping my style." He mimes

slicking his hair back with both hands and smiles at me. "But also, I didn't ask for all that. I like having you both here. I like seeing my granddaughter grow up. It would be too quiet without you."

As if on cue, Polly, who was fast asleep on the love seat, jolts up and starts barking loudly. My body tenses at the sound because she rarely barks, perfectly content to creep up behind us without warning and let the mail lady pass without any fanfare. Her head twists around, focusing on nothing in particular.

Dad points to her and arches an eyebrow. "Also, who would train that dog? You'd let her get away with too much."

I roll my eyes and lean my head on his shoulder. "I love you, Dad."

"I love you, too, Maves."

A heavy knock at the door breaks through Polly's barking, interrupting our little father-daughter bonding moment. So I guess Polly really was making all this noise for a reason. But who would be here this late? I feel a twist of panic in my belly, remembering the last time Polly was barking like this . . .

Dad gets up. "Make sure you check the peep—" I start, but he's already swinging the door open wide like he *hasn't* watched every single episode of *Law & Order* that's ever aired.

"Ms. Joyce!" he says with a smile, but quickly his brow furrows. "Are you all right?"

Ms. Joyce doesn't wait to be invited in. She rushes into the entryway, past my dad, talking fast. "Sorry to bother you so late, but I have something really troubling to share. *Disturbing!*" She plops down next to me and adjusts the blue geometric-printed scarf on her head. It matches her robe. "But you know how it is, I can't go to the police," she continues, her voice getting more frenzied with each word. "You know they're not on our side!"

I clutch her arm, my heartbeat speeding up. "Ms. Joyce, what is it?"

"What happened?" Dad asks, sitting down on her other side.

She lets out a long, heavy sigh and pats her chest, like she's trying to slow her own heart down. "It's—it's—"

"What?" I look around for my phone, ready to call for help, but it's still in the kitchen.

"It's that woman next door. Mavis's little friend—"

Oh.

"Mackenzie Skinner?" my dad asks, still worried. "Is *she* all right?"

"She's not my little friend," I clarify.

"Hmmm." Ms. Joyce gives me a look to let me know what she thinks about that. "Anyway, she's spying on me. I realized tonight."

"Spying on you?" I ask. Dad's face is all twisted—he's clearly trying to catch up.

"Yes," Ms. Joyce says, letting out another belabored sigh. "She set up this camera on her door. I saw the light when I was taking out my cans just now. And then, when I walked around, I saw more of them! A camera on the side of her house, by her trash cans, and one on the back, too!"

"How did you see the cameras on the back of her house?" I ask.

"I think those little doorbell cameras are a pretty normal thing, aren't they, Joyce?" Dad chimes in.

She chooses to hear only Dad, though. "Normal for *who*? You're telling me you got a camera?"

It's clear she already knows the answer to that second question, but Dad still shakes his head in response.

"They are getting more common, especially for all these new people moving in," I say, with a shrug. My heart rate has slowed down, and now I'm just holding in a laugh because I know Ms. Joyce won't hesitate to swat me across the knee. "They want to see what's going on around their investment properties, you know? They have a little app where they share the videos for the whole neighborhood."

As soon as the Realtor sign gets taken down, it's like clockwork. Brass address numbers go up next to the door, along with some new landscaping, heavy on succulents—and then the Ring camera. Jasmine showed me the app and all the foolish drama that blows up on there. After the Knoll Elementary Parents Facebook group, it's her next favorite source of entertainment. People complaining about stolen packages and catalytic converters, people complaining about suspicious activity (usually someone with a little melanin walking by)—even people complaining about the kids yelling on the playground too loudly. I remember laughing about that one with Jasmine, because, like, what did they expect—teachers to tell the kids to play quieter, so they don't disrupt *The View*?

I feel a pang in my chest at the thought of Jasmine. I miss my friend. I know I need to fix things between us. She'd love to hear about Ms. Joyce's newest complaint that those doorbell cameras are everywhere . . .

Those doorbell cameras are everywhere.

Could there be one on a house facing the school? The *school* cameras went down, but did anyone think to check for those?

I need to be done with this. So I can move on and focus on being the best mom I can be to Pearl.

But in order to be done with this for good, Jack and I need evidence that Trisha was there that night. *Real* evidence, other than just my word, that we can pass on to Mrs. Smith, and maybe the authorities. And looking around for Ring cameras sure beats having to go digging in Trisha's yard.

Could it really be that easy?

"Now what is this face?" Ms. Joyce's honey voice knocks me out of my thoughts, and when I look up, she has me locked in her assessing stare. "Looking like the cat that got the cream."

"I just—I need to go text a friend," I say, standing up.

"Hmmm."

"Not Mackenzie Skinner!"

"I didn't say nothing, but it suuuuure is interesting how your mind went there. Hmmm."

WHEN JACK AND I WALK UP TO THE SPANISH-STYLE BUNGA-low directly across from the school the next afternoon and see the residents sitting outside, I almost turn right back around.

These are not new residents of Beachwood, harbingers of the Erewhon apocalypse. No, these people have *been* here. Sitting in two orange rocking chairs on the front porch is a couple. One woman has a wispy cloud of white hair and pastel-pink glasses. She's wearing a floral-printed button-down with matching lavender capris. The other woman has a long gray braid over the shoulder of her Los Angeles Clippers T-shirt and a tall, twiggy frame. As we walk up their path, I notice a book of crossword puzzles in enlarged print on the table between them, which they're both squinting at, Ticonderogas in hand.

So, yeah, definitely not the brass-address-number, succulent-garden, doorbell-camera type.

But then the sunlight hits at just the right angle, and there's a glint next to their big wooden door. It's a Ring doorbell, al-ready with a festive faceplate for Halloween, even though it's still September.

I nudge Jack with my elbow, and his eyes widen with excitement. He brushes my wrist with his fingers, guiding me along after him. This could be it.

The women look up when we reach their front steps, and Jack starts talking immediately. "Good afternoon, ma'ams. We are, um, doing some research into doorbell cameras in the area and assessing . . . how well they function. So we were wondering—if you consent to it, of course—if we could take a look at footage on yours. Specifically from two weeks ago."

The woman with the glasses smiles wearily, and the Clippers fan narrows her eyes in suspicion. And I don't blame them. Maybe we shoulda brought Derek.

"I'm sorry, but we don't want to buy anything, dears."

"And we have a 'No Solicitors' sign down there on the gate that you just walked past."

Okay, I guess this is gonna be up to me. Should I use the mentor angle again? Yeah, because that was *so* successful last time . . .

No. It's time to accept that we're just not good at this whole undercover-investigating thing. It *could* backfire, but I'm thinking honesty is the best policy here.

"Hi, sorry, we're not selling anything, I promise." I show them my empty hands as proof. "My name is Mavis Miller, and this is my, uh, friend, Jack Cohen. He's the school psychologist over at Knoll." I point to the school across the street, and the woman with the glasses brightens, her guardedness melting away.

"Oh, such a special school, isn't it?" she coos. "Our grandson, Calvin, went there. He's very talented, very bright. Won the science fair in fifth grade, and now he's an engineer on computers, isn't that something? Do they still have the science fair?" She doesn't wait for us to answer, just keeps talking. "And oh, you all have been through it lately, haven't you? With your poor principal missing! Has anyone figured out what happened? I'm Edith, and this is my wife, Bonnie, by the way."

Bonnie nods at us but doesn't say anything, clearly a woman of few words. Which, I guess she has to be when Edith has so many of them.

"It's nice to meet you both, and actually, that's why we're here," I say. "We're looking into the disappearance, and we were hopeful that you might allow us to look at your Ring footage from that night—the last time he was seen."

"Did anyone ask you to do that?" Bonnie asks. So she has some words then . . . inconvenient ones. Luckily Edith cheerfully jumps right back in, undeterred by that, okay, *pretty* rational question.

"Yes, our grandson, Calvin, got that for us! The computer engineer," she says, holding her arms out toward the jack-o'-lantern-covered Ring like she's Vanna White. "He said it would keep our house secure, but we don't have to worry much about all that around here. So I mostly use it to watch the squirrels. Oh, they're such a hoot!" She slaps her knee to accentuate her point. "Calvin even got me the premium account so I could save the videos and send them to the family. There's a lighter one with a really thick coat and white spots on her right side. I call her Trixie—and she must love the camera, because she's always out here doing little flips and tricks. Hence the name! With the premium account, I can send the videos of Trixie to the whole family!"

I'm momentarily at a loss for words myself at the introduction of Trixie, but thankfully Jack is less stunned by the fact that this lady is out here naming squirrels and swoops in as the closer.

"So, could we see some of those videos then? From Tuesday two weeks ago?"

Bonnie starts to grunt in protest, but Edith is already on her feet. "Yes, of course! Come in, dears."

We follow Edith through the cozy, cluttered house, to a massive gray computer monitor, set up on a mahogany desk. It looks like something from another time—I can almost hear the phantom dial-up tone of my youth.

"Here we go," Edith says, pushing a large circular button on the monitor to switch it on. Bonnie stands at a distance with her arms crossed. "Calvin set the application up for me on here because the phone screen is too small for me, you know, to really see the details. And oh! Are you hungry? I just made some cottage cheese cups!" She swishes over to the kitchen counter with surprising speed and presents us with a tray of—from what I can tell—cottage cheese in muffin liners, accented with sliced Maraschino cherries.

"Oh, that's so kind of you, Edith, but I actually just ate."

"Yes, I'm sorry. Me too. Those do look delicious, though," Jack quickly chimes in.

But Edith just keeps standing there, smiling, with her arm outstretched, as if she can't hear us. So Jack slowly reaches forward and takes one of the disgusting-looking snacks, and then another one for good measure.

"You're going to love them!" Edith chirps, instantly reanimated. She puts the tray back and then sits down in front of her computer. "Now, let's see what we can find, dears. Two weeks ago, you said?"

She scrubs back through the footage, which *does* contain quite a bit of squirrel content. And okay, I'll admit, some of it is impressive, even in rewind. Like, I'm pretty sure I just saw Trixie do a cartwheel.

When it's clear that that method is taking a while, she begins to click through days of footage at a time, speeding backward, until finally she's on that Tuesday night. Then she lets the short captured videos, triggered by movement, play out moment by moment. We watch as parents enter the PTA meeting in the fading evening light and then leave the meeting when the sky has darkened. Corinne is first out of the front gates, in her lavender sweats and green Crocs, because she left early, and there I am shortly after, speed walking away after what I overheard in the bathroom. A big crowd leaves later—including Trisha, I notice. So, she *did* leave with all the other parents . . . but then she came back?

There's a man in a baseball hat walking his golden retriever, and a teenage couple holding hands as they strut in step, and then . . .

"There! Right there!"

Principal Smith comes out of the front office, checks to make sure the gate is locked, and then quickly walks down the front path, turning right down the sidewalk and out of view.

"Can you play that again?" Jack asks.

"Sure, dear."

This time I study him more carefully. He's wearing that same dorky outfit I saw him in at the meeting—a polo tucked into jeans, with brown tasseled loafers. And he doesn't seem bothered in any way. He's not running and doesn't appear to be in danger. Actually, he looks . . . excited, even? There's a smile spreading across his face, and his eyes are alight—you can tell, even from the grainy video.

"And there you go, just like we showed the other lady," Bonnie says from her spot in the corner of the room.

"Wait." My brain rushes to catch up. "What other lady?"

I raise my eyebrows at Jack, who looks just as confused as me.

Edith stands up. "You know, the other lady. Aren't you all working together? The one with the blond hair, dyed I think, and the puffy lips—" She sticks her own out in a duck-lip pout to demonstrate. "And the honkers out to here!" She juts out her chest, completing a visual I wish I'd never seen. But I know who she's talking about.

"That's Mrs. Smith. His wife."

"Yes, nice lady. *She* ate the cottage cheese cups." Edith flicks her eyes at me. "She came last week and asked if she could watch the footage. You all really should get yourselves organized, you know, with a spreadsheet or something. Calvin taught me how to use the Excel."

My stomach sinks. Here I thought we may have a promising new lead, a chance to break this thing open, but now I just feel stupid. We're behind. We have nothing valuable to offer Mrs. Smith . . . nothing that will get us any reward money.

"Well, thank you so much, Edith and Bonnie," Jack says. At least he has the composure to be polite when accepting our failure. "These are really delicious. I'll have to get the recipe from you."

"They're surprisingly easy to make." Edith beams at him, standing up from the desk.

Except . . . "Wait!" Three pairs of eyes turn my way. Bonnie looks like she regrets letting these possibly deranged strangers into her house. "What was the time stamp on that video?"

I don't wait for the answer. I sit down in Edith's black plastic computer chair and find it myself: 8:57 p.m. Principal Smith walked out of the school at 8:57 p.m.

That was before I took Polly out for a walk. Before I saw Trisha.

My body feels electric as the adrenaline rushes through me.

"Can I fast-forward a little—" But I'm already clicking, already moving the video to where I know it needs to be. I can't remember the exact time I was out there with Polly, but it had to be later. I did all of my mom second shift, dishes and laundry and packing lunch, before I went out the door again. It was late—that's why Ms. Joyce gave me the judgy eyes and the "Hmmm."

And sure enough, a van pulls up to the front of the school at 10:06 p.m., in perfect view of Edith and Bonnie's Ring camera. Its lights shut off, and Trisha springs from the driver's side. In her left hand she's clutching a loosely filled black trash bag, and there's the shadow of more under her other arm. She walks confidently, as if she already knows the school's cameras are down . . . because she took care of them herself when she was here earlier.

"Oh, the other lady definitely didn't watch this, dear. *Who* is that? She looks angry."

I ignore Edith's question and click forward some more. I need to get to the moment I saw. I need to prove to myself that it actually happened.

Jack's face is close to mine, and I can feel his sharp intake of breath when we both see Trisha again on the screen, now sporting yellow rubber gloves and blue mesh booties over her shoes. She slips through the front gate, locking it behind her and wiping it with a cloth that she shoves into one of the bags. After retying it, she starts to lug the three lumpy bags out, grimacing with the effort. My skin pricks with panic all over again, as if I'm right back there with Polly, hidden behind the bougainvillea bush around the corner.

"What is that woman doing?" Even Bonnie is intrigued now.

I lean in closer, my nose nearly touching the screen. I don't want to miss any detail.

There's that same sound of clattering plastic I heard that night, faintly picked up on the Ring's microphone. I see Trisha cursing and angrily picking up the cleaning supplies, shoving them into one of the bags. And then she freezes. That *must* be when Polly starts howling. If I listen closely, I can hear it, and I remember again how I felt in that moment, desperate to get away, even before I knew the danger I was actually in.

Trisha leaves her bags behind and runs around the side of the school to look. I can see only the back of her head from this angle, so I can't know for sure if she spotted me. But her escalating threats since that night make me almost certain that she did.

She looks even more pissed when she comes back. She grabs the bags and starts dragging again, and I'm watching Trisha's face so closely that I see it there first—*something is wrong*. Then I notice the bag at her feet. It's ripped open, and its contents are spread across the sidewalk.

"Is that . . . what I think it is?" I ask, my brain rushing to catch up.

"Yes, it is," Jack confirms.

Edith gasps. "Oh my god."

Knoll Elementary Parents Facebook Group

Leslie Banner

I thought the next PTA meeting wasn't until next month, but this calendar invite says tonight?

Trisha Holbrook

It is next month. And the schedule is available on our website if you're ever worried about being a bother! ☺

Leslie Banner

Oh wait, this invite says for parents in the PTA, not a PTA meeting. So, is this something different? Sorry, I'm new here, so I'm still learning about all the meetings! You guys sure do hold a lot of them, haha!

Trisha Holbrook

What are you talking about? There is no meeting tonight. What did the invite say? Who was it from?

Charlie Lee

I got it too! The email address is "ThetruthaboutTrisha" . . . ? Are you playing a joke on us, mama? Lol

Ruth Gentry

Fake PTA meetings are no laughing matter, Charlie. Clearly someone is bullying Trisha. We need to investigate this immediately.

Florence Michaelson

Is anyone else worried about how this hacker got our personal email addresses? That information should be confidential??

Trisha Holbrook

This is unauthorized! The auditorium is NOT available! PLEASE FORWARD ME THIS EMAIL AND THEN DELETE.

Della Lively

The email says it's being held in the library . . .

EIGHTEEN

I'M ABOUT TO HOST MY FIRST PTA MEETING, AND I AM freaking out.

Or, I'm sorry, *meeting for parents who are in the PTA.* Dyvia insisted we word it that way. Even after everything Jack and I told her, the video footage we shared—she *still* didn't want to break any of the PTA bylaws. I think we left bylaw territory a long-ass time ago, but Dyvia is the one who had access to the email addresses.

Whatever this meeting is called, I feel like I'm going to throw up.

"Did you check to make sure the projector is set up?" Dyvia asks, pacing back and forth across Jack's office.

"Yes," Jack confirms from the leather chair behind his desk. "Well, I went in there to check, at least, and Mrs. Nelson shooed me away. She's very particular about her projector settings."

As soon as we filled her in on what we discovered, Mrs. Nelson was eager to help, too, and offered the library as a venue. Trisha would have wrapped chains around all of the auditorium's door handles if we even attempted to hold this meeting there—she probably did anyway, just as a precaution.

"And do we have a backup of the video? In case she cuts the school's internet?"

I raise an eyebrow at Dyvia, but she raises one right back. "She did it during the last election, when Samantha Collier tried to run against her for PTA president—and Samantha had a chance. People liked her maybe even more than they feared Trisha. But we had to switch to paper ballots at the last minute, and Trisha won in a landslide. No one heard from Samantha again."

A shock of cold hits me in the chest. My eyes widen.

"Because she moved to Temecula," Dyvia clarifies. "But the stakes are even higher tonight."

Jack pulls a flash drive from his desk drawer. "I've got it here. Did you contact Debra at Beachwood Council PTA?"

Dyvia nods. "Of course. And you called the school board president?"

"I did." Jack sighs and bites his bottom lip. "Now, is he actually going to come? I don't know. But I tried to communicate how important this is."

"She's friends with him, you know," I say. I remember the picture of the two of them posing together in her office, and another wave of nausea hits. "Do you think this is the right thing to do?"

"Yes," Dyvia says. "People need to know who she really is."

I think back to when Jack and I showed Dyvia the Ring video last night, and, after the initial shock, the anger that took over her face. It's still burning there now, along with complete certainty and determination. I wish I could bottle up some of that confidence and drink it like medicine. Or maybe try to talk her into doing this instead of me again and see if she cracks this time. Because all I feel right now is absolute terror. That, somehow, Trisha will spin this. That she'll bury it and make everyone forget. Which you wouldn't think would be possible, considering what she's done and the undeniable proof that we have, but . . . that lady is capable of anything. That's very clear now.

But that's why Dyvia insisted we had to do it like this, in front of everyone. And it *had* to be me, the closest thing we have to an eyewitness. (She also very kindly didn't point out that this would have been cleared up a long time ago if I had just listened to her.)

I don't know how convincing I'm about to be, though, if I start straight hyperventilating at the sight of our culprit.

"Breathe. It's going to be okay." Dyvia moves in close to me, patting a soothing rhythm on my back.

I follow directions, leaning into her touch. "I don't know how you can be so nice to me," I croak out between big gulps of air. "When I was such an asshole to you."

She smiles at me slyly. "Well, you were busy."

"I'm so sorry, Dyvia! I can't say it enough."

"You've said it plenty," she says, nodding with finality. "And now, we're going to make everything right."

"We are," I say firmly. "Here *and* with our DEI committee. This has all made it so clear how much work there is to do at Knoll. And I promise I'm going to help you do that work. Our kids deserve it."

"I *guess* you can be my cochair," she mutters with a small laugh, and I almost join in. But the door to Jack's office swings open, and I swear my hair grazes the ceiling from jumping so high. It's not Trisha coming to take care of me like the contents of those trash bags, though. No, it's Corinne. She's breathing just as heavily as I am, like she's been running. She quickly closes the distance between us and clutches my arm.

"What is happening? I just saw the email because I never read my email, but—what—did you figure it out? Did Trisha . . ." Her eyes flash, full of meaning. "You know."

"Yes. Oh, wait, no . . . no! Well, yes, but not—"

"Mavis, she's here," Dyvia interrupts, her tone urgent. "I just saw her storming down the hallway. She's going to take over if you don't do this right now."

I can think of a lot more things I'd rather do in this moment. Get my annual Pap smear. Do my taxes. Clean slime out of a rug. Listen to that song about sharks on repeat for the rest of my life . . .

"Hey." I'm not sure how long I'm standing there contemplating fleeing, but all of a sudden Jack is right there next to me instead of Dyvia and Corinne, his voice a warm whisper in my ear, just for me. "We're only here because of you—because you saw what no one else could see. You've got this, Benson."

He threads his fingers through mine and brushes his lips against my cheek. His rough stubble stings my skin and makes my belly ache and tug. And I don't know if it's that or the knowledge of what I'm about to do, but I feel like my head is full of helium as I make my way out the door and down the hallway. I don't walk, I float out to my place at the front of the library.

The room is packed. Parents are perched in the little-kid chairs, pressed against the rainbow of spines, filling up every inch of available space. I see faces I know—Ruth's pinched scowl and Angela's barely concealed delight at the incoming gossip—but mostly faces I don't, dozens, and I find myself searching them all, looking for someone in particular. But my chest gets tight as it hits me. Jasmine's not here. It's my fault. I should have invited her, should have mended this rift between us already, but I didn't.

It's fine. This is going to be fine. All these other people are here, and soon they're going to know what I know. All of this will finally be over—or at least my part in it will be.

I scan the room for the comfort of Jack. Can he hold my hand while I'm up here? Or, you know, maybe we can just run away from here altogether and explore what comes next if something as chaste as a cheek kiss already does all that to my body.

But my searching eyes land on Trisha, right there in the front row. She's wearing a navy bouclé jacket with sharp shoulders and big gold buttons over a white shift dress, as if she's running for office. She's perched at the edge of her tiny plastic chair with perfect posture, her head held high and her hands crossed in her lap. Her annoyed expression and her rapidly tapping foot almost make it seem like she has somewhere better to be—that I'm wasting her time. But her blue eyes burn bright when they lock with mine, and a cascade of wrinkles appears across her forehead. She narrows her eyes at me, an unsettling smile finding her lips. And I think it's supposed to be a warning, but it feels more like a challenge. A rush of resolve falls over me, settling my nerves. Trisha is not going to win. I won't let her.

Dyvia places a microphone in my hand and then nods. It's time.

"Thank you all for coming tonight," I say. I sound steady and clear. I sound like someone you should believe. "I know how hard it can be to make it to one of these meetings on a school night. *I* hate going to them myself." There's a gasp in the front row, and my eyes find Ruth, covering her mouth in shock like *that* was the big reveal. Well, hold on to your frankincense, Ruthie. "But it was urgent that we meet tonight. Because I have irrefutable evidence that our PTA president, Trisha Holbrook, has committed a crime."

This time, it's more than just Ruth gasping—though she's doing that, too, along with reeling her head back so fast that her little plastic chair topples over. Next to her, Felicia's mouth drops open, and Angela looks like she might pass out from pure giddiness as she takes out her phone to record the scene. Trisha's sharp voice cuts straight through the buzz of confusion and chaos.

"This is ridiculous!" She stands up, pointing at me with a shaky finger, and then spins it around the room. "Come on, you all know this is ridiculous, right? I mean, do any of you even know *her*?" Her fiery glare turns back to me. "You have a lot of nerve, Mavis, after everything I've done for you. You're going to regret—"

"I have a video!" I shout, cutting her off. And I hope Angela got footage of that news creeping across Trisha's face—the twist of her lips, the color draining from her cheeks, and her eyes bugged out with a mountain range of ridges above them. Because I want to watch it every day for the rest of my life.

"This video was taken two weeks ago," I continue. "After the PTA meeting, Trisha returned to the school—"

"I did not!" She stomps her foot like a toddler.

"*She returned to the school* and she did something . . . well, truly evil."

"Now, really, is anyone going to—"

"What I'm about to show you is troubling, but I think it's important that everyone sees this. And I hope once you see who Trisha *truly* is and what she's capable of that you'll join me in calling for her immediate removal as PTA president."

I think she should face criminal charges, too—*obviously*. But the only authority we have in the room is Debra from Beach-wood Council PTA, who Dyvia is sitting next to and enthusi-astically gesturing her head toward, so that'll have to do for now.

I nod at Mrs. Nelson, who is standing in a front corner of the room, next to a display of Rick Riordan books. She nods back and turns off the light. I push play on the computer and watch as the video of what really happened that night is projected for everyone to see.

My pulse speeds up as Trisha's minivan pulls up to the curb in front of the school in the dark video, as if I hadn't already watched this in Edith and Bonnie's house yesterday—and on constant repeat since then. To make sure I was getting this right, without a doubt, and that there was no way for her to explain it away.

"Sorry it's a little grainy, but this was taken by the Ring camera across the street from the school." I glance at Trisha, who is still standing up, making everyone behind her lean to the side. Her eyes flash at me. "Because *something* happened to the school's security cameras, this is all the footage we have. I think we can all still tell who that is, though."

She doesn't bother to deny it.

I click on the screen, scrubbing forward to the moment Trisha reappears outside of the school, carrying her three trash bags. It's dark, but her face is unmistakable. I scan the expressions of the people in the room: furrowed brows, sucked-in lips, and frowns. I wonder if their minds have already jumped to the same alarming conclusion as I did, hiding in the bushes. I wonder if they're noticing the sharp angles that jut out from the bags—a detail I missed that night when my only instinct was to run—and matching those angles to their own, doing the morbid math.

A dad in a slim gray suit jumps in his seat at the faint sound of the cleaning bottles clattering to the ground. In front of him, Felicia whispers something in Ruth's ear.

"Maybe Gloria took the night off," Ruth snaps back.

And now here's the moment. Trisha in the video has run around the corner and seen me taking off with Polly. I half expected present Trisha to run right on out of here, too, but no—she's standing unnaturally still in the middle of the front row, ready to face what's coming.

In the video she starts dragging the bags again, and my whole body tenses in anticipation. One pull and then another and—the bag tears open.

Its contents spill out across the concrete.

Books.

Dozens of books.

Books that were cataloged in the color-coded spreadsheet Dyvia emailed me two weeks ago.

Trisha gathers what she can back into the trash bag and picks up the rest in small batches, furiously flinging them into the trunk of her minivan. When they're all loaded, she pushes a button, and the door slowly clicks shut. Then she runs to the driver's side and peels off into the night.

I turn off the video with a flick of my hand that even I can admit is slightly dramatic, and as the lights turn back on, I wait for the outrage to ensue. Lord, after that clear evidence, maybe I can just step aside—the parents will take over and run her out of town with pitchforks all on their own.

But instead of the anger I was expecting, I'm met with blank faces and slow-blinking eyes. Instead of pissed off . . . they just look confused. Trisha sits down and crosses her arms, her face twisted into a sickeningly smug smile.

A woman in the back wearing a Knoll Fun Run sweatshirt raises her hand. "I don't get it. You brought us all here . . . just for . . . *books?*"

"Books are the very foundation of our school!" Mrs. Nelson yells out. "Today's readers are tomorrow's leaders!" She pumps her fist in the air with a wild look in her eyes that shows she's a great librarian, yeah, but, uh . . . probably isn't helping our case here. And oh god, do I look like that, too? Standing up here, presenting this video like it's a smoking gun? I mean, I thought it was . . .

Ruth lets out a high laugh that echoes across the silent room. "God, Mavis, the way you were acting, I would have thought there were body parts in the bag or something!"

Which, okay, *is* what I initially thought. But this is all pretty bad, too. Yeah, it's not murder, but Trisha *still* committed a crime. She still deserves to face consequences . . .

And. Oh no. I may have misjudged this.

I'm suddenly in one of my stress dreams, the kind that makes me grind my teeth and load up on magnesium and melatonin. But instead of realizing I have to take a final for a class I didn't even realize I was enrolled in or rushing to get Pearl to school before the late bell, I am standing in front of a group of parents who think I'm crazy. Or immature. Or stupid. Probably all three. And there's no waking up from this.

I want to pinch myself so hard I leave a mark. I want to run away and never come back. But as my head starts swiveling, checking for the nearest exit, my eyes land on Jack. His gaze is so intense that it feels tangible, like a solid tether between him and me, or an embrace. He nods at me reassuringly and then gives me one of his sunburst smiles.

I can fix this. I just need to help them understand. I need to connect the dots, just like Dyvia helped Jack and me to do last night.

"These aren't just any *books*," I explain. My voice shakes, but I keep going. "Dyvia Mehta, one of the longtime board members of our PTA, has been working hard for months to get more diverse books for our school's library—books that represent all of Knoll's students." She started the process after she heard about my complaints at the book fair last school year—and that's why she was so excited to work with me on this DEI committee. Which I would have known if I ever truly listened to her instead of just writing her off. "Dyvia got a major grant to purchase hundreds of books. Books with kids of color and kids with disabilities. Books that featured LGBTQ kids and families. Books our school *really* needed. But after the shipment arrived here, they went missing. And no one would help her find them or replace them because we've all been so preoccupied with Principal Smith's disappearance—myself included." I find Dyvia again in the crowd and flash her another apologetic smile. "It wasn't until I saw this video and finally listened to Dyvia that I realized what happened. Trisha stole these books that belonged to the school, and tried to cover it up by cutting the school's security cameras after the PTA meeting and cleaning up any traces she left behind."

I think the Clorox and blue mesh booties and gloves were a little overkill, because no one was about to go dusting for fingerprints for some missing books, but Trisha is nothing if not extra.

"What I'm still trying to figure out is why, though," I say, focusing my gaze on Trisha, who is still just sitting there looking annoyed and inconvenienced. "Why this whole big plot just to steal some library books? Why do these books *for children* threaten you so much?"

"Yeah, what do you have to say for yourself?!" Mrs. Nelson shouts—again, coming in a little too hot, but I appreciate the enthusiasm. That doesn't seem to be the consensus among the room, though. Even after everything I just shared, most of the crowd still looks confused . . . or even worse, bored.

And Trisha knows it, too. I can see it in the easy way she stands up and the dismissive giggle she pretends to try to control as she comfortably takes her spot at the front of the room. She beams a benevolent smile out to the audience, as if she called the meeting in the first place.

"See, I told you this was ridiculous," she says, with a commiserating sigh. "I'm just so sorry, everyone, that your time was wasted like this. I can assure you there is no scandal here, no nefarious intentions. All I did was get rid of some . . . *inappropriate* titles that were purchased for our school by a parent that wanted to do good." She sends a placating look in Dyvia's direction. "But was, unfortunately, just a little misguided. I'm not sure why it called for this disruptive and, quite frankly, *slanderous* response."

In the front row, Felicia raises her hand but starts talking before she's called on. "Did Dyvia pay for them herself? You can just pay her back, and then this is all settled, right?"

"No, she got a grant." Trisha's forehead wrinkles, but her smile remains. "But it was really just a small amount—"

"Uh-uh!" Dyvia cuts her off. "It was for five thousand dollars."

Someone in the crowd whistles, and Corinne, bless her, shouts out, "I don't know about y'all, but five thousand dollars definitely isn't a small amount to me!"

There's a slight grumbling, but Trisha continues before it can take hold. "Yes, but it wasn't a good *use* of the money. Those kinds of books just don't belong here in our beloved Knoll library, because they lack educational value—"

The dad in the slim suit snort-laughs, and Trisha winces. "Educational value? I'm pretty sure those are just ninety percent poop jokes." He points to a graphic novel series about cats that's taking up an entire shelf in the corner. "But who cares? My daughter loves them. And she's reading."

I catch a couple of nods of agreement. Trisha shoots him a look that wouldn't kill but could definitely maim. She clears her throat. "Like I said, though, they were not appropriate. They were pushing a political agenda—"

"What kinds of books *were* they?" Ruth asks. She looks at Dyvia with wide eyes, like she belongs on some list.

"Picture books and novels. For children," Dyvia says, staring right back at her. "They were all recommended by the American Library Association. Some were Newbery and Coretta Scott King award winners."

There are even more nods this time from parents who seem to find this acceptable. And there's something else, too. A visible unease from a few people—the man in the suit is squirming slightly in his seat, and two more moms in the back row exchange uncomfortable glances. Because the more Trisha talks, the more it's clear what she might have found inappropriate about these books.

Maybe . . . maybe I don't have to do anything here. Maybe if I just let Trisha keep going, she'll take herself down.

"What agenda do picture books push, exactly?" Jack asks. His expression is serious, but I can see the spark of mischief in his eyes when they briefly dance my way. We're on the same page here.

"I don't know what their plans are, but not a *good* one, that's for sure." Trisha lets out a sharp exhale and shakes her head. "You should have seen some of these things. They were—were—*CRT*." She spits out the acronym quiet and sharp, like a curse.

My pleasant customer service mask cracks, and I make one of those faces my dad used to insist were going to get stuck that way. "Do you even know what that stands for?"

"Cultural re-re . . . replacement—you know what, it doesn't even matter." She waves her hands like she can wipe the slates of our minds clean. "It's *my* responsibility to do what's best for our kids. So I had to get rid of these books that have no business in our school. All they were going to do was make our kids feel sad and guilty, and hurt their self-esteem. Is *that* what you want?"

A woman in the middle with glossy black hair held back by a pastel-pink headband stands up.

"What kids are 'our kids'?" Her voice is quiet compared to Trisha's increasingly shrill tone, but it commands the room just as easily. "Because from what Mavis and Dyvia have said . . . I think it would help *my* kids' self-esteem to have these books. In fact, now that I think about it, Sophie and Eleanor haven't had many books in their classes with Korean characters. It makes me sad that I *haven't* really thought about it before . . . and even more sad, Trisha, that you would go to such extremes to keep these books from *our* kids."

"Oh, Charlie, that's not—you know what I—I *am* thinking of all of our kids! And I'm almost certain that Mrs. Seller's class read that book about the girl and the paper cranes last year, so let's—let's check on that! We wouldn't want you to spread false information, right?" Seeing Trisha cycle from worry to rage to faux concern in the span of seconds is truly a marvel. Her Botox has clearly given up and ceded her forehead to the wrinkles. "And—and just, look around! We already have plenty of books for the . . . the norm—the kids! I'm sure Mrs. Nelson would love to do her job and help even the pickiest of readers. But the books we have are fine. More than fine—they're wonderful! That's why they've been around for so long. You got a problem with *Charlotte's Web*? You think you're too good for Roald Dahl? Dr. Seuss? I mean, really! At least ALL kids can enjoy them instead of these other . . . specialty books." Her lips stretch farther back into a snarl with each word, and her eyes flicker with hot blue flames. Her perfect polish has rubbed away, revealing something ugly underneath. "We don't need to woke-ify our kids this young! We need to protect them!"

Her words ring out across the room, and I can see the effect as they land on each person, like drops of rain falling from the sky. The man in the suit who was squirming earlier is now holding his hands up in disbelief. The woman Trisha called Charlie stares at Trisha with angry, narrowed eyes. Angela looks like she's about to leap out of her seat, as far away from Trisha as possible, as if the Caucasity is contagious and spreading fast. Even Ruth is sweating.

Trisha glares around wildly, daring anyone to challenge her, and it's Dyvia who stands up.

"I see you now for who you are, Trisha. And I'm just sorry I didn't see it sooner. Before you wasted all of our time." She rolls her eyes and lets out a long sigh. "What I don't understand, though, is why you even let me get the grant, if this was how you felt? I told you every step of the way."

"Well, I couldn't tell you no, could I? Not without it being a big thing, especially here in Beachwood—*snowflake city*!" She laughs as she shakes her head. "I mean, look at all the parents in other states, shouting and making a scene at school board meetings. So undignified! If I told you what I thought, no matter how logical, you'd've had me on MSNBC, too, and that wouldn't be acceptable. No, I needed a more subtle approach."

That's her problem with the parents trying to ban books in other states? Sure, it's okay to be racist. Or homophobic. No big deal, but, oh goodness, don't be undignified about it! Better to protect little Cayden and Anabella from the scary books with kids of color by secretly stealing them from the elementary school library in the middle of the night. Yeah, that makes *perfect* sense.

"I will not stay silent here! I will use my privilege to stand in front of you all and say this is wrong!" Angela shouts, practically quivering with excitement at this opportunity to put her reading of *White Fragility* to good use.

But she's not the only person looking at Trisha with anger

and disgust. The uneasiness in the room has now shifted fully to the outrage I expected from the start. Maybe because they actually feel that way all on their own, or maybe because they read the same books as Angela and know they're supposed to. Regardless, parents are standing up and shaking their heads. Debra from Beachwood Council PTA shoots Trisha a look so venomous that it's clear her days are numbered. And then the shouting starts.

"What gives you the right?!"

Trisha flinches at the first question, like it's a dart landing on her chest.

"Are you going to pay the school back?"

"When are you going to resign?"

"What's wrong with you?!"

She blinks furiously at the audience, as if she can will them back into the adoring crowd she's used to, the one she expects.

"What did you do with them?"

"Did you burn them?"

For some reason, that's the question she chooses to answer.

"No, of course not! God, I'm not a monster! I recycled them."

LATER, AFTER TRISHA TRIED TO FIELD QUESTIONS AND THEN finally stormed out when it was clear it was not going to go her way, and I'm thanked and congratulated and told that I am my ancestors' wildest dreams (one guess who that was from), I walk out Knoll's front gates with Jack, Dyvia, and Corinne.

"Mavis, that was truly a sight to behold." Corinne lets out a low whistle. "A Trisha takedown. Never thought I'd see the day!"

"You *were* an asshole, Mavis." Dyvia smiles at me playfully and then squeezes my shoulder. "But you came through. Thank you."

I jab a finger at Jack. "This guy helped me, too."

He quickly waves that away. "None of this would have happened without you." His hand brushes my lower back, and he looks at me with something like awe.

And I know I should feel good. I know I should be basking in this accomplishment. I know I should be celebrating this win. But . . . I don't feel like I thought I would.

I solved a mystery, yeah, but it was one I didn't even realize was happening. My instincts were right and Trisha *did* commit a crime, but not the big one.

And maybe there isn't even a big one. Maybe Principal Smith really just skipped town to get a break from his wife and mistress. Maybe he had a whole nother mistress he went to go see. There's no evidence that shows otherwise. Because with Trisha out of the equation . . . what's left? No more suspects, no more clues that haven't already been explained away.

So how good were my instincts, really? Because I was convinced that Trisha killed our principal, and I couldn't have been further from the truth. My neck gets hot with shame as I think about just how wrong I really was, how I was wasting my time chasing money that was never going to be mine.

Maybe, subconsciously, I knew that. Maybe I just wanted to be distracted from my messy life by digging into someone else's mess.

But there are no more distractions now. This is over. And I need to accept that and find my way back to normal.

My plate was too full, and look, here's something I can scrape right off it into the trash can. This is *a relief.* And maybe if I keep telling myself that, I'll start to believe it.

Knoll Elementary Parents Facebook Group

Della Lively

Are we going to get a new moderator for this group? Because obviously we can no longer trust the person who has been in charge around here . . .

Angela Hart

I volunteer! I'd love to help make this a safe space, especially for all the BIPOC people at Knoll!!

Ruth Gentry

In these trying times, I think we'll all need help processing our feelings. And that's why I'm happy to offer a special promotion on my emotional wellness oil blend! If you buy neroli and bergamot for full price, you'll get patchouli for 50% off! Wow, what a deal!!

Jasmine Hammonds

Can the first order of business for our new moderators be banning MLMs?

Ruth Gentry

I thought we banned you . . .

Jasmine Hammonds

Leslie Banner

Okay I'm caught up on everything with Trisha and the stolen books, but what does all of this have to do with Principal Smith??

Felicia Barlow

Nothing.

NINETEEN

THE LATE BELL RANG FIVE MINUTES AGO, BUT PEARL AND I are taking our time walking up to Knoll's front gate.

"Mommy, I think I'm gonna open a doggy day care," she says, swinging our joined hands between us.

"When you grow up?"

"No. This weekend."

I smile at her sweet, serious face. "Oh yeah? Where will this doggy day care be located?"

"In my room. And in the backyard when they need to go potty or play outside."

"That might be a little crowded?"

"Well, we can use your room, too, if we have to," she says with a shrug. "And I can teach them how to do tricks, like how I teached Polly. High five and roll over and play dead. Maybe you can even make them those special blueberry muffins."

Even though we're late, I woke up extra early this morning. So there was time to do Pearl's hair just how she wanted it, four braided buns with pink butterfly clips, *and* I baked—*baked!*—blueberry muffins. From a box mix, but *still*—that's way fancier than Cheerios. If I can't do anything else right, at least I can love on my baby and be the best mom I can be.

"They weren't the most delicious for humans, but dogs might eat them," she adds.

Okay, maybe not the *best* mom, but a perfectly adequate one. I laugh and squeeze her hand.

"How much are you going to charge the dog owners?"

"I don't know." She taps her cheek and puckers her lips. "Maybe twenty? Fifty?"

"For the whole day?"

"Per hour." She smiles, showing off her dimple. "And I'll give you some of the money, but only a little bit. Because it was my idea, of course."

"Oh, of course." We reach the main office, and I slide her sparkly rainbow backpack from my shoulder to hers. I brace myself for one of Lilliam's life-crushing looks as I open the door.

"Good morning, Ms. Lilliam!" Pearl chirps cheerfully. She knows exactly how this goes—be cute and kind, and then Lilliam can't be too mad at us, at least not at her.

"Good morning, Pearl," Lilliam says, smiling through a sigh. She turns to me, pulling out her big attendance binder from beneath the front counter. "You're late." But then something happens that makes me worried I actually slept through my alarm and I'm still dreaming now. She smiles.

I look to Pearl to make sure she didn't somehow transform into Polly or melt into a puddle on the ground, but no. This appears to be real life.

"I'm sorry," I squeak out, my normal response.

"Mm-hmm." Lilliam continues to smile and then adds a little conspiratorial wink. I almost fall right over. "I'll let it slide this time."

"Um. Thank you?"

Is this because of last night? What I revealed to everyone about Trisha? I'm scared to make any sudden movements, scared to do anything that'll mess up this moment. But then Lilliam just waves me away and walks over to her desk in the back. "This time, Ms. Miller. Don't expect any special treatment tomorrow, mm-hmm."

I kneel down in front of Pearl, who was watching this all with a wrinkly-nosed grin.

"How are you feeling?" I ask. Everything with SoSo is still so fresh, and my stomach churns with anxiety as I send her in there, knowing I can't control what may happen.

"I feel great, Mommy." She reaches up and pats my cheek. "Have a good day!"

She skips through the doorway to the school, all light and easy, and I hope that she stays that way all day. I hope I can be like that, too. I wave goodbye to Lilliam, who doesn't smile again but at least doesn't outright frown, so it's definitely a step up. When I'm outside the front gate, though, I hear a familiar, tinkling-bell voice that immediately dashes all my hopes for a light and easy morning.

"Do you really have to follow me so close like that? Honestly, I'm not some kind of *criminal*!"

I see her out of the corner of my eye, wearing a royal-blue pantsuit and carrying a big cardboard box. Behind her is a campus security guard, who *is* standing especially close, right behind her elbow. I gotta get out of here. The last thing I need is a run-in with her this morning.

"Yoo-hoo!"

So much for that.

I turn around slowly, my heartbeat thumping in my ears.

"Hi, Trisha."

She stalks over to me, the security guard following behind at a careful distance. "Don't 'Hi, Trisha' me after that little performance last night!" she snaps, eyes flashing. She lets out a long, belabored sigh, like this is all some terrible inconvenience to her. "God, I knew you were onto me, the way you were always creeping around corners and being all nosy. That's why I tried to politely hint that you should back off."

Politely hint or threaten? Somehow I don't think she'd be open to debating semantics right now.

"But you didn't listen, did you? And *blech*, I didn't know you were going to be so dramatic about it," she scoffs. "What a scene you made, and for what? You could have shown *some* tact."

And I don't know if it's just the ridiculousness of the person who stole library books from an elementary school in the middle of the night telling *me* to have some tact, or just, like, the general comedown from the past two weeks. But the words are flying out of my mouth before I can stop myself.

"The reason I was *creeping* around was because I thought you killed Principal Smith!"

Trisha's jaw drops open. "What?!"

"Ma'am." The security guard's eyes are wide as he cautiously steps closer to Trisha. "If you have reason to believe that Mrs. Holbrook—"

"Oh, stay out of this, Eugene!" Trisha shouts, flinging a palm in his direction. "You thought I—I *what*?"

"I thought you killed Principal Smith. Because I saw you here that night. And then the next day, he was gone." It feels so strange to finally say it all out loud, like I'm breaking a spell that's had a hold on me for so long.

"You—you—" And then she's cracking up. She throws her head back in laughter, her dark hair falling back on shaking shoulders. "You thought I killed him! How—what—what would I have done with the body? Chopped it up and thrown it in the—the school dumpster?" she chokes out between manic giggles, wiping tears from her eyes. "Or, no. No! Weighed it down and tossed it into the—the—*ocean!*"

She falls forward, clutching her sides in delight.

"So, just to clarify, you *didn't* do this . . . right, Mrs. Holbrook?" Eugene asks, nervously fingering his walkie-talkie.

"Of course I didn't!" She shoots him a hostile glare, but just as quickly, her pleased smirk is back. "What would even be my motive? I barely know the man!"

"You were . . . you were just so mad about the gifted school, how Principal Smith stopped it from happening." The theory I felt so sure of before quickly deflates when met with her amused smile. "I—I . . . thought whatever you were up to, it had to be related to that."

She laughs again, her eyes wide and wild. "Oh, I'm going to take care of that, too. Don't you worry. Well, as soon as I get this 'banned from school premises' nonsense handled." She curls her fingers into quotation marks and glowers at the security guard. "Principal Reed is on my side."

"You don't think Principal Smith is coming back?"

"Definitely not," she says with finality, but then she sees Eugene's and my concerned faces, and another round of giggles bubbles up.

"Not because I *killed* him. My goodness, can both of you just *relax?*"

Eugene runs his hand over his bald head, which is considerably shinier than when this roller coaster of a conversation started. My nerves are so fried that I'm definitely gonna have to raid the Project Window tea stash again. But I have one more thing I have to know before I can let this go for good.

"There's something I still don't get. Why did you come to me for a DEI committee? Obviously you didn't want that, so why not just . . . ignore the requirement? Or put yourself in charge?"

"Well, because you're—" She stops herself, a single ounce of sense left in her.

"I didn't think you would actually *do* anything," she finally says with a huff. "You barely talk to anyone at the gate. You take off running when I try to even say hello to you. Sure, you *complained*, but complaining's easy." She snorts and shakes her head. "I didn't expect you to go all Harriet the Spy on me."

"You know what . . . we never thought of that one. Does she have a sidekick?" And then I laugh because what else can I do?

"It's time to go, Mrs. Holbrook," Eugene cuts in. "I'm under strict orders from the superintendent. You were only supposed to be given thirty minutes to clean out your office."

"Strict orders from the superintendent," Trisha says in a high-pitched tone that sounds nothing like Eugene, and then explodes into another round of unsettling laughter. "Bob has a lot of nerve, considering what I know about that Memorial Day weekend in Downey. And *you*! You're going to regret this, too, when I have you fired next week, Eugene!"

"Sure, Mrs. Holbrook," he says with a small smile, leading her by the elbow to her minivan.

WHEN I SEE WHO IS NEXT TO MY PRIUS, I TAKE OFF running.

"Hey. Hey!"

In between my car and the white-and-orange sedan labeled *Parking Enforcement* that's pulled up in front of it, a man is hunched forward, already writing down my license plate number.

"This isn't a no-parking zone. I checked!"

He doesn't even bother to turn around. "It's Thursday, ma'am. There's no parking here from eight to noon on Thursdays for street sweeping."

I squint at the sign a couple of houses down, which I didn't even look at, because Pearl was giving me the play-by-play of her dream about llamas, and anyway I knew it was far enough to not be a *school* no-parking zone. But yes. He's right.

"Oh. It's you."

When I look back at the parking enforcement officer, he is narrowing his eyes at me and stroking his big bushy mustache. I know that mustache. Or at least, I had a memorable interaction with its owner.

And from the way he's slowly backing up now, with his palms up in front of him, it seems it was memorable for him, too.

"Listen, I don't want any trouble," he says warily. "I'm just doing my job here."

"Trouble? You're the one who brings *me* trouble. I'm just trying to get my daughter to school in the morning, even though the city has apparently decided to forbid parking on every single block surrounding it." I groan and throw my hands up. "The street sweeper doesn't even come by until, like, nine thirty, because even *they* know that everyone parks here for drop-off."

I look around at the block that's, of course, empty except for my car.

"I swear they do," I mumble.

He's looking around, too, but it's not in the snarky way he did last time. He looks almost . . . nervous?

"Your friend with the anger management issues isn't nearby, is he?"

"Friend with anger management . . . ?" I snort when the realization hits. "Wait. You mean Jack?"

A smile tugs on my lips as I think about that first meeting.

It seems so long ago, Jack swooping in to save me from that parking ticket like a knight in mud-stained armor—mostly because I know him so well now. Even then, he was willing to take a risk for me, willing to do something a little bonkers—just like he did with this whole investigation. The outcome of our sleuthing may be a little disappointing, but at least I still have him and what's blossoming between us.

"Is Jack the Ken-doll-looking guy who likes to go around starting fights?"

"Starting fights!" I try to hold in my laugh of disbelief, but it escapes. "Come on, man. He kicked some mud. The only casualty was my car."

The officer lets out a sharp exhale and shakes his head. "Well, there was that *and* the fight with the other guy that morning. Your buddy was yelling and getting in his face. I thought for sure he was going to punch him—he would have if he didn't see me there. He knew I would be a witness to the assault." The officer strokes his mustache again and then shakes his finger at me. "You know what, that's probably why he went to the extreme with your *well-deserved* ticket. He was trying to send me a message. Guy's definitely got a pattern."

"W-what? That doesn't . . . that doesn't make any sense."

I can't even imagine Jack raising his voice at someone, let alone almost getting into a physical altercation—especially in front of the school.

"Who was this other guy?"

"I don't know who he was, ma'am. Can't you just ask your friend?" My unblinking stare must be answer enough to that question, because he sighs and looks up at the sky. "Okay, he had dark hair, I think? And a mustache . . . yeah, definitely a mustache, but not as full-bodied as mine—though, few are. And . . . oh! I remember he was wearing a blue polo tucked into jeans.

That stuck out to me because I was watching this fashion show on Netflix with the missus the night before and they were talking about the French tuck? Have you heard of that? It's supposed to be more flattering on the ol' gut than tucking your shirt in all the way." He pats his own belly to prove the point, and I almost laugh at his white uniform shirt French tucked into his Dickies because some Netflix fashion expert told him to do so. But the laughter quickly dies in my chest when I realize who he's describing. Principal Smith.

"Are you sure it was that morning?" It can't be. Jack would have mentioned it. Jack would have mentioned *any* argument that he had with Principal Smith . . . or he should have.

"One hundred percent," the officer confirms with a confident nod. "I remember that day well. Most people just accept their tickets and go. They don't think they're above the law, so yeah. It stuck out to me. Which reminds me—" He tears off a sheet from the front of the thick pad in his hands and gives it to me. My ticket.

"Have a good day now, ma'am," he says, waving and shooting me a satisfied smirk as he walks back to his car.

"You too," I mumble. Or at least I think I do. My brain is already spiraling, and it's hard to process anything.

This isn't true. It can't be true. I mean, my parking enforcement nemesis seems to be pretty sure it's true . . . but if it is, that means Jack lied to me. Or intentionally withheld information from me, which is the same thing.

It feels like a knife in the stomach. I've trusted him more than anyone, told him everything. How could he do this? And even more alarming, *why*?

I came to him that Wednesday morning frantic and scared, convinced that Trisha did something to make Principal Smith disappear, and he didn't tell me he got into an argument with the missing person *just the morning before*? It *had* to be for a specific reason, because if it was nothing, why wouldn't he just mention it? Unless . . .

It's too disturbing to even put into words. Like, if I even allow my brain to formulate the sentence, I've turned a corner I can never come back from.

But we still don't know where Principal Smith is. We still don't know if he left on his own, or if someone *did* something to him. Jack is always so calm and collected—at least the Jack I thought I knew. What was he so mad at Principal Smith about? And could they have run into each other again that night? Could it have gone too far?

A chill prickles my skin as I start to see our first meeting in Jack's office with a new lens. I can practically hear Keith Morrison narrating the moment, highlighting my every misstep. Jack was so quick to believe me and that made me feel so good, so seen, but . . . could it all have been a ploy to distract me? Was he laughing on the inside as I went on this wild-goose chase after Trisha? Is that why he encouraged me throughout the investigation, step after step in the wrong direction? Is that why *he* suggested not going to the cops?

No. No, that doesn't fit at all with the Jack I know. He wouldn't hurt anyone. And what we have, it's real. I feel it in his touch, in the way he looks at me. But then why this deception? How can anything between us be *real* if there's that massive red flag, waving from the very beginning?

It doesn't make sense. None of this does.

The only thing I do know for sure: I need to talk to Jack. Soon. And get some fucking answers to my questions.

TWENTY

BUT FIRST I HAVE TO GO TO WORK.

Somehow, our morning team meeting lasts only twenty minutes, and normally that would be a good thing—I can be alone with my thoughts in my little office, getting real work done instead of just talking about doing work. But the last thing I want to do right now is be alone with my thoughts. Because my thoughts are consumed with reanalyzing every interaction I've had with Jack and trying to imagine him hurting someone with those hands that have touched me so gently, and spiraling over my inability to really know anyone.

When he texts midmorning—Can we see each other again this weekend? I'll call Carl to reserve Candy Land—I jump out of my seat and speed over to the combination break room / copy room / storage closet, like I'm running from the decisions I'll have to make very soon.

I'm making a cup of tea (Relaxing Rooibos Dandelion—at least *that* decision was easy) when Rose swings her head into the room, knocking on the doorframe.

"Knock, knock!" she exclaims, as if the actual knocking

wasn't enough. Her blond curls are pulled up into a topknot, and she's wearing a vaguely ethnic printed scarf draped over her blazer. "I heard you might be leaving us soon!"

"What?" I nearly drop my cup of murky-looking tea on the floor.

Rose winks. "Because you're gonna come into some money."

My eyes go wide. "I don't know what you—"

"Oh my god, your face! I'm just messing with you!" She laughs, stepping farther into the room. "Nelson told me you were looking into the disappearance of a principal at your kid's school? And that there was some big reward? My word—it's like something off the TV, isn't it? Now, do you watch—"

"He—he . . . told you that?"

"Yes, he did." Her eyebrows jump slightly at being interrupted, but then she smiles again. "He said you even interviewed him. How fun! Though, next time, maybe don't do that during working hours. We want to set a good example for Nelson, you know! But I told him, I said, 'If anyone is going to solve a mystery in her free time, it's Mavis!'" The disbelief must be clear on my face, because she reaches forward and pats my arm. "It's true! Everything you do, you do it well. And I mean that. Being our little worker bee here at Project Window, being an awesome mom—I don't know how you do it, Mavis! But we're so lucky to have you keeping our ship afloat."

Is it luck on their part—or just stupidity on my own? Because I am their little worker bee, doing every menial task that's asked of me even though I'm qualified for much more, and then smiling graciously to make them feel better when they promote someone over me. I've made it so easy for them over these seven years, all because I'm too scared to find out if this is as good as it gets for me.

"Well, I'm not going to do it anymore," I blurt out, without thinking. And the shocked look on her face makes me want to scoop all the words up and shove them back down my throat.

"Huh?" Rose blinks at me.

"I just mean . . . the mystery. It's over. I solved it."

Her overly lined lips drop open. "Did you get all that money?!"

"No." And that's why I'll be here, making everyone marvel at my ability to do it all, for the foreseeable future. "I solved the wrong mystery."

And I may have a lead for the *right* mystery, but . . . I hope I'm wrong. I'm going to have a lot to reckon with if I'm *not* wrong.

"The wrong mystery!" She laughs again, big and loud, like I told the best joke ever. It's hard not to feel like all of this *is* just a sick joke. "Well, selfishly, I'm happy about that. What would we do without you?"

"I don't know," I say with a sigh, taking a sip of my tea. It tastes disgusting. "Good thing you won't have to find out."

BY THE TIME FIVE O'CLOCK ROLLS AROUND, I KNOW I CAN'T take this for another day—another second. I need to settle this for my own sanity. So I text Corinne to see if Pearl can come over for another playdate. (Dad's out attempting to record his first podcast episode with Bert, and I still haven't patched things up with Jasmine, even though I know I should.) Then I tell Jack that it can't wait until this weekend. I need to see him as soon as possible. The red heart he sends back makes my stomach drop to my toes.

"Thanks again for doing this," I say to Corinne as Pearl runs past me into the now familiar home. "You keep saving me."

"That's what friends are for!" Corinne says, waving it away. "But you better not bat an eye when I pull up in front of your house one day, shove the boys out the sliding door of my minivan, and speed off."

I force out a laugh, but my hands are already getting clammy as I think about the task ahead of me.

"Stay out late! Please! I'll feed her dinner and give her the time of her life until bedtime," Corinne continues. "Lord knows I wish I could be out on the town with a beautiful man, so at least I can facilitate it for you."

She raises her eyebrows suggestively and laughs, but her playful grin drops when I join in a beat too late. "Okay, now, why do I look more excited about this than you?"

She puts her hand on her hip and raises a stern eyebrow. I check behind her, and Pearl is long gone, but I don't want to say too much. Not until I know for sure.

"I found out . . . something," I admit. "Something between Jack and Principal Smith that just—it doesn't make any sense."

Her jaw drops. "You think he was involved?"

"No," I say quickly. "I don't know. I need to talk to him."

She tuts and lets out a long sigh. "Mavis, just—make sure you're not sabotaging your own happiness here. I think we both know very well that Jack wasn't involved in whatever happened to Principal Smith. Are you just . . . looking for *something* to be a problem?"

I want to know that very well. I do. But the nagging thought just won't go away, like a gnat buzzing in my ear: *Why didn't he tell me?* I shrug.

"My advice," she continues. "And you can tell me to shut the hell up if you want to. But my advice: let this go. Wherever Tom Smith went—it doesn't have to be your burden. And as far as Jack goes—that man adores you. It's so clear."

And I wish that was enough. But I know I can't let this go until I have some answers.

"Thank you, Corinne," I say, pulling her into a hug so I don't have to look her in the eye, and thankfully, she squeezes me tight instead of pushing any more.

Jack suggested another dinner at Boards and Brews, which I should have agreed to because, really, it's better to do this in a public place if there's any chance Jack *could* have something to do with Principal Smith's disappearance. But even now, I can't get over my fear of causing a public scene, and I'm pretty sure there's going to be a scene. So I invited Jack over to my house.

When my doorbell rings, though, I'm questioning for the millionth time whether that was a good decision. As I open the door, my eyes catch on Ms. Joyce's curtains flicking. I guess at least I've got her snooping if anything goes sideways. Which it won't . . . I hope.

"Hey."

"Hey."

His smile, like golden sunshine, takes over his face, and he steps over the threshold, pulling me into an easy hug. It feels like falling into a warm bath, and I want to let it wash over me. But I know I shouldn't feel this way. I need to keep my focus.

Polly rushes between us for her own greeting, and as he kneels down to pet her, I notice a manila folder tucked under his arm. I point to it. "What's that?

"Oh, I should have texted you," he says, his green eyes lighting up. "It's—wait, what's wrong? Are you okay?"

I thought I had the storminess going on inside hidden. But as much as I try to keep myself in neutral, to be palatable, he's someone who sees right through that. That used to be a comfort . . . a sign of what could be between us.

"Mavis, what is it?"

I can't find the right words yet, so I reach behind him and shut the door. It's only after I do it that I realize it's probably a stupid move. If this was an episode of *Law & Order*, Dad and I would be screaming at the screen. But here I am, making the unbelievable choice that would have us hollering, and then walking farther away from the exit and sitting down on the living room couch. Wordlessly, Jack follows me.

I stare at my hands instead of his searching eyes, picking at the ragged cuticle on my thumb, and finally force the words out. "I ran into the parking officer. The one from that first day . . . with the ticket and the mud."

I can feel Jack's relief as he lets out a big laugh, his head falling back. "He was probably so happy to see you," he says with a sly smile, but it quickly dims. "What . . . what did he say?"

"It's most likely nothing. I hope it's nothing."

"Just tell me." A line appears between his brows, and he reaches forward to brush his fingers against mine. "Please, Mavis."

I take a steadying breath. I'm never going to get answers unless I make myself say it. But this is the moment where everything could change. Forever.

It all comes out quickly, like a drink knocked over and spilled across the counter. "He said he saw you, that morning. He said you were arguing with Principal Smith, yelling at him and— and maybe even about to hit him? He said you were really mad. And, like, I've never seen you mad in the way he said you were mad. And I don't even know how to process that, because you never even mentioned this, and that seems like a hell of a thing not to mention, Jack."

The words hang in the air between us, and it's silent except for the long, heavy sigh that Jack lets out. He runs his fingers through his hair and then looks me right in the eye.

"I did get into it with Principal Smith that morning," he admits, and I wince. "It was one of those things that felt so big in the moment, but after everything that happened . . . well, not so much. I did yell at him, though, and I would do it again, because he was wrong and needed to be told he was wrong. I'd just found out that morning that he'd started the process to transfer one of our students with an IEP to another school. This kid has a disability that requires a lot of expensive services, and Principal Smith wanted to pass on that cost to another school. I called him on it, and how he didn't even talk to me or the special education teachers about it, and he—he called it a burden. The kid or the services—I don't even remember, because I immediately saw red. I lost it for a moment and forgot where I was. But . . . that language. It reminded me of what people used to say about Derek. And I just couldn't keep my cool."

The relief immediately washes over me, smoothing the tension throughout my body, because I believe him. Thank god, *I believe him*. There's still the issue of him keeping this from me, but at least I feel nearly certain that he's telling me the truth now. That he didn't do the unthinkable. Still, I need to be *fully* certain.

"And that's the last time you both talked about that, right? You didn't see him . . . later? Right?"

"Yes, because I ran into you, and then I ended up staying in my office the rest of the school day because of my pants." He starts to smile again, but then his eyes narrow. "Why do you ask that?"

"I just didn't know why you didn't tell me!" I rush to explain. "It caught me off guard when this man I don't even know told me something about you . . . I didn't know what to think."

He wrinkles his nose. "I didn't think it was related. And it involved a student's privacy."

That excuse makes me bristle. "I mean, you didn't have to tell me what it was about. But it *should* have come up, Jack. Don't you see that? It feels like you were—were lying to me . . ."

"I'm sorry," he says immediately, his face full of remorse. "That wasn't my intention, Mavis, and I can see where you're coming from. I can. And I promise it wasn't anything . . . untoward. But you found out this morning and you've been holding it in all day? Why didn't you just text me right then, right when you talked to him?" I can see the exact moment the realization hits. His eyes widen and his lips part. Slowly, he begins to shake his head. "You—you didn't think I . . . ? Oh my god, Mavis. You know me!"

"But I don't. Not really." My throat feels thick and tight as I choke the words out. "It's been a couple weeks, Jack. You could be anyone. And I've moved into this so fast. Maybe—I don't know . . . Maybe I was just making you into who I've wanted you to be . . ."

Even as I'm saying it, I'm not sure I believe it myself. What's between us has felt so real but so rare—like a constellation you can only catch in the night sky at the exact right moment. But that's scary. What have I been risking by letting myself feel this way?

"I don't know what to believe." My hollow words make his face crack open in pain, and I immediately want to reach for him and make it better. But I'm the one who did that.

He clears his throat and braces his hands on his thighs. "I should go."

"Jack, no," I say quickly, and let myself clutch his hands. I don't know precisely what I want, but I know, urgently, it's not *that*. It's not Jack leaving.

"I know how I feel about you." His voice is soft but steady.

"And if you're not there yet . . . that's totally fine. I understand. But the fact that you could even consider I would—" His words catch, and he bites his lip. He lets out a long exhale as he rubs his hands down his face. "I think I just need to take a beat. To process all of this."

He stands up, and my hands fall from his. Before he leaves, though, his eyes land on the folder he brought with him. It ended up on the coffee table, on top of Pearl's Chromebook.

"I brought this for you." He picks it up and holds it out toward me. "I kept looking into Paul McGee. I just couldn't let it go. And I wanted this for us—" He clears his throat again. "For you."

"He was Principal Smith's friend from childhood. Back in Florida." I say what we already know, what I discovered from that high school reunion Facebook group. It's easier than talking about what's actually happening here, everything falling apart. "So, he was probably just sending him an email to catch up . . . right? It probably wasn't related."

"Yes, probably. But I did a little more digging and printed out this stuff, just in case. His posts and a few pictures from Facebook. And some local news articles about Paul's family. They're a big deal in Bradley County, where they're from, I guess. His dad is a longtime mayor, and his mom is a philanthropist. She seems to be on the board of nearly every organization there."

He holds out the folder again, but I don't take it. I know what will happen when I do.

"Let's look at it together." I hate the desperate edge to my voice, but I can't help it. My stomach feels tight and sick at the thought of him leaving. "I'm sorry. I'm so sorry, Jack. I never should have—can we just rewind? And go back to, like, fifteen minutes ago?"

His green eyes lock on mine, and I think I see the glint of sunshine there, a smile that's about to rise. But then he shakes his head and gently places the folder on the couch next to me.

"I hope it helps you, but I think—I think I'm done playing detective, Mavis."

Then he walks away without looking back.

TWENTY-ONE

WELL, I FUCKED THAT UP.

Jack is the one person who has been on my side, unwaveringly, since the beginning of all this, and I just went ahead and accused him of committing a crime that *I don't even know actually took place*!

And now I've lost him and completely made a mess of things, which appears to be my general pattern lately. With Pearl, with Jasmine, with work . . . with the goddamn PTA.

And for what? Money that's clearly not coming? Or maybe I just wanted to feel important and valuable and like I'm doing anything that matters, for once? I let myself get so obsessed and one-track minded that I was racing down a road, ignoring all the warning signs and flashing lights, until I slammed straight into a wall.

I want to drink a beer. I want to watch endless episodes of *Bachelor in Paradise* until my vision blurs. I want to fall apart.

But I can't. I don't get to fall apart. Not right now, not ever. Because falling apart takes time, and I don't have it.

Maybe I can fit in a ten-minute meditation before I pick up Pearl, with that stupid app Project Window gave us instead of mental health coverage in our insurance plan last year. *Maybe.* I'm not sure that deep breathing along with this unnaturally calm-voiced lady is going to fix the fact that all of the pieces of my life currently lie shattered on the ground around me, destroyed by my own hand. But still, I reach for my phone on the coffee table. I can try.

Before I can even pull up Tanya or Dakota or whatever the meditation app guru's name is, though, I see a text on my screen from Jasmine.

My chest feels tight as I quickly unlock my phone.

> Hey sis, just checking in! I heard all
> about your meeting and what was
> revealed about Miss Trish. Okay Law
> and Order! Okay relentless pursuit
> of the truth!! I'm proud of you.

I call her before I can talk myself out of it, and my mouth starts moving as soon as she says, "Hello."

"I'm sorry! I'm so, so sorry, Jasmine! I should have listened to you, I shouldn't have gotten so defensive. Because I was wrong and you were right. And—and . . . I'm just such a mess. A fucking mess! And not even Tanya can help me now, because I think I'm *too* much of a mess to clean up at this point. And I'm sorry— did I already say I was sorry? Because I was not a good friend when you were being the *best* friend and showing up for me even when I was acting totally and completely insane."

I stop talking, because it turns out I also have to breathe, and that gives Jasmine a second to speak.

"Girl, what?"

"W-what?"

"Not that I don't like to be groveled to, don't get me wrong," she laughs. "But I don't know, just a small hunch . . . It seems like maybe there's something else happening here?"

So I fill her in on everything that's happened since our blowup on her front porch. My run-in with Dyvia and the video from the Ring doorbell camera that brought everything together. Solving a mystery, but the *wrong* mystery, and the clue from my parking nemesis that made me convinced, momentarily, that maybe Jack knew more about the *right* mystery all along. And how he just answered for himself right now, but our relationship was probably a casualty of me even asking the question.

"Let me get this straight: You thought Jack coulda killed Principal Smith?" Jasmine asks when I'm done. "Because I woulda thought he was a little too 'let's hold hands and talk about our feelings' for murder, but I guess there are a shit ton of Netflix documentaries about just that type, huh?"

"No!" I feel the word so forcefully that I jump out of my seat, knocking Jack's folder of documents to the ground in the process. Polly pads over to investigate. "I mean . . . yes. I thought that briefly . . . but—oh my god. I am questioning my judgment all around here. Like, I thought *Trisha* killed Principal Smith, and she was just stealing books with Black kids in them. Clearly, I am not reliable here."

"See, uh-uh, Trisha has the murder-y vibes, though!" she says. "And say Jack didn't do it. *Regardless*, I'm gonna get him."

"What? Why?" I ask. I cradle the phone on my shoulder as I bend down to pick up the mess of papers and pictures on the ground that Polly is sniffing with suspicion. At the top is a news article about Mayor McGee setting a record for the most non-consecutive terms served in Bradley County.

"Um, because he led you on! How are you going to act like

you were really in it if you bounce at the first accusation of murder, huh?"

I snort out a laugh as I scoop up some more pictures and articles about Paul McGee I didn't find in my own googling.

"Let's go egg his house—or no! Let's go egg all his neighbors' houses, so he's the only one *not* egged, and then they'll blame him!"

I giggle along with Jasmine's increasingly ridiculous yet brilliant schemes as I continue to stack up all the scattered documents. They fill in the gaps between that homecoming with the *Dumb and Dumber* suits and the more recent picture I saw on his Facebook page. Becoming a partner in the McGee family's law office, a marriage announcement in the local paper, an opinion piece from just a few weeks ago predicting that he's set to run for mayor with his dad's recently announced retirement. And in all the pictures, his blue eyes are equally piercing. They seem to stare out right at me, and it makes me uneasy. I close the folder.

"You know I have the hookup with urine samples, but it's possible they could get traced back to me. So, maybe option three is better?"

"I'm gonna be honest, I have no idea what you're even talking about anymore. But I missed you, Jasmine. And again, I'm so sorry."

"I missed you, too. Now tell me again how I'm the best friend ever. And give a little more supporting evidence this time."

When we get off the phone twenty minutes later, I feel lighter than I did before. Not *better*, because I don't think that's in my foreseeable future, but at least I no longer feel like crumpling up into a pile on the ground. I can get up. I can go get Pearl. I can get through the rest of this day.

As I stand to leave, I notice one more photo that I missed on the ground, held protectively between Polly's paws. I take it from her, ignoring her look of betrayal, and I have a flash of recognition. It's the same one from the Facebook page with the blue and orange suits and cheesy pose.

God, I really need to get all of this out of here so my dad and Pearl don't find any of it and start asking questions I do not want to answer. I should just toss it all in the trash.

But wait . . . This picture is a little different. It's the same shot, but wider, like the other one was cropped. There's another boy off to the right, a skinny kid in a too-big suit, with his head back in laughter. And on the left is a girl, much closer to Thomas and Paul. She's facing the camera, but her eyes are off to the side, looking at the boys, like one of them told a joke and her amused gaze flicked to them at the last second.

She's wearing a shiny purple strapless dress, and she has a cloud of ginger curls that fall to her shoulders and puff up in the front in unfortunate bangs. Her face, full of freckles, is stretched into a wide, friendly smile, and as I lean in closer, I see that it shows off her two bottom incisors, which stick up like bunny ears.

An icy chill ripples across my whole body, and as my hands begin to shake, the picture floats to the ground.

I know that face well.

It belongs to the person who's currently watching my baby girl.

I grab my keys and run out the door.

TWENTY-TWO

"CORINNE! CORINNE!" I POUND ON THE DOOR WITH MY fist, matching the speed of my racing heart. My knuckles sting, and I know I'm only moments away from them splitting open and marking her door with blood. But I need to get in that house. Now. "Corinne!"

Suddenly, her heavy oak door swings open, and I nearly fall over. The rainbow beaded bracelets on Corinne's wrist cheerfully jingle as she puts her hand on her hip and considers me with a confused smile.

"Mavis, what in the devil is going on here? You nearly gave me a—" Her head tilts to the side as she looks at me, and then her lids drop down low. "So you've finally figured it out, have you?"

She sighs and steps back, waving me in. "Well, come on in then. We can have a drink. Lord knows I'm gonna need one if I'm about to tell you all this."

"Pearl. I need to see Pearl." My voice is low and hoarse and seems to come from deep within me. My whole body aches for my baby. I weave my head around, trying to see past Corinne into the house, but I don't see any sign of her. "Where is she?"

"I would never do anything to Pearl, Mavis. You should know that." Corinne's voice is almost chastising. She huffs. "Now, I already invited you in. Come and see for yourself." She holds her arm out again, with an edge of impatience this time. And for a second, I hesitate. Is it really smart to enter the house of someone who basically just admitted to killing someone? Is this another one of those moves that would have my dad and me yelling at the TV screen? But Pearl is in there. It doesn't matter what's smart.

I carefully step across the threshold, tensing when Corinne firmly shuts the door behind me. She walks across the living room, scattered with backpacks and Nerf guns, and down the hallway. And as I follow her, I can hear the shouts and laughter of the Ackerman boys—and then Pearl's infectious giggle. She's fine. She's happy. My eyes well up in relief.

When we walk into the room, Pearl, River, and Mason are crowded around the tiny screen of a Nintendo Switch, which is propped up on a stack of novels and a Chromebook on top of a small desk. All three of them hold controllers, and while Mason and River are intensely focused on a round of *Mario Kart*, Pearl is excitedly bouncing behind them as her Princess Peach car on the screen aimlessly wanders the track.

"Hey, baby! Hey, baby girl!" I go to scoop her up into my arms, but Corinne steps in between us. She flashes me a warning look.

"Okay, how much screen time have y'all had?" she says, and the boys groan, their eyes not leaving the screen. "Hey, Mavis, can I see your phone to check?"

"M-my phone?" I choke out, and her dark eyes flash at me again, their message clear.

I can't give her my phone. It's my only way to get help if something goes wrong—and oh god, why the hell didn't I do that before rushing over here in the first place? Now *that* was a stupid move from a pre-credits scene in *Law & Order*. I need to get us out of here. I need to at least let someone know where we are. But I also don't know what Corinne will do, what she's capable of. I don't want Pearl to be scared or to see me get hurt—or, even worse, get hurt herself. I don't have a choice.

"Okay," I say and hand Corinne my phone.

She checks the screen, probably to make sure I haven't texted anyone, and then makes an exaggerated show of checking the time. But the kids aren't even paying attention. "Looks like you can have a little bit longer. Ms. Mavis and I are going to have a grown-up chat for a bit in the kitchen. So, stay in here, okay, kiddos?"

River and Mason both grunt in acknowledgment, but Pearl's eyes actually drift from their race.

"Have fun on your mommy playdate!" Pearl says, beaming at me with her one-dimpled smile. My throat feels tight, and a single tear rolls down my cheek, but Pearl's gaze has already returned to the screen. As Corinne closes their door and leads me back into the kitchen, standing close behind me to ensure I don't run, I'm struck with the thought that I may never see that smile again.

How did I get this so wrong?

"Please sit," Corinne says quietly, gesturing to one of her barstools. I follow directions. "Do you want a beer?"

I find myself nodding, as if this is just a normal evening with a mom friend, catching up over a drink. As if I'm not taking a mental inventory of everything in this room that could be used as a weapon. The block full of fancy knives, the meat tenderizer, the glass coffeepot . . .

She sticks my phone in her back pocket and takes two lavender glass goblets out of the cabinet. Then she gets a tall can out of the fridge and cracks it open. Her movements are so quick that she's facing me again before I can even process that her back was to me. My pulse pounds in my ears as she calmly pours the IPA, carefully tilting the glasses to prevent too much foam.

Her voice is barely above a whisper when she finally speaks. "I remember the first time he hit me. I didn't even flinch."

Her brown eyes appear nearly black. It feels like she's looking right through me.

"I thought, of course. Because this is what they do," she continues. "Just like my daddy used to, until the day Mama didn't get back up." Her eyelids flutter and she shakes her head. "I knew I had to find my way out then. And I thought I had—with him. He loved me. He took care of me. Until he turned out to be just like the rest of them."

"I—I don't understand." But I do know that if we're talking, she's staying far away from Pearl. And there's more time for someone, maybe, to realize where I am . . . though as I tick through everyone in my mind, I know that's a long shot. Dad won't be home until late, and I just got off the phone with Jasmine. Jack certainly won't be looking for me anytime soon. But . . . Corey. Pearl is supposed to have her nightly FaceTime with Corey! In the chaos of everything today, I forgot to reschedule. He'll call. He always does. If I can just keep Corinne occupied for a little while longer, he'll get worried, call my dad, *something*. Unless he just assumes I dropped the ball again . . .

Still, I have to try.

"Are you talking about Principal Smith? Is he the one who hit you?"

She lets out a low, bitter laugh. "Not Tom, though he was no saint either. He knew what was going on." Her expression turns hard again. "No, Paul. Brody's dad."

"Brody's dad?"

"Yes, Brody's dad. As in not Mason and River's dad," she speaks slowly, enunciating each syllable, and her eyes flicker with annoyance. "God, Mavis, I'm gonna need you to keep up, because I'm pretty damn sure that we don't have a lot of time. Did your little boyfriend finally put the pieces together for you here? Is he on his way?"

"No. Jack doesn't know. He's . . . We're not . . . He walked away."

She slams the empty can on the counter, and I startle in my seat. She shoots out a shaky finger in my face. "Don't you lie to me!"

I put my hands up. "I'm not. I swear, Corinne. I should have told someone I was coming here . . . but I didn't. We both know I'm a fucking mess and don't know what the hell I'm doing half the time. I can barely even get my kid to school before the late bell."

She nods at that, and I actually feel a flash of indignation. Because the way it works with mom friends is that we insult ourselves and then the other person insists we're wrong because *you're perfect and magical and totally the best mom ever!* But I mean, I *guess* social norms go out the window when your mom friend is confessing to murder or whatever. A desperate laugh almost escapes my lips, but I press them together tightly.

"Well, good. But I'm still not planning to hang around here much longer. I thought maybe Tom's wife would just let it go, especially once the affair came out, and that letter they found. I thought I would have some time to get things in order, explain to Ben what happened . . . and then I could make an anonymous phone call about Tom's location on our way out. But then she offered that reward." She rolls her eyes and takes a swig from her goblet. "Some people just don't know what's good for them. I did her a favor."

"So, he's—he's dead then? Principal Smith?"

"Of course he's not dead! Ha!" She slaps the counter, like I just told a good joke. "What kind of person do you think I am? I've been waiting on him like a servant, bringing him PB&Js, making sure his wrists and ankles aren't getting infected from the restraints."

Well, I'd hardly classify that as waiting on him like a servant. But it's probably in my best interest if I let that go.

"I'm so confused, Corinne. Can you just start from the beginning? And tell me what happened? I'm sure you had a good reason . . ."

I'm not sure of that at all, but it's important that she thinks I am.

She pulls my phone out of her pocket again, either to check the time or to make sure no one is texting me. I can't see the screen to tell if Corey has called, and her face doesn't give anything away.

"Let's drink first. I'm waiting for it to get a little darker. I don't need any lookie-loos, and Brody is supposed to be at his band practice until nine."

I feel myself start to sweat. Because aren't I, like, the ultimate lookie-loo? If she's not worried about me, well . . . then she must have a plan for me already. And it most likely doesn't end with me leaving here, able to tell the tale of all I've lookie-d and loo-ed.

Corinne pushes the glass goblet toward me, and I start to

sweat. *That* would be an easy way to take me out. I don't think I saw her drop anything into the drink, but was I watching close enough? Probably not. I was too busy taking inventory of all the knives. And Pearl—my chest aches at the thought of her. I *know* Corinne wouldn't do anything to Pearl. Not the Corinne I know . . . but I guess I don't actually know her at all.

"Do you think I'm gonna poison you?" She smiles like it's a joke, but her voice is too sharp for it to land. "We're friends, Mavis. I'm not going to hurt you." She nods to the drink again, and it's clear I don't have a choice. I take a big gulp.

"Tell me what happened," I say, wiping the foam from my lip.

She takes another sip and then lets out a long exhale, like she's been holding her breath for a long time. "I started dating Paul my sophomore year of high school. I didn't really know him before that football game when he walked up to me and asked me to the movies—but I knew *of* him. Everyone in Bradley County knows the McGees. Their names are on practically all the buildings. And I remember feeling so special that he chose me. Paul could have any girl and he wanted me—a foster kid whose daddy was in jail. I made him my whole life, because I knew that's what was expected of a girl that was with one of the McGee boys. And he was so nice in the beginning—bringing me flowers to homeroom just because, taking me to all the fundraisers and fancy events the McGees were invited to. And he never made me feel bad when he had to cover my dress or the cost at the beauty parlor—he said it was his honor." A small smile flickers on her face, but then her dark eyes turn stormy. "That's what I held on to when he started being not so nice. When he called me a whore, or a slut, for smiling at the wrong person. Or when he pinched me or hit me or kicked me—where no one could see the marks, of course, because we didn't want people talking. And if I was alert, if I paid attention,

I could stop him before it got too bad . . . I could make him happy." She sighs and runs her hands over her face. "I told myself I could put up with his little spells because the good times were so good."

I remember her mentioning an abusive ex at the playdate . . . should I have asked more questions? I didn't want to make her feel uncomfortable, and she just so easily brushes everything off. But still, maybe we wouldn't be here now if I had. I guess she'd already done . . . whatever she did at that point, though.

"I'm so sorry, Corinne."

She waves that away, her calm, cool exterior back in place. "We all have our lot in life, and I did my best with mine. Until I got pregnant. With Brody, my senior year. I knew then that I couldn't just go along anymore, not for his sake. No, he was something to fight for—and it was my job to protect him. He didn't deserve this life, to continue this cycle that my daddy, and probably my daddy's daddy, started. He deserved only the best."

"So you ran."

She takes another drink of her beer and then nods. "I ran. I had no other choice. There's no way they would have let me *not* marry him, to keep a *McGee* boy from them. They would have used all their resources to come after me. So, I caught a Greyhound. I changed my name. It's surprisingly easy if you have the money—and I did. I'd been skimming some from Paul since the day I first got the positive. But I don't think there was anything criminal about that. The McGees definitely weren't wanting for anything." She looks at me expectantly, like she's waiting for validation.

"Yes," I say quickly. "You did what you had to do."

"I did. And eventually, I made it all the way to California. I didn't know anything about California, except for what I saw on TV. Like—like . . . *Saved by the Bell*, all those shows on Saturday mornings? The kids in them seemed so happy and carefree, their biggest problem was getting a date to the dance or a zit on their noses, you know? That's the life I wanted for him."

Her eyes go hazy and unfocused as she tells her story, almost as if she's telling it just for herself. I want to get up, make a run for Pearl, but I know I need to be careful, be sure. I still have no idea what she did to Principal Smith—what she's fully capable of.

"I found a women's shelter just for pregnant teens. And after I gave birth to Brody, the director, Joan, connected me with another program that let me stay on for another year, as I got on my feet. I worked as a house cleaner, mostly, but I did other jobs that paid under the table—whatever I had to do. And I took some community college classes—well, I never actually enrolled, because I wasn't sure how my new identity would hold up. But I would sit in the back and listen and dream about being just another student in those classes. When I was little, I used to say I wanted to be a doctor, can you believe that? I wanted to help people." She smiles again, but this time it lingers. I follow her gaze to a gallery wall of family photos, and my eyes catch on something I didn't notice before. Her phone, on the far edge of the kitchen counter.

"And that's where I met Ben. He looked like he walked right out of a California dream, with his sun-bleached hair and tan skin. He even surfed! He didn't seem real. And the way he treated me and Brody . . . it took me a long time to trust him, but he was a decent man. Not just for show, but all the time. We got married in months and eventually had the boys. And I made a life for myself. A good one. Until . . ."

Could I reach the phone without her noticing? But then what would I even do with it?

"Until you saw Principal Smith at the PTA meeting," I finish for her.

I think back to that night, when we met for the first time, making fun of the other moms. I thought she was distracted, lost in the silly drama, but she was scared. And then she disappeared before the meeting was over . . . I didn't think there was anything suspicious about it. I just made it about myself, and how she might not want to be my friend.

"I knew it was Tom Smith as soon as I saw him." Her lip curls in disgust. "I always wondered if I should have dyed my hair, made more of an attempt to disguise myself. But I was too vain. This is my best feature." She chuckles and flips her thick red hair. "I tried to decide what to do, trying to convince myself that he didn't see me, too. I knew, deep down, that I should run, but the boys, and Ben—" Her voice cracks when she says her husband's name, and she closes her eyes, steadying herself. "I knew I should run, but I started telling myself these wild stories—that I could just get them a nanny, and she could take them back and forth to school. Or I could move them to private—it was only two years! And the whole time I was doing the laundry, the dishes—as if *that* was important." She sighs and shakes her head. "And then he showed up at my door. He always was Paul's little pet."

I could probably reach the phone in one lunge, if she turned around again. I won't be able to dial anything, but isn't there a button you can press to go straight to an emergency line? God, I need to keep her talking while I figure this out, which she seems happy to do.

I clear my throat. "W-what did he say to you?"

"He said he looked me up in the school's system. He threatened to tell the McGees where I was after all this time. Said,

'Oh, wouldn't Marjorie just be overjoyed to know she had another grandchild?'" Her words are laced with venom. "He had obviously been drinking. He didn't even bother to hide the joy he was getting from wielding this power over me—that he'd get to deliver me and Brody to the McGees like a prize."

"That must have been so scary, Corinne . . ."

"*Then* he alluded that he might be willing to keep it between us." She keeps going as if she didn't even hear me. Maybe I can just tilt to the side and quickly grab the phone without her noticing. "If I would do something for him, that is. The look on his face, Mavis, the way he was *leering* at me—it made me sick. He always wanted what Paul had, because he was *always* second best to him in Bradley."

"Then what happened?" I lean on my arm, like I'm enthralled in her story, inching closer to the phone.

"He—he stepped toward me—he grabbed my arm. So tight. I still have the bruise. And—and—I didn't think. I just reacted. He was on the ground before I knew what I had done. That wasn't my plan when I brought the pan with me to the door, I promise. I was just doing the dishes." Her eyes flick to the stove, where the lid of her fancy Instagram pan is still sitting, but she's focused back on me again before I can make my move. "But I don't regret it. He deserved what happened to him."

"And what about River and Mason? They didn't wake up?" I turn my body around to face their closed door, hoping that she'll mimic me. She doesn't.

"They're heavy sleepers just like me, always have been. I was that annoying mom that bragged about my three-month-old sleeping through the night." She smiles sheepishly at me, and I instinctively smile back. Even as we're talking about, at a minimum, second-degree assault.

"What happened then?" I lean another inch, then two.

"Well, he was out cold. So I dragged him inside, shut the door. I almost called Ben right then and there, told him everything—but I didn't know if Tom was going to make it. And I couldn't do that to Ben, couldn't ruin his life, too. Better to have some distance between him and . . . the body. And then I remembered the empty house next door, and I slowly but surely got him all the way over there—it was a real bitch on my back, I'll tell you. I've been popping ibuprofens like candy since then. And, well . . . let's see, I checked his pulse, he was alive—he's *stayed* alive. So I locked him in their fancy-ass wine room, tied his wrists and ankles with some zip ties that the construction workers just left lying around. And then I came back here and basically waited for the police that night. I was sure it couldn't have been that easy—someone must have seen or figured it out. But no one did . . . until you."

Her words hang in the air between us. Until me. I'm the only one who knows what she's done, the only one in the way of this good life she's created for herself. Well, except for Principal Smith, but it's inevitable that she'll have to take care of him soon, right? I don't buy the run-away-and-make-an-anonymous-phone-call plan.

If I could just distract her for a moment and reach that phone, Pearl and I might have a chance.

"I—I understand why you'd do this. You were looking out for your boys. We'd all do whatever we'd have to do for our kids." My hand is so close. And I think it's the side button and one of the volume buttons I have to push at the same time. Yeah, that's it. "I won't tell anyone, Corinne." Even if she realizes what's happening, I can do that before she reaches me. I hope. "I promise, Corinne. Please."

Corinne begins to shake her head sadly. And then, faster than I can even process what's happening, she grabs her phone just out of my grasp and throws it down onto the tile floor. The screen shatters, and then she stomps on it for good measure. I never had a chance.

She reaches into her back pocket, and I think she's about to do the same with my phone, but instead there's the glint of something silver in her hand.

"Mavis, you know I can't just let you leave."

TWENTY-THREE

"STAND UP AND WALK TO THE BOYS' ROOM." HER VOICE IS hard, and I know I need to listen. But even though I'm sending the message to my limbs to *get up right now, what the hell are you doing, you fool*, I can't make myself move. I'm frozen.

"Now," she orders, and as she points, I see that it's a pocket-knife in her hand.

A pocketknife? I could take her with just that, a tiny voice inside of me insists. But that also may be the voice that told me to run over here without telling anyone as soon as I saw that picture, so I'm a little hesitant to trust it. No, better to be cautious. To think clearly. If she goes after Pearl, though, that voice is going to win out, no question, and I know what I'll do—what I'll *have* to do.

I slowly stand up, and Corinne rushes to stand behind me. I don't feel the point of the small knife in my back, but I can feel its presence as we walk together down the hall.

Pearl turns to us as soon as we open the door, and I slap on an *everything is fine, nothing to see here* smile.

"Mommy, I don't want to go home yet!" she shouts, pouting in frustration. "I'm going to win!"

She is most definitely not going to win, as Princess Peach is currently spinning in circles in a lava pit on the screen. And also, there's the whole, I don't know, lady-with-a-knife thing!

But all three of them are screen zombies and seem to have no idea what's been going down in the kitchen. I've always wondered if Pearl would even notice if I slipped and fell, or a masked madman came running into our house and took me hostage, when she's deep into her favorite show. And I guess now I have my answer.

"Pearl, you don't have to leave." Corinne is now standing next to me, and the knife is put away, or maybe tucked under her sleeve. I can't tell. But I quickly rush to Pearl's side on the floor and pull her into a tight hug. Corinne smiles to keep her cover, but I can see the warning there. "You can stay over as long as you want!"

"I can?" Pearl asks, squirming in my arms. She looks at me for confirmation, and I nod, careful to keep my mask in place.

"Yes, you sure can!" Corinne has walked farther away from us, to the closet, but she's still watching me carefully, and I don't dare move. She reaches behind her and pulls out two small blue duffel bags from the corner behind their shoe rack.

"The boys and I do have to go pick up Brody," she continues. "But, Pearl, your mommy says she wants to stay here and play Guess Who with you. Doesn't that sound like fun?"

That makes Mason tear his eyes away from the screen. "Aww, Mom! I don't want to pick up Brody! I want to finish this match."

"Yeah," River chimes in. "Can't Ms. Mavis just watch us, too?"

"Guess Who! I love Guess Who!" Pearl cheers, throwing her hands up in excitement. But then she frowns. "When are you going to be back, though?"

"Brody said he has a special treat for you two," Corinne says, expertly unplugging the Switch in the same moment. She throws it into one of the duffel bags and zips it up as the boys groan. "And, Pearl, your mommy said she could beat you at Guess Who but I told her, 'I bet that's not true!'"

Pearl crosses her arms and shoots me a betrayed look, so she doesn't even notice Corinne shooing the boys out with the same icy glare she gave me earlier.

"You can't, Mommy! I always win!"

Corinne rushes over to the doorway, but before she leaves, she pauses and considers me with a sad smile.

"Goodbye, Mavis."

Then she shuts the door. A second later, I hear the click of the lock.

I'VE OFTEN FELT LIKE I WAS BEING HELD CAPTIVE, PLAYING endless rounds of Guess Who with Pearl, but this is the first time that's actually an accurate description of my circumstances.

"Do you have a mustache?"

"No. Do you have a wig?"

"How am I supposed to know if it's a wig, Pearl?"

"You just know."

It's been at least forty-five minutes. Well, I don't know for sure without my phone or a clock, but we've played six rounds of this game.

"Do you have glasses?"

"Define *glasses*."

"Baby girl, I think there's only one definition of *glasses*."

I wanted to wait for them to be gone for sure. I didn't want to give Corinne any reason to change her mind about sparing us and come back to get rid of the only witnesses. And also . . .

maybe there's a small part of me, deep down, that wants her to get away. I don't agree with her choices, but there's no debate about the fact that she was dealt a bad hand.

And who knows how far I would go if there was a chance Pearl could be taken away from me?

"Do you have a pretty face?" Pearl asks.

"Um—I think so? Yes. And are you . . . Joe?"

Pearl flattens all the people on her board. "Mommy, I'm bored now. Can we play something else?"

I think they're gone. They have to be at this point, if Corinne is serious about getting away. I stand up and press my ear to the door again. I don't hear anything, and Mason and River are definitely not the quiet type.

I turn back to Pearl and smile. "Hey, I know something fun we can do. Let's play a game called bang on the window!"

Her eyes light up, and her lips stretch into a mischievous grin. "For real?"

"For real! And let's scream while we do it, too!"

The window is locked. I tried right away to pull it open, but it wouldn't budge—and then I remembered how Corinne said it was busted by the boys.

But the night is quiet. Surely someone will hear us if we're loud enough.

I walk to the window and begin to pound on it with my fists, hollering as loud as I can. Pearl joins me, jumping and giggling with excitement that I'm letting her do something that would never fly at home.

But after just a few minutes, and seemingly no response outside, Pearl sits down on one of the boys' beds. "Okay, I'm done now. Also I'm hungry. Can you make me a snack?"

"No, not yet," I chirp. I swear this child would ask me for a snack on my deathbed. But for once I'm grateful, because this means she still has no idea that we're trapped in here. And I want to keep it that way. I need to protect her from this, whatever it takes. "Maybe . . ." I begin to look around the room for anything I missed before, anything that could get us out of here. "Oh, where are River's and Mason's backpacks? Maybe they have snacks in there?"

And possibly cell phones, too. At drop-off, I've made judgy eyes at the fifth graders who flash their iPhones that are newer than mine, but now I hope Corinne is one of those moms.

"River and Mason left their backpacks out there." She points to the closed door. "Can't we go in the kitchen? Ms. Corinne buys the good fruit snacks that you said were too sugary."

Yeah, and Ms. Corinne also had your principal tied up next door for weeks and just threatened me with a pocketknife! But I keep my too-cheerful smile plastered on.

"First, let's find something else to play with! There's so many fun things here!" I clap my hands together, which is definitely overkill, and Pearl raises a suspicious eyebrow at me, less than convinced. But then her eyes go wide at something behind me.

"Oh! Oh, can I use that Chromebook? I think they would be fine with that." She blinks and bites her lip. "Um, not to send any messages or write any lists, of course. But to play, um . . . scholarly games!"

"Sure," I sigh. Giving her more screen time is probably the best option right now. It'll keep her happy and distracted, while I keep looking for a way out of here. And honestly, the *least* of my worries in this moment is her emailing little SoSo Hart . . .

Emails. That's it. I can send an email through the boys' school-issued Chromebook!

The email program is restricted to within the school district, but there's someone I know who works in the district. Someone who I hope will come right away, despite how we left things.

"Pearl, can you show me how to open up the messages?"

"Fine. But then can I use it?" She starts to whine, and I'm surprised it's taken this long. "Because, because. Mommyyyyyy, I asked firrrrrst!"

"Yes, baby girl. Just give me two seconds."

"One, two," she says quickly and then smirks.

I take a deep breath. "Okay, uh, like . . . two hundred and fifty-six seconds."

"Fine! But I'm counting. One, two, three, four . . ."

"I'm gonna need you to count a little slower than that, girl-friend."

"Five, six, seven . . ."

TWENTY-FOUR

I DON'T FALL ASLEEP. I REMAIN *FIRMLY* AWAKE.

It's just . . . there are only so many hours your body can stay on high alert before your heart rate *has* to come down. So you might start to stare at the space-printed bedspread, counting how many times Saturn repeats in the pattern. And maybe you use a giant dinosaur Squishmallow as a pillow because the hardwood floor is tough on your muscles, which are tense from being in fight-or-flight mode for so long. And when you close your eyes, it's just to say a quick prayer that help is on the way, not for any other reason. And minutes later—probably seconds—your daughter is perched over you, giving you an excellent view of her nostrils.

"I think someone is having a party."

I jolt up from the ground, where I've been awake and alert and ready to defend my daughter this whole time.

"They're playing weird music and flashing lights, Mommy," she says, tugging on my arm. "Can we go? Also, I'm still hungry."

"W-what!" I jump up and throw my arm in front of Pearl,

bracing for a fight. But Corinne isn't back. There's no one here in the room with us. There are flashing lights, though . . . blue and red. And that isn't weird music, it's sirens. While those two things usually strike fear into my heart, especially on the 405 freeway, right now they might as well be a chorus of angels singing. And then, cutting through it all, I hear our names being called—faint at first, then much louder. Closer.

"Mavis! Pearl!"

I start to bang on the bedroom window. "Here! We're in here!"

Pearl huffs and rolls her eyes. "Are we playing *that* boring game again?"

"Yes, we are!" I shout, and she rolls her eyes one more time, just in case I missed it the first time. And I start to laugh—in disbelief at the absolute absurdity of this situation, in relief that my kid feels comfortable enough to *roll her eyes* at me and has no idea of the danger we were just in, in overwhelming joy that I was able to keep us safe.

Because we're safe now. Because I know those voices. I recognize them even through a closed window, in a siren-filled night. They're my people. And they showed up for us.

"Maves! Pearl! We're coming for you! Don't worry, Papa is here!" My dad's face appears at the window. I can see the worry in his furrowed brow and wide, bleary eyes, and it makes my own eyes burn. But I hold in my tears and put my palm up to the window.

"Look at that, Pearl. Papa is here!"

"So, Papa's at the party, too?"

There's a crash somewhere in the house, followed by loud, quick footsteps.

"Stand back!" a muffled voice shouts on the other side of the door, and after just a few heavy thumps, the door crashes open.

A man with a crew cut, wearing a navy uniform and black boots, leads the rescue team.

"Are you okay?" he shouts, and I nod, dazed. "Is there anyone else in the house?"

"No, just us."

"What about Ms. Corinne?" Pearl's tiny, concerned voice next to me startles me more than the chaos surrounding us.

"They went on their trip . . . remember?"

Her eyes flicker with fear, and she bites her lip. She knows this isn't right, isn't fun anymore, and my chest aches with the need to take her away from all this and wipe the worry from her brow. I pick her up, settling her on my hip like I used to do when she was a baby, and take her outside, shielding her from the scene as best I can. And there, on the front lawn, we see Jack, Jasmine, and my dad waiting for us.

Dad runs forward, pulling Pearl and me into a hug so tight it feels like we'll be stuck together forever. As he kisses both of our heads, I can feel the tears on his cheeks.

"My girls, I love you so much," he chokes out in between sniffles.

"I love you, too, Dad. We're okay."

"I love you, Papa," Pearl says as she wiggles out of my arms and drops down to the grass. "But I'm hungry. Mommy wouldn't let me eat fruit snacks, and then she fell asleep."

My head falls back in startled laughter, and my dad joins in, too, wiping his damp face.

"I'm sorry, baby." My voice cracks, and I get down on my knees in front of her, stroking her soft curls and smooth skin. I say a little prayer of gratitude that she's here and she's safe and she's complaining about fruit snacks.

"It's okay," she says, patting my head.

"You can have all the fruit snacks you want!"

"Really?" I can tell by the twinkle in her dark brown eyes that she's actively committing that to memory and never letting it go. "Like . . . infinity fruit snacks?"

"Infinity times infinity fruit snacks," I confirm, and she starts to jump up and down in excitement. But the street is lined with police cars, and officers are hovering close by, clearly waiting on some answers. Pearl begins to look around more carefully, and she's smart. I know she's starting to figure this out, despite my promises of infinity fruit snacks.

And I know there's a time coming, very soon, when I'll need to explain all this to her. It's my duty to her to be transparent and answer all her questions—but that time is not now. I can protect her for a little while longer.

"Dad," I say, flashing him a meaningful look. "Can you take Pearl to get her fruit snacks right now?"

"And cheese pizza and Doritos?" Pearl adds.

"And cheese pizza and Doritos."

Pearl beams at both of us. She may not know exactly what's going on, but she knows she's getting away with something—and she's going to milk it. I kiss both of her cheeks and hug her one more time. Dad bends down to pick her up, his knees popping in the process. She smiles and waves over his shoulder as he carries her down the street, past all the police cars and neighbors standing on their lawns, and to his car.

"Ma'am, I'm going to need you to remain on the premises and tell us what happened." The same officer who busted open the bedroom door is now standing right next to me.

"I will, but first you need to check that house." I point to the mid-century modern construction site next door to Corinne's. "The woman who lived here, who locked us up—she has Knoll Elementary's principal held captive in that house. He should be in the wine room. And he's going to need medical attention as soon as possible. He's been there for weeks."

He takes off across the lawn, alerting his team on the way, and I turn my attention back to my friends. Jack's lips hang open in shock as he runs his hands through his hair, and Jasmine is shaking her head, impressed.

"Girl! You did that!" She claps to emphasize each word.

And I know I've just been through the most traumatic thing of my life and I'm sure that's going to come out in other ways very soon. But again, I start to laugh, falling forward and letting myself be enveloped by both of them.

"I'm sorry I didn't see your email sooner," Jack says. "Derek and I—we were . . . watching *The Price Is Right*."

That just makes me laugh even harder.

"This guy wouldn't have told us what was happening until the morning if I hadn't called him to give him a piece of my mind!"

I pull back from them, raising an eyebrow at Jasmine. "You—what?"

"Yeah, after you told me that he dumped you!"

Jack's face flames, and I feel my neck heat up, too. "Um, I don't think I said—"

"After he *dumped* you. RUDE!" She shoots Jack a playful side-eye. "I called this man to tell him he made a bad choice and needed to fix it immediately."

Jack rubs the back of his neck as he studies the ground.

"How did you even get his number?" I ask.

"I have my ways," she says, fluttering her eyelashes. "And when I talked to him, he said he'd already realized his grave mistake and had been trying to call you but didn't get an answer. Then *I* tried to call you and couldn't get an answer. So we both drove by your house and found your dad. Papa Miller didn't know where you were, either, and he and Corey were worried because it was so late and you missed your FaceTime! Then my girl Ms. Joyce—you know I love her—she said she saw you running like you were being chased by the devil. So that's when we started to get *real* worried. And then *this one*"—she jabs an accusatory thumb Jack's way—"finally got around to checking his email!"

"To be fair," Jack adds sheepishly, "I'm trying to have a better work-life balance."

"T'uh. Oh-kay," Jasmine says, hitting him with an up-down look, but I can tell she's just messing with him. Mostly. "Anyway, that's when we found out that you had gone and got yourself hostaged. And we—"

"We came as soon as we could," Jack cuts in, putting a warm, steady hand on my back. "Are you okay?"

"Yes." And obviously that's not true, because I'm pretty sure Jack's touch is the only thing keeping me standing right now. "No . . . I don't know."

There's a commotion of voices and gasps, and we all turn to see Principal Smith being wheeled out on a stretcher to a waiting ambulance. His face is pale, and his clothes are filthy. But he's alive.

"I—I hope he's okay," I say aloud. *And I also hope Corinne and her boys are okay*, I finish in my head. It feels strange to hold both those feelings at the same time. It's too much—and it comes out as tears and shaky limbs and breaths that I just can't catch. Jack hugs me tightly, as Jasmine tenderly pats my back. I'm not okay. But with them, I think I will be eventually.

After the ambulance speeds away and my breathing slows down, Jack rests his forehead against mine. "I'm so happy you're safe, Mavis. I don't know what I would have done if you—" His voice catches, and I squeeze his hand in understanding. "And I'm just so . . . in awe. You solved all this. You got Principal Smith out alive." He shakes his head, looking at me like I'm the biggest treasure. "You can really do anything."

"I can," I agree, slightly dazed.

But . . . just because I *can* do anything, doesn't mean I should. I want to do less.

Or, at least, prioritize better. And put *myself* closer to the top of those priorities. That doesn't mean I don't care about my community, about other people's business, but I think it's also okay to care about just my own business sometimes. Like—there's that whole thing they tell you on planes, about putting on your own mask first. Well, I've been putting on everyone's mask— multitasking, all at the same time—so none of these goddamn things are secured properly and we're all passing out in the aisles. I'm ready to try another way and see if it leads to all of us being a little more happy.

"What do you need right now? How can we help you?" Jack asks, thinking about me, putting me first, just like he has since I met him.

So I press my lips to his, and it's electric all the way down to the tips of my toes. I cradle his cheeks with both of my hands, and he puts his palm on my hip, pulling me flush with him. And the rest of the world is gone, it's just him and me and his soft, urgent lips and gentle touch. And it's possible I could linger in this moment forever, where the only thing I have to do is exactly what I want. But eventually, reluctantly, we break away to breathe.

"I needed that," I murmur, brushing my hands against my swollen lips to make sure they're still there, that our perfect kiss actually just happened. He smiles with flushed cheeks and sunbursts next to his eyes.

"I needed that, too."

"All right, that was just too cute," Jasmine squeals. "I'm gonna need to take a lap! Or maybe throw up."

I laugh. And then I take a long, deep breath. Because I'm not done, and this still doesn't come easy to me. It probably won't without a lot of practice—and I plan to do just that.

"Now, I want . . . no, I need—"

"Yes?" Jack asks, threading his fingers through mine.

"I need to go to sleep."

"Oh, girl, you are gonna *sleep*! And I mean, *sleep* sleep!" Jasmine laughs and claps her hand on my shoulder. "Don't worry, I got drop-off for you tomorrow."

EPILOGUE

FIVE WEEKS LATER

"CAN WE GO OUT ALREADY?" PEARL'S FACE IS PRESSED UP against the front window, creating little circles of fog.

"No, baby girl, it's still too early." I've lost count of how many times I've repeated this exact phrase, but she lets out a deep sigh again to make her suffering clear. "We have to wait until it's dark."

"Looks pretty dark to me!" she insists in a singsong voice.

I walk over to where she's perched on the sill in her sparkly black dress and pointy witch hat and make an exaggerated show of squinting at the sky. The bright blue of the afternoon has faded to a swirling mix of bubblegum and lavender, but the sun is still unmistakably there. She squints, too, her eyes barely visible because of the thick purple eyeshadow she insisted on putting on herself, and then turns back to me.

"It's sooooo dark! I can't even see Ms. Joyce's house!"

We've been doing this same dance since she got home from school and immediately put on her costume—in between rounds of the *separate* dance of her sneaking candy from her class goody bag and me pretending I don't see. And every time, she pleads her case, really commits, like there's a chance I'm going to give in this round. I guess I have to admire the persistence . . . but I'm still not letting her go trick-or-treating until it's *actually* dark.

"Look! Someone's out there!" Langston runs up next to Pearl, jumping up and down in his Black Panther costume.

"And she's dressed as a pumpkin!" Pearl leaps off the sill and grabs her plastic ghost bucket. "See, see! Let's go!"

"Uh-uh, slow your roll, girlfriend," I say, hooking my arm around her waist before she takes off. "That's just Mrs. Skinner."

Yes, she *is* in a neon-orange sports bra and legging set, but that's just her jogging outfit, not a costume.

"Miss Thang is really showing out, isn't she?" Jasmine asks, joining us at the window, so now Mackenzie Skinner has four people spying on her—well, five, if you count Ms. Joyce, who is definitely doing the same thing across the street.

I look Jasmine up and down slowly. She's gone full Angela Bassett in a tall, wide hat and custom-made gown. "Showing out, huh?"

She flutters her eyelashes and preens and then waggles her finger in my direction. "And what do you call this costume? Mom detective? Or no—*local celebrity*!"

She laughs, and I join in, looking down at the same button-up and Old Navy Pixie pants that I wore to work today. I call this costume . . . I forgot to actually get a costume. But not because I was too busy with work or the DEI committee or all the other things that are still on my plate. No, because I chose to use most of my nights the past few weeks to lie in bed and binge-watch *Bachelor in Paradise* instead. I have a lot of rose ceremonies to catch up on.

"What if I give you, um, this many pieces of candy?" Pearl continues, picking up three packs of Skittles from the pile next to her, which I *know* was a lot bigger before. She reconsiders and puts one back. "*This* many. And, Mommy, we don't want to be the last ones!"

"That's when only the reject candy is left," Langston concurs. His mask makes him look extra serious.

"And—*and* those candies have more germs, too! Because more kids have touched them." Pearl crosses her arms, fixing me with her shimmery purple gaze. "You don't want me to get sick. Do you, huh? Do you?"

"Whoo! I need to start adding more to that college fund for law school. Because this child is going to make a good attorney someday!" My dad kisses the top of Pearl's head, stealing a 100 Grand off the top of her pile for himself. He's wearing black dog ears and a pink collar, with face paint done by Pearl. When he sits down on the couch, his twin, Polly, immediately jumps onto his lap.

"Hey, maybe we'll see River and Mason while we're trick-or-treating!" Pearl shouts, clapping her hands together.

"Maybe," I say. "But probably not. They might be with their glamma tonight."

That's where Corinne left her two youngest boys, after locking Pearl and me in their room and leaving town. And no one has been able to locate her or Brody since. Out of all the decisions she had to make, I know that one was probably the most difficult, dropping off two of her babies with her mother-in-law and not looking back. But if she hadn't, there would be two families after her instead of just the McGees. And even though I know I probably shouldn't, I can't help but wish her the best— that she'll stay safe, that she'll be reunited with her family sometime in the future. She did bad things, but she also had a lot of bad things done to her. And through all the deception, she was still my friend.

I haven't reached out to her husband, Ben, to see how he's doing, picking up the pieces. Partly because he hasn't brought the boys back to Knoll yet—which I understand. Between all the gossip and Principal Smith returning, with no consequences for his own wrongs, *awkward* is an understatement. But partly because I just don't know what to say to him. *Sorry for your loss! And also I'm totally not holding a grudge that your wife held me against my will because I figured out her secret identity and that whole other person she was holding against* their *will! It's okay—all moms have bad days!* Yeah, I'm not ready for that conversation yet.

Of course, I told Pearl all of this, or at least the seven-year-old-friendly version. But she keeps bringing them up, trying to get me to explain it again, more—to make it make sense this time. And I get it, because it doesn't make sense, what happened. Corinne was someone she thought she knew, someone she trusted. I'm heartbroken she's lost that trust, that she's now less likely to give it so freely.

"Do you know what you need to go with that beautiful eyeshadow, Pearl?" Jasmine says. "Some black lipstick!"

"Black lipstick?" My dad balks. "Now what are you trying to do to my grandbaby, Jasmine?"

Jasmine winks at him. "It's Halloween, Papa Miller!"

But, of course, there are still a lot of good people in our lives who have her back, who will show her she can trust again.

"Yes!" Pearl squeals, her eyes lighting up. "I only did that once before, but then Mommy told me I couldn't do it again." She gives me the side-eye, leaning into Jasmine.

I sigh. "That's because you did it with permanent marker."

"Can I have some, too?" Langston asks, pulling up his mask.

"Yes, sir," Jasmine says, twirling her finger at him. "That's about to bring this whole look together, little man."

They crowd around Jasmine's makeup bag on the couch as Leon and Derek round the corner from the kitchen.

"So you're a what, again? A whopper?" Leon asks. His bare chest is covered with dozens of fake scars that must have taken forever to draw on. The Hammondses really went all out.

"A Whammy!" Derek clarifies, gesturing to his red face paint and yellow mask. "Like, no Whammy, no Whammy!"

"Right, right. And those are from . . . *The Price Is Right*?"

"*Press Your Luck*! But *The Price Is Right* is the superior show."

"Can't argue with that," Leon says, putting his arm around Derek's shoulders and steering him into the living room. "Now, tell me your thoughts on Steve Harvey . . ."

My chest feels like it's full of light as I see all of my favorite people gathered together in one room. Well, *almost* all of my favorite people. The very last one walks in from the kitchen next, smiling like sunshine, and my belly aches with longing. And it's not just because of the big bowl of fun-size candy bars he's holding.

"I've got a costume for you," Jack murmurs as he pulls a little ID badge out of his back pocket and clips it to my collar. It reads *Olivia Benson*, to match the *Stabler* one on his shirt.

"It's perfect. Though, I'm not trying to be a detective again anytime soon . . . or ever."

He laughs, low and rumbly. "We're on the same page there."

He slides his arm around my waist, and I rest my head on his shoulder. I find my eyes flicking to Pearl on the couch, where Jasmine is applying black lipstick to her puckered lips. It's still so new, being like this with him in front of her.

I asked him if he was sure this was what he wanted, if this was going to be something serious. I had to know he was all in before telling Pearl.

"I think I've already made it pretty clear that I can't help but say yes to you," he replied, without hesitation.

"That was, like, life or death, though—a possible murder!"

"So saying yes to being your boyfriend is the easiest thing in the world."

And it has been so much easier this past month, having him by my side. Dyvia has tried her best as interim PTA president to temper gossip, in person and online, but she can only do so much. Plus, she's been busy enough with Ruth and Felicia, or the Trisha Truthers, as we like to call them—making sure they stayed far away from the double order of replacement books (our DEI committee's first order of business) and squashing all their rumblings about the gifted school (luckily, Principal Smith's firm stance didn't change on that one). But still, the judgy looks and whispers from moms at drop-off, and the decisions I have to make—and soon—about what to do with this reward money from Mrs. Smith, and the episodes of panic I've been experiencing since that night . . . well, it all feels a little more manageable when Jack's there to hold my hand.

The doorbell rings, and Polly bounds toward the door, whimpering in excitement. Pearl isn't far behind.

"See, I told you it wasn't too early!"

For the record, it *is* still too early. But I guess I can't blame this mom for trying to fast-track this chaotic, sugar-filled night and hustle everyone to bedtime.

"Okay," I say, holding my hands up in surrender. "Let's do this."

Pearl eagerly unlocks the door, and Jack comes in with the assist, holding up the candy bowl for her. But when the door swings open, there aren't any kids standing there.

No, it's Chewbacca. A six-foot-something, broad-chested

Chewbacca. I look behind him to see if maybe there's a shy Baby Yoda or R2-D2 hidden behind there, but no. Just Chewbacca.

"Trick or treat!" Chewbacca calls out in a *definitely* adult man voice.

And then Chewbacca takes off his head.

"Daddy!"

Chewbacca is Corey.

I shouldn't be shocked. I knew he would be back by November. But I swear he still had a few more dates on this leg of the tour before his replacement flew in. And even then, I insisted we couldn't promise Pearl anything until he had a lease, a solid plan.

My eyes lock with his dark, sparkling gaze, and my stomach dips, my heart begins to race. Am I . . . nervous? Excited? I don't have a clue how I feel.

It's clear how Pearl feels, though, as she hops onto his side and squeezes him tight, talking a mile a minute. "Daddy, okay, Daddy, so you're going to go trick-or-treating with me, and I'm going to show you the house that I'm pretty sure is haunted and also all the cool tricks I've taught Polly. Plus, I have to show you my Chromebook and the drawing I did of Armando and his whole family and—and the hole in the fence that looks sorta like a heart. So we better start right now because it's already dark! Mommy, how many hours until bedtime? Can I stay up extra, extra late tonight?"

Corey kisses the top of her witch hat and both of her cheeks. "That all sounds like a lot of fun, but we don't have to rush everything tonight, my Pearl girl. We have all the time we need."

"Are you staying for a *whole month*?" she asks, smiling big, and he flashes her his identical grin.

"More than a month. For good. Because I'm moving back to

Beachwood. From now on, I'm going to be here for every day and every thing."

Pearl screams in delight, and Corey lifts her up into the air, spinning her around. I can't remember the last time I've seen her this happy.

My stomach dips again, like I'm at the top of the tallest roller coaster and going down. And it's confusing—thrillingly, infuriatingly *confusing*—but it looks like I've got time to figure it out. I grab a fun-size Milky Way from the big bowl in Jack's arms, avoiding his inquisitive smile, and then take another handful and shove them into my pocket for good measure. I'm going to need them.

ACKNOWLEDGMENTS

This book exists because of two people. (And I guess because of me, too, but I've already thanked myself with cake and new dresses.)

First: Taylor Haggerty, my fiercely bright and incredibly patient agent. Taylor, you always said I'd write a novel for adults, and I always said, "Yeah, sure," because there was absolutely no way *that* was going to happen. Until a phone call one Friday afternoon, when I was feeling so stuck in my creativity and career, and I was whining about a lot of things, one of which being how I could never write a novel for adults, because I could *never* write a sex scene that my dad would read. And you said (among a lot of other great pieces of advice): "Well, it doesn't have to be the adult version of your YA books." It totally unlocked something in my brain, and by Monday I had this whole book sketched out (and you had several increasingly unhinged emails waiting for you in your inbox). Five years into this partnership, I can look back in awe at all the ways you've advocated for me, protected me, and guided my career. I am forever grateful.

And second: Joe, my bighearted, strong, steady, and *also incredibly patient* husband. The only reason I could go from the kernel of a "What if?" on a Friday to a fully fleshed out oh-my-god-is-this-a-real-thing by Monday is because of your unending belief in my ability and your willingness to drop everything and dream with me for hours. You make me believe in myself because you treat all my ideas with reverence, marvel at everything I'm too anxious and cynical to see clearly, and laugh at all of my jokes. I'm so lucky to be loved by you. (Also, you make dinner every night, so our girls don't have to survive on cheese plates and cereal. You deserve a medal just for that.)

Esi Sogah, I knew from our very first phone call that you understood my vision for this book and that I could trust it in your hands. I've never experienced such a creative shorthand with someone, and I've felt so affirmed, supported, and fortunate throughout the whole process. Thank you for pushing me with your brilliant edits, while still ensuring that my voice shined through. I hope we get to meet in person someday soon and have some cake!

I'm still starry-eyed that I get to publish with Berkley. Thank you to all the people who have made every step along the way a dream, including Sareer Khader, Genni Eccles, Elisha Katz, Loren Jaggers, Kaila Mundell-Hill, Emily Osborne, Sarah Oberrender, Christine Legon, Megan Elmore, Angelina Krahn, George Towne, Jeanne-Marie Hudson, Craig Burke, Claire Zion, Christine Ball, and Ivan Held. And Camila Pinheiro, thank you for the beautiful cover art, especially Mavis's perfect side-eye.

Many thanks also to Jasmine Brown, Stacy Jenson, Holly Root, and everyone else at Root Literary. The world of publishing is big and scary, and you all make me feel at home (or at least *much* less panicked).

My gratitude to all the authors and reviewers who read my book and shared their love, from blurbs to blogs to social media. Your support means the world to me.

I'm so grateful to all of the people in our community who make it possible for me to write, by taking such good care of me and my kids: Shavonne James, Dr. Noreen Hussaini, Dr. Mireya Hernandez, Shannon Kennedy, Lyndsey and Keith Yeomans, Kyle Becker, Alexa King, Bonnie Woodside, Nicole Garcia, Karen Huanosto, and Sonia Ramirez.

Mom, you're responsible for my love of mysteries. (And *also* responsible for my constant fear of getting murdered, because seriously, I was way too young for *Law & Order* and Faye Kellerman. What were you thinking?) When you read this book in two days and told me that it was great, it felt bigger than anything from my career highlight reel so far. Dad, I hope you can see your fingerprints all over this story, too. I'm always trying to make you proud, and man, it's a lot of pressure! I'm tired! But it's also pushed me to achieve so many things, like living out my childhood dreams, so I *guess* I'll keep at it or whatever. Rachal, thank you for being my soft place to land and also the first to call me on my shit. Bryan, thank you for being my guaranteed dose of joy (and trivia).

Coretta and Tallulah, being your mom (and your chauffeur and snack-maker and cringey backup singer) is truly the greatest joy of my life. Every day is an adventure because I never know if you're going to summon a ghost, or write a beautiful poem, or say something so kind it makes me cry, or change the world, or decide to solve the mystery of what exactly happened at Roanoke. And every day I wake up very tired but very excited to do it again because, wow, how lucky am I to be a witness? You're my favorite people, and I love you more than anything in the whole wide world.

Thank you to my readers for supporting me through some of the worst years to release a book and for following me to something new. I carried many of you in my heart as I wrote this book, and I hope you can feel it.

And finally, I've been fortunate to work alongside so many smart, selfless, and dedicated parents during my years in the PTA, including Julie Guzman, Celine Malanum, Christine Koehring, Ebony Brown, Sheila Hernandez, and Malis Mam. You do so much to make sure all of the kids in our community have the very, very best. I promise Trisha isn't based on any of you.

IT'S ELEMENTARY

ELISE BRYANT

READERS GUIDE

ELISE'S SUMMER READING LIST

When No One Is Watching by Alyssa Cole

Finlay Donovan Is Killing It by Elle Cosimano

Vera Wong's Unsolicited Advice for Murderers by Jesse Q. Sutanto

The Mamas by Helena Andrews-Dyer

The Thursday Murder Club by Richard Osman

Such a Fun Age by Kiley Reid

Like a Sister by Kellye Garrett

The Bodyguard by Katherine Center

Killing Me by Michelle Gagnon

What Never Happened by Rachel Howzell Hall

1. Mavis has proudly "mastered the swift, no-small-talk drop-off." Why is she so reluctant to interact with the other parents at Knoll? If you have kids, do you avoid eye contact like Mavis, or are you a card-carrying member of the PTA?

2. Throughout the book, we see all the work that Mavis does at night, after Pearl goes to sleep. Can you relate to this "second shift"? Is this labor respected and valued in our society?

3. Mavis is constantly worried about being seen as a Bad Mom, and she makes many decisions based on how she'll be perceived by others. Do you worry about getting the Bad Mom label, too? Do moms hold themselves (and other moms) to unfair standards?

4. After being out of the dating game for a while, Mavis makes an instant connection with Jack. Why is she so drawn to him? Is he a good partner for her? What do you predict will happen now that Corey has reentered the picture?

5. Mavis complains about how DEI roles and responsibilities are often delegated to Black women. She describes it as "free

labor to be given willingly to fix problems that we didn't create" and "exhausting work—trying to prove to everyone else that you and your kids belong." Do you agree or disagree with Mavis? Should Black parents be responsible for this work in the school setting?

6. The controversy over the gifted program at Knoll and Trisha's reaction show how these classes and programs can sometimes serve as a status symbol for parents. Does a kid's placement in a gifted program actually reflect on the parents? Are gifted programs fair and beneficial to all kids?

7. Even though Mavis is unhappy at Project Window and has been passed over for a promotion she thinks she deserved, she doesn't make any moves to find a new job. Why do you think she is scared to leave? What do you think she should do?

8. Pearl doesn't ask for help with her bullying problem because she observes Mavis not asking for help with her own problems. Which patterns do you see repeating from your parents? Or with your own kids? How do we make sure our kids don't pick up our worst habits?

9. Mavis's father reminds her of the Gwendolyn Brooks quote "We are each other's business." Do you agree with this? We see how gentrification is changing Beachwood from the city Mavis grew up in. What does this do to the sense of community? Do people still make each other's business their own?

10. Even though she wasn't a murderer, Trisha was still guilty of something. What do you think about the severity of her

crime? Why do you think she resorted to such extreme measures over children's books?

11. Corinne escapes in the end, but she has to leave behind two of her kids and her husband. She also reveals how she was a victim, too, during her confession. She suffers consequences—do you think they match the seriousness of her actions? What are your predictions for what will happen next?

12. Mavis, Corinne, and Trisha are all doing what they think is best for their kids, in their own way. What do you think about their choices? How far would you go to do what's best for your child?

Author photo by Joseph Sebastia Photograph

Elise Bryant is the NAACP Image Award–nominated author of *Happily Ever Afters, One True Loves,* and *Reggie and Delilah's Year of Falling.* For many years, Elise had the joy of working as a special education teacher, and now she spends her days reading, writing, and eating dessert. She lives with her husband and two daughters in Long Beach, California.

VISIT ELISE BRYANT ONLINE

EliseBryant.com

EliseMBryant

Ready to find
your next great read?

Let us help.

Visit prh.com/nextread